In Praise of *The Notebooks of Don Rigoberto*

"No one would accuse the outrageous characters in Mario Vargas Llosa's latest novel of lacking runaway imaginations. *The Notebooks of Don Rigoberto*, which re-explores the erotic escapades and fetishtic fantasies of Vargas Llosa's 1990 novel, *In Praise of the Stepmother*, is one of the most titillating—if strangest—novels to have come this reader's way in a long time."　　　　　　　　　　　　　　—*The Miami Herald*

"The narration is . . . in the style of eighteenth-century erotica. . . . *The Notebooks of Don Rigoberto* abounds with comic invention and glitters with intellectual brilliancy."　　　　　　　—*The Wall Street Journal*

"A wonderful new novel, a comic joy, with erotica galore, more than a touch of philosophy and an unblinking look at life in the city of Lima today. It is one of his finest creations since *Aunt Julia and the Scriptwriter*. . . . Sex, philosophy, art history, delusion, ranting, and big, big laughs—it takes a genius like Vargas Llosa to put them together in one novel."
　　　　　　　　　　　　　　　　—*Newark Star-Ledger*

"A comedy of Eros that raises fetishism and fantasy to the level of sublimely Epicurean philosophical discourse. An outrageous delight."
　　　　　　　　　　　　　　—*Raleigh News & Observer*

"Vargas Llosa's most enjoyable novel since his *Aunt Julia and the Scriptwriter* . . . It's all so outrageously entertaining that one must concentrate scrupulously to notice how brilliantly Vargas Llosa uses Don Rigoberto's notebooks to comment on a daunting variety of general cultural as well as sexual topics. An Anatomy of Eros unlike any other fiction . . . all the reader needs is the time and place (preferably bed) to sample its very considerable pleasure."　　　—*Kirkus Reviews* (starred review)

"As in much of his writing, Vargas Llosa creates a certain timelessness, a dream-like play on the present. The more he leaves sex to the imagination, the more erotic and beautifully suggestive it becomes."
　　　　　　　　　　　　　　　　—*Publishers Weekly*

PENGUIN BOOKS

THE NOTEBOOKS OF DON RIGOBERTO

Mario Vargas Llosa, Peru's foremost writer, is the author of many novels, including *The Notebooks of Don Rigoberto*, *Death in the Andes*, *In Praise of the Stepmother*, *The Storyteller*, *Aunt Julia and the Scriptwriter*, and *The War of the End of the World* (all available from Penguin), as well as *Conversation in the Cathedral* and *The Green House*. He has also written the memoir *A Fish in the Water* (Penguin), three plays, and several volumes of literary essays including *Making Waves*, which won the National Book Critics Circle Award. He has been awarded the Cervantes Prize, the Spanish-speaking world's most distinguished literary honor, and the Jerusalem Prize, which is given to writers whose work expresses the idea of freedom of the individual in society. He now lives in London.

Edith Grossman has translated the poetry and prose of major contemporary Latin American writers, including Gabriel García Márquez and Alvaro Mutis, as well as Vargas Llosa's novel *Death in the Andes*.

BY MARIO VARGAS LLOSA

The Cubs and Other Stories
The Time of the Hero
The Green House
Captain Pantoja and the Special Service
Conversation in The Cathedral
Aunt Julia and the Scriptwriter
The War of the End of the World
The Real Life of Alejandro Mayta
The Perpetual Orgy
Who Killed Palomino Molero?
The Storyteller
In Praise of the Stepmother
A Fish in the Water
Death in the Andes
Making Waves
The Notebooks of Don Rigoberto

The
Notebooks of
Don Rigoberto

MARIO VARGAS LLOSA

Translated by Edith Grossman

PENGUIN BOOKS

PENGUIN BOOKS
Published by the Penguin Group
Penguin Putnam Inc., 375 Hudson Street,
New York, New York 10014, U.S.A.
Penguin Books Ltd, 27 Wrights Lane,
London W8 5TZ, England
Penguin Books Australia Ltd, Ringwood,
Victoria, Australia
Penguin Books Canada Ltd, 10 Alcorn Avenue,
Toronto, Ontario, Canada M4V 3B2
Penguin Books (N.Z.) Ltd, 182–190 Wairau Road,
Auckland 10, New Zealand

Penguin Books Ltd, Registered Offices:
Harmondsworth, Middlesex, England

First published in the United States of America by Farrar, Straus and Giroux 1998
Published in Penguin Books 1999

1   3   5   7   9   10   8   6   4   2

Originally published in Spanish in 1977 under the title
Los cuadernos de don Rigoberto by Alfaguara, Madrid.

PUBLISHER'S NOTE
This is a work of fiction. Names, characters, places, and incidents either are the
product of the author's imagination or are used fictitiously, and any resemblance
to actual persons, living or dead, events, or locales is entirely coincidental.

ISBN 0-374-22327-0 (hc.)
ISBN 0 14 02.8359 5 (pbk.)
(CIP data available)

Printed in the United States of America
Set in Adobe Garamond
Designed by Jonathan D. Lippincott

Man, a god when he dreams, barely a beggar when he thinks.
—Hölderlin, *Hyperion*

I cannot keep a record of my life through my actions; fortune has buried them too deep: I keep it through my fantasies.
—Montaigne

The
Notebooks of
Don Rigoberto

I

The Return of Fonchito

The doorbell rang, Doña Lucrecia went to see who was there, and like a portrait in the open doorway, with the twisted gray trees of the Olivar de San Isidro as the background, she saw the golden ringlets and blue eyes of Fonchito's head. The world began to spin.

"I miss you very much, Stepmamá," chirped the voice she remembered so well. "Are you still angry with me? I came to ask your forgiveness. Do you forgive me?"

"You, it's you?" Still holding the doorknob, Doña Lucrecia had to lean against the wall. "Aren't you ashamed to come here?"

"I sneaked out of the academy," the boy insisted, showing her his sketchbook, his colored pencils. "I missed you very much, really I did. Why are you so pale?"

"My God, my God." Doña Lucrecia staggered and dropped to the faux-colonial bench next to the door. White as a sheet, she covered her eyes.

"Don't die!" shouted the boy in fright.

And Doña Lucrecia—she felt herself passing out—saw the small, childish figure cross the threshold, close the door, fall to his knees at her feet, grasp her hands, and rub them in bewilderment. "Don't die, don't faint, please."

She made an effort to collect her wits and regain her self-control. She took a deep breath before speaking. Her words came slowly, for she thought her voice would break at any moment. "Nothing's wrong, I'm fine now.

Seeing you here was the last thing I expected. How did you have the nerve? Don't you feel any remorse?"

Still on his knees, Fonchito tried to kiss her hand.

"Say you forgive me, Stepmamá," he begged. "Say it, say it. The house isn't the same since you left. I came here so many times after school just to catch a glimpse of you. I wanted to ring the bell but I didn't have the courage. Won't you ever forgive me?"

"Never," she said firmly. "I'll never forgive what you did, you wicked boy."

But, belying her own words, her large, dark eyes scrutinized with curiosity, some pleasure, perhaps even with tenderness, the tousled curls, the thin blue veins in his neck, the tips of his ears visible among the blond ringlets, the slim graceful body tightly encased in the blue jacket and gray trousers of his school uniform. Her nostrils breathed in that adolescent odor of soccer games, hard candies, and d'Onofrio ice cream; her ears recognized the high-pitched breaks, the changing voice that still echoed in her memory. Doña Lucrecia's hands resigned themselves to being dampened by the baby-bird kisses of that sweet mouth.

"I love you very much, Stepmamá," Fonchito whimpered. "And even if you don't think so, my papá does too."

Just then Justiniana appeared, a lithe, cinnamon-colored figure wrapped in a flowered smock, with a kerchief around her head and a feather duster in her hand. She stood, frozen, in the hallway leading to the kitchen.

"Master Alfonso," she murmured in disbelief. "Fonchito! I can't believe it!"

"Imagine, imagine!" Doña Lucrecia exclaimed, determined to display more indignation than she actually felt. "He has the gall to come to this house. After ruining my life and hurting Rigoberto so. To ask for my forgiveness and shed his crocodile tears. Have you ever seen anything so shameless, Justiniana?"

But even now she did not pull away the slender fingers that Fonchito, shaken by his sobs, continued to kiss.

"Go on, Master Alfonso," said the girl, so confused that without realizing it she now began to address him with the more familiar *tú*. "Can't you see how much you're upsetting the señora? Go on, leave now, Fonchito."

"I'll go if she says she forgives me," pleaded the boy, sighing, his head resting on Doña Lucrecia's hands. "And you, Justita, you don't even say

4

hello, you start right in insulting me? What did I ever do to you? I love you too, a lot; I love you so much I cried all night when you left."

"Quiet, you liar, I don't believe a word you say." Justiniana smoothed Doña Lucrecia's hair. "Shall I bring you a cloth and some alcohol, Señora?"

"Just a glass of water. Don't worry, I'm all right now. But seeing the boy here in this house gave me such a shock."

And, at last, very gently, she withdrew her hands from Fonchito's grasp. The boy remained at her feet, not crying now, struggling to suppress his sobs. His eyes were red and tears had streaked his face. A thread of saliva hung from his mouth. Through the mist that fogged her eyes, Doña Lucrecia observed his chiseled nose, well-defined lips, small, imperious cleft chin, the brilliant whiteness of his teeth. She wanted to slap him, scratch that Baby Jesus face. Hypocrite! Judas! Even bite his neck and suck his blood like a vampire.

"Does your father know you're here?"

"What an idea, Stepmamá," the boy answered immediately, in a conspiratorial tone. "Who knows what he'd do to me. He never talks about you, but I know how much he misses you. I swear you're all he thinks about, night or day. I came here in secret, I sneaked out of the academy. I go three times a week, after school. Do you want me to show you my drawings? Say you forgive me, Stepmamá."

"Don't say anything, throw him out, Señora." Justiniana had come back with a glass of water; Doña Lucrecia took several sips. "Don't let him fool you with his pretty face. He's Lucifer in person, and you know it. He'll play another evil trick on you worse than the first one."

"Don't say that, Justita." Fonchito looked ready to burst into tears again. "I swear I'm sorry, Stepmamá. I didn't know what I was doing, honest. I didn't want anything to happen. Do you think I wanted you to go away? That I wanted my papá and me to be left all alone?"

"I didn't go away," Doña Lucrecia muttered, contradicting him. "Rigoberto threw me out as if I were a whore. And it was all your fault!"

"Don't say dirty words, Stepmamá." The boy raised both hands in horror. "Don't say them, they don't suit you."

Despite her grief and anger, Doña Lucrecia almost smiled. Cursing didn't suit her! A perceptive, sensitive child? Justiniana was right: he was Beelzebub, a viper with the face of an angel.

The boy exploded with jubilation. "You're laughing, Stepmamá! Does that mean you forgive me? Then say it, say you have, Stepmamá."

He clapped his hands, and in his blue eyes the sadness had cleared and a savage little light was flashing. Doña Lucrecia noticed the ink stains on his fingers. Despite herself, she was touched. Was she going to faint again? How absurd. She saw her reflection in the foyer mirror: her expression had regained its composure, but a light blush tinged her cheeks, and her breast rose and fell in agitation. With an automatic gesture she closed the neckline of her dressing gown. How could he be so shameless, so cynical, so perverse, when he was still so young? Justiniana read her thoughts. She looked at her as if to say, "Don't be weak, Señora, don't forgive him. Don't be a fool!" Hiding her embarrassment, she took a few more sips of water; it was cold and did her good. The boy quickly grasped her free hand and began to kiss it again, talking all the while.

"Thank you, Stepmamá. You're so good, but I knew that, that's why I had the courage to ring the bell. I want to show you my drawings. And talk to you about Egon Schiele, about his life and his paintings. And tell you what I'll be when I grow up, and a thousand other things. Can you guess? A painter, Stepmamá! That's what I want to be."

Justiniana shook her head in alarm. Outside, motors and horns disturbed the San Isidro twilight, and through the sheer curtains in the dining alcove, Doña Lucrecia caught a glimpse of the bare branches and knotted trunks of the olive trees; they had become a friendly presence. Enough indecisiveness, it was time to act.

"All right, Fonchito," she said, with a severity her heart no longer demanded of her. "Now make me happy. Please go away."

"Yes, Stepmamá." The boy leaped to his feet. "Whatever you say. I'll always listen to you, I'll always obey you in everything. You'll see how well I can behave."

His voice and expression were those of someone who has eased himself of a heavy burden and made peace with his conscience. A golden lock of hair brushed his forehead, and his eyes sparkled with joy. Doña Lucrecia watched as he put a hand into his back pocket, took out a handkerchief, blew his nose, and then picked up his book bag, his portfolio of drawings, his box of pencils from the floor. With all that on his shoulder, he backed away, smiling, toward the door, not taking his eyes off Doña Lucrecia and Justiniana.

"As soon as I can, I'll sneak away again and come and visit you, Stepmamá," he warbled from the doorway. "And you too, Justita, of course."

When the street door closed, both women stood motionless and silent.

Soon the bells of the Virgen del Pilar Church began to ring in the distance. A dog barked.

"It's incredible," murmured Doña Lucrecia. "I can't believe he had the nerve to show his face in this house."

"What's incredible is how good you are," the girl replied indignantly. "You've forgiven him, haven't you? After the way he tricked you into fighting with the señor. There's a place reserved for you in heaven, Señora!"

"I'm not even certain it was a trick, or that he planned it all out ahead of time."

She was walking toward the bathroom, talking to herself, but she heard Justiniana chiding her. "Of course he planned everything. Fonchito is capable of the most awful things, don't you know that yet?"

Perhaps, thought Doña Lucrecia. But he was a boy, only a boy. Wasn't he? Yes, at least there could be no doubt about that. In the bathroom she splashed cold water on her forehead and looked at herself in the mirror. Agitation had sharpened her nose and made it twitch uneasily, and there were bluish circles under her eyes. Between her partially opened lips she could see the tip of the sandpaper her tongue had turned into. She recalled the lizards and iguanas in Piura; their tongues were always bone-dry, like hers was now. Fonchito's presence in her house had made her feel stony and ancient, like those prehistoric relics of the northern deserts. Without thinking, acting automatically, she untied her belt, and with a movement of her shoulders shrugged off her dressing gown; the silk slid down her body like a caress and fell with a whisper to the floor. Flat and round, the dressing gown covered her insteps, like a gigantic flower. Not knowing what she was doing or what she was going to do, breathing heavily, her feet stepped across the barrier of clothing that encircled them and carried her to the bidet, where, after lowering her lace panties, she sat down. What was she doing? What are you going to do, Lucrecia? She was not smiling. She tried to inhale and exhale more calmly while her hands, moving independently, turned the taps, the hot, the cold, testing them, mixing them, adjusting them, raising or lowering the jet of water—lukewarm, hot, cold, cool, weak, strong, pulsating. Her lower body moved forward, moved back, leaned to the right, the left, until it found just the right spot. There. A shiver ran down her spine. "Perhaps he didn't even realize, perhaps he didn't know what he was doing," she repeated to herself, feeling sorry for the boy she had cursed so often during these past six months. Perhaps he wasn't bad, perhaps he wasn't. Mischievous, naughty, conceited, irresponsible, a thousand other things. But not evil, no. "Perhaps not." Thoughts burst inside her head like bubbles in a pot of boiling water. She recalled the day she had met Rigoberto, the widower with the great Buddha ears and outrageous nose whom she would marry a short while later, and the first time she had seen her stepson, a cherub in a blue sailor suit—gold buttons, a little cap with an anchor—and all she had discovered and learned, the unexpected, imaginative, intense nocturnal life in the little house in Barranco that Rigoberto had built to begin their life together, and the arguments between the architect and her husband which had marked the construction of what would become her home. So much had happened! The images came and went, dissolved, changed, entwined, followed one after the other, and it was as if the liquid caress of the nimble jet of water reached to her very soul.

Instructions for the Architect

Our misunderstanding is conceptual in nature. You have created this attractive design for my house and library based on the supposition—one that is extremely widespread, unfortunately—that people, not objects, are the primary consideration in a residence. I do not criticize you for having made this opinion your own, since it is indispensable for any man in your profession not resigned to doing without clients. But my conception of my future home is just the opposite. To wit: in the small constructed space that I will call my world and that will be ruled by my whims, we humans will be second-class citizens; books, pictures, and engravings will have first priority. My four thousand volumes and one hundred canvases and prints should constitute the primary rationale for the design I have hired you to make. You must subordinate the comfort, safety, and space allotted human occupants to what is needed for those objects.

An absolutely essential factor is the fireplace, which must have the capacity to serve, at my discretion, as a crematorium for unwanted books and prints. For this reason, it must be placed very close to the bookshelves and within reach of my chair, since it pleases me to play inquisitor to literary and artistic calamities while seated. Let me explain. The four thousand volumes and one hundred prints in my possession are invariable numbers. In order to avoid excessive abundance and disorder, I will never own more,

8

but they will not always be the same, for they will be replaced constantly until my death. Which means that for each book I add to my library, I eliminate another, and each image that enters my collection—lithograph, woodcut, xylograph, drawing, engraving, mixed media, oil painting, watercolor, et cetera—displaces the least favorite among all the others. I will not conceal from you that choosing the victim is difficult, at times heartrending, a Hamletian dilemma that torments me for days, weeks, and then becomes part of my nightmares. At first I presented the sacrificed books and prints to public libraries and museums. Now I burn them, which accounts for the importance of the fireplace. I chose this drastic method, which seasons the discomfort of selecting a victim with the spice of committing a cultural sacrilege, an ethical transgression, on the day, or, I should say, the night when, having decided to replace a reproduction of Andy Warhol's multi-colored Campbell's soup can with a beautiful Szyszlo inspired by the sea of Paracas, I realized it was stupid to inflict on other eyes a work I had come to consider unworthy of mine. And then I threw it in the fire. As I watched the pasteboard scorch and burn, I confess to experiencing a vague remorse. This no longer happens. I have consigned dozens of romantic and indigenist poets to the flames, and an equal number of conceptualist, abstract, informalist, landscapist, portraitist, and sacred works of art in order to maintain the *numerus clausus* of my library and art collection, and I have done so not with regret but with the stimulating sense that I was engaging in literary and artistic criticism as it should be practiced: radically, irreversibly, and flammably. Let me add, to bring this digression to a close, that the pastime amuses me, but since it in no way serves as an aphrodisiac, I consider it limited, minor, merely spiritual, lacking bodily repercussions.

I trust you will not interpret what you have just read—the greater importance I attribute to pictures and books than to flesh-and-blood bipeds—as a sudden whim or cynical pose. It is neither, but rather a deep-rooted conviction, the result of certain extremely difficult but also highly pleasurable experiences. It was in no way easy for me to adopt a position that contradicted the ancient traditions—with a smile on our lips, let us call them humanistic—of anthropocentric philosophies and religions in which it is inconceivable that a real human being, an organism of perishable flesh and bone, can be considered less worthy of interest and respect than the invented one that resides (if it makes you more comfortable, let us say it is reflected) in the imagery of art and literature. I will spare you the details of this story and move directly to the conclusion I reached, which I now proclaim with no embarrassment. It is not the world of cunning cattle that you and I are part of which interests me and brings me joy or suffering, but the myriad beings animated by imagination, desire, and artistic skill, the beings present in the paintings, books, and prints that I have collected with the patience and love of many years. The house I am going to build in Barranco, the project you are going to redesign from beginning to end, is for them rather than for me or my new bride or young son. The trinity formed by my family, no blasphemy intended, is in the service of these objects, as you must be when, after reading these lines, you lean over the drawing board to correct the mistake you have made.

What I have just written is the literal truth, not an enigmatic metaphor. I am building this house to suffer and find pleasure with *them* and by *them* and for *them*. Make an effort to imitate me during the limited time you will be in my employ.

And now, draw up your plans.

The Night of the Cats

Faithfully keeping the appointment, Lucrecia came in with the darkness, talking of cats. She herself resembled a beautiful Angora in the whispering ermine that reached down to her feet and concealed her movements. Was she naked under her silvery wrap?

"Did you say cats?"

"Little cats, I mean," she mewed, striding resolutely around Don Rigoberto, who was reminded of a bull that has just emerged from the pen and is taking the bullfighter's measure. "Kitty cats, pussycats, kittens. A dozen, maybe more."

They were frolicking on the red velvet bedspread. They pulled back and extended their little paws beneath the cone of brutal light that fell, like stardust, from the invisible ceiling onto the bed. The scent of musk filled the air, and baroque music, with its abrupt diapasons, came from the same corner as the dry, commanding voice.

"Get undressed."

"Absolutely not," Doña Lucrecia protested. "You want me there with those animals. I'd rather die, I can't stand them."

"He wanted you to make love to him in the middle of all those kittens?"

Don Rigoberto did not miss a single moment of Doña Lucrecia's progress around the soft thick carpet. His heart awoke as the Barrancan night became less humid, more lively.

"Imagine," she replied softly, stopping for an instant and then resuming her circular pacing. "He wanted to see me naked in the middle of those cats. And I find them so disgusting! I get gooseflesh just thinking about it."

Don Rigoberto began to discern their shapes, his ears began to hear the weak mewing of the swarm of cats. Segregated by shadows, they began to appear, become corporeal, and on the fiery bedspread, beneath the shower of light, the gleams and reflections and dark contortions made him dizzy. He sensed that at the tips of those shifting limbs there was a suggestion of aqueous, curved, infant claws.

"Come, come here," the man in the corner ordered in a quiet voice. And at the same time he must have turned up the volume, because clavichords and violins swelled, assaulting his ears. Pergolesi! Don Rigoberto recognized the composer. He understood why that sonata had been chosen: the eighteenth century was not only the time of disguises and confusion of the sexes; it was also the century par excellence of cats. Hadn't Venice always been a feline republic?

"Were you naked by this time?" Listening to himself, he realized that desire was quickly taking control of his body.

"Not yet. He undressed me, as always. Why do you ask when you know that's what he likes best?"

"And do you too?" he interrupted in a honeyed tone.

Doña Lucrecia laughed, a little forced laugh.

"It's always nice to have a valet," she whispered, inventing a charming modesty for herself. "Though this time it was different."

"Because of the cats?"

"Of course because of the cats. They made me so nervous. My nerves were all on edge, Rigoberto."

And still, she had obeyed the order of the lover hidden in the corner. Docile, curious, aroused, she stood beside him and waited, not for a second forgetting the pack of felines knotted together, arching their backs, rolling over, licking with their tongues, displaying themselves in the obscene yellow circle that held them prisoner in the center of the flaming bedspread. When she felt his two hands on her ankles, moving down to her feet and removing her shoes, her breasts grew as taut as two bows. Her nipples hardened.

Meticulously he removed her stockings, kissing, without haste and with great care, every inch of exposed skin. He murmured something that Doña Lucrecia thought at first were tender or vulgar words dictated by excitement.

"But no, it was not a declaration of love, or any of the filthy things that sometimes occur to him." She laughed again, the same little disbelieving laugh, and stopped within reach of Don Rigoberto's hands. He did not attempt to touch her.

"What, then," he stammered, struggling with his recalcitrant tongue.

"Explanations, a whole felinesque lecture," and she laughed again between stifled little screams. "Did you know that the thing kittens like best in the world is honey? And that at their backsides they have a sac that produces perfume?"

Don Rigoberto sniffed at the night with dilated nostrils.

"Is that the scent you're wearing? Isn't that musk?"

"It's civet. Cat perfume. I'm covered with it. Does it bother you?"

The story was slipping away from him, he was losing his hold on it, he had thought he was inside and now he found himself on the outside. Don Rigoberto did not know what to think.

"And why had he brought the jars of honey?" he asked, fearing a game or a joke that would undermine the gravity of the ceremony.

"To smear on you," said the man, and he stopped kissing her. He continued to undress her; he had finished with her stockings, jacket, and blouse. Now he was unfastening her skirt. "I brought it from Greece, from the bees on Mount Hymettus. The honey that Aristotle speaks of. I saved it for you, thinking about tonight."

He loves her, thought Don Rigoberto, moved despite his jealousy.

"No, you won't," Doña Lucrecia protested. "Absolutely not. That dirty stuff's not for me."

Her defenses weakened by the contagious will of her lover, she spoke without authority, in the tone of one who knows she is defeated. Her body had begun to divert her thoughts from the high-pitched noises on the bed, had begun to quiver, to focus her attention on the man who had stripped away her last articles of clothing and, kneeling at her feet, continued his caresses. She allowed him to go on, attempting to abandon herself to the pleasure he gave her. His lips and hands left flames wherever they touched. The kittens were always there, grayish-green, lethargic or lively, wrinkling the bedspread. Meowing, frolicking. Pergolesi had subsided into a distant breeze, a sonorous swoon.

"Smear your body with honey from the bees on Mount Hymettus?" Don Rigoberto repeated, spelling out each word.

"So that the kittens would lick it off, can you imagine? Even though the damn things make me sick, even though I'm allergic to cats and can't stand to touch sticky things (She never chewed gum, Don Rigoberto thought with gratitude) even with the tip of my finger. Can you imagine?"

"It was a great sacrifice, you did it only because . . ."

"Because I love you," she interrupted. "You love me too, don't you?"

With all my heart, thought Don Rigoberto. His eyes were closed. He had finally reached the state of absolute lucidity he had been striving for. He could orient himself without difficulty in that labyrinth of dense shadows. Very clearly, with a touch of envy, he could see the skill of the man who, without hurrying or losing control of his fingers, freed Lucrecia of her slip, her bra, her panties, while his lips delicately kissed her satin skin, feeling the light granulation—from cold, uncertainty, apprehension, disgust, desire?—that enervated her, and the warm exhalations, summoned by his caresses, that appeared on those same parts of her body. When he felt on the tongue, teeth, and palate of the lover the curly thatch of hair, and the spicy aroma of her juices ascended to his brain, he began to tremble. Had he begun to apply the honey? Yes. With a painter's fine brush? No. With a cloth? No. With his bare hands? Yes. Or rather, with each of his long, bony fingers and all the knowledge of a masseur. His fingers spread the crystalline substance on her skin—the sugary scent rose, cloying, through Don Rigoberto's nostrils—and verified the consistency of thighs, shoulders, and breasts, pinched those hips, passed over those buttocks, penetrated and separated those puckered depths. The music of Pergolesi capriciously returned. It resounded, hiding Doña Lucrecia's muffled protests and the agitation of the kittens, who could smell the honey and, guessing at what was going to happen, had begun leaping and yowling, running along the bedspread, their jaws open, impatient.

"It was more hunger," Doña Lucrecia corrected him.

"Were you excited?" panted Don Rigoberto. "Was he naked? Did he put honey on his own body too?"

"Yes, yes, yes," Doña Lucrecia intoned. "He smeared me, he smeared himself, he had me smear his back where his hand couldn't reach. Naturally those little games are very exciting. He isn't made of wood, and you wouldn't want me to be made of wood either, would you?"

"Of course not," Don Rigoberto agreed. "My darling."

"Naturally we kissed, we touched, we caressed," his wife stated with precision. She had resumed her circular pacing, and Don Rigoberto's ears could detect the whisper of ermine at each step. Did it inflame her, remembering? "I mean, without our leaving the corner. For a long while. Until he picked me up and carried me, all covered with honey, to the bed."

The vision was so clear, the definition of the image so explicit, that Don Rigoberto became fearful. "I may go blind." Like those hippies during the psychedelic years, stimulated by the synesthesias of LSD, who defied the California sun until the rays burned their retinas and they were condemned to see life with their ears, their sense of touch, their imagination. There they were, smeared and dripping with honey and their own secretions, Hellenic in their nakedness and grace, advancing toward the cattish swarm. He was a medieval knight armed for battle and she a wood nymph, a ravished Sabine woman. She kicked her golden feet and protested, "I don't want to, I don't like it," but her arms amorously encircled the neck of her raptor, her tongue struggled to enter his mouth, and she sipped his saliva with pleasure. "Wait, wait," Don Rigoberto implored. An accommodating Doña Lucrecia stopped, and it was as if she had disappeared into those complicitous shadows while her husband evoked in memory the languid girl by Balthus (*Nu avec chat*), seated on a chair, her head voluptuously thrown back, one leg extended, the other bent, her slim heel resting on the edge of the chair, arm outstretched to stroke a cat that lies on the top of a dresser and, with half-closed eyes, calmly awaits his pleasure. Digging deeper, searching—in the book by the Dutch animalist Midas Dekkers?— he also recalled seeing but not paying much attention to the *Rosalba* by Botero (1968), an oil painting in which a small black feline, crouching on a nuptial bed, prepares to share sheets and mattress with a voluptuous, curly-haired prostitute who is finishing her cigarette; and a woodcut by Félix Vallotton (*Languor*, circa 1896?) in which a girl with vivacious buttocks, among flowered bolsters and a geometric quilt, scratches the erogenous neck of an aroused cat. Apart from these uncertain approximations, in the arsenal of his memory no image coincided with this one. He was childishly intrigued. His excitement had ebbed, without disappearing altogether; it appeared on the horizon of his body like one of those cold suns in a European autumn, his favorite season for traveling.

"And?" he asked, returning to the reality of his interrupted dream.

The man had placed Lucrecia beneath the cone of light, and firmly freeing himself from the arms that tried to hold him, ignoring her pleas, he stepped back. Like Don Rigoberto, he contemplated her from the darkness. It was an uncommon sight and, once he was past the initial discomfiture, incomparably beautiful. After moving away in fright to make room for her and observe her, crouching, uncertain, always on the alert—green sparks, yellow ones, tense little whiskers—the tiny animals sniffed at her and leaped onto that sweet prey. They scaled, laid siege to, and occupied the honeyed body, mewing with happiness. The noise wiped out the breathless protests, the stifled little laughs, the exclamations of Doña Lucrecia. Her arms crossed over her face to protect her mouth, eyes, and nose from their eager licking, and she was at their mercy. Don Rigoberto's eyes followed the greedy, iridescent creatures, slipped with them along her breasts and hips, slid along her knees, stuck to her elbows, climbed along her thighs, indulged, like those little tongues, in the liquid sweetness forming pools on the full moon of her belly. The gleam of honey seasoned with the saliva of the cats gave her white body a semi-liquid appearance, and the little starts and shivers that traced the stepping and tumbling of the animals had something of the soft movements of bodies in water. Doña Lucrecia was floating, she was a living vessel cutting a wake through invisible waters. How beautiful she is! he thought. Her body with its firm breasts and generous hips, well-defined buttocks and thighs, was on the very edge of what he admired above all else in a feminine silhouette: the abundance that suggests but just avoids an undesirable obesity.

"Open your legs, my love," asked the faceless man.

"Open them, open them," pleaded Don Rigoberto.

"They're very small, they don't bite, they won't hurt you," the man insisted.

"Were you enjoying it?" asked Don Rigoberto.

"No, no," replied Doña Lucrecia, who had again resumed her hypnotic walking. The murmurous ermine reawakened his suspicions: was she naked beneath the fur? Yes, she was. "The tickling drove me crazy."

But in the end she had consented, and two or three felines rushed eagerly to lick the hidden backs of her thighs, the little drops of honey that sparkled on the silken black hairs of her mound of Venus. The chorus of licking tongues seemed like celestial music to Don Rigoberto. Pergolesi returned, faintly now, sweetly, moaning slowly. The firm body, licked clean, lay still, in deep repose. But Doña Lucrecia was not sleeping, for Don Rigoberto's ears could detect the discreet eddies escaping, without her realizing it, from her depths.

"Were you over your revulsion?" he inquired.

"Of course not," she replied. And, after a pause, with some humor: "But it didn't matter so much anymore."

She laughed, this time with the open laugh she reserved for him on their nights of shared intimacy, the fantasy without awkwardness that made them happy. Don Rigoberto desired her with all the mouths of his body.

"Take off the coat," he pleaded. "Come, come to my arms, my queen, my goddess."

But he was distracted by the vision that at precisely this instant had doubled. The invisible man was no longer invisible. His long, oiled body silently infiltrated the image. Now he was there too. Dropping onto the red cover, he embraced Doña Lucrecia. The screeching of the kittens squashed between the lovers and struggling to escape with bulging eyes, wide-open jaws, tongues hanging out, hurt Don Rigoberto's eardrums. He covered his ears, but he could still hear them. And though he closed his eyes, he saw the man covering Doña Lucrecia. He seemed to sink into the robust white hips that received him with pleasure. He kissed her with the avidity displayed by the kittens when they licked her, and he moved on her, with her, imprisoned by her arms. Doña Lucrecia's hands clenched his back, and her raised legs fell on his and her proud feet rested on his calves, one of Don Rigoberto's most erogenous zones. He sighed, struggling to control an overwhelming desire to cry. He caught sight of Doña Lucrecia slipping away toward the door.

"Will you come back tomorrow?" he asked anxiously.

"And the day after and the day after that," the silent, vanishing figure replied. "Have I even left?"

The kittens, recovered from their surprise, returned to their duties and dispensed with the final drops of honey, indifferent to the couple's fierce struggles.

The Name Fetishist

I have a name fetish, and your name captivates me and drives me mad. Rigoberto! It is virile, it is elegant, it is Bronzinian, it is Italian. When I say it quietly, just for myself, a shiver snakes all the way down my spine and these rosy heels that God (or Nature if you prefer, unbeliever!) gave me turn to ice. Rigoberto! A laughing cascade of transparent waters. Rigoberto! The yellow joy of a goldfinch celebrating the sun. Wherever you may be, I am there too. Silent and loving, I am there. Do you sign a bill of exchange or a promissory note with the four syllables of your name? I am the dot over the *i*, the tail of the *g*, the little horns on each side of the *t*. The spot of ink on your thumb. Do you appease the heat with a glass of mineral water? I am the tiny bubble that refreshes your palate, the cube of ice that makes your viper-tongue shiver. I, Rigoberto, am the laces in your shoes, the cherry-extract lozenge you take each night to prevent constipation. How do I know this detail of your gastroenterological life? She who loves, knows, and considers everything that concerns her love as worthwhile knowledge, sanctifying the most trivial aspect of his person. Before your portrait I cross myself and pray. To learn about your life I have your name, the numerology of the Cabalists, the divinatory arts of Nostradamus. Who am I? One who loves you as the foam loves the wave and the cloud the rosy dawn. Seek, seek and find me, beloved.

Yours, yours, yours,
The Name Fetishist

II

Egon Schiele's Things

"Why are you so interested in Egon Schiele?" asked Doña Lucrecia.

"It makes me sad that he died so young and that they put him in prison," Fonchito replied. "His pictures are really beautiful. I spend hours looking at them in my papá's books. Don't you like them, Stepmamá?"

"I don't recall them very well. Except for the poses. The bodies are strained and twisted, aren't they?"

"And I like Schiele because, because . . ." The boy interrupted her, as if he were about to reveal a secret. "I'm afraid to tell you, Stepmamá."

"You know how to say things very well when you want to, so don't play the fool."

"Because I have a feeling that I'm like him. That I'm going to have a tragic life, like his."

Doña Lucrecia laughed out loud. But then a feeling of uneasiness came over her. How did the boy ever think up an idea like that? Fonchito continued to look at her, very seriously. After a while, making an effort, he smiled. He was sitting cross-legged on the floor of the dining alcove; he was still wearing the blue jacket and gray tie of his uniform but had taken off the peaked cap, which lay beside him along with his book bag and the portfolio and box of pencils from the academy. Just then, Justiniana came in with the tea tray. Fonchito welcomed her with glee.

"Toasted sweet buns with butter and marmalade." He clapped his hands, suddenly freed from care. "What I love best in the whole world. You remembered, Justita!"

"I didn't fix this for you, it's for the señora," Justiniana lied, pretending severity. "Not even a burned crumb for you."

She began to serve the tea, arranging the cups on the coffee table in the living room. In the Olivar some boys were playing soccer, and their enthusiastic silhouettes could be seen through the curtains; inside the house they could hear, in muted form, their curses, resounding kicks, and shouts of triumph. Soon it would be dark.

"Won't you ever forgive me, Justita?" The boy grew sad. "Learn from my stepmamá; she's forgotten what happened and now we get along fine, just like before."

No, not just like before, thought Doña Lucrecia. A hot wave lapped at her all the way from her feet to the ends of her hair. She concealed it and sipped at her tea.

"I guess the señora is very, very good and I'm very, very bad," Justiniana said mockingly.

"Then you and I are alike, Justita. Because you think I'm very, very bad, don't you?"

"You win, that's another goal for you," the girl said in parting as she disappeared into the hallway to the kitchen.

Doña Lucrecia and the boy did not speak as they ate their buns and drank their tea.

"Justita just says she hates me," Fonchito declared when he had finished chewing. "But deep down I think she's forgiven me too. Don't you think so, Stepmamá?"

"Maybe, maybe not. She doesn't let herself be taken in by your goodlittle-boy ways. She doesn't want what happened to happen again. And even though I don't like to think about it, I suffered a great deal because of you, Fonchito."

"Do you think I don't know that, Stepmamá?" The boy turned pale. "That's why I'm going to do everything, everything, to make it up to you."

Was he serious? Or was he playing a part, using words that were too mature for him? There was no way to tell in that young face, where the eyes, mouth, nose, cheekbones, ears, even the tousled hair, seemed the work of a scrupulous aesthete. He was as beautiful as an archangel or a little pagan god. And the worst thing, the very worst thing, Doña Lucrecia thought, was that he seemed the incarnation of purity, a model of innocence

20

and virtue. "The same halo of chastity that Modesto had," she said to herself, recalling the engineer, so fond of sentimental songs, who had courted her before she married Rigoberto, and whom she had rejected, perhaps because she could not truly appreciate his propriety and goodness. Or had she turned down poor Pluto precisely because he was so good? Because what appealed to her heart were those murky depths sounded by Rigoberto? With him, she had not hesitated for an instant. In the excellent Pluto, his chaste expression was a reflection of his soul; in this little devil Alfonso, it was a strategy for seduction, a siren song calling her down to the abyss.

"Do you love Justita very much, Stepmamá?"

"Yes, very much. She's more than an employee to me. I don't know what I would have done without Justiniana all these months, when I had to get used to living alone again. She's been a friend, an ally. That's how I think of her. I don't have the stupid prejudices against servants that other people in Lima have."

She almost told Fonchito about the eminently respectable Doña Felicia de Gallagher, who boasted at her tea and canasta parties that she had forbidden her chauffeur, a robust black man in a navy-blue uniform, to drink water when he was working so that he would not feel the need to urinate and have to stop the car, find a bathroom, and leave his employer alone in those streets crawling with thieves. But she stopped herself, sensing that even an indirect allusion to a bodily function in front of the boy would be like stirring up the fetid waters of a swamp.

"Shall I pour you more tea? The buns are delicious," said Fonchito, flattering her. "When I can get away from the academy and come here, I feel happy, Stepmamá."

"You shouldn't cut so many classes. If you really want to be a painter, you'll find those classes very useful."

Why, when she spoke to him like a child—which is what he was—why was she overcome by a feeling of duplicity, of lying? But if she treated him like a young man, she had identical misgivings, the same sense of mendacity.

"Do you think Justiniana is pretty, Stepmamá?"

"Yes, yes I do. She's a very Peruvian type, with her cinnamon skin and pert look. She must have broken a few hearts along the way."

"Did my papá ever tell you he thought she was pretty?"

"No, I don't think he ever did. Why so many questions?"

"No reason. Except you're prettier than Justita, prettier than all of them,

Stepmamá," the boy exclaimed. And then, frightened, he immediately begged her pardon. "Was I wrong to say that? You won't get angry, will you?"

Señora Lucrecia tried to keep Rigoberto's son from noticing how perturbed she was. Was Lucifer up to his old tricks? Should she pick him up by the ear and throw him out and tell him never to come back? But now Fonchito seemed to have forgotten what he had just said and was looking for something in his portfolio. At last he found it.

"Look, Stepmamá," and he handed her the small clipping. "Schiele when he was a boy. Don't I look like him?"

Doña Lucrecia examined the painfully thin adolescent with the short hair and delicate features, tightly encased in a dark turn-of-the-century suit with a rose in the lapel and a high stiff collar and bow tie that seemed to be strangling him.

"Not at all," she said. "You don't look anything like him."

"Those are his sisters standing beside him. Gertrude and Melanie. The smaller one, the blonde, is the famous Gerti."

"Why famous?" asked Doña Lucrecia, feeling uncomfortable. She knew very well she was entering a minefield.

"What do you mean why?" The rosy little face showed amazement; his hands made a theatrical gesture. "Didn't you know? She was the model for his best known nudes."

"Oh, really?" Doña Lucrecia's discomfort intensified. "I see you're very familiar with Egon Schiele's life."

"I've read everything there is about him in my papá's library. Lots of women posed naked for him. Schoolgirls, streetwalkers, his lover Wally. And also his wife, Edith, and his sister-in-law, Adele."

"All right, all right." Doña Lucrecia looked at her watch. "It's getting late, Fonchito."

"Didn't you know he had Edith and Adele pose for him together?" the boy went on enthusiastically, as if he hadn't heard her. "And the same thing happened when he was living with Wally, in the little village of Krumau. He posed her naked with some schoolgirls. That's why there was such a scandal."

"I'm not surprised, if they were schoolgirls," Señora Lucrecia remarked. "Now, it's getting dark and you'd better go. If Rigoberto calls the academy, he'll find out you're missing classes."

"But the whole thing was unfair," the boy continued, carried away by

22

excitement. "Schiele was an artist, he needed inspiration. Didn't he paint masterpieces? What was wrong with having them undress?"

"I'll take the cups into the kitchen." Señora Lucrecia rose to her feet. "Help me with the plates and the breadbasket, Fonchito."

The boy quickly brushed the crumbs scattered on the table into his hand. Obediently he followed his stepmother. But Señora Lucrecia had not succeeded in tearing him away from his subject.

"Well, it's true he did things with some of the women who posed naked for him," he said as they walked down the hall. "For example, with his sister-in-law Adele. But he wouldn't have with his sister Gerti, would he, Stepmamá?"

The cups had begun to clatter in Señora Lucrecia's hands. The damn kid had the diabolical habit of turning the conversation to salacious topics, playing the innocent all the while.

"Of course not," she replied, feeling her tongue stumbling over the words. "Certainly not, what an idea."

They had walked into the small kitchen, its floor tiles gleaming like mirrors. The walls sparkled too. Justiniana observed them, intrigued. A light fluttered like a butterfly in her eyes, animating her dark face.

"With Gerti, maybe not, but he did with his sister-in-law," the boy insisted. "Adele herself admitted it after Egon Schiele died. The books say so, Stepmamá. I mean, he did things with both sisters. That's probably where his inspiration came from."

"What good-for-nothing are you talking about?" asked the maid. Her expression was very lively. She took the cups and plates, rinsed them in running water, then put them in the washbasin, full to the brim with soapy, blue-tinged water. The odor of bleach permeated the kitchen.

"Egon Schiele," whispered Doña Lucrecia. "An Austrian painter."

"He died when he was twenty-eight, Justita," the boy explained.

"He must have died of all those things he did," Justiniana said as she washed plates and cups and dried them with a red-checkered towel. "So behave yourself, Foncho, or the same thing will happen to you."

"He didn't die of the things he did, he died of Spanish influenza," replied the boy, impervious to her mockery. "His wife too, three days before him. What's Spanish influenza, Stepmamá?"

"A fatal flu, I guess. It must have come to Vienna from Spain. All right, you have to go now, it's late."

"Now I know why you want to be a painter, you bandit," an irrepressible

23

Justiniana interjected. "Because painters seem to have so much fun with their models."

"Don't make those kinds of jokes," Doña Lucrecia reprimanded her. "He's only a boy."

"A nice big boy, Señora," she replied, opening her mouth wide and showing her dazzling white teeth.

"Before he painted them, he played with them." Fonchito took up the thread of his thought again, not paying attention to the dialogue between the señora and her maid. "He had them take different poses, trying things out. Dressed, undressed, half-dressed. What he liked best was for them to try on stockings. Red, green, black, every color. And lie on the floor. Together, separately, holding one another. And pretend they were fighting. He spent hours and hours looking at them. He played with the two sisters as if they were his dolls. Until his inspiration came. Then he painted them."

"That's quite a game," Justiniana said, teasing him. "Like kids' strip poker, but for grown-ups."

"Enough! That's enough!" Doña Lucrecia's voice was so loud that Fonchito and Justiniana stood there openmouthed. More quietly, she said, "I don't want your papá to start asking you questions. You have to go."

"All right, Stepmamá," the boy stammered.

He was white with shock, and Doña Lucrecia regretted having shouted. But she could not allow him to go on talking so passionately about the intimate details of Egon Schiele's life; her heart warned her that a trap, a danger lay there, one she absolutely had to avoid. What had gotten into Justiniana to make her egg him on that way? The boy left the kitchen. She heard him picking up his book bag, portfolio, and pencils in the dining alcove. When he came back, he had straightened his tie, put on his cap, and buttoned his jacket.

Standing in the doorway, looking into her eyes, with utter naturalness he asked, "May I kiss you goodbye, Stepmamá?"

Doña Lucrecia's heart, which was returning to normal, began to race again; but what disturbed her most was Justiniana's little smile. What should she do? It was ridiculous to refuse. She nodded, bending her head down. A moment later she felt a baby bird's peck on her cheek.

"May I kiss you too, Justita?"

"Make sure it's on the mouth," and the girl burst out laughing.

This time the boy joined in the joke, laughed, and stood on tiptoe to kiss Justiniana on the cheek. It was foolish, of course, but Señora Lucrecia did not dare to meet the eyes of her servant or reprimand her for carrying her tasteless jokes too far.

"I could kill you," she said finally, half seriously, half in jest, when she heard the street door close. "Have you lost your mind, making jokes like that with Fonchito?"

"Well, there's something about that boy," Justiniana apologized with a shrug. "I don't know what it is, but it fills your head with sin."

"Whatever," said Doña Lucrecia. "But where he's concerned, it's better not to throw fuel on the fire."

"Fire is what's on your face, señora," replied Justiniana, with her customary impudence. "But don't worry, you look terrific in that color."

Chlorophyll and Dung

I am sorry I must disappoint you. Your impassioned arguments in favor of preserving nature and the environment do not move me. I was born, I have lived, and I will die in the city (in the ugly city of Lima, to make matters worse), and leaving the metropolis, even for a weekend, is a servitude to which I submit occasionally because of family or professional obligations, but always with distaste. Do not count me as one of those bourgeois whose fondest wish is to buy a little house on a southern beach where they can spend summers and weekends in obscene proximity to sand, salt water, and the beer bellies of other bourgeois identical to themselves. This Sunday spectacle of families fraternizing beside the sea in a *bien pensant* exhibitionism is, in the ignoble annals of gregariousness, one of the most depressing offered by this pre-individualist country.

I understand that for people like you a landscape peppered with cows grazing on fragrant grasses or nanny goats sniffing around carob trees gladdens your heart and makes you experience the ecstasy of a boy seeing a naked woman for the first time. As far as I am concerned, the natural destiny of the bull is the bullring—in other words, it lives in order to face the matador's cape and cane, the picador's lance, the banderillero's dart, the sword—and as for the stupid cows, my only wish is to see them carved, grilled, seasoned with hot spices, and set down before me bloody and rare and surrounded by crisp fried potatoes and fresh salads, and the goats should be pounded, shredded, fried, or marinated, depending on the recipe for

25

northern *seco*, one of my favorite of all the dishes offered by our brutal Peruvian gastronomy.

I know I am offending your most cherished beliefs, for I am not unaware that you and your colleagues—yet another collectivist conspiracy!—are convinced, or are almost convinced, that animals have rights and perhaps a soul, all of them, not excluding the malarial mosquito, the carrion-eating hyena, the hissing cobra, and the voracious piranha. I openly admit that for me, animals are of edible, decorative, and perhaps sporting interest (though I state specifically that I find love of horses as unpleasant as vegetarianism, and consider horsemen, their testicles shrunken by the friction of the saddle, to be a particularly lugubrious type of human castrato). I respect, at a distance, those who attribute an erotic function to animals, but I personally am not seduced (on the contrary, it makes me smell nasty odors and presume a whole series of physical discomforts) by the idea of copulating with a chicken, a duck, a monkey, a mare, or any species with orifices, and I harbor the enervating suspicion that those who find gratification in such gymnastic feats are, in the marrow of their bones—and please do not take this personally—primitive ecologists and unknowing conservationists, more than capable in the future of banding together with Brigitte Bardot (whom I too, let it be said, loved as a young man) and working for the survival of the seals. Although, on occasion, I have had unsettling fantasies of a beautiful naked woman rolling on a bed covered with kittens, the fact that sixty-three million cats and fifty-four million dogs are household pets in the United States alarms me more than the host of atomic weapons stored in half a dozen countries of the former Soviet Union.

If this is what I think of quadrupeds and mangy birds, you can well imagine the feelings awakened in me by murmuring trees, dense forests, delicious foliage, singing rivers, deep ravines, crystalline peaks, and so forth and so on. All these natural resources have significance and justification for me if they pass through the filter of urban civilization; in other words, if they are manufactured and transmuted—it does not matter to me if we say denaturalized, but I would prefer the currently discredited term humanized—by books, paintings, film, or television. To be sure we understand each other, I would give my life (this should not be taken literally since it is obvious hyperbole) to save the poplars that raise their lofty crowns in Góngora's "Polyphemus," the almond trees that whiten his "Solitudes," the weeping willows in Garcilaso's "Eclogues," or the sunflowers and wheat fields that distill their golden honey onto the canvases of Van Gogh, but I would not shed a tear in praise of pine groves devastated by summer fires, and my hand would not tremble as I signed an amnesty for the arsonists who turn Andean, Siberian, or Alpine forests to ashes. Nature that is not passed through art or literature, Nature *au naturel*, full of flies, mosquitoes, mud, rats, and cockroaches, is incompatible with refined pleasures such as bodily hygiene and elegance of dress.

For the sake of brevity, I will summarize my thinking—my phobias, at any rate—by explaining that if what you call "urban blight" were to advance unchecked and swallow up all the meadows of the world, and the earth were to be covered by an outbreak of skyscrapers, metal bridges, asphalt streets, artificial lakes and parks, paved plazas, and underground parking lots, and the entire planet were encased in reinforced concrete and steel beams and became a single, spherical, endless city (but one abounding in bookstores, galleries, libraries, restaurants, museums, and cafés), the undersigned, *homo urbanus* to his very bones, would applaud.

For the reasons stated above, I will not contribute one cent to the Chlorophyll and Dung Association, over which you preside, and will do everything in my power (very little, don't worry) to keep you from achieving your ends and to prevent your bucolic philosophy from destroying the object that is emblematic of the culture which you despise and I venerate: the truck.

Pluto's Dream

In the solitude of his study, awake in the cold dawn, Don Rigoberto repeated from memory the phrase of Borges he had just found: "Adultery is usually made up of tenderness and abnegation." A few pages after the Borgesian citation, the letter appeared before him, undamaged by the corrosive passage of years:

Dear Lucrecia:

    Reading these lines will bring you the surprise of your life, and perhaps you will despise me. But it doesn't matter. Even if there were only one chance that you would accept my offer against a million that you would reject it, I would take the plunge. I will summarize what would require hours of conversation, accompanied by vocal inflections and persuasive gestures.

Since leaving Peru (because you turned me down), I've been working in the United States and have done fairly well. In ten years I have become a manager and member of the executive board of a thriving electrical-conductor factory in the state of Massachusetts. As an engineer and entrepreneur, I have made my way in this, my second country, for I became an American citizen four years ago.

I wanted to let you know that I have just resigned my position and am selling my stock in the firm, from which I expect to make a profit of $600,000—with luck, a little more. I am doing this because I have been offered the presidency of TIM (Technological Institute of Mississippi), the college I attended and with which I have maintained a close relationship. A third of the student body is now Hispanic (Latin American). My salary will be half of what I earn here. I don't care. I look forward to devoting myself to the education of young people from the two Americas, who will build the twenty-first century. I always dreamed of dedicating my life to Academe, and this is what I would have done if I had remained in Peru, that is, if you had married me.

"What's the point of all this?" you must be asking yourself. "Why has Modesto returned after ten years to tell me this story?" I'm getting there, my darling Lucrecia.

I have decided that during the week between my departure from Boston and my arrival in Oxford, Mississippi, I will spend $100,000 of my $600,000 on a vacation. I have, by the way, never taken a vacation and do not plan to take one in the future, because, as you may remember, I've always liked working. My job is still my favorite diversion. But if my plans materialize, as I hope they do, this week will be something quite out of the ordinary. Not the conventional Caribbean cruise or beaches with palm trees and surfers in Hawaii. Something very personal, and unrepeatable: the fulfillment of an old dream. This is where you come in, right through the front door. I know you are married to an honorable Limenian gentleman, a widower and an insurance executive. I am married too, to a gringa, a physician from Boston, and I am happy to the modest extent that marriage allows. I am not proposing that you divorce and take up a new life, not at all. Only that you join me for this ideal week, cherished in my mind for so many years, which circumstances now permit me to make a reality. You will not regret sharing these seven days of illusion with me, days you will remember fondly for the rest of your life, I promise.

We will meet on Saturday the 17th at Kennedy Airport in New York, where you will arrive from Lima on Lufthansa, and I will fly in from Boston. A limousine will take us to the suite at the Plaza Hotel, which I have already reserved, along with the flowers I have selected to perfume it. You will have time to rest, have your hair done, visit a sauna, or go shopping on Fifth Avenue, which is literally at your feet. That night we have tickets to the Metropolitan Opera to see Puccini's Tosca, with Luciano Pavarotti as Mario Cavaradossi and the Metropolitan Orchestra under the direction of Maestro Edouardo Muller. We will dine at Le Cirque, where, with luck, you can rub elbows with Mick Jagger, Henry Kissinger, or Sharon Stone. We will end the evening at the glamorous and exciting Regine's.

The Concorde to Paris leaves at noon on Sunday, and there will be no need for us to rise early. Since the flight takes less than three and a half hours—apparently one is hardly aware of the passage of time, thanks to the luncheon delicacies prepared under the supervision of Paul Bocuse—it will still be day when we reach the City of Light. After we have registered at the Ritz (a view of the Place Vendôme guaranteed), there will be time for a stroll along the bridges over the Seine, enjoying the mild evenings of early autumn, the loveliest season, according to connoisseurs, as long as it doesn't rain. (I have failed in my efforts to determine the chances of fluvial precipitation in Paris on Sunday and Monday, since NASA, which is to say the science of meteorology, predicts the whims of heaven only four days in advance.) I have never been to Paris, and I hope you have not either, so that on our evening walk from the Ritz to Saint-Germain we will discover together what is, by all accounts, an astonishing itinerary. On the Left Bank (in other words, the Parisian Miraflores) we can look forward to a performance of Mozart's unfinished Requiem at the Abbey of Saint-Germain des Prés, and supper chez Lipp, an Alsatian brasserie where the choucroute is obligatory (I don't know what that is, but as long as it has no garlic, I'll like it). I've assumed that when supper is over you will probably wish to rest in order to be fresh for our busy schedule on Monday, and therefore that night we will not be caught up in a whirl of discotheques, bars, boîtes, or caves that stay open until dawn.

The next morning we will visit the Louvre to pay our respects to La Gioconda, have a light lunch at La Closerie de Lilas or La Coupole (the restaurants in Montparnasse so revered by snobs), and in the afternoon we will dip into the avant-garde at the Centre Pompidou and make a quick visit to the Marais, famous for its eighteenth-century palaces and contemporary faggots. We will have tea at La Marquise de Sévigné, at La Madeleine, before returning to the hotel for a refreshing shower. Our program that night is completely frivolous: an apéritif at the Ritz Bar, supper in the modernist decor of Maxim's, and to round off the festivities, a visit to that cathedral of striptease the Crazy Horse Saloon, with its brand-new revue, It's So Hot! (Tickets have been purchased, tables reserved, and maîtres d's and doormen bribed to assure the best locations, tables, and service.)

On Tuesday morning a limousine, less showy but more refined than the one in New York, complete with driver and guide, will take us to Versailles to visit the palace and gardens of the Sun King. We will eat a typical meal (steak and fried potatoes, I'm afraid) at a bistro along the way, and before the opera (Verdi's Otello, with Plácido Domingo, of course) you will have time for shopping on the Faubourg Saint-Honoré, very close to the hotel. We will have a simulacrum of supper, for purely visual and sociological reasons, at the Ritz, where—dixit the expert—the sumptuous ambiance and elegant service compensate for an unimaginative menu. We will have our real supper after the opera, at La Tour d'Argent, from whose windows we will bid a fond farewell to the towers of Notre Dame and the lights of the bridges reflected in the flowing waters of the Seine.

The Orient Express to Venice leaves on Wednesday at noon, from the Gare Saint Lazare. We will spend that day and night traveling and resting, but according to those who have engaged in this railway adventure, passing through the landscapes of France, Germany, Austria, Switzerland, and Italy in those belle époque compartments is relaxing and instructive, stimulating but not fatiguing, exciting but in moderation, and entertaining, if only for archaeological reasons, because of the tastefully restored elegance of the compartments, restrooms, bars, and dining cars of that legendary train, the setting for so many novels and films of the years between the wars. I will bring with me Agatha Christie's novel Murder on the Orient Express, in both English and Spanish, in case you wish to enhance your view of the locales where the action occurs. According to the prospectus, for our supper à la chandelle that evening, formal wear and deep décolletage are de rigueur.

Our suite at the Hotel Cipriani, on the island of Giudecca, has a view of the Grand Canal, the Piazza di San Marco, and the swelling Byzantine towers of its church. I have hired a gondola and the man considered by the agency to be the best-informed (and only good-natured) guide in the lacustrine city, so that on Thursday morning and afternoon he can familiarize us with the churches, plazas, convents, bridges, and museums, including a short break at noon for a snack—a pizza, for example—surrounded by pigeons and tourists on the terrazza of the Florian. We will have a drink—an inevitable concoction called a Bellini—at the Hotel Danieli, and our supper at Harry's Bar, immortalized in a wretched novel by Hemingway. On Friday we will continue the marathon with a visit to the Lido and an excursion to Murano, where glass is still shaped by human breath (a technique that preserves tradition as it strengthens the lungs of the natives). There will be time for souvenirs and a furtive glance at a villa by Palladio. At night, a concert on the isle of San Giorgio—I Musici Veneti—performing music by Venetian baroque composers, of course: Vivaldi, Cimarosa, and Albinoni. Supper will be on the terrazza of the Danieli, where, if the sky is clear, we can watch (I cite the guidebooks) the lights of Venice like a mantle of fireflies. We will take our leave of the city and the Old Continent, my dear Lucre, if our bodies permit, surrounded by modernity in the discotheque Il Gatto Nero, which attracts old, middle-aged, and youthful jazz fans (something you and I have never been, but one of the requirements of this ideal week is to do what we have never done, subject as we are to the servitude of the mundane).

The following morning—the seventh day, with the word "end" looming on the horizon—we will have to rise early. The plane to Paris leaves at ten, connecting with the Concorde to New York. As we fly over the Atlantic, we will sort through the images and sensations stored in our memories, selecting those that deserve to endure.

We will say goodbye at Kennedy Airport (your flight to Lima and mine to Boston leave at almost the same time), no doubt never to see one another again. I do not think our paths will cross a second time. I will not return to Peru, and I do not believe you will ever set foot in the remote corner of the Deep South that, beginning in October, will boast of the only Hispanic college president in this country (the 2,500 others are gringos, African Americans, or Asians).

Will you come? Your passage is waiting for you in the offices of Lufthansa in Lima. You don't need to send me a reply. On Saturday the 17th I will be at the appointed place. Your presence or absence will be your response. If you do not come, I will follow this itinerary alone, fantasizing that you are with me, making real this whim that has been my consolation for years, thinking of a woman who, despite the rejection that changed my life, will always be the very heart of my memory.

Need I point out that this is an invitation to honor me with your company and does not imply any obligation other than your presence? I am in no way asking you, during the days of our travels together—I can think of no other euphemism for saying this—to share my bed. My darling Lucrecia, my only desire is that you share my dream. The suites reserved in New York, Paris, and Venice have separate bedrooms with doors under lock and key, and if your scruples demand it, I can add daggers, hatchets, revolvers, and even bodyguards.

31

But you know none of that will be necessary, and for the entire week this virtuous Modesto, this gentle Pluto, as they called me in the neighborhood, will be as respectful of you as I was years ago in Lima, when I tried to persuade you to marry me and barely had the courage to touch your hand in darkened movie theaters.

Until we meet at Kennedy, or goodbye forever, Lucre,

Modesto (Pluto)

Don Rigoberto felt assailed by the high temperature and tremors of tertian fever. How would Lucrecia respond? Would she indignantly reject this letter from Lazarus? Or would she succumb to frivolous temptation? In the milky light of dawn, it seemed to him that his notebooks were waiting for the denouement as impatiently as his tormented spirit.

Imperatives of the Thirsty Traveler

This is an order from your slave, beloved.

Before a mirror, on a bed or sofa adorned with hand-painted silks from India or Indonesian batik with circular eyes, you will lie on your back, undressed, and loosen your long black hair.

You will raise your left leg, bending it until it forms an angle. You will rest your head on your right shoulder, partially open your lips, and, crushing a corner of the sheet in your right hand, you will lower your eyelids, feigning sleep. You will imagine a yellow river of butterfly wings and stardust descending from heaven and entering you.

Who are you?

The *Danaë* of Gustav Klimt, naturally. No matter the model he used to paint this oil (1907–8), the master anticipated you, foretold you, saw you just as you would come into the world, just as you would be half a century later, on the other side of the ocean. He believed he was re-creating a figure from Hellenic mythology with his brushes, when he was actually pre-creating you, future beauty, loving wife, sensual stepmother.

Only you among women, in this painterly fantasy, combine an angel's virtuous perfection, innocence, and purity with a boldly terrestrial body. Today I pass over the firmness of your breasts and the assertiveness of your hips to pay exclusive homage to the consistency of your thighs, a temple

32

to whose columns I would like to be tied, then whipped because I have misbehaved.

All of you brings joy to my senses.

Velvet skin, aloe saliva, oh delicate lady of unwithering elbows and knees, awaken, regard yourself in the mirror, tell yourself, "I am worshipped and admired above all others, I am desired as watery mirages in the desert are longed for by the thirsty traveler."

Lucrecia-Danaë, Danaë-Lucrecia.

This is a plea from your master, slave.

The Ideal Week

"My secretary called Lufthansa and, in fact, your paid passage is waiting there," said Don Rigoberto. "Round trip. First class, of course."

"Was I right to show you the letter, my love?" exclaimed Doña Lucrecia in great alarm. "You're not angry, are you? We promised never to hide anything from each other, and I thought I ought to show it to you."

"You did just the right thing, my queen," said Don Rigoberto, kissing his wife's hand. "I want you to go."

"You want me to go?" Doña Lucrecia smiled, looked somber, then smiled again. "Are you serious?"

"I beg you to go," he insisted, his lips on his wife's fingers. "Unless the idea displeases you. But why should it? Even though the plan is that of a rather vulgar nouveau riche, it has been worked out in a spirit of joy and with an irony not at all frequent in engineers. You will have a good time, my dear."

"I don't know what to say, Rigoberto," Doña Lucrecia stammered, making an effort not to blush. "It's very generous of you, but . . ."

"I'm asking you to accept for selfish reasons," her husband explained. "And you know that selfishness is a virtue in my philosophy. Your trip will be a great experience for me."

Doña Lucrecia knew from Don Rigoberto's eyes and expression that he was serious. And so she did take the trip, and on the eighth day she returned to Lima. At Córpac she was met by her husband and Fonchito, who was holding a cellophane-wrapped bouquet of flowers with a card that read: *Welcome home, Stepmamá.* They greeted her with many displays of affection,

33

and Don Rigoberto, to help her conceal her discomfort, asked endless questions about the weather, going through customs, changes in schedule, jet lag and fatigue, avoiding anything approaching sensitive material. On the way to Barranco he provided her with a meticulous accounting of events at the office and Fonchito's school, and their breakfasts, lunches, and dinners during her absence. The house sparkled with extravagant order and cleanliness. Justiniana had even had the curtains washed and the fertilizer in the garden replaced, tasks usually reserved for the end of the month.

The afternoon was spent unpacking suitcases, talking to the servants about practical matters, and answering phone calls from friends and relations who wanted to know how she had enjoyed her trip to Miami to shop for Christmas presents (the official version of her adventure). The atmosphere was absolutely uncharged when she took out gifts for her husband, her stepson, and Justiniana. Don Rigoberto liked the French ties, the Italian shirts, and the sweater from New York, and Fonchito looked marvelous in the jeans, leather jacket, and athletic gear. Justiniana gave a cry of enthusiasm when she tried on the duck-yellow dress over her smock.

After supper, Don Rigoberto withdrew to the bathroom and took less time than usual with his ablutions. When he emerged, he found the bedroom in darkness cut by indirect lighting that illuminated only the two engravings by Utamaro depicting the incompatible but orthodox matings of the same couple, the man endowed with a long, corkscrew member, the woman with a Lilliputian sex, the two of them surrounded by kimonos billowing like storm clouds, paper lanterns, floor mats, low tables holding a porcelain tea service, and, in the distance, bridges spanning a sinuous river. Doña Lucrecia lay beneath the sheets, not naked, he discovered when he slipped in beside her, but in a new nightgown—purchased and worn on her trip?—that allowed his hands the freedom necessary to reach her most intimate corners. She turned on her side, and he could slide his arm under her shoulders and feel her from head to foot. He did not crush her to him but kissed her, very tenderly, on the eyes and cheeks, taking his time to reach her mouth.

"Don't tell me anything you don't want to," he lied into her ear with a boyish coquetry that inflamed her impatience as his lips traced the curve of her ear. "Whatever you have a mind to. Or nothing at all, if you prefer."

"I'll tell you everything," Doña Lucrecia murmured, searching for his mouth. "Isn't that why you sent me?"

"That's one reason," Don Rigoberto agreed, kissing her on the neck, the hair, her forehead, returning again and again to her nose, cheeks, and chin. "Did you enjoy yourself? Did you have a good time?"

"Whether it was good or bad will depend on what happens now between you and me," said Señora Lucrecia hurriedly, and Don Rigoberto felt his wife become tense for a moment. "Yes, I enjoyed myself. Yes, I had a good time. But I was always afraid."

"Afraid I would be angry?" Now Don Rigoberto was kissing her firm breasts, millimeter by millimeter, and the tip of his tongue played with her nipples, feeling them harden. "That I would make a scene and be jealous?"

"That you would suffer," Doña Lucrecia whispered, embracing him.

"She's beginning to perspire," Don Rigoberto observed to himself. He felt joy as he caressed her increasingly responsive body, and he had to bring his mind to bear to control the vertigo that was overtaking him. He whispered into his wife's ear that he loved her more, much more than before her trip.

She began to speak, pausing as she searched for the words—silences meant to conceal her awkwardness—but little by little, aroused by his caresses and amorous interruptions, she gained confidence. At last, Don Rigoberto realized she had recovered her natural fluency and could tell her story by assuming a feigned distance from the account, clinging to his body, her head resting on his shoulder. The couple's hands moved from time to time to take possession or verify the existence of a member, a muscle, or a piece of skin.

"Had he changed very much?"

He had become very much a gringo in the way he dressed and spoke, for he continually used English words. But though his hair was gray and he had put on weight, he still had the same long, melancholy Pluto face, and all the timidity and inhibitions of his youth.

"Seeing you arrive must have been like a gift from heaven."

"He turned so pale! I thought he was going to faint. He was waiting for me with a bouquet of flowers bigger than he was. The limousine was one of those silver-colored ones that gangsters have in movies. With a bar, a television, a stereo, and—this will kill you—leopardskin seat covers."

"Poor ecologists," Don Rigoberto responded with enthusiasm.

"I know it's very parvenu," Modesto apologized while the chauffeur, an extremely tall Afghani in a maroon uniform, arranged their luggage in the trunk. "But it was the most expensive one."

"He's able to laugh at himself," Don Rigoberto declared. "That's nice."

"On the ride to the Plaza he paid me a few compliments, blushing all the way to his ears," Doña Lucrecia continued. "He said I looked very young and even more beautiful than when he asked me to marry him."

"You are," Don Rigoberto interrupted, drinking in her breath. "More and more, every day, every hour."

"Not a single remark in bad taste, not a single offensive insinuation," she said. "He was so grateful to me for joining him that he made me feel like the good Samaritan in the Bible."

"Do you know what he was wondering while he was being so gallant?"

"What?" Doña Lucrecia slipped her leg between her husband's.

"If he would see you naked that afternoon, in the Plaza, or if he would have to wait until that night, or even until Paris," Don Rigoberto explained.

"He didn't see me naked that afternoon or that night. Unless he peeked through the keyhole while I was bathing and dressing for the Metropolitan Opera. What he had said about separate rooms was true. Mine overlooked Central Park."

"But he must have at least held your hand at the opera, in the restaurant," he complained, feeling disappointed. "With the help of a little champagne, he must have put his cheek to yours while you were dancing at Regine's. He must have kissed your neck, your ear."

Not at all. He had not tried to take her hand or kiss her during that long night, though he did not spare the compliments, but always at a respectful distance. He was very likable, in fact, mocking his own lack of experience ("I'm mortified, Lucre, but in six years of marriage I've never cheated on my wife"), and admitting to her that this was the first time in his life he had attended the opera or set foot in Le Cirque and Regine's.

"The only thing I'm sure of is that I must ask for Dom Pérignon, sniff at the glass of wine as if I suffered from allergies, and order dishes with French names."

He looked at her with immeasurable, canine gratitude.

"To tell the truth, I've come out of vanity, Modesto. And curiosity too, of course. After ten years of our not seeing each other, of our not being in touch at all, is it possible you're still in love with me?"

"Love isn't the right word," he pointed out. "I'm in love with Dorothy, the gringa I married, who's very understanding and lets me sing in bed."

"For him you meant something more subtle," Don Rigoberto declared.

"Unreality, illusion, the woman of his memory and desires. I want to worship you the same way, the way he does. Wait, wait."

He removed her tiny nightgown and then positioned her so that their skin would touch in more places. He reined in his desire and asked her to continue.

"We returned to the hotel just as I was beginning to yawn. He said good night at a distance from my door. He wished me pleasant dreams. He behaved so well, he was so much a gentleman, that the next morning I flirted with him just a little."

When she appeared for breakfast in the room that separated the two bedrooms, she was barefoot and wearing a short summer wrapper that left her legs and thighs exposed. Modesto was waiting for her, shaved, showered, and dressed. His mouth fell open.

"Did you sleep well?" he managed to articulate, slack-jawed, pulling out a chair for her at the breakfast table, which held fruit juice, toast, and marmalade. "May I say that you look very attractive?"

"Stop." Don Rigoberto cut her off. "Let me kneel and kiss the legs that dazzled Pluto the dog."

On the way to the airport, and then as they ate lunch in the Air France Concorde, Modesto returned to the attentive adoration he had displayed on the first day. He reminded Lucrecia, in an undramatic way, of how he had decided to leave the School of Engineering when he became convinced she would not marry him, and had gone to Boston to seek his fortune; of his early difficulties in that city of cold winters and dark red Victorian mansions, where it took him three months to find his first permanent job. His heart had been broken, but he was not complaining. He had achieved the security he needed, he got along well with his wife, and now that a new phase of his life was about to begin with his return to the university, which was something he had always missed, he was making his fantasy, the grown-up game that had been his refuge all these years, come true: his ideal week with Lucre, when he would pretend to be rich in New York, Paris, and Venice. Now he could die happy.

"Are you really going to spend so much of your savings on this trip?"

"I would spend the three hundred thousand that are mine, because the rest belongs to Dorothy," he affirmed, looking into her eyes. "And not for the entire week. Just for having seen you at breakfast, just for seeing those legs, those arms, those shoulders. The most beautiful in the world, Lucre."

"What would he have said if he had seen your breasts and your sweet ass?" Don Rigoberto kissed her. "I love you, I adore you."

"This was when I decided that in Paris he would see the rest." Doña Lucrecia moved away slightly from her husband's kisses. "I made the decision when the pilot announced that we had broken the sound barrier."

"It was the least you could have done for so proper a gentleman," said Don Rigoberto approvingly.

As soon as they were settled in their respective bedrooms—the view from Lucrecia's windows included the dark column on the Place Vendôme, so high she could not see the top, and the glittering display windows of the jewelry shops all around it—they went out for a stroll. Modesto had memorized the route and calculated the time it would take. They passed through the Tuileries, crossed the Seine, and walked toward Saint-Germain along the quays on the Left Bank. They reached the abbey half an hour before the concert. It was a pale, mild afternoon, autumn had already turned the leaves on the chestnut trees, and, from time to time, the engineer would stop, guidebook and map in hand, to give Lucrecia a bit of historical, urbanistic, architectural, or aesthetic information. On the uncomfortable little seats in a church filled to capacity for the concert, they had to sit very close together. Lucrecia enjoyed the lavish melancholy of Mozart's *Requiem*.

Later, when they were at a small table on the first floor of Lipp's, she congratulated Modesto. "I can't believe this is your first trip to Paris. You know streets, monuments, directions, as if you lived here."

"I've prepared for this trip as if it were the final exam for a degree, Lucre. I've consulted books, maps, travel agencies, and talked to travelers. I don't collect stamps or raise dogs or play golf. For years my only hobby has been preparing for this week."

"Was I always in it?"

"Another step along the road of flirtation," Don Rigoberto noted.

"Always you and only you," said Pluto, blushing. "New York, Paris, Venice, operas, restaurants, all the rest, were merely the background. The important thing, the central thing, was to be alone with you in that setting."

They returned to the Ritz in a taxi, tired and a little tipsy from the champagne, the Burgundy wine, and the cognac with which they had anticipated, accompanied, and bidden farewell to the *choucroute*. When they said good night, standing in the small room that divided their bedrooms, Doña Lucrecia, without the slightest hesitation, announced to Modesto,

"You're behaving so well that I want to play too. I'm going to give you a present."

"Oh, really?" Pluto's voice broke. "What's that, Lucre?"

"My entire body," she sang out. "Come in when I call you. But just to look."

She did not hear Modesto's reply but was sure that in the darkened room, as he nodded, speechless, his joy knew no bounds. Not certain exactly what she would do, she undressed, hung up her clothes, and, in the bathroom, unpinned her hair ("The way I like it, my love?" "Exactly the same, Rigoberto"), walked back into the room, turned out all the lights except the one on the night table, and moved the lamp so that its illumination, softened by a satin shade, fell on the sheets that the chambermaid had turned down for the night. She lay on her back, turned slightly to the side in a languid, uninhibited pose, and settled her head on the pillow.

"Whenever you're ready."

She closed her eyes so as not to see him come in, thought Don Rigoberto, moved by that touch of modesty. With absolute clarity he could see in the blue-tinged light, from the perspective of the hesitant, yearning engineer who had just crossed the threshold, the shapely body that, without reaching Rubenesque excesses, emulated the virginal opulence of Murillo as she lay on her back, one knee slightly forward to hide the pubis, the other presented openly, the full curves of the hips stabilizing the volume of golden flesh in the center of the bed. Though he had contemplated, studied, caressed and enjoyed that body so many times, through another man's eyes he seemed to see it for the first time. For a long while—his breathing agitated, his phallus stiff—he admired it. Reading his mind, not saying a word to break the silence, from time to time Lucrecia moved in slow motion with the abandon of one who thinks she is safe from indiscreet eyes, and displayed to the respectful Modesto, frozen two paces from the bed, her flanks and back, her buttocks and breasts, her hair-free underarms and the little forest of her pubis. At last she began to open her legs, revealing her inner thighs and the half-moon of her sex. "In the pose of the anonymous model of *L'Origine du monde*, by Gustave Courbet (1866)," Don Rigoberto sought and found the reference, overcome by emotion to discover that the exuberance of his wife's belly, the robust solidity of her thighs and mound of Venus, coincided millimeter by millimeter with the headless woman in the oil painting that was the reigning prince of his private collection. Then eternity dissolved.

"I'm tired, and I think you are too, Pluto. It's time to sleep."

"Good night" was the immediate reply of a voice at the very peak of ecstasy, or agony. Modesto stepped back, stumbled, and seconds later closed the door.

"He was capable of restraining himself, he did not throw himself at you like a ravening beast," exclaimed an enchanted Don Rigoberto. "You were controlling him with your little finger."

"It's hard to believe," Lucrecia said with a laugh, "but that docility of his was also part of the game."

The next morning a bellboy brought a bouquet of roses to her bed, with a card that read: *Eyes that see, a heart that feels, a mind that remembers, and a cartoon dog that thanks you with all his heart.*

"I want you too much," Don Rigoberto apologized as he covered her mouth with his hand. "I must make love to you."

"Then imagine the night poor Pluto must have spent."

"Poor?" Don Rigoberto pondered after love, as they, exhausted and satisfied, were recovering their strength. "Why poor?"

"I'm the happiest man in the world, Lucre," Modesto declared that night in the interval between two striptease shows at the Crazy Horse Saloon, which was packed with Japanese and Germans, and after they had consumed a bottle of champagne. "Not even the electric train that Father Christmas brought me on my tenth birthday can compare to your gift."

During the day, as they had walked through the Louvre, lunched at La Closerie de Lilas, visited the Centre Pompidou, or lost their way in the narrow, reconstructed streets of the Marais, he had not made the slightest allusion to the previous night. He continued to act as her well-informed, devoted, obliging traveling companion.

"The more you tell me, the better I like him," remarked Don Rigoberto.

"The same thing happened to me," Doña Lucrecia acknowledged. "And so that day I went a step further, to reward him. At Maxim's he felt my knee against his during the entire meal. And when we danced, my breasts. And at the Crazy Horse, my legs."

"I envy him," exclaimed Don Rigoberto. "To discover you serially, episodically, bit by bit. A game of cat and mouse, after all. A game not without its dangers."

"No, not if it's played with gentlemen like you," Doña Lucrecia said coquettishly. "I'm glad I accepted your invitation, Pluto."

40

They were back at the Ritz, drowsy and content. They were saying good night in the sitting room of their suite.

"Wait, Modesto," she improvised, blinking. "Surprise, surprise, close your little eyes."

Pluto obeyed instantly, transformed by expectation. She approached, pressed against him, kissed him, lightly at first, noticing that he hesitated to respond to the lips brushing his, and then to the thrusts of her tongue. When he did, she sensed that with this kiss the engineer was giving her the love he had felt for so long, his adoration and fantasy, his well-being and (if he had one) his soul. When he caught her around the waist, cautiously, prepared to let go at the first sign of rejection, Doña Lucrecia allowed him to embrace her.

"May I open my eyes?"

"You may."

And then he looked at her, not with the cold eyes of the perfect libertine, de Sade, thought Don Rigoberto, but with the pure, fervent, impassioned eyes of the mystic at the moment of his ascent and vision.

"Was he very excited?" The question escaped his lips, and he regretted it. "What a stupid question. Forgive me, Lucrecia."

"He was, but he made no attempt to hold me. At the first hint, he moved away."

"You should have gone to bed with him that night," Don Rigoberto admonished her. "You were being abusive. Or perhaps not. Perhaps you were doing just the right thing. Yes, yes, of course. The slow, the formal, the ritualized, the theatrical—that is eroticism. It was a wise delay. Rushing makes us more like animals. Did you know that donkeys, monkeys, pigs, and rabbits ejaculate in twelve seconds, at the most?"

"But the frog can copulate for forty days and nights without stopping. I read it in a book by Jean Rostand: *From Fly to Man*."

"I'm envious." Don Rigoberto was filled with admiration. "You are so wise, Lucrecia."

"Those were Modesto's words." His wife confused him, returned him to an Orient Express hurtling through the European night on its way to Venice. "The next day, in our *belle époque* compartment."

And the words were reiterated by a bouquet of flowers waiting for her at the Hotel Cipriani, on sun-filled Giudecca: *To Lucrecia, beautiful in life and wise in love.*

"Wait, wait." Don Rigoberto brought her back to the rails. "Did you share the compartment on the train?"

"It had two beds. I was in the upper berth and he was in the lower."

"In other words . . ."

"We literally had to undress on top of one another," she completed the sentence. "We saw each other in our underclothes, though it was dark, because I turned out all the lights except the night-light."

"Underclothing is a general, abstract concept," Don Rigoberto fumed. "Give me precise details."

Doña Lucrecia did. When it was time to undress—the anachronistic Orient Express was crossing German or Austrian forests, passing an occasional village—Modesto asked if she wanted him to leave. "There's no need, in this darkness we're no more than shadows," Doña Lucrecia replied. The engineer sat on the lower berth, taking up as little room as possible in order to give her more space. She undressed, not forcing her movements or stylizing them, turning round where she stood as she removed each article of clothing: dress, slip, bra, stockings, panties. The illumination from the night-light, a little mushroom-shaped lamp with lanceolate drawings, caressed her neck, shoulders, breasts, belly, buttocks, thighs, knees, feet. Raising her arms, she slipped a Chinese silk pajama top, decorated with dragons, over her head.

"I'm going to sit with my legs uncovered while I brush my hair," she said, and did so. "If you feel the urge to kiss them, you may. As far as my knees."

Was it the torment of Tantalus? Or the garden of earthly delights? Don Rigoberto had moved to the foot of the bed, and anticipating his wish, Doña Lucrecia sat on the edge so that, like Pluto on the Orient Express, her husband could kiss her insteps, breathe in the fragrance of the creams and colognes that refreshed her ankles, nibble at her toes and lick the hollows that separated them.

"I love you and admire you," said Don Rigoberto.

"I love you and admire you," said Pluto.

"And now to sleep," ordered Doña Lucrecia.

They reached Venice on an Impressionist morning, the sun strong and the sky a deep blue, and as the launch carried them to the Cipriani through curling waves, Modesto, Michelin in hand, provided Lucrecia with brief descriptions of the palaces and churches along the Grand Canal.

"I'm feeling jealous, my dear," Don Rigoberto interrupted her.

"If you're serious, we'll erase it, sweetheart," Doña Lucrecia proposed.

"Absolutely not," and he recanted. "Brave men die with their boots on, like John Wayne."

From the balcony of the Cipriani, over the trees in the garden, one could see the towers of San Marco and the palaces along the canal. They went out in the gondola-with-guide that was waiting for them. It was a whirl of canals and bridges, greenish waters and flocks of gulls that took flight as they passed, dim churches where they had to strain their eyes to make out the attributes of the gods and saints hanging there. They saw Titians and Veroneses, Bellinis and del Piombos, the horses of San Marco and the mosaics in the cathedral, and they fed a few grains of corn to the fat pigeons on the piazza. At midday they took the obligatory photograph at a table at Florian's while they ate the requisite pizzetta. In the afternoon they continued their tour, hearing names, dates, and anecdotes they barely listened to, lulled by the soothing voice of the guide from the agency. At seven-thirty, when they had bathed and changed, they drank their Bellinis in the salon with Moorish arches and Arabian pillows at the Danieli, and at precisely the right hour—nine o'clock—they were in Harry's Bar. There they saw the divine Catherine Deneuve (it seemed part of the program) come in and sit at the next table. Pluto said what he had to say, "I think you're more beautiful, Lucre."

"And?" Don Rigoberto pressed her.

Before taking the vaporetto back to Giudecca, they went for a walk, Doña Lucrecia holding Modesto's arm, through narrow, half-deserted streets. They reached the hotel after midnight. Doña Lucrecia was yawning.

"And?" Don Rigoberto was impatient.

"I'm so exhausted after our walk and all the nice things I've seen, I won't be able to close my eyes," lamented Doña Lucrecia. "Fortunately, I have a remedy that never fails."

"What's that?" asked Modesto.

"What remedy?" echoed Don Rigoberto.

"A Jacuzzi, alternating cool and warm water," explained Doña Lucrecia, walking toward her bedroom. Before she disappeared inside, she pointed toward the huge, luminous bathroom with its white tiled walls. "Would you fill the tub for me while I put on my robe?"

Don Rigoberto moved in his place, as restless as an insomniac: And? She went to her room, slowly undressed, folding each article of clothing, one piece at a time, as if she had all eternity at her disposal. Wearing a terrycloth robe and another little towel as a turban, she came back. The round tub bubbled noisily with the pulsations of the Jacuzzi.

"I put in bath salts." Then Modesto asked timidly, "Was that right?"

"That's perfect," she said, testing the water with the toes of one foot.

She let the yellow robe fall to her feet, and keeping on the towel that served as a turban, she stepped in and lay down in the water. She leaned her head on a pillow that the engineer hurriedly handed her. She sighed in gratitude.

"Shall I do anything else?" Don Rigoberto heard Modesto asking in a strangled voice. "Shall I go? Shall I stay?"

"How delicious, this cool water massage is so delicious." Doña Lucrecia stretched her legs and arms with pleasure. "Then I'll add warmer water. And then to bed, as good as new."

"You were roasting him over a slow fire," Don Rigoberto bellowed approvingly.

"Stay if you like, Pluto," she said at last, wearing the intense expression of one who derives infinite pleasure from the caress of the water going back and forth across her body. "The tub is enormous, there's plenty of room. Why don't you bathe with me?"

Don Rigoberto's ears registered the strange hoot of an owl? howl of a wolf? trill of a bird? that greeted his wife's invitation. And, seconds later, he saw the naked engineer sinking into the tub. His fifty-year-old body, saved in the nick of time from obesity by his practice of aerobics, and jogging that brought him to the threshold of a heart attack, lay only millimeters from his wife.

"What else can I do?" he heard him ask, and he felt his admiration for him growing at the same rate as his jealousy. "I don't want to do anything you don't want. I will not take any initiative. At this moment I am the happiest and most unfortunate creature on earth, Lucre."

"You may touch me," she said with a sigh, in the cadence of a bolero, not opening her eyes. "Caress me and kiss me, my body and my face. Not my hair, because if it gets wet, tomorrow you'll be ashamed of me, Pluto. Don't you see that in your program you didn't leave a free moment for the hairdresser?"

"I too am the happiest man in the world," whispered Don Rigoberto. "And the most unfortunate."

Doña Lucrecia opened her eyes.

"Don't be like that, so timid. We can't stay in the water very long."

Don Rigoberto squinted to see them better. He heard the monotonous bubbling of the Jacuzzi and felt the tickle, the rush of water, the shower of drops spattering the tiles, and he saw Pluto, taking precaution to the extreme in order not to seem crude, as he eagerly applied himself to the soft body that let him kiss, touch, caress, that moved to facilitate access for his hands and lips to every area but did not respond to his caresses or kisses and remained in a state of passive delight. He could feel the fever burning the engineer's skin.

"Aren't you going to kiss him, Lucrecia? Aren't you going to embrace him, not even once?"

"Not yet," replied his wife. "I too had my program, I had planned it very carefully. Don't you think he was happy?"

"I've never been so happy," said Modesto, his head, between Lucrecia's legs, rising from the bottom of the tub before submerging again. "I'd like to sing at the top of my lungs, Lucre."

"He's saying exactly what I feel," Don Rigoberto interjected, then permitted himself a joke: "Wasn't he risking pneumonia with all that hydroerotic exertion?"

He laughed and immediately regretted it, again remembering that humor and pleasure repel each other like water and oil. "Please excuse the interruption," he apologized. But it was late. Doña Lucrecia had begun to yawn in such a way that the diligent engineer, summoning all his fortitude, stopped what he was doing. On his knees, dripping water, his hair streaming down in bangs, he feigned resignation.

"You're tired, Lucre."

"I'm feeling all the weariness of the day. I can't stay awake anymore."

She leaped lightly from the tub and wrapped herself in the robe. From the door of her room she said good night with words that made her husband's heart skip a beat: "Tomorrow is another day, Pluto."

"The last one, Lucre."

"And the last night, as well," she said with precision, blowing him a kiss.

They began Friday morning half an hour late, but they made up for it on their visit to Murano, where, in hellish heat, artisans in T-shirts with prison stripes were blowing glass in the traditional manner, turning out decorative or household objects. The engineer insisted that Lucrecia, who did not want to make further purchases, accept three little transparent animals: a squirrel, a stork, and a hippopotamus. On the way back to Venice the guide enlightened them about two villas by Palladio. Instead of lunch, they had tea and cakes at the Quadri, enjoying a blood-red twilight that set roofs, bridges, water, and bell towers on fire, and they reached San Giorgio for the concert of baroque music with enough time to stroll around the little island and view the lagoon and the city from different perspectives.

"The last day is always sad," Doña Lucrecia remarked. "Tomorrow this will end forever."

"Were you holding hands?" Don Rigoberto wanted to know.

"We were, and during the entire concert as well," his wife confessed.

"Did the engineer weep great tears?"

"He was extremely pale. He squeezed my hand and his sweet eyes glistened."

"In gratitude and hope," thought Don Rigoberto. The "sweet eyes" reverberated along his nerve endings. He decided that from this moment on he would be silent. While Doña Lucrecia and Pluto ate supper at Danieli's, contemplating the lights of Venice, he respected their melancholy, did not interrupt their conventional conversation, and suffered stoically when he realized, in the course of the meal, that Modesto was not alone in his lavish attentions. Lucrecia presented him with toast that she had buttered, with her own fork she offered him mouthfuls of her rigatoni, and she willingly gave her hand when he raised it to his mouth to rest his lips on it, once on the palm, once on the back, once on the fingers, and each one of her nails. With a fearful heart and an incipient erection, he waited for what was bound to happen.

And in fact, as soon as they entered the suite at the Cipriani, Doña Lucrecia grasped Modesto's arm, put it around her waist, brought her lips up to his, and, mouth to mouth, tongue to tongue, she murmured, "To say goodbye, we'll spend the night together. With you I will be as compliant, as tender, as loving as I've been only with my husband."

"You said that?" Don Rigoberto swallowed strychnine and honey.

"Did I do wrong?" his wife asked in alarm. "Should I have lied to him?"

"You did the right thing," Don Rigoberto howled. "My love."

In an ambiguous state in which arousal clashed with jealousy and each fed on the other retrospectively, he watched them undress, admired the self-confidence displayed by his wife, enjoyed the clumsiness of that fortunate mortal overwhelmed by a joy that compensated, on this last night, for his timidity and obedience. She would be his, he would love her: his hands fumbled at the buttons of his shirt, caught the zipper on his trousers, stumbled when he took off his shoes, and when, wild-eyed, he was about to climb into the bed where that magnificent body lay waiting for him in the dark, in a languid pose—Goya's *Naked Maja*, Don Rigoberto thought, though her thighs are wider apart—he banged his ankle on the edge of the bed and squealed "Owwowoww!" Don Rigoberto enjoyed listening to the hilarity the mishap provoked in Lucrecia. Modesto laughed too as he knelt in the bed: "Emotion, Lucre, pure emotion."

The burning coals of his pleasure cooled when, stifling her laughter, he saw his wife abandon the statue-like indifference with which she had received the caresses of the engineer on the previous day and begin to take the initiative. She embraced him, she obliged him to lie beside her, on top of her, beneath her; she entwined her legs in his legs, she searched for his mouth, she thrust her tongue deep inside, and—oh, oh, Don Rigoberto protested—she crouched down with amorous intent, fished with gentle fingers for his startled member, and, after stroking the shaft and head, brought it to her lips and kissed it before taking it into her mouth. Then, at the top of his voice, bouncing in the soft bed, the engineer began to sing—to bellow and howl—"*Torna a Sorrento*".

"He began to sing '*Torna a Sorrento*'?" Don Rigoberto sat up violently. "At that very moment?"

"At exactly that moment." Doña Lucrecia burst into laughter again, then controlled herself and apologized. "You astonish me, Pluto. Are you singing because you like it or because you don't?"

"I'm singing so I will like it," he explained, tremulous and bright red, between false notes and arpeggios.

"Do you want me to stop?"

"I want you to continue, Lucre," a euphoric Modesto implored. "Laugh, I don't care. I sing to make my happiness complete. Cover your ears if it distracts you or makes you laugh. But by all you hold most dear, don't stop."

"And he went on singing?" Don Rigoberto exclaimed, intoxicated, mad with satisfaction.

"Without stopping for a second," Doña Lucrecia affirmed, between giggles. "While I was kissing him, when I was on top, when he was on top, while we made love both orthodox and heterodox. He sang, he had to sing. Because if he didn't sing, fiasco."

"And always *'Torna a Sorrento'*?" Don Rigoberto delighted in the sweet pleasure of revenge.

"Any song of my youth," the engineer sang, leaping with all the power of his lungs from Italy to Mexico. *"Voy a cantarles un corrido muy menta-dooo . . ."*

"A potpourri of cheap music from the fifties." Doña Lucrecia was very specific. " '*O sole mio*,' '*Caminito*,' '*Juan Charrasqueado*,' '*Allá en el rancho grande*,' and even Agustín Lara's '*Madrid*.' Oh, it was so funny!"

"And without all that musical vulgarity, fiasco?" Don Rigoberto asked for confirmation, a visitor to seventh heaven. "It's the best part of the night, my love."

"You haven't heard the best part yet, the best part came at the end, it was the height of absurdity." Doña Lucrecia wiped away her tears. "The other guests began to bang on the walls, the front desk called saying we should turn down the TV, the phonograph, nobody in the hotel could sleep."

"In other words, neither of you ever finished . . ." Don Rigoberto suggested, with faint hope.

"I did, twice," said Doña Lucrecia, bringing him back to reality. "And he, at least once, I'm sure of that. When he was all set for the second one, that's when the complaints started and he lost his inspiration. Everything ended in laughter. What a night. Worthy of Ripley."

"Now you know my secret," said Modesto, once their neighbors and the front desk had been placated, and their laughter had subsided, and their impulses had quieted, and they were wrapped in the white Cipriani bathrobes and had begun to talk. "Do you mind if we don't speak of it? As you can imagine, it embarrasses me . . . Well, let me tell you one more time that I'll never forget our week together, Lucre."

"Neither will I, Pluto. I'll always remember it. And not only for the concert, I swear."

They slept the sleep of the just, knowing they had fulfilled their obligations, and they were on the dock in good time to catch the vaporetto to the airport. Alitalia was meticulous as well, and the plane left with no delays, allowing them to connect with the Concorde from Paris to New York, where they said goodbye, knowing they would never see each other again.

"Tell me it was a horrible week, that you hated it," Don Rigoberto suddenly moaned, grasping his wife around the waist and pulling her down on him. "Didn't you, Lucrecia, didn't you?"

"Why don't you try singing something at the top of your lungs," she suggested in the velvety voice of their finest nocturnal encounters. "Something really vulgar, darling. '*La flor de la canela*,' '*Fumando espero*,' '*Brasil, terra de meu coração*.' Let's see what happens, Rigoberto."

III

The Picture Game

"How funny, Stepmamá," said Fonchito. "Your dark green stockings are exactly the same color that one of Egon Schiele's models wore."

Señora Lucrecia looked at the heavy wool stockings covering her legs up past the knee.

"They're very good for Lima's damp weather," she said, stroking them. "They keep my feet nice and warm."

"*Reclining Nude in Green Stockings*," the boy recalled. "One of his most famous pictures. Do you want to see it?"

"All right, show it to me."

While Fonchito hurried to open the bag that he had dropped, as usual, on the rug in the dining alcove, Señora Lucrecia felt the vague uneasiness the boy tended to arouse in her with his sudden outbursts of enthusiasm, which always seemed to conceal some danger beneath their apparent innocence.

"What a coincidence, Stepmamá," said Fonchito as he leafed through the book of Schiele reproductions that he had just taken out of his book bag. "I look like him and you look like his models. In lots of ways."

"What ways, for example?"

"The green or black or maroon stockings you wear. And the checked cover on your bed."

"My goodness, how observant you are!"

"And then, you're so regal," Fonchito added, not looking up, absorbed in searching for *Reclining Nude in Green Stockings*. Doña Lucrecia did not know if she should laugh or make fun of him. Was he aware of the affected gallantry or had he said it accidentally? "Didn't my papá always say you were regal? And that no matter what you did, you were never vulgar? Only through Schiele could I understood what he meant. His models lift their skirts, show everything, assume very strange poses, but they never seem vulgar. They always look like queens. Why? Because they're regal. Like you, Stepmamá."

Confused, flattered, irritated, alarmed, Doña Lucrecia both wanted and did not want to put an end to his talk. Once again, she was beginning to feel insecure.

"What silly things you say, Fonchito."

"Here it is!" the boy exclaimed, handing her the book. "Do you see now what I'm saying? Isn't she in a pose that would seem bad in any other woman? But not in her. That's what being regal means."

"Let me see." Señora Lucrecia took the book, and after examining *Reclining Nude in Green Stockings* for a time, she agreed. "You're right, they're the same color as the ones I'm wearing."

"Don't you think it's nice?"

"Yes, very pretty." She closed the book and quickly handed it back to him. Again she was devastated by the idea that she was losing the initiative, that the boy was beginning to defeat her. But in what battle? Her eyes met his: Alfonso's eyes were shining with an equivocal light, and the first signs of a smile played across his untroubled face.

"Could I ask you for a big favor? The biggest in the world? Would you do it for me?"

He's going to ask me to take off my clothes, she thought in terror. I'll slap his face and never see him again. She hated Fonchito and she hated herself.

"What favor?" she murmured, trying to keep her smile from turning grotesque.

"Would you pose like the lady in *Reclining Nude in Green Stockings*?" intoned the mellifluous young voice. "Just for a minute, Stepmamá!"

"What are you saying?"

"Without undressing, of course," the boy reassured her, moving eyes and hands, wrinkling his nose. "Just the pose. I'm dying to see it. Would you do that big, big favor for me? Don't be mean, Stepmamá."

"Don't play so hard to get when you know very well you'll enjoy it," said Justiniana, walking in and displaying her usual high spirits. "And since tomorrow is Fonchito's birthday, let this be his present."

"Brava, Justita!" The boy clapped his hands. "Between the two of us, we'll persuade her. Will you give me this present, Stepmamá? But you do have to take off your shoes."

"Admit you want to see the señora's feet because you know they're very pretty," Justiniana teased, bolder than she had been on other afternoons. She placed the Coca-Cola and the glass of mineral water they had requested on the table.

"Everything about her is pretty," the boy said candidly. "Go on, Stepmamá, don't be embarrassed with us. If you want, just so you won't feel uncomfortable, Justita and I can play the game too and imitate another picture by Egon Schiele."

Not knowing how to respond, what joke to make, how to feign an anger she did not feel, Señora Lucrecia suddenly found herself smiling, nodding, murmuring, "All right, you willful child, it will be your birthday present," removing her shoes, leaning back, and stretching out on the settee. She tried to imitate the reproduction that Fonchito had unfolded and was showing to her, like a director giving instructions to the star of the show. The presence of Justiniana made her feel safe, even though this madwoman had gotten it into her head to take Fonchito's part. At the same time, her presence as a witness added a certain spice to the outlandish situation. She attempted to make a lighthearted joke out of what she was doing—"Is this it? No, the shoulder's a little higher, the neck's stretched like a chicken's, the head's straighter"—while she leaned back on her elbows, extended one leg and flexed the other, carefully imitating the model's pose. Justiniana and Fonchito looked back and forth from her to the page, from the page to her, the girl's eyes laughing, the boy's filled with deep concentration. This is the most serious game in the world, Doña Lucrecia thought.

"That's it exactly, Señora."

"Not yet," Fonchito interrupted. "You have to raise your knee a little more, Stepmamá. I'll help you."

Before she had a chance to forbid it, the boy handed the book to Justiniana, walked to the sofa, and placed both hands under her knee at the place where the dark green stocking ended and her thigh began. Very gently, paying close attention to the reproduction, he raised and moved her leg.

The touch of his slender fingers on her bare flesh stirred Doña Lucrecia. The lower half of her body began to tremble. She felt a palpitation, a vertigo, something overpowering that brought both distress and pleasure. And just then she met Justiniana's glance. The eyes burning in that dark face spoke volumes. She knows the way I am was her mortified thought. The boy shouted just in time to save her: "Now we have it, Stepmamá! Isn't that perfect, Justita? Stay that way for a second, please."

Sitting cross-legged on the rug like an Oriental, he looked at her in rapture, his mouth partly open, his eyes as round as full moons, ecstatic. Señora Lucrecia let five, ten, fifteen seconds go by, lying absolutely still, infected by how solemnly the boy played the game. Something had happened. The suspension of time? A presentiment of the absolute? The secret of artistic perfection? She was struck by a suspicion: "He's just like Rigoberto. He's inherited his tortuous imagination, his manias, his power of seduction. But, fortunately, not his clerk's face, or his Dumbo ears, or his carrot nose." She found it difficult to break the spell.

"Enough. Now it's your turn."

Disappointment overcame the archangel. But his response was instantaneous: "You're right. That's what we agreed."

"Get to work," Doña Lucrecia spurred them on. "What picture are you going to do? I'll choose it. Give me the book, Justiniana."

"Well, there are only two pictures for Justita and me," Fonchito advised her. "*Mother and Child* and the *Nude Man and Woman Lying Down and Embracing*. The others are just men, or just women, or two women together. Take your pick, Stepmamá."

"What a know-it-all!" exclaimed a stupefied Justiniana.

Doña Lucrecia examined the images, and in fact, those mentioned by Alfonsito were the only ones they could imitate. She rejected the second, since how believable would it be if a beardless boy played the part of the bearded redhead identified by the author of the book as the artist Felix Albrecht Harta, who looked out at her from the photograph of the oil painting with an imbecilic expression, indifferent to the faceless nude in red stockings who slithered like an amorous snake beneath his bent leg. At least in *Mother and Child* the age difference was similar to the one that separated Alfonso and Justiniana.

"That mommy and baby are in a nice little pose!" The maid pretended to be alarmed. "I suppose you won't ask me to take off my dress, you rascal."

"Only to put on black stockings," the boy replied with absolute seriousness. "I'll take off just my shoes and shirt."

There was no nasty undercurrent in his voice, not a shadow of malicious intent. Doña Lucrecia sharpened her ears and scrutinized his precocious face with suspicion: no, not a shadow. He was a consummate actor. Or merely an innocent boy and she an idiotic, dirty old woman? What was the matter with Justiniana? In all the years she had known her, she could not recall seeing her so impertinent and bold.

"How can I put on black stockings when I don't even own any?"

"My stepmamá will lend you some."

Instead of cutting the game short, as her reason told her to, she heard herself saying, "Of course." She went to her room and returned with the black wool stockings she wore on cold nights. The boy was removing his shirt. He was slim and well proportioned, his skin between white and gold. She saw his torso, his slender arms, his thin shoulders with the fine little bones protruding, and Doña Lucrecia remembered. Had it all really happened? Justiniana had stopped laughing and was avoiding her eyes. She must be on edge as well.

"Put them on, Justita," the boy urged her. "Shall I help you?"

"No, thanks very much."

The girl had also lost the naturalness and assurance that rarely abandoned her. Her fingers were fumbling, and the stockings were crooked when she put them on. As she straightened and tugged at them, she bent over in an effort to hide her legs. She stood on the rug next to the boy, looking down and moving her hands, to no discernible effect.

"Let's begin," said Alfonso. "You're facedown, resting your head on your arms; they're crossed, like a pillow. I have to be on your right. My knees on your leg, my head on your side. Except, since I'm bigger than the boy in the painting, my head reaches to your shoulder. Are we getting it, Stepmamá?"

Holding the book, caught up in a desire for perfection, Doña Lucrecia leaned over them. His left hand had to be under Justiniana's right shoulder, his face turned more this way. "Lay your left hand on her back, Foncho, let it rest on her. Yes, now you're getting it."

She sat on the sofa and looked at them, without seeing them, lost in her own thoughts, astonished at what was happening. He was Rigoberto. Improved and corrected. Corrected and improved. She felt impetuous, and changed. The two of them lay still, playing the game with utter gravity.

Nobody was smiling. The pose revealed only one of Justiniana's eyes, and it no longer flashed mischievously but was like a pool, languid and indolent. Was she excited too? Yes, yes, like her, even more so. Only Fonchito— eyes closed to heighten the resemblance to Schiele's faceless child—seemed to play the game openly, with no hidden agenda. The atmosphere had thickened, the sounds from the Olivar were muffled, time had slipped away, and the little house, San Isidro, the world, had evaporated.

"We have time for one more," Fonchito said at last as he got to his feet. "Now you two. What do you think? It can only be—turn the page, Stepmamá—it can only be that one, it's perfect. *Two Girls Lying in an Embrace*. Don't move, Justita. Just turn a little, that's it. Lie down beside her, Stepmamá, hover over her, your back to me. Your hand like this, under her hip. You're the one in the yellow dress, Justita. Imitate her. This arm here, and your right arm, just pass it under my stepmamá's legs. Bend a little, let your knee brush against Justita's shoulder. Raise this hand, put it on my stepmamá's leg, spread your fingers. That's it, that's it. Perfect!"

They were silent, obedient, bending, straightening, turning on their sides, extending or withdrawing legs, arms, necks. Docile? Bewitched? Enchanted? "Defeated," Doña Lucrecia admitted to herself. Her head was resting on her maid's thighs and her right hand held her waist. From time to time she pressed it to feel the moist heat emanating from her, and in response to that pressure, Justiniana's fingers clasped her right thigh and made her feel what she was feeling. She was aroused. Of course she was; that intense, heavy, disturbing odor, where would it come from if not Justiniana's body? Or did it come from her? How had they ever gone so far? What had happened? How, without realizing it—or realizing it, perhaps—had the boy made them play this game? Now she didn't care. She felt content to be in the picture. To be with her, her body, Justiniana, in this situation. She heard Fonchito leaving.

"What a shame I have to go. Everything was so nice. But you two go on playing. Thanks for the present, Stepmamá."

She heard him open the door, she heard him close it. He had gone. He had left them alone, lying entwined, abandoned, lost in a fantasy of his favorite painter.

I understand, Señora, that the feminist sect which you represent has declared a war of the sexes, and that the philosophy of your movement is based on the conviction that the clitoris is morally, physically, culturally, and erotically superior to the penis, ovaries more noble than testicles.

I grant that your theses are defensible. I do not attempt to make the slightest objection to them. My sympathies for feminism are profound, though subordinate to my love for individual freedom and human rights, which means that those sympathies are bounded by limits I should specify so that my subsequent remarks make sense. Speaking generally, and beginning with the most obvious point, I will state that I am in favor of eliminating every legal obstacle to a woman's accepting the same responsibilities as a man, in favor of the intellectual and moral struggle against the prejudices upon which restrictions to women's rights rest, and let me add, among these I believe the most important, for women as well as men, is not the right to employment, education, health, and so forth, but the right to pleasure, and here, I am certain, is where our first disagreement arises.

But the principal and, I fear, irreversible difference that opens an unfathomable abyss between you and me—or, to move into the realm of scientific neutrality, between my penis and your vagina—has its roots in the fact that, from my point of view, feminism falls into the collectivist intellectual category; that is, it is a piece of specious reasoning that attempts to subsume within a generic, homogeneous concept a vast collection of heterogeneous individuals in whom differences and disparities are at least as important (surely more important) than the clitoral and ovarian common denominator. I mean to say, without a shred of cynicism, that having a penis or a clitoris (artifacts whose parameters are blurred, as I will prove to you below) seems less important for differentiating one being from another than other attributes (vices, virtues, or hereditary defects) that are specific to each individual. Forgetting this is the reason ideologies create leveling forms of oppression that are generally worse than the despotisms against which they rebelled. I fear that feminism, in the variant which you support, will follow the same path in the event your theses triumph, and from the point of view of the condition of women, this will simply mean, in vulgar parlance, exchanging drool for snot.

These are, in my opinion, considerations of a moral and aesthetic nature, and there is no reason for you to share them. Fortunately, I also have science on my side. You will discover this if you look, for example, at the works of Dr. Anne Fausto-Sterling, Professor of Genetics and Medical Science at Brown University, who has, for many years, been demonstrating to a mob made imbecilic by conventions and myths, and blinded to the truth, that there are not two human genders—feminine and masculine—as we have been led to believe, but at least five, and perhaps more. Though I object for phonetic reasons to the names chosen by Dr. Fausto-Sterling (*herms, merms,* and *ferms*) for the three intermediate stages between masculinity and femininity that have been noted by biology, genetics, and sexology, I welcome her research and the research of scientists like her—powerful allies for those who believe, as does this coward writing to you, that the Manichaean division of humanity into men and women is a collectivist illusion marked by conspiracies against individual sovereignty—and therefore against liberty—a scientific falsehood enthroned by the traditional insistence of states, religions, and legal systems on maintaining a dualist system that is opposed to nature and contradicts it at every turn.

The imagination of an utterly free Hellenic mythology knew this very well when it created the being that combined Hermes and Aphrodite; the adolescent Hermaphroditus, when he fell in love with a nymph, fused his body with hers, becoming a man-woman or woman-man (each of these formulas, *dixit* Dr. Fausto-Sterling, represents a subtly different combination, in a single individual, of gonads, hormones, and the composition of chromosomes, and consequently gives rise to sexes different from the ones we know as man and woman, to wit, the cacophonous and weedy-sounding *herms, merms,* and *ferms*). The important thing to realize is that this is not mythology but concrete reality, for both before and after the Greek Hermaphrodite, intermediate beings have been born (neither male nor female in the usual sense of the word) and condemned by stupidity, ignorance, fanaticism, and prejudice to live in disguise or, if discovered, to be burned, hanged, exorcised as spawn of the devil and, in modern times, to be "normalized" in their infancy through surgery and the genetic manipulations of a science obedient to a fallacious nomenclature that accepts only the masculine and the feminine, and hurls, beyond the limits of normality and into the deepest hell of the anomalous, the monstrous, the physically freakish, these delicate intersexual heroes—all my sympathy lies with them— endowed with testicles and ovaries, clitorises like penises or penises like clitorises, urethras and vaginas, and who, on occasion, emit sperm at the same time they menstruate. For your information, these rare cases are not so rare; Dr. John Money, of Johns Hopkins University, estimates that intersexuals constitute 4 percent of born hominids (add it up and you will see that by themselves they could populate an entire continent).

The existence of this large, scientifically established human population (about whom I have learned by reading works that have, for me, a particularly erotic interest) living at the margins of normality, and for whose liberation, recognition, and acceptance I also struggle in my futile way (I mean, from my solitary corner where I, a libertarian hedonist, a lover of art and the pleasures of the body, am shackled behind the anodyne breadwinner, the insurance executive) by fulminating against those, like you, who insist on separating humanity into watertight compartments based on sex: penises here, clitorises there, vaginas to the right, scrotums to the left. This slavish schematic does not correspond to the truth. With regard to sex, we humans represent a gamut of variants, families, exceptions, originalities, subtleties. To grasp the ultimate, untransferable human reality in this domain, as in all others, one must renounce the herd instinct, the crowd view, and have recourse to the individual.

In summary, let me say that any movement that attempts to transcend (or relegate to the background) the struggle for individual sovereignty, to place greater importance on the interests of a collective—class, race, gender, nation, sex, ethnicity, vice, or profession—seems to me a conspiracy to rein in even further an abused human freedom. A freedom that reaches its deepest significance only in the sphere of the individual, that warm, indivisible homeland which we embody, you with your assertive clitoris and I with my sheathed penis (I have my foreskin and so does my son Alfonso, and I am opposed to the religious circumcision of the newborn—but not to that chosen by rational beings—for the same reasons I condemn the excision of the clitoris and vaginal labia practiced by many African Muslims) and which we should defend, above all, against the efforts of those who wish to absorb us into the amorphous, castrating conglomerations manipulated by persons hungry for power. Everything seems to indicate that you and your followers are part of that herd, and therefore it is my duty to inform you of my antagonism and hostility by means of this letter, which, incidentally, I do not intend to mail.

To lighten somewhat the funereal solemnity of my missive and end it with a smile, I would like to refer you to the case of the pragmatic androgyne Emma (should I, perhaps, say androgynette?) as reported by the urologist Hugh H. Young (also of Johns Hopkins), who treated her/him. Emma was reared as a girl, despite having a clitoris the size of a penis, as well as a hospitable vagina, which allowed her to have sexual exchanges with women and men. When she was unmarried, she had most of her encounters with girls, playing the male part. Then she married a man and made love as a woman, though this role did not give her as much pleasure as the other; and therefore she had women lovers, whom she happily drilled with her virile clitoris. When she consulted him, Dr. Young explained that it would be very easy to intervene surgically and transform her into a man, since that seemed to be her preference. Emma's response is worth whole libraries on the narrowness of the human universe: "You'd have to take away my vagina, wouldn't you, Doctor? I don't think I'd like that, since it's my meal ticket. If you operate, I'd have to leave my husband and find a job. And if that's the case, I prefer to stay the way I am." The anecdote is cited by Dr. Anne Fausto-Sterling in *Myths of Gender: Biological Theories about Women and Men*, a book I recommend to you.

Farewell and fine fucking, my friend.

Drunkenness with Hangover

In the stillness of the Barrancan night, Don Rigoberto sat up in his bed with the speed of a cobra summoned by a snake charmer. There was Doña Lucrecia, absolutely beautiful in her décolleté, sheer silk black dress, shoulders and arms bare, smiling, tending to a dozen guests. She gave instructions to the butler, who was serving drinks, and to Justiniana, who, in her blue uniform with the starched white apron, was passing around trays of canapés—cassava chunks with Huancayan sauce, cheese sticks, pasta shells à la parmigiana, stuffed olives—with an assurance worthy of the mistress of the house. Don Rigoberto's heart skipped a beat, however, for what threatened to dominate the entire scene in his indirect memory of the event (he had been notably absent from that party, which he knew about through Lucrecia and his own imagination) was the singular voice of Fito Cebolla. Drunk already? Well on his way, for whiskeys passed through his hands like rosary beads between the fingers of a devout woman.

"If you had to travel"—Doña Lucrecia buried herself in his arms—"we should have canceled the cocktail party. I told you that."

"Why?" asked Don Rigoberto, adjusting his body to his wife's. "Did something happen?"

"A lot of things." Doña Lucrecia laughed, her mouth against his chest. "But I won't tell you. Don't even think about it."

"Did someone behave badly?" Don Rigoberto warmed to the topic. "Did Fito Cebolla cross the line?"

"Who else?" His wife gave him pleasure. "Of course it was him."

Fito, Fito Cebolla, he thought. Did he love or hate him? It wasn't easy to tell, for he awakened in Don Rigoberto the kind of diffuse, contradictory emotion that seemed to be his specialty. They had met at a directors' meeting, when it was decided to name him head of public relations for the company. Fito had friends everywhere, and though he was clearly in decline and on the road to slobbering dipsomania, he was very good at what his high-sounding appointment suggested: having relations and being public.

"What outrageous thing did he do?" he asked eagerly.

"He put his hands on me," an embarrassed Doña Lucrecia replied evasively. "And practically raped Justiniana."

Don Rigoberto had known him by reputation and was sure he would detest him the moment he appeared in the office to take up his new post. What else could he be but a despicable swine whose life was defined by recreational activities—his name was associated, Don Rigoberto vaguely recalled, with surfing, tennis, golf, with fashion shows or beauty contests where he was one of the judges, with frequent appearances on the society pages: his carnivorous teeth, his skin tanned on all the beaches of the world, dressed in formal clothes, sports clothes, Hawaiian clothes, evening, afternoon, dawn and dusk clothes, a glass in hand and surrounded by very pretty women. He expected complete imbecility in its high Limenian society variant. His surprise could not have been greater when he discovered that Fito Cebolla, who was precisely and utterly what he had expected—a frivolous, high-class pimp, a cynic, scrounger, and parasite, an ex-sportsman and ex-lion of the cocktail-party circuit—was also an original, unpredictable man and, until his alcoholic collapse, extremely amusing. He had, at one time, been a reader, and had profited from those pages, citing Fernando Casós —"In Peru what does not happen is admirable"—and, with admonitory laughter, Paul Groussac: "Florence is the artist-city, Liverpool the merchant-city, and Lima the woman-city." (In order to verify this statement statistically, he carried a little book in which he took notes on the ugly and pretty women who crossed his path.) Soon after they met, while they were having a drink with two other men from the office at the Club de la Unión, the four of them had a contest to see who could utter the most pedantic sentence. Fito Cebolla's ("Every time I pass through Port Douglas, Australia, I put away a crocodile steak and fuck an Aborigine") was declared the unanimous winner.

In his solitary darkness, Don Rigoberto suffered an attack of jealousy that made his pulses pound. His fantasy clicked away like a typist. There was Doña Lucrecia again. Beautiful, with smooth shoulders and splendid arms, standing in her sandals with the stiletto heels, her shapely legs carefully depilitated, conversing with the guests, explaining to each couple in turn that Don Rigoberto had been urgently called away to Río de Janeiro that afternoon on company business.

"And why should we care?" Fito Cebolla gallantly joked, kissing the hand of his hostess after he had kissed her cheek. "It's all we could desire."

He was flabby despite the athletic prowess of his younger years, a tall, strutting man with batrachian eyes and a mobile mouth that stained each word with lasciviousness. He had, of course, come to the cocktail party without his wife—knowing that Don Rigoberto was flying over the Amazon jungle? Fito Cebolla had squandered the modest fortunes of his first three legitimate wives, whom he had divorced as he drained them dry, taking his leisure at the best spas in all the world. When the time came for him to rest, he settled for his fourth and, undoubtedly, final wife, whose dwindling inheritance would guarantee him not the luxurious excesses of travel, wardrobe, and cuisine but simply a decent house in La Planicie, a reasonable larder, and enough Scotch to nourish his cirrhosis, providing he did not live past seventy. She was delicate, small, elegant, and apparently stupefied by her retrospective admiration for the Adonis that Fito Cebolla had once been.

Now he was a bloated man in his sixties who went through life armed with a notebook and a pair of binoculars, and with these, on his walks around the center of the city and at red lights when he was behind the wheel of his old maroon Cadillac, he would observe and make notes, not only general information (were the women ugly or pretty?), but more specific data as well: the bounciest buttocks, pertest breasts, shapeliest legs, most swanlike necks, sensual mouths, and bewitching eyes that the traffic brought into view. His research, the most meticulous and arbitrary imaginable, sometimes devoted an entire day, and even as long as a week, to one portion of the passing female anatomies, in a manner not too different from the system devised by Don Rigoberto for the care and cleaning of body parts: Monday, asses; Tuesday, breasts; Wednesday, legs; Thursday, arms; Friday, necks; Saturday, mouths; Sunday, eyes. At the end of each month, Fito averaged out the ratings on a scale from zero to twenty.

The first time Fito Cebolla allowed him to leaf through his statistics, Don Rigoberto began to sense a disquieting similarity in their unfathomable seas of whims and manias, and to admit to an irrepressible sympathy for any specimen who could indulge his extravagances with so much insolence. (Not so in his case, for his were hidden and matrimonial.) In a certain sense, even setting aside his own cowardice and timidity—qualities lacking in Fito Cebolla—Don Rigoberto intuited that this man was his equal. Closing his eyes—useless, since the darkness in the bedroom was total—and lulled by the nearby sound of the sea at the base of the cliff, Don Rigoberto could make out that hand with its hairy knuckles, wedding band, and gold pinky ring, treacherously coming to rest on his wife's bottom. An animal groan that could have awakened Fonchito was torn from his throat: "Son of a bitch!"

"That's not how it happened," said Doña Lucrecia, fondling him. "We were talking in a group of three or four people, Fito among them, and he'd already had a good number of whiskeys. Justiniana was passing a serving platter and then he, as fresh as he could be, began to flirt with her."

"What a good-looking maid," he exclaimed, his eyes bloodshot, his lips dribbling a thread of saliva, his voice thick. "The little *zamba* half-breed's a knockout. What a body!"

"Maid's an ugly word, it's derogatory and somewhat racist," responded Doña Lucrecia. "Justiniana is an employee, Fito. Like you. Rigoberto, Alfonsito, and I are very fond of her."

"Employee, favorite, friend, protégée, whatever, I mean no disrespect," Fito Cebolla went on, not taking his eyes off the young woman as she moved away. "I'd like to have a little *zamba* like that in my house."

And at that moment Doña Lucrecia felt—unequivocal, powerful, slightly damp and warm—a man's hand on the lower part of her left buttock, the sensitive spot where it descended in a pronounced curve to meet her thigh. For a few seconds she did not react, move it away, move away herself, or become angry. He had taken advantage of the large croton plant near the place where they were talking to make his move without anyone else noticing. Don Rigoberto was distracted by a French expression: *la main baladeuse*. How would you translate that? The traveling hand? The nomadic hand? The wandering hand? The slippery hand? The passing hand? Without resolving the linguistic dilemma, he became indignant again. An impassive Fito looked at Lucrecia with a suggestive smile while his fingers began to move, crushing the crepe of her dress. Doña Lucrecia moved away abruptly.

"I was faint with rage and I went to the pantry for a glass of water," she explained to Don Rigoberto.

"What's wrong, Señora?" Justiniana asked.

"That revolting pig put his hand on me, right here. I don't know how I kept from hitting him."

"You should have, you should have broken a flowerpot over his head, scratched him, thrown him out of the house." Rigoberto was furious.

"I did, I did hit him, and break the pot, and scratch him, and throw him out." Doña Lucrecia rubbed her nose against her husband's, like an Eskimo. "But that was later. First, some other things happened."

The night is long, Don Rigoberto thought. He had become interested in Fito Cebolla, as if he were an entomologist studying a rare, collectible insect. He envied the crass humanity that so shamelessly displayed tics, fantasies, everything a moral code not his own would call vices, failings, degeneracy. Through an excess of egotism, without even realizing it, that fool Fito Cebolla had achieved greater freedom than he had, for he realized everything but was a hypocrite and, to make matters worse, an insurance man (like Kafka and the poet Wallace Stevens, he excused himself to himself, but in vain). With amusement Don Rigoberto recalled their conversation in César's bar—recorded in his notebooks—when Fito Cebolla confessed that the greatest excitement he had felt in his life had been provoked not by the statuesque body of one of his infinite lovers or the show girls at the Folies-Bergère in Paris but in austere Louisiana, at the chaste State University in Baton Rouge, where his misguided father had enrolled him in the hope he would take a degree in chemical engineering. There, on a window ledge in his dormitory one spring afternoon, he had witnessed the most formidable sexual encounter since the dinosaurs had fornicated.

"Between two spiders?" Don Rigoberto's nostrils flared and continued to quiver ferociously. His great Dumbo ears fluttered too, in an excess of excitement.

"They were this big." Fito Cebolla mimed the scene, raising and crooking his ten fingers obscenely, bringing them close. "They saw one another, desired one another, and each advanced on the other prepared to make love or die. I should say, to make love until they died. When one leaped on the other, there was the thunder of an earthquake. The window, the whole dormitory, filled with a seminal odor."

"How do you know they were copulating?" Don Rigoberto taunted him. "Why not just fighting?"

"They were fighting and fornicating at the same time, as it must be, as it has always had to be." Fito Cebolla danced in his seat; his hands had locked and his ten fingers rubbed hard against one another, the joints cracking. "They sodomized each other with all their legs, rings, hairs, and eyes, with everything they had in their bodies. I never saw such happy creatures. Nothing has ever been that exciting, I swear by my sainted mother in heaven, Rigo."

According to him, the excitation produced in him by arachnidian coitus had resisted an aerial ejaculation and several cold showers. After four decades and countless adventures, the memory of those hairy little beasts clutching at one another beneath the inclement blue sky of Baton Rouge still returned to disturb him, and even now, when his years recommended moderation, whenever that distant image came suddenly to mind, it gave him more of a hard-on than a swig of yohimbine.

"Tell us what you did at the Folies-Bergère, Fito," Teté Barriga requested, knowing perfectly well the risk she was taking. "Even if it's a lie, it's so funny!"

"That was asking for it, like holding your hand to the flame," Señora Lucrecia remarked, drawing out the story. "But Teté loves to play with fire."

Fito Cebolla stirred in the seat where he sprawled, almost overcome by whiskey. "What do you mean, a lie! It was the only pleasant job I ever had in my life. Even though they treated me as badly as your husband treats me at the office, Lucre. Come, sit with us, pay some attention to us."

His eyes were glazed, his voice lewd. The other guests were glancing at their watches. Doña Lucrecia, summoning all her courage, sat down next to Teté Barriga and her husband. Fito Cebolla began to evoke that summer. He had been stranded in Paris without a cent, and through a girlfriend he got a job as nippler at the "historic theater on the rue Richer."

"That's nippler, not nibbler," he explained, showing the obscene tip of his reddish tongue, half-closing his salacious eyes, as if to see more clearly what he was looking at ("And what he was looking at was my cleavage, my love." Don Rigoberto's solitude became populated, and feverish). "Though my work was the most menial, the worst paid, the success of the show depended on me. And that was a damned big responsibility!"

"What, what was it?" Teté Barriga urged him on.

"To stiffen the nipples of the chorus girls just before they went onstage."

And for that, in his nook behind the curtains, he had a bucket of ice. The girls, decked out in plumes, adorned with flowers, exotic hairdos, long eyelashes, false fingernails, invisible mesh tights, and peacock tails, their buttocks and breasts bare, bent over Fito Cebolla, who rubbed each nipple and the surrounding corolla with an ice cube. Then they, giving a little shriek, leaped out onstage, their breasts like swords.

"Does it work, does it work?" insisted Teté Barriga, eyeing her sagging bosom while her husband yawned. "If you rub them with ice they get . . . ?"

"Hard, firm, erect, proud, haughty, arrogant, overbearing, bristling, enraged." Fito Cebolla was prodigal with his synonymatic knowledge. "They stay that way for fifteen minutes by the clock."

"Yes, it works," Don Rigoberto repeated to himself. A faint ray of light slipped through the blinds. Another dawn far from Lucrecia. Was it time to wake Fonchito for school? Not yet. But wasn't she here? As she had been when he had verified the Folies-Bergère formula on her own beautiful breasts. He had seen her dark nipples harden in their golden areolas and offer themselves, as cold and hard as stones, to his lips. The process of verification had cost Lucrecia a cold that had infected him as well.

"Where's the bathroom?" asked Fito Cebolla. "I just want to wash my hands, don't think anything dirty."

Lucrecia led him to the hall, keeping a prudent distance. She feared she would feel that cupping hand again at any moment.

"Seriously, I really liked your little *zamba* half-breed," Fito stammered as he stumbled over his own feet. "I'm democratic, they can be black, white, or yellow, as long as they're hot. Will you give her to me? Or sell her, if you'd prefer. I'll pay you."

"There's the bathroom," Doña Lucrecia stopped him. "Wash your mouth out too, Fito."

"Your wish is my command," he drooled, and before she could move away, his damned hand went straight to her breasts. He pulled it back immediately and walked into the bathroom. "Excuse me, excuse me, I tried to open the wrong door."

Doña Lucrecia returned to the living room. The guests were leaving. She trembled with rage. This time she would throw him out of the house. She exchanged the conventional courtesies and said goodbye to them in the garden. "This is the last straw, the last straw." The minutes passed and Fito Cebolla did not appear.

"Do you mean he had left?"

"That's what I thought. That when he left the bathroom he had gone out, discreetly, through the service entrance. But no, he hadn't. The awful man had stayed behind."

The guests were gone, the hired waiter had left, and, after they helped Justiniana to collect glasses and plates and closed the windows, turned out the lights in the garden, and set the alarm, the butler and cook said good night to Lucrecia and retired to their remote bedrooms in a separate wing behind the swimming pool. Justiniana, who slept on the top floor, next to Don Rigoberto's study, was in the kitchen putting dishes in the washer.

"Fito Cebolla was hiding in the house?"

"In the sauna, perhaps, or in the garden. Waiting for the others to leave and for the cook and butler to go to bed before sneaking into the kitchen. Like a thief!"

Doña Lucrecia sat on a sofa in the living room, tired and still disturbed by the unpleasant experience. That reprobate Fito Cebolla would never set foot in this house again. She was wondering if she should tell Don Rigoberto what had happened when she heard the scream. It came from the kitchen. She jumped to her feet and ran. At the door of the white pantry —tile walls gleaming beneath the pharmaceutical light—what she saw paralyzed her. Don Rigoberto blinked several times before fixing his gaze on the pale light at the blinds that announced the dawn. He could see them: Justiniana, sprawled on the pine table to which she had been dragged, struggling with hands and legs against the soft corpulence that was crushing her, lavishing kisses on her, making gurgling noises that were, that had to be, obscenities. In the doorway, her face distorted, her eyes wide, stood Doña Lucrecia. Her paralysis did not last long. There she was—the heart of Don Rigoberto beat wildly, filled with admiration for the Delacroixian beauty of that fury who seized the first thing she could find, the rolling pin, and threw herself on Fito Cebolla, shouting insults at him. "You abusive, miserable, filthy drunkard!" She hit him without mercy, wherever the rolling pin landed, on his back, his fat neck, his balding head, his buttocks, until she forced him to let go of his prey and defend himself. Don Rigoberto could hear the blows falling on the bones and muscles of the interrupted ravisher, who, finally defeated by the beating and by the intoxication that hindered his movements, turned, his hands outstretched toward his attacker, stumbled, slipped, and slid to the floor like jelly.

"Hit him, you hit him too, get back at him," shouted Doña Lucrecia, dealing violent blows with the tireless rolling pin to the blob in the soiled blue suit who, attempting to stand, raised his arms to fend off the blows.

"Justiniana smashed the stool on his head?" asked an overjoyed Don Rigoberto.

It broke and splinters flew up to the ceiling. She raised it with both hands and brought it down with all the weight of her body behind it. Don Rigoberto saw the slender figure, blue uniform, white apron, rising up like a meteor. The stentorian "Ohhhh!" of a horrified Fito Cebolla almost shattered his eardrums. (But not the cook's, or the butler's, or Fonchito's?) He covered his face, and there was blood on his hands. He passed out for a few seconds. Perhaps the shouts of the two women, who were still insulting him, brought him back to consciousness: "You degenerate, drunken, abusive faggot!"

"Revenge is so sweet." Doña Lucrecia laughed. "We opened the back door and he crawled away. On all fours, I swear. Whimpering, 'Oh, my poor head, oh, they've cracked it open.' "

At that moment the alarm went off. What a scare. But not even that woke up Fonchito or the butler or the cook. Hard to believe? No. But very convenient, thought Don Rigoberto.

"I don't know how we turned it off, but we went back inside, locked the door, and reset the alarm." Doña Lucrecia was laughing, without restraint. "Until, little by little, we began to calm down."

Then she realized what that brute had done to poor Justiniana. He had ruined her dress. The girl, still terrified, burst into tears. Poor thing. If Doña Lucrecia had gone up to her bedroom, she wouldn't have heard her screams, since the butler and the cook and the boy hadn't heard anything either. That pig would have raped her to his heart's content. She consoled her, she embraced her: "It's over now, he's gone, don't cry." The girl's body, pressed against hers—she seemed much younger like this, so close—trembled from head to foot. She could feel her heart beating and how she tried to control her sobs.

"It made me sad," whispered Doña Lucrecia. "Besides ruining her uniform, he had hit her."

"He got what he deserved," Don Rigoberto said with a gesture. "He left humiliated and bleeding. Well done!"

"Look what he's done to you, that wretch." Doña Lucrecia held the girl at arm's length. She examined the uniform that hung in tatters, she lovingly stroked the face that now showed not a trace of its usual exuberant good humor; fat tears were running down Justiniana's cheeks, a grimace convulsed her lips. Her eyes were dimmed.

"Did anything happen?" Don Rigoberto insinuated, very discreetly.

"Not yet," Doña Lucrecia replied, just as discreetly. "In any case, I didn't realize what was happening."

She didn't realize. She thought the feeling of restlessness, the nervous exaltation were the result of fear, and they undoubtedly were, in part; she felt an overpowering sense of affection and compassion, she longed to do something, anything, to get Justiniana out of the state she was in. She took her by the hand and led her to the stairs. "Come take off those clothes, we'd better call a doctor."

As they left the kitchen, she turned off the downstairs light. In darkness, holding hands, one step at a time, they climbed the circular staircase that led to the study and bedroom. When they were halfway up, Señora Lucrecia put her other arm around the girl's waist. "What a fright you've had." "I thought I would die, Señora, but I'm feeling better now." It wasn't true; she clutched at her employer's hand and her teeth were chattering, as if she were cold. Holding hands, their arms around each other's waist, they made their way past the shelves filled with art books, and in the bedroom they were greeted by the lights of Miraflores spread across the window, the streetlamps along the Seawalk, the white crests of waves advancing toward the cliffs. Doña Lucrecia turned on the floor lamp, which illuminated the spacious crimson chaise longue with its clawed feet, the small table with its magazines, the Chinese porcelains, the pillows and poufs strewn over the carpet. The wide bed, the bedside lamps, the walls covered with Persian, Tantric, and Japanese engravings were in darkness. Doña Lucrecia went to the dressing room. She handed a robe to Justiniana, who remained standing, covering herself with her arms, somewhat embarrassed.

"We have to throw those clothes into the trash and burn them. Yes, burn them, the way Don Rigoberto burns the books and pictures he doesn't like anymore. Put this on, and I'll see what I can find to make you feel better."

In the bathroom, while she was soaking a cloth in cologne, she saw herself in the mirror ("Beautiful," Don Rigoberto complimented her). She too had been frightened out of her wits. She looked pale, and there were dark circles under her eyes; her makeup was smeared, and she had not realized that the zipper on her dress had broken.

"I'm one of the wounded too, Justiniana." She spoke through the door. "Because of that revolting Fito, my dress is torn. I'm going to put on a robe. Come in, there's more light here."

When Justiniana came into the bathroom, Doña Lucrecia, who was stepping out of her dress—she wore no bra, just the triangle of black silk panties—could see her reflected in the mirror over the sink and repeated in the one by the tub. In the white robe that reached to her thighs, she seemed slimmer and darker. Since there was no belt, she held the robe closed with her hands.

Doña Lucrecia took down her Chinese after-bath wrap—"the red silk, with two yellow dragons joined by the tail on the back," Don Rigoberto insisted—put it on, and called to her, "Come a little closer. Are you bruised anywhere?"

"No, I don't think so, just two little ones." Justiniana extended a leg through the folds of the robe. "These black-and-blue marks, where I banged into the table."

Doña Lucrecia bent down, rested one of her hands on the smooth thigh, and delicately rubbed the purplish skin with the cloth soaked in cologne.

"It's nothing, it'll go away before you know it. And the other one?"

On her shoulder and part of her arm. Opening the robe, Justiniana showed her the bruise, which was beginning to swell. Doña Lucrecia saw that the girl wore no bra either. Her chest was very close to Doña Lucrecia's eyes. She saw the tip of her nipple. It was a young, small breast, well formed, with a light granulation on the corolla.

"This looks more serious," she murmured. "Does it hurt here?"

"Just a little," said Justiniana, not pulling back the arm that Doña Lucrecia rubbed carefully, more attentive now to her own perturbation than to the bruises on her employee.

"In other words," insisted, implored Don Rigoberto, "something happened then."

"Yes, something happened then," his wife conceded this time. "I don't know what, but something. We were so close, in robes. I'd never had intimacies like that with her. Or perhaps it was because of what happened in the kitchen. Whatever the reason, suddenly I was no longer myself. I was on fire from head to toe."

"And she?"

"I don't know, who knows, I don't think so." Doña Lucrecia seemed bewildered. "Everything had changed, I know that. Do you understand, Rigoberto? After a fright like that. Imagine what was happening to me."

"That's the way life is," Don Rigoberto murmured aloud, listening to his words resonate in the solitude of the bedroom filled with daylight. "That is the wide, unpredictable, marvelous, terrible world of desire. Dear wife, I have you so close to me, now that you are so far."

"Do you know something?" said Doña Lucrecia to Justiniana. "What you and I need to calm us after all the excitement is a drink."

"So we won't have nightmares about that animal." The employee laughed, following her into the bedroom. Her expression was animated. "The truth is, I think getting drunk is the only way I won't dream about him tonight."

"Let's both get drunk, in that case." Doña Lucrecia walked toward the little bar in the study. "Do you want whiskey? Do you like whiskey?"

"Anything, whatever you're going to have. Leave it, leave it, I'll bring it to you."

"You stay there," Doña Lucrecia interrupted her from the study. "Tonight I'll do the serving."

She laughed, and the girl did the same, amused. In the study, feeling that she could not control her hands, not wanting to think, Doña Lucrecia filled two large glasses with a generous amount of whiskey, a splash of mineral water, and two ice cubes. She came back, slipping like a feline among the pillows scattered on the floor. Justiniana was resting against the back of the chaise longue, but her feet were still on the floor. She made a move to stand up.

"Just stay there," Doña Lucrecia interrupted her again. "Move over, we'll both fit."

The girl hesitated, disconcerted for the first time, but immediately regained her composure. Taking off her shoes, she raised her legs and moved toward the window to make room for Doña Lucrecia, who lay down beside her. She arranged the pillows beneath her head. There was room for both of them, but their bodies brushed lightly. Shoulders, arms, legs, hips were sensed, and touched briefly.

"What shall we drink to?" asked Doña Lucrecia. "The beating we gave that animal?"

71

"My stool." Justiniana had recovered her high spirits. "I was so angry I could have killed him, I swear. Do you think I split his head open?"

She sipped again at her drink and was overcome by laughter. Doña Lucrecia began to laugh too, a little half-hysterical laugh. "You split it, and with my rolling pin I split a few other things for him." And so they passed the time, like two friends sharing a good-natured, rather risqué confidence, shaken by outbursts of laughter. "I promise you that Fito Cebolla has more black-and-blue marks than you do, Justiniana." "And what excuses do you think he'll give to his wife for all those cuts and bruises?" "That he was attacked by muggers who kicked him." In a counterpoint of banter and laughter, they finished their glasses of whiskey. They grew calmer. Little by little they caught their breath.

"I'm going to pour two more," said Doña Lucrecia.

"I'll do it, let me, I swear I know how to fix them."

"All right, go on; I'll put on some music."

But instead of getting up from the chaise longue to let the girl by, Señora Lucrecia took her by the waist with both hands and helped Justiniana slide across her, not holding her back but slowing her down in a motion that, for a moment, meant that their bodies—the mistress below, the employee above—were entwined. In the semidarkness, as she felt Justiniana's face over hers—her breath warming her face, entering her mouth—Doña Lucrecia saw an alarmed light flash in the girl's jet-black eyes.

"And at that moment, what was it you noticed?" Don Rigoberto prompted her in a strangled voice, feeling Doña Lucrecia move in his arms with the animal sloth her body sank into when they made love.

"She wasn't offended; maybe just a little frightened. Though not for long," she said, her voice husky. "Frightened that I had taken those liberties, holding on to her waist and sliding her over me. Maybe she realized. I don't know, I didn't know anything, I didn't care about anything. I was flying. But I do know one thing: she didn't get angry. She took it with good grace, with that mischievousness she brings to everything. Fito was right, she is attractive. Even more so half-naked. Her *café con leche* skin contrasting with the white silk . . ."

"I would have given a year of my life to see the two of you at that moment." And Don Rigoberto found the reference he had been seeking for some time: *Sloth and Lust, or The Dream*, by Gustave Courbet.

"Aren't you seeing us now?" Doña Lucrecia asked mockingly.

With absolute clarity, despite the fact that unlike his daylit bedroom, this one was nocturnal, and the part of the room beyond the circle of light shed by the floor lamp lay in darkness. The atmosphere had grown heavy. That penetrating, dizzying perfume intoxicated Don Rigoberto. His nostrils breathed it in, exhaled it, reabsorbed it. In the background he heard the sound of the sea and, in the study, Justiniana preparing the drinks. Half hidden by the plant with narrow, tapering leaves, Doña Lucrecia stirred and, as if shaking off her lassitude, started the phonograph; the music of Paraguayan harps and a Guaraní chorus floated through the room, while Doña Lucrecia returned to her place on the chaise longue and, with lowered eyelids, waited for Justiniana with an intensity that Don Rigoberto could smell and hear. The Chinese robe revealed a white thigh and bare arms. Her hair was tousled, her eyes watchful behind their silky lashes. An ocelot stalking her prey, thought Don Rigoberto. Justiniana appeared, carrying the two glasses, smiling, moving easily, accustomed now to their complicity, to not maintaining a proper distance from her employer.

"Do you like this Paraguayan music? I don't know what it's called," murmured Doña Lucrecia.

"Yes, I do, it's pretty, but you can't dance to it, can you?" Justiniana commented as she sat on the edge of the chaise longue and handed her a glass. "Is that all right, or does it need more water?"

She did not dare to slide over her, and Doña Lucrecia moved toward the corner that the girl had occupied before. With a gesture she encouraged her to take her place. Justiniana did, and when she lay down beside her, the robe slipped so that her right leg was also uncovered, just millimeters from the bare leg of her señora.

"*Cin-cin,* Justiniana," said Doña Lucrecia, tapping her glass against hers.

"*Cin-cin,* Señora."

They drank. As soon as they moved their glasses away, Doña Lucrecia joked, "Fito Cebolla would have given a lot to have the two of us the way we are now."

She laughed, and Justiniana laughed too. Their laughter rose and fell. The girl dared to make a joke: "If at least he had been young and good-looking. But with that frog-face, and drunk besides, who would let him do anything?"

"At least he has good taste." Doña Lucrecia's free hand ruffled Justiniana's hair. "You really are very pretty. It doesn't surprise me that you drive men wild. Only Fito? I'll bet you've made a lot of conquests out there."

She continued to stroke her hair as she extended her leg until it touched Justiniana's. Justiniana did not move hers away. She lay still, her mouth fixed in a half smile. After a few seconds Señora Lucrecia's heart skipped a beat when she realized that Justiniana's foot was moving, slowly, very slowly, until it made contact with hers. Timid fingers were passing over hers in an imperceptible scratching motion.

"I love you very much, Justita," she said, calling her for the first time by the nickname that Fonchito used. "I realized tonight. When I saw what that fat slob was doing to you. It made me so angry! As if you had been my sister."

"I love you too, Señora," Justiniana whispered as she turned slightly, onto her side, so that now, in addition to their feet and thighs, their hips, arms, and shoulders were also touching. "I don't know how to say it, but I'm so envious of you. Because of the way you are, because you're so elegant. The best-looking woman I've ever known."

"Will you let me kiss you?" Señora Lucrecia lowered her head until it brushed against Justiniana's. Their hair became entwined. She could see her deep, wide-open eyes, observing her without blinking, without fear, but with some uneasiness. "Can I? Can we? Like friends?"

She felt uncomfortable, regretful, for the seconds—two, three, ten?—that it took Justiniana to reply. And her soul returned to her body—her heart beating so fast she could hardly breathe—when, at last, the dear face beneath hers nodded and moved upward, offering her lips. As they kissed, passionately, their tongues intertwining, separating and reuniting, their bodies embracing, Don Rigoberto exulted. Was he proud of his wife? Of course. More in love with her than ever? Naturally. He drew back in order to see and hear them.

"I have to tell you something, Señora," he heard Justiniana whisper into Lucrecia's ear. "For a long time I've had a dream. The same dream, again and again, until I wake up. I dream that one night it's cold and the señor is away on a trip. You're afraid of thieves and ask me to stay with you. I want to sleep on this chair and you say, "No, no, come here, come here." And you have me lie down with you. And when I dream that, while I'm dreaming, I don't know how to tell you, I get wet. I'm so embarrassed!"

"Let's do the dream." Señora Lucrecia stood up, pulling Justiniana after her. "Let's sleep together, but in the bed, it's softer than the chaise longue. Come, Justita."

Before they slipped under the sheets they took off their robes and left them at the foot of the king-size bed, which was covered with a spread. The harps had been followed by an old-fashioned waltz, violins whose rhythms were attuned to the rhythm of their caresses. What did it matter that they had turned off the light as they were playing and loving, hidden beneath the sheets, and that the busily moving bedspread twisted, wrinkled, swayed back and forth? Don Rigoberto did not miss a single detail of their onslaughts and attacks; he entangled and disentangled along with them; he was at the side of the hand that encircled a breast, in each finger that caressed a buttock, in the lips that, following several skirmishes, dared at last to sink into that hidden darkness, searching out the crater of pleasure, the warm hollow, the throbbing entrance, the small, quivering muscle. He saw everything, smelled everything, heard everything. His nostrils were enraptured by the perfume of their skin, his lips drank in the juices that flowed from the charming pair.

"She had never done that before?"

"And neither had I," Doña Lucrecia confirmed. "Neither of us had, not ever. A couple of novices. We learned on the spot. I enjoyed it, we both enjoyed it. That night I didn't miss you at all, my love. Do you mind my telling you that?"

"I like your telling me," and her husband embraced her. "And she, did she feel regret afterward?"

Not at all. She displayed a naturalness and discretion that impressed Doña Lucrecia. Except for the next morning, when the bouquets of flowers arrived (the card for the employer read: *From beneath his bandages, Fito Cebolla sends heartfelt thanks for the well-deserved lesson received from his beloved and admired friend Lucrecia,* and for the employee: *Fito Cebolla greets and humbly begs the pardon of the Cinnamon Flower*) and they showed them to one another, the subject was never mentioned again. Their relationship, the way each behaved toward the other and treated the other, did not change for those who observed them from the outside. True, Doña Lucrecia occasionally showed a certain weakness for Justiniana, giving her new shoes or a dress or taking her along on her outings, but though this caused some jealousy in the butler and cook, it came as no surprise to anyone, since the entire household, from the chauffeur to Fonchito and Don Rigoberto, had noticed for some time that with her quick wit and ready flattery, Justiniana had completely won over the señora.

Flying-Ears Love

Eyes for seeing, a nose for smelling, fingers for touching, and ears like horns of plenty for stroking with fingertips, like the hunchback's hump or the Buddha's belly—they bring luck—and then for licking and kissing.

I adore you, Rigoberto, you and only you, but more than anything else about you I adore your flying ears. I would like to get down on my knees and peer into those dear openings that you clean each morning (I know what I know) with a little cotton-tipped stick, whose little hairs you pluck with a tweezer—strand ah by strand ooh in front of the mirror ow—on the days when it is their turn for purification. What would I see down those deep little caverns? A precipice. And then I would learn your secrets. What, for example? That without knowing it, you already love me, Rigoberto. Would I see anything else? Two baby elephants with their trunks raised. Dumbo, dear, sweet Dumbo, how I love you.

We each love what we love. Though some say that because of your nose and ears you could win a contest as the Elephant Man of Peru, for me you are the most attractive, best-looking man in the world. Go on, Rigoberto, take a guess: if I had to choose between Robert Redford and you, who do you think would be my heart's desire? Yes, my darling ears, yes, my precious nose, yes, my Pinocchio: it would be you, you.

What else would I see if I peeked into your auditory abysses? A field of clover, all with four leaves. And bouquets of roses, every petal with a portrait on its velvety whiteness of a face in love. Whose? Mine.

Who am I, Rigoberto? Who is the mountain climber who loves you, adores you, and one day in the not-too-distant future will scale your ears as others scale the Himalaya or the Huascarán peak?

Yours, yours, yours forever,
Mad About Your Ears

IV

Fonchito in Tears

Fonchito had been dejected and pale since his arrival at the house in San Isidro, and Doña Lucrecia was sure his dark circles and his evasive eyes had something to do with Egon Schiele, the invariable topic of their afternoon conversations. He barely opened his mouth while they were having tea, and for the first time in weeks failed to praise Justiniana's toasted sweet buns. Poor grades at school? Or had Rigoberto discovered he was missing classes at the academy to visit her? Enclosed in gloomy silence, he bit at his knuckles. At one point he had muttered something terrible about Adolf and Marie, the parents or relatives of his beloved painter.

"When something is eating away at you inside, it's a good idea to talk about it," Doña Lucrecia proposed. "Don't you trust me? Tell me what's wrong, perhaps I can help you."

The startled boy looked into her eyes. He was blinking and seemed about to burst into tears. His temples were throbbing and Doña Lucrecia could see the fine blue veins in his neck.

"Well, it's just that I've been thinking," he said at last. He looked away and fell silent, having second thoughts about what he was going to say.

"About what, Fonchito? Go on, tell me. Why are you so worried about those two? Who are Adolf and Marie?"

"Egon Schiele's folks," said the boy, as if he were speaking about a classmate. "But it's not Señor Adolf I'm worried about, it's my papá."

"Rigoberto?"

"I don't want my papá to end up like him." The boyish face grew even more somber, and he made a strange gesture with his hand, as if he were frightening away a ghost. "It scares me and I don't know what to do. I didn't want to worry you. You still love my papá, don't you, Stepmamá?"

"Of course I do," she agreed, disconcerted. "I'm really confused now, Fonchito. What does Rigoberto have to do with the father of a painter who died on the other side of the world half a century ago?"

At first she had found it amusing and very typical of him, this strange game, this passion for the pictures and life of Egon Schiele, studying them, learning about them, identifying with the painter until he believed, or claimed to believe, he was the reincarnation of Egon Schiele, and like him would also die tragically, after a brief, brilliant career, at the age of twenty-eight. But now the game had gone too far.

"His father's fate is being repeated in my papá," Fonchito stammered, swallowing hard. "I don't want him to go crazy with syphilis like Señor Adolf, Stepmamá."

"But that's so foolish," she tried to reassure him. "First of all, lives aren't inherited or repeated. Where'd you ever get a silly idea like that?"

The boy's face contorted, and incapable of controlling himself, he burst into tears, his thin body shaken by sobs. Señora Lucrecia leaped from her chair, sat beside him on the carpet in the dining alcove, put her arms around him, kissed his hair and forehead, dried his tears with her handkerchief, and had him blow his nose. Fonchito held her tight. His chest heaved with deep sighs, and Doña Lucrecia felt his heart pounding.

"Calm down now, it's all right, don't cry, that's nothing but nonsense." She was smoothing his hair, kissing his hair. "Rigoberto is the healthiest, most sensible man I've ever known."

Egon Schiele's father was syphilitic and had died insane? Her curiosity piqued by Fonchito's constant allusions, Doña Lucrecia had gone to The Green House bookshop, just a few steps from her house, to learn more about Schiele, but she found no monographs, only a history of Expressionism that devoted no more than a chapter to him. She did not recall any mention at all of his family. The boy nodded, his lips pursed, his eyes half-closed. From time to time a shudder ran down his spine. But he was calmer, and without moving away, huddling against her, happy, one might almost say, to be sheltered in Doña Lucrecia's arms, he began to speak. Didn't she know the story of Señor Adolf Schiele? No, she didn't know it; she hadn't been able to find a biography of the painter. But Fonchito had read several in his papá's library and consulted the encyclopedia. A terrible story, Step-mamá. They said if you didn't know about Señor Adolf Schiele and Señora Marie Soukup, you couldn't understand Egon. Because their story hid the secret of his painting.

"All right, all right," said Doña Lucrecia, trying to depersonalize the subject. "Then what's the secret of his painting?"

"His papá's syphilis," replied the boy, with no hesitation. "The madness of poor Señor Adolf Schiele."

Biting her lip, Doña Lucrecia contained her laughter, not wishing to hurt the boy. She seemed to hear Dr. Rubio, an acquaintance of Don Rigoberto's who was an analyst, and very popular with her women friends ever since he began to undress during sessions—citing the example of Wilhelm Reich—in order to better interpret the dreams of his female patients. He would always say things like that at cocktail parties, and with the same conviction.

"But, Fonchito," she said, blowing on his forehead, for it gleamed with perspiration, "do you even know what syphilis is?"

"A venereal disease; that means it comes from Venus, the goddess of something or other," the boy confessed with disarming sincerity. "I couldn't find her in the dictionary. But I know where Señor Adolf caught it. Shall I tell you what happened?"

"Only if you calm down. And stop torturing yourself with absurd fantasies. You're not Egon Schiele and Rigoberto has nothing to do with his father, you silly goose."

The boy made no promises, he did not respond at all. For a time he remained silent, within her protective arms, his head resting on his step-mother's shoulder. When he began to tell her the story, he supplied a quantity of dates and details, as if he had been a witness to the events he was narrating. Or a protagonist, for he spoke with all the emotion of one who had experienced them personally. As if he had not been born in Lima at the end of the twentieth century but were Egon Schiele, a lad from the last generation of Austro-Hungarian subjects, the generation that would see the so-called *Belle Epoque* vanish in the catastrophe of the First World War, along with the Empire, that brilliant society—cosmopolitan, literary, mu-sical, and artistic—which Rigoberto loved so dearly and about which he had instructed Doña Lucrecia so patiently during the early years of their marriage. (Now Fonchito was giving the lessons.) The generation of Mahler, Schoenberg, Freud, Klimt, Schiele. In the alarming account, and setting aside anachronisms and a certain childishness, a story was beginning to take shape. A village called Tulln, on the banks of the Danube, in the outskirts of Vienna (twenty-five kilometers away, he said), and the wedding, in the final years of the century, of the imperial railway official Adolf Eugen Schiele, a Protestant of German origin, just turned twenty-six, and Marie Soukup, a Catholic adolescent of Czech origin, seventeen years of age. A scandalous, unconventional marriage, due to the opposition of the bride's family. ("Was your family opposed to your marrying my papá?" "Not at all, they were delighted with Rigoberto.") It was a puritanical time and full of prejudices, wasn't it, Stepmamá? Yes, certainly. Why? Because Marie Soukup didn't know anything about life; she hadn't even been told how babies are made, the poor girl thought storks brought them from Paris. (His stepmamá couldn't have been that innocent when she married? No, Doña Lucrecia already knew all she had to know.) Marie was so innocent she didn't even know she was pregnant and thought her discomfort was caused by eating too many apples, which she loved. But that's getting ahead of the story. We have to go back to their honeymoon. That's where it all began.

"What happened on their honeymoon?"

"Nothing," said the boy, sitting up to blow his nose. His eyes were swollen, but he had lost his pallor and was involved, body and soul, in his story. "Marie was afraid. For the first three days she wouldn't let Señor Adolf touch her. The marriage was not consummated. What are you laughing at, Stepmamá?"

"Hearing you talk like an old man when you're still a little boy. Don't be angry, I'm very interested. All right, for the first three days of their marriage nothing, nothing at all, between Adolf and Marie."

"It's no laughing matter." Fonchito grew sad. "It's something to cry over. The honeymoon was in Trieste. In memory of their parents' trip, Egon Schiele and Gerti, his favorite sister, made an identical trip in 1906."

In Trieste, during the frustrated honeymoon, the tragedy began. Since his wife would not allow him to touch her—she would cry, kick and scratch him, make a huge scene every time he tried to get close enough to kiss her—Señor Adolf went out. Where did he go? To console himself with bad women. And in one of those places Venus infected him with syphilis. That was when the disease began to kill him, slowly. It made him lose his mind and brought misfortune to the entire family. A curse fell on the Schieles. Adolf, without realizing it, infected his wife when he was finally able to consummate the marriage, on the fourth day. And that was why

80

Marie's first three pregnancies miscarried; and that was why Elvira died, the little girl who lived only ten short years. And that was why Egon was so weak and sickly. In fact, when he was a boy they thought he would die because he spent so much time seeing doctors. In the end, Doña Lucrecia could visualize him: a solitary child playing with his toy trains, drawing, drawing all the time in his school notebooks, in the margins of the Bible, even on pieces of papers he pulled from the trash.

"You see, you're nothing like him. You were the healthiest child in the world, according to Rigoberto. And you liked to play with planes, not trains."

Fonchito refused to joke. "Shall I finish the story or are you getting bored?"

She wasn't bored, she was enjoying it, less because of the vicissitudes of Austro-Hungarian characters at the turn of the century than for the passion with which Fonchito evoked them: trembling, moving his eyes and hands, using melodramatic inflections. The awful thing about the disease was that it came slowly and stealthily, and it brought disgrace to its victims. That was why Señor Adolf never acknowledged that he suffered from it. When his relatives advised him to see the doctor, he would protest: "I'm healthier than any of you." But he wasn't. He had begun to lose his mind. Egon loved him, they got on very well, he suffered when his father grew worse. Señor Adolf would sit down to play cards as if his friends had come for a visit, but he was all alone. He would deal the cards, chat with them, offer them cigarettes, and there was nobody sitting at the table in the house in Tulln. Marie, Melanie, and Gerti tried to make him see reality: "But, Papá, there's nobody here to talk to, to play cards with, don't you know that?" Egon would contradict them: "It's not true, Father, don't pay attention to them, here's the chief of police, the postmaster, the schoolteacher. Your friends are here with you, Father. I see them too, just like you." He didn't want to accept the fact that his father was hallucinating. Without warning Señor Adolf would put on his dress uniform, his cap with the gleaming visor, his boots shining like mirrors, and he would stand at attention on the railway platform. "What are you doing here, Father?" "I'm waiting to receive the Emperor and Empress, my son." He was completely mad. He couldn't go on working for the railway, he had to retire. The Schieles were so ashamed they moved from Tulln to a town where no one knew them: Klosterneuburg. In German it means: "new convent town." Señor Adolf grew worse, he forgot how to speak. He spent his days in his room, never saying a word. Did she see? Did she? Fonchito was suddenly overcome by an anguished agitation.

"Just like my papá," he cried, his voice breaking. "He comes home from the office and shuts himself in and doesn't talk to anybody. Not even me. Even on Saturdays and Sundays he does the same thing; the whole darn day in his study. When I try to talk to him, it's 'Yes,' 'No,' 'All right.' That's all he says."

Could he have syphilis? Was he going crazy? And for the same reason as Señor Adolf. Because he was left all alone when Señora Lucrecia went away. He went to one of those bad houses and Venus infected him. He didn't want his papá to die, Stepmamá!

He started to cry again, this time silently, to himself, covering his face, and this time it was harder for Doña Lucrecia to soothe him. She comforted him, what an absurd idea, she petted him, there was nothing wrong with Rigoberto, she cradled him, he was saner than Fonchito and her put together, she felt the tears from that rosy face dampening the bodice of her dress. After a good deal of fondling, she managed to calm him. Rigoberto liked to shut himself away with his pictures and books, with his notebooks, to read and listen to music, to write his citations and reflections. Didn't he know him yet? Hadn't he always been like that?

"No, not always." The boy denied this firmly. "Before, he used to tell me about the lives of the painters, he explained their pictures, he showed me things. And he read to me from his notebooks. With you he used to laugh, go out; he was normal. But he changed when you left. He became sad. Now he doesn't even care about my grades; he signs my report card without looking at it. The only thing he cares about is his study. He shuts himself in there for hours and hours. He'll go crazy, just like Señor Adolf. Maybe it's happened already."

The boy had thrown his arms around her neck and was resting his head on his stepmother's shoulder. In the Olivar there were children calling and playing as they did every afternoon when the schools let out and the boys from the area flocked to the park from countless street corners to smoke, hiding from their parents, and kick the ball, and flirt with the neighborhood girls. Why didn't Fonchito ever do those things?

"Do you still love my papá, Stepmamá?" The same question, this time full of apprehension, as if someone's life or death depended on her answer.

"I've already told you, Fonchito. I never stopped loving him. What's that have to do with anything?"

"He's the way he is because he misses you. Because he loves you, Stepmamá, and he hasn't gotten over your not living with us anymore."

"Things happened the way they happened." Doña Lucrecia struggled against a growing uneasiness.

"You're not thinking about getting married again, are you, Stepmamá?" the boy suggested timidly.

"The last thing I would ever do in this life is get married again. Never, never. Besides, Rigoberto and I aren't even divorced, we're only separated.".

"Then you can make up," Fonchito exclaimed with relief. "When people fight, they can make up. I fight and make up every day with the kids at school. You could come back, Justita too. Everything would be the way it was before."

"And we could cure your papá's craziness," Doña Lucrecia thought. She was annoyed. Fonchito's fantasies no longer amused her. Wordless anger, bitterness, rancor overwhelmed her as her mind dusted off unpleasant memories. She took the boy by the shoulders and moved him away. She observed him, their faces close, indignant that those blue eyes, swollen and red, so innocently withstood her reproachful look. Could he really be so cynical? He wasn't even an adolescent yet. How could he talk about the break between her and Rigoberto as if it were not his affair, as if he had not been the cause of everything? Hadn't he arranged for Rigoberto to find out the whole story? His tear-streaked face, his artfully drawn features, pink lips, curly eyelashes, small firm chin, looked at her with virginal innocence.

"You know better than anyone what happened," said Señora Lucrecia between clenched teeth, trying to keep her indignation from exploding. "You know very well why we separated. Don't pretend to be a good little boy who feels bad about that separation. You were as much to blame as me, maybe even more."

"That's exactly why, Stepmamá," Fonchito interrupted. "I made you fight, and that's why it's up to me to make you friends again. But you have to help me. You will, won't you? Say you will, Stepmamá."

Doña Lucrecia did not know how to answer; she wanted to slap him and kiss him at the same time. Her cheeks were hot. And to make matters worse, that impudent Fonchito, in an abrupt change of mood, seemed happy now. Suddenly he began to laugh.

"You're all red," he said, throwing his arms around her neck again. "Then the answer's yes. I love you so much, Stepmamá!"

"First you cry and now you're laughing," said Justiniana, appearing in the hallway. "Just what is going on here?"

"We have wonderful news," said the boy by way of greeting. "Shall we tell her, Stepmamá?"

"You're the one who has a screw loose, not Rigoberto," said Doña Lucrecia, hiding her embarrassment.

"Venus must have infected me with syphilis too." Fonchito laughed, looking away. And, in the same tone, he said to the girl, "My papá and my stepmamá are going to make up, Justita! What do you think of that?"

Diatribe against the Sportsman

I understand that in summer you surf the rough waves of the Pacific and spend the winters skiing down the Chilean trails at Portillo, the Argentine trails at Bariloche (since the Peruvian Andes do not permit such affectations), that you sweat every morning doing aerobic exercises at the gym, or running around athletic tracks or parks or streets, encased in a thermal suit that squeezes your ass and belly like the old-fashioned corsets that asphyxiated our grandmothers, that you never miss a soccer game or the classic encounter between Alianza Lima and Universitario de Deportes or a boxing match for the South American, Latin American, North American, European, or World title, and that on these occasions, glued to the television set and making the show even more agreeable with beer, cuba libres, or whiskey on the rocks, you yell at the top of your lungs, turn red in the face, howl, wave your arms, or become depressed with every triumph or failure of your idols, as befits a loyal sports fan. More than enough reasons, Señor, to confirm my worst suspicions regarding the world in which we live, and to classify you as a brainless, mentally defective shithead. (I use the first and third terms as metaphors; the second is to be taken literally.)

Yes, it's true, in your atrophied intellect a light has come on: I consider the practice of sports in general, and the cult of sports in particular, as radical forms of the imbecility that brings human beings close to sheep, geese, and ants, three extreme examples of animal gregariousness. Control your wrestler's impulse to tear me to pieces and listen; in a moment we'll talk about the Greeks and the hypocritical *mens sana in corpore sano*. First, I should tell you that the only sports I do not find ridiculous are those of the table (excluding Ping-Pong) and the bed (including, of course, mastur-bation). As for the rest, contemporary culture has transformed them into obstacles to the development of spirit, sensibility, and imagination (and, consequently, of pleasure). And above all, of consciousness and individual freedom. In our time nothing, not even ideology and religion, has contrib-uted so much to the rise of contemptible mass-man, a robot full of con-ditioned reflexes, or to the resurrection of the culture of the tattooed primate in a loincloth which lies concealed behind the façade of modernity, as the glorification of physical exercise and games by our society.

Now we can speak of the Greeks, so you won't pester me anymore about Plato and Aristotle. But I warn you, the spectacle of young Athenian boys smearing themselves with oils in the gymnasium before testing their physical dexterity, or hurling the discus and the javelin beneath the pure blue of the Aegean sky, will be of no help to you but will force you deeper into ig-nominy, you, a buffoon whose muscles have been hardened at the expense of a lowered testosterone level and a plummeting IQ. Only blows to the head with a soccer ball or the punches received in the boxing ring or the mind-numbing turn of the cyclist's wheels and the premature senile de-mentia (in addition to sexual dysfunction, incontinence, and impotence?) which they tend to provoke can explain the attempt to establish a direct line between the tunicked youths of Plato anointing themselves with resins after their sensual and philosophical physical displays and the drunken hordes roaring in the stands of modern stadiums (before setting them on fire) at contemporary soccer games, in which twenty-two clowns, deperson-alized by garishly colored uniforms and running wildly after a ball on a grassy rectangle, serve as the pretext for exhibitions of collective insanity.

In Plato's day, sport was a means, not the end it has become in these municipalized times. It served to enrich human pleasure (masculine plea-sure, since women did not engage in sports), stimulating and prolonging it with the representation of a beautiful, smooth, oiled, well-proportioned, harmonious body, inciting it with pre-erotic calisthenics and certain move-ments, postures, frictions, bodily exhibitions, exercises, dances, touches, in-flaming desire until participants and spectators were catapulted into coupling. That these encounters were eminently homosexual neither adds to nor subtracts from my argument, nor does the fact that in the sexual realm Yours Truly is boringly orthodox and loves only women—indeed, only one woman—and is totally disinterested in active or passive pederasty. Understand me, I have no objections at all to what gays do. I am delighted that they enjoy themselves, and I support their campaigns against discriminatory laws. Beyond that I cannot go, for very practical reasons. Nothing related to what Quevedo called the "eye of the ass" gives me pleasure. Nature, or God, if He exists and wastes His time on these matters, has made that concealed aperture the most sensitive of all the orifices that pierce my body. Suppositories wound it, and the tip of the enema syringe makes it bleed (once, during a period of stubborn constipation, one was forced into me, and it was terrible), and so the idea that certain bipeds enjoy having a virile member inserted there fills me with horrified amazement. I am certain, in my case, that along with howls and screams, I would experience a true psychosomatic cataclysm if that aforementioned opening were to be penetrated by an erect penis, even if it were a Pygmy's. The only punch I ever threw in my life was aimed at a physician who, without warning and on the pretext of determining if I had appendicitis, attempted to commit upon my person a form of torture disguised by the scientific label "rectal examination." Despite this, I am theoretically in favor of human beings making love inside out, upside down, alone or in couples or in promiscuous collective (ugh!) matings in which men copulate with men, and women with women, and both with ducks, dogs, watermelons, bananas, cantaloupes, and every imaginable disgusting thing if it makes them agreeable to the pursuit of pleasure, not reproduction, an accident of sex which one must accept as a minor inconvenience but in no way sanctify as the justification for carnal joy (this imbecility on the part of the Church exasperates me as much as a basketball game). But I digress: the image of aging Hellenes, wise philosophers, august legislators, battle-scarred generals, or high priests frequenting gymnasiums in order to revive their libidos with the sight of youthful discus throwers, wrestlers, marathon runners, or javelin hurlers—that image moves me. The kind of sport that panders to desire I condone and would not hesitate to engage in if my health, age, sense of the ridiculous, and leisure time were to permit it.

There is another instance, even further removed from our cultural environment (I don't know why I include you in this fraternity since, as a result of soccer's kicks and blows to the head, cycling's sweaty exertions, karate's throws to the ground, you have been excluded from it), when sport also has an excuse. And that is when a human being, by engaging in it, transcends his animal nature, touches the sacred, and rises to a plane of intense spirituality. If you insist on our using the dangerous word "mystic," then so be it. Obviously such cases, by this time extremely rare—an exotic reminiscence is the warlike sacrifice of the Japanese sumo wrestler, fed from childhood on a fierce vegetarian diet that elephantizes him and condemns him to die, his heart bursting, before the age of forty, and to spend his life trying not to be expelled by another mountain of flesh exactly like him from the small magic circle to which his life is confined—cannot be compared to those idols of the mob that post-industrial society calls "martyrs to sport." Where is the heroism in being turned to mush at the wheel of a racing car propelled by motors that do all the work for humans, in regressing from a thinking being to a mental defective with brains and testicles mangled by the practice of intercepting goals or striving to achieve them, just so that maddened crowds can be desexed by ejaculations of collective egotism at each point scored? For contemporary man, the physical exercises and skills called sports bring him no closer to the sacred and the religious; they distance him from the spirit, and brutalize him by catering to his most ignoble instincts: tribalism, machismo, the will to dominate, the dissolution of the individual ego in an amorphous gregariousness.

I know of no lie more base than the phrase taught to children: "A sound mind in a sound body." Who ever said that a *sound mind* is a desirable goal? In this case, "sound" means stupid, conventional, unimaginative, and unmischievous, the vulgar stereotype of established morality and official religion. Is that a "sound" mind? It is the mind of a conformist, a pious old woman, a notary, an insurance salesman, an altar boy, a virgin, a Boy Scout. That is not health, it is an impairment. A rich, independent mental life demands curiosity, mischief, fantasy, and unsatisfied desires, which is to say a "dirty" mind, evil thoughts, and the blossoming of forbidden images and appetites that stimulate exploration of the unknown, renovation of the known, and systematic disrespect toward received ideas, common knowledge, and current values.

Furthermore, it is not even true that engaging in sports in our day creates sound minds in the banal sense of the word. Just the opposite occurs, and you know that better than anyone, for in order to win the hundred-meter dash on Sunday you would put arsenic and cyanide in your competitor's soup, swallow every vegetable, chemical, or magical drug to guarantee your victory, corrupt or blackmail the judges, devise medical or legal schemes to disqualify your rivals, and live hounded by your neurotic fixation on the victory, the record, the medal, the dais; this has turned you, the professional sportsman, into an artificial creation of the media, an antisocial, nervous, hysterical psychopath, the polar opposite of that sociable, generous, altruistic, "healthy" individual to which imbeciles wish to allude when they still dare to use the expression "sportsmanship" in the sense of a noble athlete filled with civic virtues, when, in fact, what lurks behind the phrase is a potential assassin willing to kill referees, murder all the fans of the other team, devastate the stadiums and cities that house them, and bring about the final apocalypse, not for the high artistic purpose that led to the burning of Rome by the poet Nero, but so that his club can win a fake silver cup or he can see his eleven idols carried to a rostrum, flagrantly ridiculous in their shorts and striped undershirts, their hands to their chests and their eyes shining as they sing the national anthem!

The Corsican Brothers

On that oppressive Sunday afternoon in winter, in his study that looked out on an overcast sky and dull, rat-gray sea, Don Rigoberto anxiously leafed through his notebooks searching for ideas to fire his imagination. The first one he came across, by the poet Philip Larkin, "Sex is too good to share with anyone else," reminded him of the many versions in art of the young Narcissus delighting in his own reflection in a pool, and of the recumbent hermaphrodite in the Louvre. But, inexplicably, this depressed him. On other occasions he had agreed with the philosophy that placed the responsibility for his pleasure exclusively on his own shoulders. Was it correct? Had it ever been correct? The truth was that even at its purest moments his solitude had been for two, a rendezvous that Lucrecia never failed to keep. A faint stirring in his spirit gave rise to new hope: she would not fail this time, either. Larkin's thesis corresponded perfectly to the saint (another page in the notebook) described by Lytton Strachey in *Eminent Victorians*: Saint Cubert was so distrustful of women that when he spoke to any of them, even the future Saint Ebba, he spent "the following hours in darkness, in prayer, submerged in water to the neck." So many colds and bouts of pneumonia for a faith that condemned the believer to a Larkinian solitary pleasure.

As if he were walking on live coals, he hurried past a page on which Azorín recalled that "caprice is derived from capra, a she-goat." He paused, fascinated, at the description by the diplomat Alfonso de la Serna of the *Farewell Symphony* by Haydn, "in which each musician, as his part ended, put out the candle that lit his music stand and stole away until only one violin was left to play the final, solitary melody." Wasn't that a coincidence? Wasn't that a mysterious joining, as if following a secret order, of the solo voice of Haydn's violin with the pleasure-seeking egotist Philip Larkin, who believed that sex was too important to share?

And yet he, though he elevated sex to the highest level, had always shared it, even during this, his time of bitterest solitude. And then, out of the blue, he was reminded of the actor Douglas Fairbanks, Jr., playing double roles in the film that had so disquieted his childhood: *The Corsican Brothers*. Of course, he had never shared sex with anyone as deeply as he had with Lucrecia. But he had also shared it, as a child, youth, and adult, with his own Corsican brother—Narciso?—with whom he had always gotten along so well despite the differences in their natures. And yet those risqué games and deceptions devised and enjoyed by the brothers did not correspond to the ironic sense in which the poet-librarian used the verb "to share." Turning page after page, he happened upon *The Merchant of Venice*:

> *The man that hath no music in himself,*
> *Nor is not mov'd with concord of sweet sounds,*
> *Is fit for treasons, stratagems, and spoils*
> (Act V, Scene 1)

"The man who has no music in his soul/And is not moved by harmonies of sweet sounds/Is likely to commit intrigue, fraud, and treason," he translated freely. Narciso had no music at all, was cut off, body and soul, from the charms of Melpomene, and could not distinguish between Haydn's *Farewell Symphony* and Pérez Prado's "Mambo Number 5." Was Shakespeare correct in decreeing that an ear deaf to the most abstract of the arts made his brother a potential schemer, swindler, and fraud? Well, perhaps it was true. The amiable Narciso had not been a model of virtue, civic, private, or theological, and would reach an advanced age boasting, like Bishop Harold (whose citation was it? The reference had been devoured by the sibylline Limenian damp, or the labors of a moth) on his deathbed, that he had practiced all the deadly sins with the regularity of his beating heart or the ringing of church bells in his bishopric. If that had not been his moral nature, Narciso never would have dared that night to suggest to his Corsican brother—Don Rigoberto could sense in his deepest being the stirrings of the Shakespearean music which he believed he carried inside himself—the daring exchange. And so they took shape before his eyes, sitting side by side in that room in the house in La Planicie that was a monument to kitsch and a blasphemous provocation to every society for the protection of animals, bristling as it was with embalmed tigers, buffalo, rhinos, and deer—Lucrecia next to Ilse, Narciso's blond wife, on the night of their adventure. The Bard was right: a deaf ear for music was a symptom (or the cause?) of a base soul. No, one could not generalize, for then one would have to conclude that their insensitivity to music had turned Jorge Luis Borges and André Breton into Judas and Cain, when it was well known that both had been very fine people, for writers.

His brother Narciso was not a devil, merely an adventurer. Endowed with a diabolical aptitude for deriving enormous profits from his wanderlust and his taste for everything forbidden, secret, and exotic. But as he was also a mythomaniac, it was difficult to know what was true and what was fantasy in the tales of his travels with which he would hold his listeners spellbound at the (sinister) hour of gala dinners, wedding banquets, or cocktail parties, the stages for his great narrative performances. For example, Don Rigoberto had never entirely believed that he had made a good part of his fortune smuggling contraband—rhinoceros horns, leopard testicles, and the penises of walruses and seals (the first two from Africa, the last from Alaska, Greenland, and Canada)—to the prosperous nations of Asia. Body parts worth their weight in gold in Thailand, Hong Kong, Taiwan, Korea, Singapore, Japan, Malaysia, and even Communist China, for connoisseurs considered them powerful aphrodisiacs and infallible remedies for impotence. On that night, in fact, while the Corsican brothers and the two sisters-in-law, Ilse and Lucrecia, were having an apéritif before supper in the Costa Verde restaurant, Narciso had entertained them with a wild story about aphrodisiacs (in it he was both hero and victim) that took place in Saudi Arabia, where he swore—backed up by precise geographical details and unpronounceable Arabic names full of guttural consonants—he had almost been decapitated in the public square in Riyadh when it was discovered that he had smuggled in a bag filled with Captagon tablets (acetophenetidin hydrochloride) to maintain the sexual potency of the lustful sheik Abdelaziz Abu Amid, who was fairly worn out by his four legitimate wives and the eighty-two concubines in his harem, and who paid him in gold for the shipment of amphetamines.

"And yobimbine?" asked Ilse, cutting off her husband's story just at the moment when he was appearing before a tribunal of turbaned ulemas. "Does it produce the effect they say in everybody who tries it?"

Losing no time, his handsome brother—without a trace of envy Don Rigoberto recalled how, after being indistinguishable as children and adolescents, adulthood began to differentiate between them, and now Narciso's ears seemed normal in comparison to the spectacular wings that he sported, and Narciso's straight, modest nose was no match for the corkscrew, or anteater's snout, with which he sniffed at life—launched into an erudite peroration on yohimbine (called yobimbine in Peru because of the lazy phonetic tendencies of the natives, for whom an aspirated *h* demanded greater buccal effort than a *b*). Narciso's lecture continued through their apéritifs—pisco sours for the gentlemen and cold white wine for the ladies—and the meal of shellfish and rice and crêpes with blancmange, and as far as he was concerned, it had the tingling effect of foreplay. At that moment—the caprices of chance—the notebook furnished him with the Shakespearean indication that turquoise stones change color to warn whoever is wearing them of imminent danger (again, *The Merchant of Venice*). Was he speaking seriously? Did he know or was he inventing knowledge in order to create the psychological climate, the amoral ambiance that would favor his subsequent proposals? He had not asked and he never would, for at this point, what did it matter?

Don Rigoberto began to laugh, and the dull gray afternoon lightened. At the bottom of the page, Valéry's Monsieur Teste boasted: "Stupidity is not my strong suit" (*La bêtise n'est pas mon fort*). Lucky for him; Don Rigoberto had already spent a quarter of a century at the insurance company, surrounded by, submerged in, asphyxiated by stupidity, making him a specialist in the subject. Was Narciso simply an imbecile? Another piece of Limenian protoplasm that calls itself decent and proper? Yes. Which made him no less amiable when he set his mind to it. That night, for instance. There he sat, the indefatigable raconteur, his face closely shaven and sporting the deep tan of the leisured, expounding on an alkaloid plant, also called yohimbine, that had an illustrious history in herbalist tradition and natural medicine. It increased vasodilatation and stimulated the ganglia that control erective tissue, and it inhibited serotonin, which, in excessive amounts, inhibits the sexual appetite. He had the warm voice of an experienced seducer; his voice and gestures were in perfect harmony with the blue blazer, gray shirt, and dark silk scarf with white dots that encircled his neck. His exposition, interspersed with smiles, adroitly respected the line between information and insinuation, anecdote and fantasy, knowledge and hearsay, diversion and excitation. Suddenly Don Rigoberto noticed the gleam in the sea-green eyes of Ilse, the dark topaz eyes of Lucrecia. Had his pretentious Corsican brother aroused the ladies? Judging by their giggles, jokes, questions, the crossing and uncrossing of their legs, and the gaiety with which they emptied their glasses of Chilean wine (Concha y Toro), yes, he had. Why wouldn't they experience the same stirring of the spirit as he? Did Narciso have his plan already prepared at this point in the evening? Of course, Don Rigoberto decreed.

And therefore, with great skill, he did not give them a chance to catch their breath, or allow the conversation to move away from the Machiavellian course he had laid out for it. From yobimbine he moved on to Japanese *fugu*, the testicular fluid of a small fish which, in addition to being an extremely powerful seminal tonic, can also cause a grisly death by poison —which is how hundreds of lascivious Japanese perish every year—and recounted the icy fear with which he had taken it, on that shimmering night in Kyoto, from the hands of a geisha in a billowing kimono, not knowing if what awaited him at the end of those opiate mouthfuls were death rattles and rigor mortis or one hundred explosions of pleasure (it was the latter, reduced by one zero). Ilse, a statuesque blonde, a former stewardess on Lufthansa, a Peruvianized Valkyrie, celebrated her husband's achievement with not a trace of retrospective jealousy. It was she who suggested (was she in on the plot?), after their floury dessert, that they conclude the evening with a drink at their house in La Planicie. Don Rigoberto said "Good idea" without a second thought, affected by the visible enthusiasm with which Lucrecia welcomed the proposal.

Half an hour later they were settled in comfortable chairs in the hideous kitsch of Narciso and Ilse's living room—Peruvian ostentation and Prussian orderliness—surrounded by dried and stuffed beasts that impassively observed them with icy glass eyes as they drank whiskey in the indirect lighting, listening to songs by Nat "King" Cole and Frank Sinatra, and contemplating the tiles in the illuminated pool through the glass doors that led to the garden. Narciso continued to display his knowledge of aphrodisiacs with all the ease of the Great Richardi—Don Rigoberto sighed as he recalled the circuses of his childhood—pulling scarves from his top hat. Combining omniscience and exoticism, Narciso asserted that in southern Italy each male consumed a ton of sweet basil in the course of his lifetime, for tradition maintains that not only the flavor of pasta but the size of the penis depends on this aromatic herb, and that in India an ointment with a base of garlic and monkey secretions was sold in the markets—he gave it to his friends when they turned fifty—and when rubbed on the proper place produced erections in succession, like the sneezes of a person suffering from allergies. He inundated them with musings on the virtues of oysters, celery, Korean ginseng, sarsaparilla, licorice, pollen, truffles, and caviar, until Don Rigoberto began to suspect, after listening to him for more than three hours, that all the animal and vegetable products in the world were probably designed to foster that joining of bodies called physical love, copulation, sin, to which human beings (himself not excluded) attached so much importance.

This was when Narciso took him by the arm and led him away from the ladies on the pretext of showing him the latest piece in his collection of walking sticks (in addition to mounted animals, what else could this priapic beast, this walking phallus, collect but walking sticks?). The pisco sours, the wine and cognac, had all had their effect. Instead of walking, Don Rigoberto seemed to float into Narciso's study, where, their pages uncut, naturally, the leatherbound volumes stood guard on the shelves: the *Britannica*, Ricardo Palma's *Peruvian Traditions*, and the Durants' *History of Civilization*, along with a paperback novel by Stephen King. Without any preliminaries, lowering his voice, Narciso spoke into his ear and asked if he remembered the tricks they had played on girls long ago in the boxes at the Leuro Cinema. What tricks? But before his brother could answer, he remembered. The switching game! The company lawyer would call it appropriating another person's identity. Taking advantage of their resemblance, emphasizing it with identical clothes and haircuts, each passed himself off as the other in order to kiss and fondle—it was called "making out" in their neighborhood—his brother's girlfriend for the duration of the movie.

"Those were the days, Brother." Don Rigoberto smiled, succumbing to nostalgia.

"You thought they didn't know, that they mixed us up," Narciso recalled. "I could never convince you they did it because they liked the game."

"No, they didn't know," Rigoberto asserted. "They couldn't have. The morality back then wouldn't have permitted it. Lucerito and Chinchilla? So proper, always going to Mass and taking Communion? Never! They would have told their parents."

"Your concept of women is too angelic," Narciso admonished him.

"That's what you think. The fact is, I'm just discreet, unlike you. But every moment I don't devote to the obligations of earning a living, I invest in pleasure."

(And just then the notebook presented him with an appropriate quotation from Borges: "The duty of all things is to give joy; if they do not give joy they are either useless or harmful." Don Rigoberto thought of a machista footnote: "Suppose we say women instead of things, then what?")

"We have only one life, Brother. You don't get a second chance."

"After the matinees we would run to Huatica Boulevard, to the block where the French girls lived," Don Rigoberto said dreamily. "In the days before AIDS, when all you got was a harmless bug and an easy cure."

"Those days aren't over. They're still here," Narciso declared. "We haven't died, and we're not going to die. That decision is irrevocable."

His eyes flamed and his voice was mellow. Don Rigoberto realized that nothing he was hearing was spontaneous; a scheme lurked behind the clever reminiscing.

"Would you care to tell me what you have in mind?" he asked, intrigued.

"You know very well, my dear Corsican brother." The fierce wolf brought his mouth to the great fluttering ear of Don Rigoberto. And without further maneuvering, he formulated his proposal: "The switching game. One more time. Today, right here, right now. Don't you like Ilse? I like Lucrecia, a lot. We'll do what we did with Lucerito and Chinchilla. Could there ever be jealousy between you and me? Let's be young again, Brother!"

In his Sunday solitude, Don Rigoberto's heart beat faster. With surprise, emotion, curiosity, excitement? And, as he had that night, he felt the urge to kill Narciso.

"We're too old and too different now for our wives to be taken in," he declared, drunk with astonishment.

"There's no need for them to be taken in," Narciso replied, very sure of himself. "They're modern women, they don't need excuses. Leave it to me, tiger."

I'll never, never play the switching game at my age, thought Don Rigoberto without opening his mouth. The rising intoxication of a moment ago had dissipated. Damn! Narciso certainly was a man of action. He had already taken his arm and was hurrying him back to the room with the mounted animals, where, cordially gossiping, Ilse and Lucrecia were tearing apart a mutual friend whose recent face-lift had left her with eyes that would be wide-open forever (at least until she was buried or incinerated). And was already announcing that the moment had come to open a bottle of the special reserve Dom Pérignon that he saved for special occasions.

A few minutes later they heard the foaming little explosion, and the four of them were toasting one another with that pale ambrosia. The bubbles going down his esophagus provoked in Don Rigoberto's spirit an idea associated with the topic that had been monopolized all night by his Corsican brother: had Narciso laced the joyful champagne they were drinking with one of the countless aphrodisiacs he said he smuggled and about which he claimed expertise? Because the laughter and bravado of Lucrecia and Ilse were increasing, seeming to favor bold moves, and even he, who five minutes earlier had felt paralyzed, confused, shocked, angered by the proposal—and yet had not had the courage to reject it—now viewed the idea with less indignation, as if it were one of those irresistible temptations that, in his Catholic youth, had driven him to commit the sins he would later describe so contritely in the confessional. Through wisps of smoke— was his Corsican brother the one who was smoking?—and the savage fangs of an Amazonian lion, he saw his sister-in-law's long white legs, crossed, carefully depilitated, and set off by the tigerskin rug in the living room– zoo–mortuary. Excitement manifested itself as a discreet itch low in his belly. And he could see her knees, rounded and satiny, the kind French gallantry called *polies*, indicating solid depths, undoubtedly wet, beneath her brown pleated skirt. Desire coursed through his body. Amazed at himself, he thought, After all, why not? Narciso had asked Lucrecia to dance, and with their arms around one another they began to sway, slowly, next to the wall hung with deer antlers and bear heads. Jealousy seasoned (but did not replace or destroy) his evil thoughts with a bittersweet flavor. He did not vacillate; he leaned over, took away the glass that Ilse was holding in her hand, and drew her toward him: "Care to dance, dear sister-in-law?" His brother had put on a series of slow boleros, of course.

He felt a pang in his heart when, through the locks of the Valkyrie's hair, he saw his Corsican brother and Lucrecia dancing cheek to cheek. His arms encircling her waist, and hers around his neck. How long had these intimacies been going on? He could recall nothing like it in ten years of marriage. Yes, that evil wizard Narciso must have spiked the drinks. While he was lost in speculation, his right arm had been drawing his sister-in-law closer to him. And she did not resist. When he felt the brush of her thighs against his, their bellies touching, Don Rigoberto told himself, not without uneasiness, that now nothing, and no one, could prevent his approaching erection. And, in fact, it came upon him at the very moment he felt Ilse's cheek against his. When the music ended it affected him like the bell during a pitiless boxing match. "Thank you, my beautiful Brunhilde," and he kissed his sister-in-law's hand. And, tripping over gruesome heads filled with stucco or papier-mâché, he moved toward the spot where Lucrecia and Narciso—with chagrin? reluctantly?—were disengaging. He took his wife in his arms and murmured pointedly, "Dear wife, may I have this dance?" He led her to the darkest corner of the room. Out of the corner of his eye he saw that Narciso and Ilse were also embracing and, in a concerted movement, had begun to kiss.

Holding the suspiciously languid body of his wife very close, his erection was reborn; now it pressed without prudery against the form he knew so well. Their lips were touching as he whispered, "Do you know what Narciso proposed?"

"I can imagine," replied Lucrecia with a naturalness that Don Rigoberto found as unsettling as her use of a verb neither of them had ever said in their conjugal intimacy. "He wants you to fuck Ilse while he fucks me?"

He longed to hurt her; instead, he kissed her, assailed by one of those moments of impassioned effusiveness to which he often gave way. Transfixed, feeling that he might begin to cry, he whispered that he loved and wanted her and could never thank her for the happiness she had brought him. "Yes, yes, I love you," he said aloud. "With all my dreams, Lucrecia." The gray Barrancan Sunday brightened, the solitude of his study softened. Don Rigoberto noticed that a tear had fallen from his cheek and blurred a very appropriate quotation from the Valéryan (valerian and Valéry, what a happy union) Monsieur Teste, which defined his own relationship to love: "*Tout ce qui m'était facile m'était indifférent et presque ennemi.*"

Before sadness could overpower him, or the warm feeling of just a moment ago sink completely into corrosive melancholy, he made an effort, and half-closing his eyes and forcing himself to concentrate, he returned to the room filled with animals and the night heavy with smoke—did Narciso smoke? did Ilse?—to dangerous mixtures of champagne, cognac, whiskey, music, and the relaxed ambiance that enveloped them, no longer divided into two stable and precise couples as they had been at the start of the evening before they went to eat dinner at the Costa Verde restaurant, but intermingled, precarious couples who separated and came together again with an ease that matched the amorphous atmosphere as changeable as the shape in a kaleidoscope. Had the light been turned off? A while ago. By Narciso, of course. The room with its dead beasts was faintly illuminated by the light from the pool, allowing only glimpses of shadows, silhouettes, anonymous contours. His Corsican brother prepared his ambushes well. Don Rigoberto's body and spirit had become dissociated; while his spirit wandered, attempting to discover if it would take the game suggested by Narciso to its ultimate consequences, his body, confident and free of scruples, was already engaged in play. Which one was he caressing as he pretended to dance and stood swaying in place, sensing vaguely that the music was stopping and starting periodically? Lucrecia or Ilse? He did not want to know. What a pleasurable sensation to have welded to him that female form whose breasts he could feel, deliciously, through his shirt, whose firm neck his lips nibbled slowly as they advanced toward an ear whose opening the tip of his tongue greedily explored. No, that cartilage or small bone was not Lucrecia's. He raised his eyes and tried to penetrate the shadows of the corner where he recalled seeing Narciso dancing just a moment before.

"They went up a while ago." Ilse's voice sounded vague and bored in his ear. He could even detect a touch of mockery.

"Where?" he asked stupidly, immediately embarrassed by his stupidity.

"Where do you think?" Ilse replied, with a perverse little laugh and German humor. "To look at the moon? Or take a piss? Have any ideas, Brother-in-law?"

"You never see the moon in Lima," Don Rigoberto stammered, releasing Ilse and moving away from her. "You can hardly see the sun in summer. It's the damn fog."

"Narciso has wanted Lucre for a long time." Ilse put him back on the rack, not giving him a chance to catch his breath; she spoke as if it had nothing to do with her. "Don't tell me you haven't noticed, you're not a moron."

His intoxication had dissipated, along with his excitement. He began to perspire. Silently, idiotically, he was asking himself how Lucrecia could have consented so easily to the machinations of his Corsican brother, when he was shaken once again by Ilse's small, insidious voice.

"Are you a little jealous, Rigo?"

"Well, yes, I am," he acknowledged. And then more frankly: "In fact, I'm very jealous."

"I was too, at first," she said, as if it were just another banal remark during a bridge game. "You get used to it, like watching the rain."

"All right, all right," he said, disconcerted. "Do you mean that you and Narciso often play the switching game?"

"Every three months," Ilse replied with Prussian precision. "Not really often. Narciso says that if you don't want this kind of adventure to lose its charm, you can only do it once in a while. Always with carefully chosen people. Because if it becomes trivialized it's no fun anymore."

He must have taken off her clothes by now, he thought. Now he's holding her in his arms. Was Lucrecia kissing and caressing his Corsican brother with the same avidity? He was still trembling as if he had Saint Vitus' dance when Ilse's next question passed through him like an electric shock: "Would you like to see them?"

She had brought her face close to speak. His sister-in-law's long blond hair was in his mouth and eyes.

"Are you serious?" he murmured in astonishment.

"Would you like to?" she insisted, brushing his ear with her lips.

"Yes, yes," he agreed. He felt as if his bones were melting, as if he were evaporating.

She grasped his right hand. "Nice and slow, very quiet," she ordered. She led him, floating, to the winding wrought-iron staircase that led to the bedrooms. It was dark, as was the hallway, though the corridor did receive some illumination from the floodlights in the garden. The deep pile of the carpet muffled their steps; they moved forward on tiptoe. Don Rigoberto felt his heart racing. What awaited him? What would he see? His sister-in-law stopped and whispered another order into his ear: "Take off your shoes," as she leaned over to remove hers. Don Rigoberto obeyed. He felt ridiculous without his shoes, like a thief in his stockinged feet, with Ilse leading him by the hand along the dim corridor as if he were Fonchito. "Don't make noise, you'll ruin everything," she said, standing still. He nodded, like a robot. Ilse started to walk again, opened a door, and had him go in ahead of her. They were in the bedroom, separated from the bed by a brick half-wall with regularly spaced diamond-shaped openings that allowed them to see the bed. It was extremely wide and theatrical. In the cone of light that fell from a ceiling fixture, he saw his Corsican brother and Lucrecia, fused together, moving rhythmically. The sound of their panting, like a quiet dialogue, reached him.

"You can sit down," Ilse indicated. "Here, on the sofa."

He did as he was told. He stepped back and dropped beside his sister-in-law on what must have been a long couch strewn with pillows and placed so that the person sitting there would not miss any part of the show. What did this mean? A chuckle escaped Don Rigoberto: "My Corsican brother is more baroque than I imagined." His mouth was dry.

Their expert positioning and perfect joining made it seem as if the couple had been making love their entire lives. The two bodies never separated; with each new posture, legs, elbows, shoulders, hips seemed to find an even better fit, and as the moments passed, each partner seemed to derive even deeper pleasure from the other. There were the beautiful full curves, the wavy jet-black hair of his beloved, the raised buttocks that made one think of a gallant promontory defying the assault of a wild sea. "No," he said to himself. Rather, the splendid rump in the gorgeous photograph *La Prière*, by Man Ray (1930). He searched through his notebooks and in a few minutes was contemplating the image. His heart sank as he recalled the times when Lucrecia had posed like this for him, in their nocturnal intimacy, sitting back on her heels, both hands supporting the hemispheres of her buttocks. Nor did he find any dissonance in the comparison to another image by Man Ray that his notebook offered next to the first, for the musical back of *Kiki de Montparnasse* (1925) was precisely the one displayed by Lucrecia as she twisted and turned. The deep inflections of her hips held him in rapt suspense for a few seconds. But the hairy arms encircling that body, the legs holding down those thighs and spreading them, were not his, nor was that face—he could not make out Narciso's features—moving now along Lucrecia's back, scrutinizing it millimeter by millimeter, the partially open mouth indecisive about where to land and what to kiss. In Don Rigoberto's agitated mind there flashed the image of two trapeze artists at the circus, the Human Eagles, who flew and were united in midair— they worked without a net—after performing acrobatic feats ten meters above the ground. Lucrecia and Narciso were just as skilled, just as perfect, just as suited to one another. He was overcome by a tripartite feeling (admiration, envy, and jealousy) and tears of emotion again rolled down his cheeks. He noticed that Ilse's hand was professionally exploring his fly.

"I don't believe it, this doesn't excite you at all," he heard her say without lowering her voice.

Don Rigoberto detected a startled movement in the bed. They had heard, of course; they could no longer pretend not to know they were being observed. They remained motionless; Doña Lucrecia's profile turned toward the openwork wall, but Narciso kissed her again and drew her back into the battle of love.

"Forgive me, Ilse," he whispered. "I'm disappointing you, and I'm sorry. But I—how shall I put it—I'm monogamous. I can make love only to my wife."

"Of course you are." Ilse laughed affectionately, and so loudly that now, under the light, Doña Lucrecia's tousled head escaped the embrace of his Corsican brother, and Don Rigoberto saw her large, startled eyes looking in fright toward the place where he and Ilse were sitting. "Just like your sweet Corsican brother. Narciso likes making love only to me. But he needs appetizers, apéritifs, prologues. He's not as uncomplicated as you."

She laughed again, and Don Rigoberto felt her moving away as she stroked his thinning hair with the kind of caress teachers give little boys who are good. He could not believe his eyes: when had Ilse taken off her clothes? There were her things on the sofa, and there she was, athletic, naked from head to foot, striding through the darkness toward the bed just as her remote ancestors, the Valkyries, strode through forests in their horned helmets hunting down bears, tigers, and men. At precisely that moment Narciso moved away from Lucrecia, ran toward the middle of the room— his face revealed indescribable happiness—and opened his arms to receive her with an animal roar of approval. And there she was now, the rejected, recanted Lucrecia withdrawing to the far side of the bed, fully aware that from now on she was not needed, looking to the left and right, searching for someone who could tell her what to do. Don Rigoberto felt pity. Without saying a word, he called her name. He watched her get out of bed on tiptoe so as not to disturb the happy couple, find her clothes on the floor, partially dress, and walk to where he was waiting for her with open arms. She huddled against his chest, trembling.

"Do you understand any of it, Rigoberto?" he heard her ask.

"Only that I love you," he replied, holding her close. "I've never seen you so beautiful. Come, come with me."

"What a pair of Corsican brothers." He heard the Valkyrie laughing in the distance, against a background of a wild boar's savage bellowing and Wagnerian trumpets.

Winged Lion Harpy

Where are you? In the Hall of Grotesques in the Museum of the Austrian Baroque on the Lower Belvedere in Vienna.

What are you doing there? You are carefully studying one of Jonas Drentwett's female creatures that bring fantasy and glory to its walls.

Which one? The one that stretches her long neck in order to better display her bosom and reveal the beautiful, sharply pointed breast with the ruddy nipple that all living beings would come to suck if you had not reserved it.

For whom? For your lover at a distance, the reconstructor of your identity, the painter who unmakes and makes you at will, your waking dreamer.

What must you do? Learn the creature by heart and emulate her in the privacy of your bedroom, preparing for the night when I will come. Do not be discouraged because you do not have a tail, or the talons of a bird of prey, or because you are not in the habit of walking on all fours. If you truly love me, you will have a tail and talons, you will walk on all fours, and gradually, through the constancy and tenacity demanded by feats of love, you will cease to be Lucrecia of the Olivar and will become the Mythological Lucrecia, Lucrecia the Winged Lion Harpy, Lucrecia who has come to my heart and my desire from the legends and myths of Greece (with a stopover at the Roman frescoes from which Jonas Drentwett copied you).

Are you like her now? With your rump tucked in, your bosom haughty, your head aloft? Do you feel how the feline tail begins to appear, the red-tinted pointed wings begin to grow? What you still lack, the diadem for your brow, the topaz necklace, the girdle of gold and precious stones where your tender bosom will rest, these will be brought to you, as a token of adoration and reverence, by one who adores you above all other things real or nonexistent.

The Lover of Harpies

V

Fonchito and the Girls

Señora Lucrecia dried her laughing eyes again, trying to gain time. She did not dare to ask Fonchito if what Teté Barriga had told her was true. She had been about to, twice, and both times she had lost her courage.

"Why are you laughing like that, Stepmamá?" the boy wanted to know, intrigued. Because from the time he had walked into the little house near the Olivar de San Isidro, Señora Lucrecia had been bursting into these unwarranted fits of laughter and devouring him with her eyes.

"Because of something a friend told me." Doña Lucrecia blushed. "I'm too embarrassed to ask you about it, but I'm dying to know if it's true."

"It must be some gossip about my papá."

"I'll tell you, even though it's very vulgar," Señora Lucrecia said decisively. "My curiosity is stronger than my good manners."

According to Teté, whose husband had been there and told her about it with a mixture of amusement and anger, it happened at one of those gatherings held every two or three months in Don Rigoberto's study. Men only, five or six childhood friends, acquaintances from school or the university or the neighborhood who continued to meet out of habit, and without enthusiasm, but who did not dare to break the ritual, perhaps because of the superstitious notion that if any one of them failed to attend, bad luck would befall the deserter, or even the entire group. And so they continued to see each other, although undoubtedly, like Rigoberto, they no longer enjoyed this bimonthly or trimonthly get-together when they would drink cognac, eat cheese turnovers, talk about those who had died, or discuss politics. Doña Lucrecia recalled that afterward Don Rigoberto's head would ache with boredom, and he would have to take a few drops of valerian. The incident had occurred at the last gathering, just a week ago. The friends—in their fifties or sixties, some of them about to retire—saw Fonchito come in, his blond hair tousled, his big blue eyes opened wide at seeing them there. The disorder of his school uniform added a touch of abandon to the beauty of his small person. The gentlemen smiled at him: Hello, Fonchito, how big you've gotten, how you've grown.

"Can't you say hello?" Don Rigoberto had gruffly admonished him.

"Yes, of course," replied the crystalline voice of her stepson. "But, Papá, please, if your friends want to hug me, tell them not to touch my bottom."

Señora Lucrecia burst into the fifth laughing fit of the afternoon.

"Did you really say something so outrageous, Fonchito?"

"But they pretend they're hugging me and all the while they never stop touching me there." The boy shrugged, not attributing too much importance to the subject. "I don't like anybody touching me there, not even as a joke, because then it itches. And whenever I itch I scratch so much I break out in a rash."

"Then it's true, you did say it." Señora Lucrecia passed from laughter to astonishment and back to laughter. "Obviously: Teté could never make up anything like that. And Rigoberto? How did he react?"

"His eyes were furious and he told me to go to my room and do my homework," said Fonchito. "Later, when they had gone, he really scolded me. And he took away my Sunday allowance."

"Those old men with their roving hands," exclaimed Señora Lucrecia, suddenly indignant. "It's disgusting. If I had ever caught them doing that, I would have thrown them out. And was your papá still so angry when you told him? But first, swear. Was it true? They touched your bottom? Could it be one of those strange things you think up?"

"Sure they touched me. Right here," and the boy showed her where, patting his buttocks. "Just like the priests at school. Why, Stepmamá? What is it about my backside that makes everybody want to touch it?"

Señora Lucrecia stared at him, trying to guess if he was lying.

"If it's true, then they have no shame, they're abusive," she exclaimed at last, still doubtful. "At school, too? Haven't you told Rigoberto, so that he can complain?"

The boy assumed a seraphic expression. "I don't want to give my papá anything else to worry about. Least of all now, when he's so sad."

Doña Lucrecia bent her head in confusion. This child was a master at saying things that made her feel bad. Well, if what he said was true, then good for him for making those dirty old men uncomfortable. Teté Barriga's husband had said that he and his friends could not move and did not dare to look at Rigoberto for a long while. Then they made jokes, though their faces were grim. In any event, enough about that. She moved on to something else. She asked Fonchito how things were going at school, if he wasn't getting into trouble at the academy when he left before classes were over, if he had gone to the movies, to a soccer game, to some party. But Justiniana, who came in with tea and biscuits, brought it up again. She had heard everything and began to give her opinion, and she had a lot to say. She was certain it was a lie: "Don't believe him, Señora. It was just more of that little devil's mischief to shame those gentlemen in front of Don Rigoberto. Don't you know him yet?" "If you didn't make such delicious sweet buns I'd be angry with you, Justita." Doña Lucrecia felt that she had been imprudent; by allowing her morbid curiosity to get the better of her —one never knew with Fonchito—perhaps she had awakened the beast. And, in effect, as Justiniana was gathering up the cups and saucers, the boy's question pierced her like the thrust of a sword.

"Why is it that grown-ups like children so much, Stepmamá?"

Justiniana slipped away, making a sound in her throat or stomach that could only be stifled laughter. Doña Lucrecia looked into Fonchito's eyes. She scrutinized them calmly, searching for a spark of malice or evil intention. No. What she saw was the luminous clarity of a diaphanous sky.

"Everybody likes children," she said hypocritically. "It's normal for a person to be affectionate with them. They're small, fragile, and sometimes very delicious."

She felt stupid, impatient to escape those great, still, limpid eyes that were resting on her.

"Egon Schiele liked them a lot," Fonchito said, nodding his agreement. "In Vienna, early in the century, there were so many abandoned little girls living on the streets. They begged in churches, in cafés."

"Just like Lima," she said, not knowing what she was saying. Once again she was overwhelmed by the sensation of being a fly lured, despite all her efforts, into the jaws of a spider.

"And he would go to Schonbrunn Park, where there were hundreds of them. He took them to his studio. He fed them and gave them money," Fonchito continued, inexorably. "Señor Paris von Güterlash, a friend whom Schiele painted—I'll show you his portrait in a minute—says there were always two or three girls from the street in his studio. They lived there at his expense. They would sleep or play while Schiele painted. Do you think there was anything wrong in that?"

"If he fed them and helped them, how could there be anything wrong?"

"But he made them get undressed and pose for him," the boy went on. There's no escape for me now, thought Doña Lucrecia. "Was it wrong for Egon Schiele to do that?"

"Well, I don't think so." His stepmother swallowed. "An artist needs models. Why have a nasty mind? Didn't Degas like to paint his *little mice*, the young dancers at the Opera in Paris? Well, young girls inspired Egon Schiele too."

Then why had he been arrested, accused of kidnapping a minor? Why was he sent to prison for circulating indecent pictures? And why had he been obliged to burn a drawing on the pretext that children had been exposed to indecency in his studio?

"I don't know why." She tried to calm him when she saw his agitation. "I don't know anything about Schiele, Fonchito. You're the one who knows everything about him. Artists are complicated people, your papá can explain it to you. They don't have to be saints. You shouldn't idealize them or demonize them. Their work is what matters, not their lives. Schiele's legacy is how he painted those girls, not what he did with them in his studio."

"He had them wear those colored stockings he liked so much," said Fonchito, putting the finishing touches on the story. "Sprawled on the sofa, on the floor. Alone or in pairs. Then he would climb a ladder so he could look down at them from a height. At the top of the ladder he would make a sketch; his notebooks have been published. My papá has the book. But it's in German. I could only look at the drawings, I couldn't read it."

"He climbed up a ladder? That's how he painted them?"

Now you were caught in the web, Lucrecia. The kid always managed it somehow. Now you didn't try to have him change the subject; you followed along, trapped. It's true, Stepmamá. He said his dream was to be a bird of prey. To paint the world from a height, to see it as a condor or buzzard saw it. And if you look closely, it was absolutely true. He would show her right now. He jumped up, rummaged in his portfolio from the academy, and a moment later he was crouching at her feet—as always, she was on the sofa and he on the floor—turning the pages of another voluminous book of Egon Schiele reproductions that he rested on his stepmother's knees. Did Fonchito really know all those things about the painter? How many of them were true? And why did he have this mania for Schiele? Had he heard things from Rigoberto? Was this painter her former husband's latest obsession? In any case, his description was accurate. Those sprawling girls and entwined lovers, those phantasmal cities without people or animals or cars, the houses crowded together and almost frozen along the banks of empty rivers, all appeared as if viewed from a height by a rapacious bird that soared above them with an all-encompassing, merciless eye. Yes, it was the perspective of a bird of prey. The angelic face smiled at her. "Didn't I tell you, Stepmamá?" She nodded in dismay. Behind those cherubic features, that innocence worthy of a religious painting, dwelled a subtle, precociously mature intelligence, its psychology as complex as Rigoberto's. And at that moment she realized what was on the page. Her face flared like a torch. Fonchito had left the book open to a watercolor in red tones and cream-colored spaces, with a mauve border, and only now did Doña Lucrecia pay attention to its subject: the artist himself in sharp outline, sitting, and between his open legs a naked girl with her back turned, holding on high, as if it were a flagpole, his gigantic virile member.

"This couple has also been painted from above," the crystalline voice informed her. "But how could he have done the sketch? He couldn't do it from the ladder, because he's the man sitting on the floor. You know that, don't you, Stepmamá?"

"I know it's a very obscene self-portrait," said Doña Lucrecia. "You'd better keep turning the pages, Foncho."

"It seems sad to me," the boy disagreed, with a good deal of conviction. "Look at Schiele's face. It's so discouraged, as if he couldn't bear any more of the sorrow he's feeling. He looks ready to cry. He was only twenty-one, Stepmamá. Why do you think he called this picture *The Red Host?*"

"You're better off not finding out, Mr. Know-it-all." Señora Lucrecia was becoming angry. "Is that what it's called? So besides being obscene, its sacrilegious too. Turn the page or I'll tear it."

"But, Stepmamá," Fonchito reproached her, "you can't be like the judge who ordered Egon Schiele to destroy his picture. You can't be that unfair and prejudiced."

His indignation seemed genuine. His eyes flashed, the fine nostrils quivered, and even his ears had sharpened. Doña Lucrecia regretted what she had just said.

"Well, you're right, in painting, in art, you have to be broad-minded." She rubbed her hands nervously. "But you make me so angry, Fonchito. I never know if you do what you do and say what you say spontaneously, or if you intend something else. I never know if I'm with a child or a dirty, perverse old man hiding behind the face of the Infant Jesus."

The boy looked at her in bewilderment; his surprise seemed to well up from the deepest part of his being. He blinked, uncomprehending. Was she the one who was shocking the child with her suspicions? Of course not. And yet, when she saw Fonchito's eyes brimming with tears, she felt responsible.

"I don't even know what I'm saying," she murmured. "Forget it, I didn't say a thing. Come, give me a kiss, let's be friends."

The boy stood and threw his arms around her neck. Doña Lucrecia could feel the fragile form trembling, the delicate bones, the small body on the verge of adolescence, that age when boys could still be mistaken for girls.

"Don't be angry with me, Stepmamá," she heard him saying into her ear. "Correct me if I do something wrong, give me advice. I want to be just what you want me to be. But don't be angry."

"It's all right, I'm not angry anymore," she said. "Let's forget it."

His slim arms around her neck held her prisoner, and he spoke so slowly and softly that she could not understand what he was saying. But all her nerves registered the tip of the boy's tongue when, like a slender probe, it entered the opening of her ear and wet it with saliva. She resisted the impulse to move him away. A moment later, she felt his finely molded lips moving across her lobe with slow, tiny kisses. And now she did move him away gently—little shudders ran up and down her body—and found herself looking into his mischievous face.

"Did I tickle you?" He seemed to be boasting of a great feat. "Your whole body started to tremble. Did you feel an electric current, Stepmamá?"

She did not know what to say. Her smile was forced.

"I forgot to tell you." Fonchito himself saved her, returning to his usual spot in front of the sofa. "I started the job, on my papá."

"What job?"

"Making you two be friends again," the boy explained, gesticulating. "Do you know what I did? I told him I saw you coming out of the Church of

108

the Virgen del Pilar, very elegant, on a gentleman's arm. And that you looked like newlyweds on their honeymoon."

"Why did you tell him lies?"

"To make him jealous. And I did. He got so nervous, Stepmamá!"

His laughter proclaimed a splendid joy in living. His papá had turned pale, and his eyes had bulged, though at first he didn't say anything. But his curiosity held the strings, and he was dying to know more, twitching like a puppet! To make things easier for him, Fonchito fired the first shot: "Do you think my stepmamá is planning to marry again, Papá?"

Don Rigoberto's face turned bitter, and he snorted in a strange way before answering. "I don't know. You should have asked her yourself." And after some vacillation, making an effort to sound natural: "Who can tell. Did the gentleman seem to be more than a friend?"

"Well, I don't know," Fonchito said uncertainly, moving his head like the cuckoo in a clock. "They were arm in arm. The gentleman was looking at her just like in the movies. And she was very flirtatious with him."

"I could kill you, you're such a lying rascal." Señora Lucrecia threw one of the pillows and hit him in the head, and Fonchito reacted with a great show of fear. "You're a fake. You didn't tell him anything, you just like making fun of me."

"I swear by all that's holy, Stepmamá." The boy giggled and kissed his fingers as they sketched a cross.

"You're the worst cynic I've ever known." She tossed another pillow, and then she laughed too. "I can imagine what you'll be like when you grow up. God protect the poor innocent who falls in love with you."

The boy became serious, in one of those abrupt changes of mood that always disconcerted Doña Lucrecia. He folded his arms across his chest and, sitting like a Buddha, looked at her with some fear.

"You were joking, weren't you, Stepmamá? Or do you really think I'm bad?"

She stretched out her hand and stroked his hair.

"No, not bad, no," she said. "You're unpredictable. A little know-it-all with too much imagination, that's what you are."

"I want you two to make up," Fonchito interrupted, with an emphatic gesture. "That's why I told him that story. I have a plan."

"Since I'm one of the parties involved, at least let me give my approval."

"Well, it's just . . ." Fonchito wrung his hands. "It's not finished yet.

You have to trust me, Stepmamá. I need to know some things about you. How you and my papá met, for instance. And how you got married."

A flood of melancholy images made that day—eleven years ago, now—present in Doña Lucrecia's memory, when, at the crowded, boring party celebrating the silver wedding anniversary of her aunt and uncle, she had been introduced to the balding gentleman with the long, melancholy face, large ears, and assertive nose. He was about fifty; a matchmaking friend, a woman committed to marrying off everybody, told her about him: "Recently widowed, has a son, he's an executive at La Perricholi Insurance, a little eccentric but from a good family, and plenty of money." At first she noticed only Rigoberto's funereal appearance and reticence, and how unattractive he was. But beginning that same night, something attracted her to this man without physical charms; she had intuited something complicated and mysterious in his life. And ever since she was a girl, Doña Lucrecia had felt a fascination for standing on the edge of the cliff and looking down into the abyss, for keeping her balance on the railing at the side of the bridge. And the attraction had been confirmed when she agreed to have tea with him at La Tiendecita Blanca, attended a Philharmonic concert with him at the Colegio Santa Ursula, and, above all, when she entered his house for the first time. Rigoberto showed her his etchings, his art books, the notebooks that contained his secrets, and he explained to her how he updated his collection, condemning the books and pictures he replaced to the flames. She had been impressed listening to him, observing how courteously he treated her, his maniacal correctness. To the astonishment of her family and friends ("What are you waiting for to get married, Lucre? Prince Charming? You can't simply turn down every one of your suitors!"), when Rigoberto proposed ("Without ever having kissed me") she accepted immediately. She had never regretted it. Not for a day, not for a minute. It had been amusing, exciting, marvelous to discover her husband's world of manias, rituals, and fantasies, to share it with him, to build their private life together over a period of ten years. Until the absurd, mad, stupid story of what she had allowed to occur with her stepson. A baby who didn't even seem to remember now what had happened. She! The woman everyone thought so judicious, so cautious, so organized, the one who always calculated every step with so much good sense. How could she have had an adventure with a schoolboy! Her own stepchild! Rigoberto had been very decent, really, avoiding a scandal, asking only for a separation and providing the financial support that permitted her to live alone. Another man would have killed her, clenched his jaws in rage and thrown her out without a cent, pilloried her publicly as a corruptor of youth. How foolish to think that Rigoberto and she could be reconciled. He would continue to be mortally offended by what had happened; he would never forgive her. Once again she felt the slender arms twining about her neck.

"What made you so sad?" Fonchito comforted her. "Did I do something bad?"

"I suddenly thought of something, and I'm a sentimental person . . . I'm all right now."

"When I saw you getting like that, I was so scared!"

The boy kissed her again on the ear, with the same tiny kisses, finishing up his caresses by wetting her earlobe again with the tip of his tongue. Doña Lucrecia felt so depressed that she didn't even have the energy to push him away.

After a while she heard him saying, in a different tone of voice, "You too, Stepmamá?"

"What?"

"You're touching my backside too, just like my papá's friends and the priests at school. Golly! Why is everybody so interested in my bottom?"

Letter to a Rotarian

Friend, I know you were offended by my refusal to join the Rotary Club, for you are an officer and promoter of that institution. And I suspect you felt somewhat distrustful as well, not at all convinced that my reluctance to be a Rotarian in no way suggests that I am going to enroll in the Lions Club or the recently established Kiwanis Club of Peru, associations with which your organization competes implacably to win first place in good works, civic spirit, human solidarity, social welfare, and other things of that nature. Don't worry: I do not belong and will never belong to any of those clubs or associations, or to anything resembling them (the Boy Scouts, the Alumni of the Jesuits, the Masons, Opus Dei, et cetera). My hostility to associations is so radical that I have stopped being a member of the Automobile Club, not to mention the so-called social clubs that gauge the ethnicity and wealth of Limenians. Since the now distant days of my membership in Catholic Action, and because of it—for this was the experience that opened my eyes to the illusory nature of all social utopias and cata-pulted me to a defense of hedonism and the individual—I have contracted such a moral, psychological, and ideological revulsion toward all forms of gregarious servitude that—this is no joke—even the line at the movies makes me feel abused, diminished in my own freedom (at times, obviously, I cannot help joining the line), and reduced to the condition of mass-man. The only concession I remember making was in response to the threat of being overweight (I am convinced, like Cyril Connolly, that "obesity is a mental disease"), which led me to join a gym, where a brainless Tarzan made fifteen imbeciles sweat for an hour a day to the rhythm of his bel-lowing and engage in certain simian contractions that he called aerobics. This gymnastic torture confirmed all my prejudices against the herd-man.

Allow me, in this regard, to transcribe for you one of the many citations that fill my notebooks, for it is a marvelous synthesis of what I believe. The author Francisco Pérez de Antón is an Asturian world traveler currently residing in Guatemala: "A herd, as everyone knows, is composed of crea-tures deprived of speech and with fairly weak sphincters. It is a proven fact, moreover, that in times of confusion, the herd prefers servitude to disorder. Which is why those who behave like crazed nanny goats do not have leaders but great goatish assholes at their head. Something in this species must be contagious, since it is so common in the human herd to find someone who can lead the masses to the edge of the reef and, once there, make them jump into the water. Unless he decides to destroy a civilization, which is something he does fairly frequently." You will say it is paranoid to detect, behind a few benign men who meet for lunch once a week and discuss in which new district they ought to put up one of those limestone pillars with the metal plaque that reads THE ROTARY CLUB WELCOMES YOU, whose erection they all contribute to, an ominous devaluation of sovereign indi-vidual into mass-man. Perhaps I exaggerate. But I cannot be negligent. Since the world is moving so quickly toward complete disindividualization and the extinction of that historical accident, the rule of the free and sovereign individual, which a series of coincidences and circumstances made possible (for a limited number of people, naturally, in an even more limited number of countries), I am mobilized and combat-ready, with all my five senses, twenty-four hours a day, prepared to delay, as much as I can and in areas that concern me, this existential calamity. It is a battle to the death, it is total warfare; everything and everyone is involved. Those associations of overfed professionals, executives, and high-level bureaucrats who show up once a week to eat a regimented meal (stuffed potato, a small steak and rice, crêpes with blancmange, all washed down with a pleasant little Tacama Reserva red wine?) are a victory for definitive robotization and obscurantism, a great advance for the planned, the organized, the obligatory, the routinized, the collective, and an even greater retreat for the spontaneous, the inspired, the creative, and the original, which are conceivable only in the sphere of the individual.

Does what you've read lead you to suspect that beneath my drab appearance as a bourgeois in his fifties there lurks a bearded antisocial anarchist? Bingo! On the nose, brother. (I've made a joke, but it's not funny: that *brother* suggests the inevitable slap on the shoulder that goes along with it, the loathsome sight of two men, their guts swollen by beer and huge quantities of spicy foods, joining together, forming a collectivist society, renouncing their innermost phantoms, their unique selves.) It is true: I am antisocial to the best of my ability, which is, unfortunately, very limited, and I resist gregarization in everything that does not endanger my survival or my excellent standard of living. That's right. To be an individualist is to be an egotist (Ayn Rand, *The Virtue of Selfishness*) but not an imbecile. As for the rest, I think imbecility is respectable if it is genetic, inherited, and not a chosen, deliberate stance. I'm afraid that being a Rotarian, or a Lion, Kiwanis, Mason, Boy Scout, or Opus Deist is (you'll forgive me) a cowardly vote in favor of stupidity.

I ought to explain this insult to you, and therefore I will soften it so that the next time company business brings us together, you won't punch me in the mouth (or kick me in the shins, a more appropriate form of aggression for people of our age). I don't know of a more accurate definition of the institutionalization of virtues and charitable feelings that these organizations represent than to call it an abdication of personal responsibility and a cheap way of acquiring a good "social" conscience (I put the word in quotation marks to emphasize how much I dislike it). In practical terms, the actions taken by you and your colleagues do not, in my opinion, help to diminish evil (or increase the good, if you prefer) to any appreciable degree. The principal beneficiaries of such collectivized generosity are you yourselves, beginning with your stomachs as you gobble down your weekly dinners, and your dirty minds, which during those evenings of fellowship (a horrifying concept!) regurgitate with pleasure, exchanging gossip and suggestive jokes, and cutting absent members to pieces. I am not opposed to such entertainments, nor, in principle, to anything that gives pleasure; but

I am opposed to the hypocrisy of not proclaiming this right openly, of seeking pleasure that is concealed behind the hygienic excuse of responsible social action. Didn't you tell me, leering like a satyr and with a pornographic nudge, that another advantage of being a Rotarian was that every week the institution provided a first-class excuse for being out of the house without alarming one's wife? And here I offer another objection. Is it law or mere custom that excludes women from your ranks? I've never seen a skirt at any of the lunches you've inflicted on me. I'm certain that not all of you are faggots, which would be the only vaguely acceptable justification for the trouserism of Rotarians (Lions, Kiwanis, Boy Scouts, et cetera). My thesis is this: being a Rotarian is a pretext for having good male times free of the vigilance, servitude, or correct behavior that is, all of you claim, imposed by cohabitation with a woman. To me this seems as anticivilized as the paranoia of the recalcitrant feminists who have declared war between the sexes. My philosophy is that in those circumstances where one is unavoidably subjected to gregariousness—school, work, entertainment—the mixing of genders (and races, languages, customs, and beliefs) is a way to ameliorate the cretinization that the mob brings with it and to introduce an element of piquancy and mischief (I am a devoted practitioner of evil thoughts) to human relationships, something which, from my point of view, elevates those relationships aesthetically and morally. I will not say that for me they are one and the same thing, since you would not understand).

All human activity that does not contribute, even indirectly, to testicular and ovarian arousal, to the meeting of sperm and egg, is contemptible. For instance, the selling of insurance, to which you and I have devoted the past thirty years, or misogynistic Rotary luncheons. As well as everything that distracts us from the truly essential purpose of human life, which, in my opinion, is to satisfy desires. I see no other reason for our being here, spinning like slow tops in a gratuitous universe. We can sell insurance, as you and I have done—and with a fair amount of success, for we have achieved notable positions in our respective companies—because we must provide food, clothing, shelter, and enough income to permit us to have and gratify desires. There is no other valid reason for selling insurance policies, or for building dams, castrating cats, or taking shorthand. I can hear you now: Suppose, unlike this lunatic Rigoberto, a man finds selling insurance against fire, theft, or sickness a fulfilling and pleasurable activity? What if attending Rotary luncheons and making small financial contributions to put up signs along highways that read SPEED KILLS is the fulfillment of his most burning desires and makes him just as happy, no more and no less, as you are when you leaf through your collection of pictures and books not suitable for young ladies or engage in the mental masturbation of writing soliloquies in your notebooks? Does not each person have a right to his own desires? Yes, he does. But if a human being's dearest desires (the most beautiful word in the dictionary) consist of selling insurance and joining the Rotary Club (or related groups), then that biped is an asshole. Agreed: this describes 90 percent of the human race. I see, insurance man, that you are beginning to understand.

You cross yourself for so little cause? Your sign of the cross moves me on to another subject, which is actually the same one. What part does religion play in this polemic? Is it also slapped in the face by this renegade from Catholic Action, this former fervent reader of Saint Augustine, Cardinal Newman, Saint John of the Cross, and Jean Guitton? Yes and no. If I am anything in these matters, I am agnostic. Suspicious of the atheist and the believer, I am in favor of people having and practicing a faith, for if not, they would have no spiritual life at all and savagery would increase. Culture—art, philosophy, all secular intellectual and artistic activity— cannot fill the spiritual vacuum left by the death of God and the eclipse of the transcendent life, except in a very small minority (of which I am a part). That vacuum makes people more destructive and bestial than they normally would be. While I am in favor of faith, religions generally make me want to hold my nose, because all of them imply processional herdism and the abdication of spiritual independence. All of them restrict human freedom and attempt to rein in desire. I acknowledge that from an aesthetic point of view, religions—Catholicism, perhaps, more than any other, with its beautiful cathedrals, rituals, liturgies, ceremonies, representations, iconographies, music—are usually superb sources of pleasure that delight the eye and the sensibility, spark the imagination, and purge us of evil thoughts. But in each of them there always lurks a censor, a commissar, a fanatic, an inquisitor's flames and pincers. It is also true that without their prohibitions, sins, and moral fulminations, desires—especially sexual desire— would not have achieved the refinement they have reached at certain times. Consequently—and this is not theoretical but practical—as the result of a modest personal survey of limited scope, I affirm that people make love much better in religious countries than in secular ones (better in Ireland than in England, in Poland than in Denmark), better in Catholic countries than in Protestant ones (better in Spain or Italy than in Germany or Sweden), and that women who have been educated in nuns' academies are a thousand times more imaginative, bold, and delicate than those who have studied at secular schools (Roger Vailland has theorized about this in *Le Regard froid*). Lucrecia would not be the Lucrecia who has filled me with a happiness I can never repay, both day and night (but especially at night) over the past ten years, if her childhood and youth had not been in the hands of extremely strict Sisters of the Sacred Heart, whose teachings included the warning that, for a little girl, it was a sin to sit with one's knees apart. Throughout history these sacrificed slaves to the Lord, with their exacerbated susceptibility and casuistry in matters of love, have educated whole dynasties of Messalinas. My blessings on them!

Well, then. Where does that leave us? I don't know where it leaves you, my dear colleague (to use another vomitous term). As for me, I am left with my contradictions, which are, after all, also a source of pleasure for an intractable and unclassifiable spirit like mine. Opposed to the institutionalization of feelings and faith, but in favor of feelings and faith. On the margins of churches, but curious about them, and envious, I diligently make use of what they can offer to enrich my world of phantoms. I tell you that I am an undisguised admirer of those princes of the Church who were capable, on the highest level, of conjoining their purple vestments and their sperm. I look through my notebooks and find, as an example, the cardinal about whom the virtuous Azorín wrote: "A refined skeptic, he privately laughed at the farce through which his person moved, and was regularly astounded at the unending human stupidity that provided money to maintain the stupendous spectacle." Is this not practically a portrait in miniature of the famous Cardinal de Bernis, the eighteenth-century French ambassador to Italy who, while in Venice, shared two lesbian nuns with Giacomo Casanova (*vide* his *Memoirs*), and in Rome entertained the Marquis de Sade, not knowing who he was, when the latter, a fugitive from France because of his libertine excesses, was traveling through Italy, with a false identity, as the Count of Mazan?

But I see you are yawning because the names I am firing at you—Ayn Rand, Vailland, Azorín, Casanova, Bernis, Sade—are, for you, incomprehensible noises, and so I will conclude this letter (and don't worry, I won't send it, either).

I wish you many luncheons and plaques, Rotarian.

In the damp night that was agitated by a churning sea, Don Rigoberto awoke with a start, bathed in sweat: the innumerable rats of the Temple of Karniji, summoned by the merry bells of the Brahmins, were gathering for their evening meal. The enormous cauldrons, the metal dishes and wooden bowls, had already been filled with bits of meat or the milky syrup that was their favorite food. From every hole in the marble walls, openings that had been made for them by the pious monks and furnished with handfuls of straw for their comfort, thousands of gray rodents greedily left their nests. Falling over one another, they raced to the containers and dove in to lick the sweet syrup, nibble at the pieces of meat, and, most exquisite of all, to tear mouthfuls of calluses and corns from bare feet with their white incisors. The priests let them do as they wished, pleased to contribute, with their excess skin, to the pleasure of the rats, who were the incarnations of deceased men and women.

The temple had been built for them five hundred years earlier in this northern corner of Rajasthan, in India, as a homage to Lakhan, the son of the goddess Karniji, a handsome youth who was transformed into a plump rat. From that time on, behind the imposing construction of silver-plated doors, marble floors, majestic walls and domes, the spectacle took place twice a day. There was the head Brahmin, Chotu-Dan, hidden beneath dozens of gray animals who climbed over his shoulders, arms, legs, back, to get to the great cauldron of syrup, for he sat on the edge. But what turned Don Rigoberto's stomach and almost made him vomit was the smell. Dense, enveloping, more pungent than mule droppings, the wind from the garbage dump, or putrefying carrion, the stink of the gray horde was now inside him. It traveled beneath his skin, in his veins and in the secretions from his glands, it soaked into the cracks in his cartilage, the marrow of his bones. His body had been turned into the temple of Karniji. "I am saturated with the smell of rats," he said in horror.

He leaped from the bed in his pajamas, not putting on his robe but only his slippers, and ran to his study to see if by leafing through a book, looking at an engraving, listening to music, or scribbling in his notebooks, other images would come to exorcise the remnants of his nightmare.

He was in luck. In the first notebook he opened, a scientific citation explained the variety of anopheles mosquito whose most outstanding characteristic is detecting the odor of their females at incredible distances. I am one of them, he thought, dilating his nostrils and sniffing. Right now, if I wish to, I can smell Lucrecia asleep near the Olivar de San Isidro, and clearly differentiate her scalp hair from that on her underarms and her pubis. But he discovered another smell—benign, literary, pleasant, fanciful—that began to dispel, as the dawn breeze dissipates nocturnal mists, the rattish stench of his dream. A holy, theological, extremely elegant smell emitted by Francis de Sales's *Introduction to the Devout Life* in the translation by Quevedo: "Lamps that use aromatic oil give off a gentler odor when their light is dimmed. In the same way, widows whose love has been pure in marriage exhale a precious, aromatic odor of the virtue of chastity when their light, that is, their husband, is dimmed by death." That aroma of chaste widows, the impalpable melancholy of their bodies condemned to physical soliloquy, the nostalgic emanation of their unsatisfied desires, aroused him. His nostrils flared diligently, trying to reconstruct, detect, extract from the atmosphere some trace of its presence. The mere idea of a widow's scent filled him with suspense. The remains of the nightmare evaporated, he felt wide awake, his spirit recovered its healthy confidence. And led him to think—why?—of Klimt's women floating among rivers of stars, those perfumed women with their dissolute faces—there was *Goldfish*, the many-colored fish-female, and *Danaë*, feigning sleep and exhibiting with great simplicity an ass as curvaceous as a guitar. No painter ever knew how to paint the odor of women as well as this decadent Viennese; his volatile, bending women had always entered his mind through his eyes and nose simultaneously. (Speaking of which, wasn't it time to begin to worry about the excessive interest another Viennese, Egon Schiele, held for Fonchito? Perhaps, but not just now.)

Had Lucrecia's body begun to give off that saintly Salesian odor when they separated? If so, she still loved him. For that odor, according to Saint Francis de Sales, bore witness to a fidelity in love that transcended the grave. That would mean she had not replaced him. Yes, she was still a "widow." The rumors, breaches of faith, accusations that had reached him—including the gossip about Fonchito—regarding Lucrecia's newfound lovers, were slander. His heart rejoiced as he furiously sniffed all around him. Was it there? Had he detected it? Was that the odor of Lucrecia? No. It was the scent of the night, the dampness, the books, oils, woods, fabrics, and leathers in the study.

Closing his eyes, he attempted to retrieve from the past, from nothingness, the nocturnal odors he had breathed in during those ten years, aromas that had given him so much pleasure, perfumes that had protected him from the surrounding pestilence and ugliness. He was overcome by depression. Some lines by Neruda came to console him as he turned another page in the same notebook:

And to see you urinate, in the dark, at the back of the house, as if you were pouring out a slender, tremulous, silvery, obstinate stream of honey, I would give up, many times over, this choir of shades I possess, and the clang of useless swords that echoes in my soul . . .

Wasn't it extraordinary that the poem those lines were taken from is called "Widower's Tango"? Without transition he caught a glimpse of Lucrecia sitting on the toilet, and listened to the merry splash of her pee in the bottom of the bowl that received it with tinkling gratitude. Of course, silent, squatting in the corner, absorbed, mystically concentrating, listening and smelling, there too was the happy beneficiary of that emission, that liquid concert: Manuel of the Prostheses! But at that moment Gulliver appeared, saving the Empress of Lilliput from her burning palace with his foaming piss. He thought of Jonathan Swift, who lived obsessed by the contrast between physical beauty and hideous bodily functions. The notebook recalled how, in his most famous poem, a lover explains with these verses why he decided to leave his lady:

*Nor wonder how I lost my wits;
Oh! Celia, Celia, Celia shits*

"What a stupid man" was his judgment. Lucrecia also shat, and this, rather than degrading her, enhanced her in his eyes and nostrils. For a few seconds, with the first smile of the night on his face, his memory inhaled the vapors reminiscent of the passage of his former wife through the bathroom. Though now the sexologist Havelock Ellis intruded, whose most secret joy, according to the notebook, was to listen to his beloved passing water, and who proclaimed in his correspondence that the happiest day of his life had been the one on which his compliant wife, in the shelter of her full Victorian skirts, irreverently urinated for him among unwitting passersby at the feet of Admiral Nelson, under the eyes of the monumental stone lions on Trafalgar Square.

But Manuel had not been a poet like Neruda, a moralist like Swift, a sexologist like Ellis. Merely a castrato. Or, perhaps, a eunuch? An abysmal difference between the two kinds of inability to fecundate. One still had a penis and an erection, the other had lost the instrument and its reproductive function and displayed a smooth, curved, feminine pubis. Which was Manuel? A eunuch. How could Lucrecia have granted that to him? Generosity, curiosity, compassion? Or vice and morbidity? Or all of them combined? She had known him before his famous accident, when Manuel was winning motorcycling championships wearing a shining helmet and a plastic face protector, straddling a mechanical steed made of tubes, levers, and wheels, always with a Japanese name (Honda, Kawasaki, Suzuki, Yamaha), catapulting himself forward with the noise of a deafening fart in a cross-country race—it was called a *motorcross*—though he also participated in idiocies named *Trail* and *Enduro*, this last competition suspiciously reminiscent of the Albigensians—at two or three hundred kilometers an hour. Flying across ditches, climbing hills, agitating stretches of sand, leaping over rocks or chasms, Manuel won trophies and had his picture in the papers uncorking bottles of champagne with models who kissed him on the cheek. Until, in one of those displays of pure stupidity, he flew through the air after racing like a shooting star up a treacherous hill; waiting for him on the other side was not, as he incautiously believed, an easy slope of cushioning sand but a rocky precipice. He was hurled into it, shouting an old-fashioned obscenity—Oh shit!—as he plummeted astride his metal charger into the depths, and seconds later he reached bottom in a resounding clamor of bones and pieces of metal being crushed, broken, and impaled. A miracle! His head was whole; his teeth intact; his vision and hearing not damaged at all; the use of his limbs somewhat painful because of broken bones and torn, bruised muscles. The liability was compensatorily concentrated in his genitals, which monopolized most of the damage. Nuts, bolts, and sharp points perforated his testicles despite the elastic supporter that guarded them, and turned them into a hybrid substance, somewhere between taffy and ratatouille, while the stalk of his virility was sliced at the root by some cutting material that perhaps—the ironies of life—did not come from the cycle of his loves and triumphs. What, then, had castrated him? The heavy, sharply pointed crucifix he wore to invoke divine protection when he perpetrated his motorcycling feats.

The skilled surgeons in Miami mended his bones, straightened what had been bent and bent what had been straightened, sewed on what had been torn away, and constructed artificial genitals, using bits of flesh taken from his gluteal muscle. It was always stiff, but that was pure show, a framework of skin over a plastic prosthesis. "Lots of smoke and no fire, or to be mathematically precise, a shell with no nuts" was Don Rigoberto's savage formulation. He could use it only to urinate, not even voluntarily but each time he drank any fluid, and since poor Manuel had no way to keep that constant flow of liquid from wetting the seat of his pants, he had to wear over it, like a grotesque little hat, a plastic bag to collect his water. Except for this inconvenience, the eunuch led a very normal life and—every madman has his madness—still served the cause of motorcycles.

"Are you going to visit him again?" Don Rigoberto asked, somewhat put out.

"He's invited me for tea, and you know he's a good friend and I feel very sorry for him," Doña Lucrecia explained. "But if it bothers you, I won't go."

"Go, go by all means," he said apologetically. "You'll tell me about it afterward?"

They had know each other since childhood. They were from the same neighborhood and had been in love in school, when being in love meant holding hands on Sundays after eleven o'clock Mass as they walked in the Parque Central in Miraflores, or in the smaller Parquecito Salazar following a swooning movie matinee of kisses and some timid, well-bred touching in the orchestra seats. And they had been sweethearts when Manuel was performing his racing feats and had his picture on the sports pages, and pretty girls were dying for him. When his flirtatiousness became too much for her, Lucrecia broke the engagement. They stopped seeing one another until the accident. She visited him in the hospital and brought him a box of Cadbury's. They re-established a relationship, a friendship, nothing more —that is what Don Rigoberto believed until he discovered the liquid truth—which continued after Doña Lucrecia's marriage.

From time to time Don Rigoberto had caught glimpses of him through the show windows of his flourishing dealership in new and used motorcycles imported from the United States and Japan (alongside the hieroglyphics of Japanese names there now stood the American Harley-Davidson and Triumph, and the Germanic BMW), which was located on the expressway just before Javier Prado. He no longer participated as a racer in any championships, but with obvious sadomasochism he maintained his connection to the sport as a promoter and patron of those vicarious massacres and butcheries. Don Rigoberto would see him on television newscasts, lowering a ridiculous checked flag with the air of someone who was starting the First World War, or standing at the starting or finishing lines at races, or handing the winner a cup covered in fake silver. The move from participant to sponsor of events assuaged—according to Lucrecia—the addictive attraction the castrato felt for these gleaming motorcycles.

And the other? The other absence? Did something or someone assuage that too? On the afternoons when they would have tea and cakes and conversation, Manuel maintained remarkable discretion regarding the matter, which Lucrecia, of course, was never imprudent enough to mention. Their talks were exchanges of news, reminiscences of a Miraflores childhood, a San Isidro youth, and of old friends from the neighborhood who married, unmarried, remarried, fell ill, had children, and occasionally died; they were sprinkled with comments on recent events: the latest film or record, the latest dance craze, a marriage or a catastrophic breakup, a recently uncovered fraud, or the latest scandal concerning drugs, adultery, or AIDS. Until one day—Don Rigoberto's hands quickly turned the pages of the notebook, trying to track down a citation that would correspond to the sequence of sharp images moving through his fevered mind—Doña Lucrecia had discovered his secret. Had she really discovered it? Or had Manuel arranged for her to believe that, when in fact she simply fell into the trap he had prepared for her? The truth is that one day, drinking tea in his house in La Planicie, which was surrounded by eucalyptus and laurels, Manuel lured Lucrecia into his bedroom. The pretext? To show her a photograph of a volleyball game at San Antonio Academy taken many years earlier. Once there, she was surprised beyond all measure. An entire bookcase of volumes dedicated to the chilling subject of castration and eunuchs! A specialized library! In every language, above all in those not understood by Manuel, who had mastered only Spanish, in its Peruvian, or, more accurately, its Mirafloran and San Isidran variant. And a collection of records and CD's that approximated or simulated the voices of castrati!

"He has become a specialist in the field," she told Don Rigoberto, for she was filled with excitement at her discovery.

"For obvious reasons," he deduced.

Had that been part of Manuel's strategy? Don Rigoberto's large head nodded agreement in the small circle of light shed by the lamp. Naturally. To create a salacious intimacy, a complicity in forbidden areas that would subsequently allow him to beg for so bold a favor. He had confessed to her—feigning embarrassment and all the hesitations of a timid man? Of course—that ever since the brutal surgery he had been obsessed by the subject until it had become the central concern of his existence. He was now a great connoisseur and could speak for hours about it, touching on its historic, religious, physical, clinical, and psychoanalytic aspects. (Had the former cyclist ever heard of the Viennese and his couch? Before, no; afterward, yes; and he had even read something by him, though he did not understand a word.) In conversations that submerged them deeper and deeper into an affectionate association over the course of those apparently innocent meetings at teatime, Manuel explained to Lucrecia the difference between the eunuch, principally a Saracen variation practiced since the Middle Ages on the guardians of seraglios, which pitilessly removed phallus and testicles, rendering them chaste, and the castrato, a Western, Catholic, Apostolic, and Roman version that consisted in removing only the jewels from the victim of the procedure—leaving the rest in place—for the purpose was not to keep him from copulating but simply to prevent the change that lowers the boy's voice by an octave when he reaches adolescence. Manuel told Lucrecia the anecdote, which both had enjoyed, of the castrato Cortona, who wrote to Pope Innocent XI requesting permission to marry. He alleged that his castration had not damaged his ability to experience pleasure. His Holiness, who was in no way an innocent, wrote in the margin of the petition: "This time do a better job of castrating him." (Those were real Popes, Don Rigoberto thought joyfully.)

He, Manuel, the great motorcycle ace, inviting her to tea and posing as a modern man critical of the Church, had explained to Lucrecia that castration with no bellicose aim, with an artistic purpose, began to be practiced in Italy in the seventeenth century because of the ecclesiastic prohibition against women's voices in religious ceremonies. This stricture created the need for a hybrid, a male with a feminized voice (a "caprine" or "falsetto" voice, "between vibrato and tremolo" was the expert Carlos Gómez Amat's explanation in the notebook), something that could be fabricated by means of a surgery that Manuel described and documented between cups of tea and bites of pastry. There was the primitive method, submerging boys with good voices in icy water to control the bleeding and crushing their balls with grinding stones ("Oh, oh!" shouted Don Rigoberto, who had forgotten all about the rats and was having a wonderful time), and the sophisticated one; to wit: the surgeon-barber, anesthetizing the boy with laudanum, used his recently sharpened razor to make an incision in the groin, and pulled out the tender young jewels. What effects did the operation have on the boy singers who survived? Obesity, thoracic swelling, a strong, piercing voice, as well as an uncommon ability to hold a note; some castrati, such as Farinelli, could sing arias for more than a minute without taking a breath. In the serene darkness of the study, with the sound of the sea in the background, Don Rigoberto was listening, more diverted and curious than joyful, to the vibration of vocal cords prolonging the fine, high-pitched tone indefinitely, like a long wound in the Barrancan night. And now, yes, yes, he could smell Lucrecia.

Manuel of the Prostheses, poisoned with death, he thought a short while later, content with his discovery. But he immediately realized he was quoting. Poisoned with death? As his hands searched through the notebook, his memory reconstructed the smoky, crowded club to which Lucrecia had dragged him on that extraordinary night. It had been one of his few memorable immersions in the nocturnal world of amusement in the foreign country, administratively his own, in which he sold insurance policies, against which he had built this enclave, and about which, as a result of discreet but monumental efforts, he had managed to learn very little. Here were the lyrics to the waltz "Desdén":

> As scornful as the gods
> I will struggle for my fate,
> ignoring the coward voices
> of men poisoned with death.

Without the guitar, the drum, and the syncopated voice of the singer, some of the lugubrious, narcissistic audacity of the bardic composer was lost. But even without music, the inspired vulgarity and mysterious philosophy were still present. Who had composed this "classic" Peruvian waltz, which is how Lucrecia described it when he had asked the question. He found out: the man was from Chiclaya and his name was Miguel Paz. He imagined an untamed Peruvian who wandered through the night with a scarf around his neck and a guitar on his shoulder, who sang serenades and woke in folkloric dives surrounded by sawdust and vomit, his throat raw from singing all night. Wild, in any case. Vallejo and Neruda together had not produced anything comparable to those lines, and what's more, you could dance to them. He chuckled suddenly and recaptured Manuel of the Prostheses, who had been getting away from him.

It had been after many late-afternoon conversations watered with tea, and after having poured his encyclopedic information regarding Turkish and Egyptian eunuchs and Neapolitan and Roman castrati all over Doña Lucrecia, that the ex-motorcyclist ("Manuel of the Prostheses, Perpetual Peepee, the Wet One, the Leaker, the Capped Cock, the Piss Bag," Don Rigoberto improvised, his mood improving as each second passed) had made his move.

"And what was your reaction when he told you?"

On the television in their bedroom they had just watched *Senso*, a beautiful Stendhalian melodrama by Visconti, and Don Rigoberto was holding his wife on his lap, she in her nightdress and he in pajamas.

"I was speechless," replied Doña Lucrecia. "Do you think it's possible?"

"If he told you wringing his hands and weeping, it must be. Why would he lie?"

"Of course, he had no reason to," she purred, writhing. "If you keep on kissing my neck that way, I'll scream. What I don't understand is why he would tell me."

"It was the first step." Don Rigoberto's mouth moved up her warm throat until it reached her ear, which he kissed as well. "The next step will be to ask you to let him watch you, or at least listen to you."

"He told me because it was good for him to share his secret." Doña Lucrecia tried to move him away, and Don Rigoberto's pulse beat wildly. "Knowing that I know made him feel less alone."

"Do you want to bet that at your next tea he'll proposition you?" Her husband insisted on kissing her ear very slowly.

"I'd leave his house and slam the door behind me." Doña Lucrecia twisted in his arms, deciding to kiss him too. "And never go back."

She had done neither. Manuel of the Prostheses had made his request with so much servile humility, and so many victim's tears and excuses and apologies, that she had not had the courage (or the desire?) to offend him. Had she said, "Have you forgotten that I'm a decent married woman?" No. Or even: "You are abusing our friendship and destroying the good opinion I had of you"? Not that either. She had simply calmed Manuel, who, pale and ashamed, begged her not to take it the wrong way, or be angry with him, or deprive him of her precious friendship. It was a highly strategic and successful move, for Lucrecia took pity on so much psychodrama and had tea with him again—Don Rigoberto felt acupuncture needles in his temples—and eventually gave him what he wanted. The man poisoned with death listened to that silvery music, was intoxicated by the liquid arpeggio. Just listening? Couldn't he have been watching too?

"I swear he wasn't," Doña Lucrecia protested, huddling against him and talking into his chest. "In absolute darkness. That was my condition. And he met it. He saw nothing. He heard."

In exactly the same position they had watched a video of *Carmina Burana*, taped at the Berlin Opera with the Peking Chorus, and conducted by Seiji Ozawa.

"That may be," replied Don Rigoberto, his imagination inflamed by the vibrant Latin of the choir (could there be castrati among the choir members with their almond-shaped eyes?). "But it may also be that Manuel has developed his vision to an extraordinary degree. And even though you didn't see him, he saw you."

"If you start conjecturing, everything is possible," Doña Lucrecia argued, though without too much conviction. "But if he did look, there was hardly anything to see."

Her odor was there, no doubt about it: corporeal, intimate, with marine touches and fruity reminiscences. Closing his eyes, he breathed it in avidly, his nostrils very wide. I am smelling the soul of Lucrecia, he thought, deeply moved. The merry splash of the stream in the bowl did not dominate this aroma; it barely colored with a physiological tint what was an exhalation of hidden glandular humors, cartilaginous exudations, secretions of muscles, which were condensed and confused in a thick, valiant, domestic discharge. It reminded Don Rigoberto of the most distant moments of his childhood—a world of diapers and talcum, vomit and excrement, cologne and sponges soaked in warm water, a prodigal tit—and of nights entwined with Lucrecia. Ah yes, how well he understood the mutilated motorcyclist. But it was not necessary to emulate Farinelli or undergo a prosthetic procedure to assimilate that culture, convert to that religion, and, like the poisoned Manuel, like Neruda's widower, like so many anonymous aesthetes of hearing, smell, fantasy (he thought of the Prime Minister of India, the nonagenarian Rarji Desai, who, when he read his speeches, paused to take little sips of his own pee; "Ah, if it had only been his wife's!"), who felt themselves transported to heaven as they watched and heard the squatting or sitting beloved creature interpret that ceremony, in appearance so trivial and functional, of emptying a bladder, who elevated it into spectacle, into amorous dance, the prologue or epilogue (for the mutilated Manuel, a substitute) to the act of love. Don Rigoberto's eyes filled with tears. He rediscovered the fluid silence of the Barrancan night, the solitude in which he found himself, surrounded by mindless engravings and books.

"Lucrecia beloved, for the sake of all you hold dear," he pleaded, kissing the unbound hair of the woman he loved, "urinate for me too."

"First, I have to make certain that with all the doors and windows closed, the bathroom is totally dark," said Doña Lucrecia, with a lawyer's meticulous attention to detail. "When the time comes, I'll call you. You'll come in without any noise, so as not to disturb me. You'll sit in the corner. You won't move or say a word. By then, the four glasses of water will begin to have their effect. Not one exclamation, not one sigh, not the slightest movement, Manuel. Otherwise I'll leave and never set foot in this house again. You can stay in your corner while I wipe myself and straighten my dress. As I walk out, you will crawl over and kiss my feet in gratitude."

Had he done that? Surely he had. He would have crawled to her along the tiled floor and brought his mouth to her shoes in doglike gratitude. Then he would wash his hands and face, and with damp eyes join Lucrecia in the living room to tell her, so unctuously, that he could not find the words, she had done so much for him, his happiness was immeasurable. And, showering her with praise, he would tell her that in reality he had been this way from the time he was a boy, not only since his leap over the precipice. The accident had allowed him to adopt as his only source of pleasure what had once produced so much shame that he had hidden it from others and himself. It had all begun when he was very young, when he slept in his little sister's room and the nanny would get up at midnight to pass water. She didn't bother to close the door; he could hear the murmuring, crystalline splash of her stream very clearly, a lullaby that made him feel like an angel in heaven. It was the most beautiful, the most musical, the most tender memory of his childhood. She understood, didn't she? The magnificent Lucrecia understood everything. Nothing in the tangled labyrinth of human desires shocked her. Manuel knew this; that is why he admired her and why he dared to make his request. If the tragedy on the motorcycle had not occurred, he never would have asked. Because until his cycle's flight into the rocky abyss, his life, as far as love and sex were concerned, had been a nightmare. What truly excited him was something he never had the courage to ask of decent girls but had negotiated only with prostitutes. And even though he paid for it, he had endured so many humiliations, so much laughter and mockery, so many contemptuous or ironic glances that inhibited him and made him feel like dirt.

That was the reason he had broken off with all those girls. All of them had failed to give him the extraordinary gift that Doña Lucrecia had just granted him: the stream of her piss. Sympathetic laughter shook Don Rigoberto. The poor wretch! Who could have imagined that the star of the *motorcross*, the man who rode steel, surrounded by statuesque beauties who came and laughed and fell in love with the sports hero, did not want to caress them or undress them, kiss them or penetrate them: he only wanted to listen to them piss. And the noble, the magnanimous Lucrecia had peed for the mutilated Manuel! That micturation would remain etched in his memory like the heroic deeds in history books, like the miracles in the lives of the saints. Dear Lucrecia! Lucrecia, so indulgent toward human frailties! Lucrecia, a Roman name that meant fortunate! Lucrecia? His hands rapidly turned the pages of the notebook and the reference soon appeared:

"Lucrecia, Roman matron renowned for her beauty and virtue. Ravaged by Sextus Tarquin, son of King Tarquin the Proud. After telling her father and husband of the crime and urging them to avenge her, she took her life in their presence, plunging a dagger into her breast. Lucrecia's suicide precipitated the expulsion of the Kings of Rome and the founding of the Republic in 509 B.C. The figure of Lucrecia came to symbolize modesty and chastity, and, above all, the virtuous wife."

It is she, it is she, thought Don Rigoberto. His wife could provoke historical cataclysms and live in perpetuity as a symbol. Of the virtuous wife? If one understood virtue in a non-Christian sense, of course. What other wife would have shared her husband's imaginings as devotedly as she? None. And Fonchito? Well, better to skirt that quicksand. In the end, hadn't it all stayed within the family? Would she have done the same as the Roman matron when she was violated by Sextus Tarquin? An icicle pierced Don Rigoberto's heart. With a grimace of horror he struggled to banish the image of Lucrecia lying on the floor, her heart pierced by a dagger. To exorcise it, he brought back the motorcyclist aroused by the flow from female bladders. Only female? Or male bladders too? Did he also get an erection at the sight of a spouting gentleman?

"Never," Manuel declared immediately, in so sincere a voice that Doña Lucrecia believed him.

Well, it wasn't entirely true that his life had been nothing but a nightmare because of his need (what name should be used to avoid calling it a vice?). Bringing color to the desert landscape of unsatisfied desires and frustrations, there were healing, effervescent moments, modest compensations for his anguish, almost always provided by chance. For example, the laundress whose face Manuel remembered with the same affection one feels when recalling the aunts, grandmothers, or godmothers most closely connected to the warmth of childhood. She came to wash clothes several times a week. She must have suffered from cystitis, because she was constantly running from the laundry room or the ironing board to the little servants' bathroom next to the pantry. And the boy Manuel was always there, alert, hiding in the garret, his face flat against the floor, his ears straining. The concert would come, the noisy, copious waterfall, a genuine flood. That woman had a bladder the size of a soccer ball, a living reservoir, given the strength, abundance, frequency, and sonority of her urination. Once— Doña Lucrecia saw the pupils of the motorcyclist with the prosthesis dilate greedily—once Manuel had seen her. Yes, seen. All right, not completely. In an act of daring he had climbed the garden trellis up to the skylight of the little servants' bathroom, and for a few glorious seconds, as he dangled in midair, he could see the bushy hair, the shoulders, the legs in woolen stockings, the flat shoes of the woman sitting on the toilet and passing her water with noisy indifference. Ah, what bliss!

And there had also been the American, blond, tanned, slightly masculine, always in boots and a cowboy hat, who came to participate in the tour of the Andes. She was so bold a motorcyclist that she almost won. But what Manuel remembered was not so much her skill on the machine (a Harley-Davidson, of course) as her forwardness and lack of prudery, which allowed her, at the rest stops, to share sleeping quarters with the other drivers and bathe in front of them if there was only one bathroom, and even go into the lavatory and do what she had to and not care if there were several motorcyclists in the same room, on the other side of a thin partition. What days those were! Manuel had lived in a state of chronic excitement, his lost organ in prolonged erection, listening to the emancipated Sandy Canal relieving herself of fluids, which transformed the race into an interminable fiesta for him. But neither the laundress nor Sandy nor any of the casual or mercenary experiences in his mythology could compare to this one, this superlative grace, this liquefying manna with which Doña Lucrecia had made him feel like a god.

Don Rigoberto smiled in satisfaction. There was no rat nearby. The temple of Karniji, its Brahmins, armies of rodents, and pots of syrup were on the other side of oceans, continents, jungles. He was here, alone, in the night that was drawing to a close, in his refuge of pictures and notebooks. There were signs of dawn along the horizon. Today, too, he would be yawning in the office. Did he smell anything? The widow odor had dissipated. Did he hear anything? The waves and, almost lost in the sound they made, the tinkle of a lady pissing.

"I," he thought, smiling, "am a man who washes his hands before, not after, he urinates."

A Superlative Menu

I know you like to eat just small quantities of food that is nice and healthy, but tasty, and I am ready to please you at a beautifully set table *as well*.

Bright and early in the morning I'll go to market and buy the freshest milk, a hot, crusty bread straight out of the oven, and the juiciest orange. I'll wake you with the prettiest breakfast tray, the most fragrant flower, the sweetest kiss. "Here is your lovely juice without seeds, your delicious toast with yummy strawberry marmalade, and your wonderful coffee with milk and absolutely no sugar, my darling señor."

For your lunch, a salad and some yogurt, just the way you like it. I'll rinse the crispy lettuce leaves until they sparkle, and I'll cut the red ripe tomatoes artistically, taking my inspiration from the pictures in your library. I'll dress them with a sprinkle of vinegar, just a touch of oil, a few drops of my saliva, and my own tears instead of salt.

And every single night, one of your favorites (I have marvelous menus for the whole blessed year, with absolutely no repetitions). Olluco root with wonderful sun-dried charqui, a perfect puree of green beans, special Indian fricassee, a spicy casserole of mashed potato, savory tripe-and-potato stew, a mouth-watering ragout of pork and kid in wine sauce, tender beefsteak Chorrillan-style, a fabulous ceviche of corvina, rich prawn stew, or phenomenal prawns Limenian-style, a magnificent rice and duck, luscious smothered rice, a delectable refried rice-and-bean omelet, spectacular stuffed chicken with garlic. But I had better stop so I won't make you hungry. And, naturally, your choice of fine red wine or refreshing, ice-cold beer.

For dessert, sweet pineapple fritters, scrumptious Limenian ladyfingers, fabulous deep-fried crullers with honey, fantastic honey-drizzled crêpes, delicious doughnuts, memorable nun's breath, marvelous marzipan, terrific twisted pastry, sensational meringues, superb golden honey candies, Doña Pepa's outstanding almond nougat, lip-smacking blue-corn pudding, and unforgettable fig turnovers with rich ricotta cheese.

Will you accept me as your gourmet cook? I'm exceptionally clean, for I take a nice bath at least twice a day. I don't chew gum, or smoke cigarettes, or have hairy underarms, and my lovely hands and feet are as perfect as my beautiful breasts and buttocks. I will work all the hours needed to keep your taste buds and tummy happy. If necessary, I will also dress you, undress you, wash you, shave you, trim your nails, and wipe your ass when you make number two. At night I'll warm you with my very own body so that you feel no nasty chill in your bed. In addition to preparing your meals, I will be your humble valet, your hot little stove, your first-class razor, your super-sharp scissors, and your downy-soft toilet paper.

Will you take me on, my darling señor?

Yours, yours, all yours,
The Stupendous Cook Without Bunions

VI

The Anonymous Letter

Instead of the anger she had felt the night before, when she had gone to bed clutching the crumpled paper in her fist, Señora Lucrecia awoke content, in a good humor. A lightly voluptuous sensation hovered around her. She stretched out her hand and picked up the missive written in block letters on pale blue textured paper, pleasing to the touch.

"Before the mirror, on a bed or sofa . . ." She had a bed, but not one covered with hand-painted Indian silks or an Indonesian batik, which meant she would not be able to fulfill that demand of her faceless master. But she could satisfy him by lying down naked, on her back, loosening her hair, raising her leg, focusing her mind on thinking she was Klimt's *Danaë* (though she didn't really believe it), and feigning sleep. And, of course, she could look into the mirror and say to herself: "I am enjoyed and admired, I am dreamed and loved." A mocking little smile and eyes flashing like fireflies were repeated in the dressing-table mirror as she pushed back the sheets and amused herself by following the instructions. But only half her body was visible, and she could not tell if she had imitated with any verisimilitude the posture in the painting by Klimt that her phantom correspondent had sent to her in a crude postcard reproduction.

As she ate breakfast and chatted distractedly with Justiniana, and then as she showered and dressed, she re-evaluated her reasons for giving only one name and one face to the author of the letter. Don Rigoberto? Fonchito? Suppose they had planned it together? How absurd! No, that made no sense at all. Logic inclined her to think this was Rigoberto's way of letting her know that despite what had happened, despite their separation, she was always present in his ecstatic passions. His way of testing the possibility of a reconciliation. No. It had all been too hard on him. He would never be able to make peace with the woman who had deceived him with his own son, in his own house. His pride, that gnawing worm, would not permit it. Well then, if the anonymous letter had not been sent by her ex-husband, the author had to be Fonchito. Didn't he have the same fascination with painting as his father? The same good or bad habit of intermingling the life of paintings with real life? Yes, it had been Fonchito. And he had given himself away when he brought up Klimt. She would let him know she knew and make him feel ashamed. That very afternoon.

The hours she spent waiting seemed very long to Doña Lucrecia. Sitting in the dining alcove, glancing at her watch, afraid that today of all days he would not come. "Good Lord, Señora, one would think your lover was visiting you for the first time," Justiniana teased her. She blushed instead of reprimanding her. As soon as he arrived, his face beautiful, his delicate body encased in a disheveled school uniform, and dropped his book bag on the rug and greeted her with a kiss on the cheek, a stern Doña Lucrecia confronted him: "You and I have something very unpleasant to talk about, young man."

She saw his intrigued expression, the troubled blue eyes opening wide. He was sitting in front of her with his legs crossed. Doña Lucrecia noticed that one of his shoelaces was untied.

"What's that, Stepmamá?"

"Something very unpleasant," she repeated, showing him the letter and postcard. "The most cowardly, most despicable thing in the world: sending anonymous letters."

The boy did not turn pale, or blush, or blink. He continued to look at her with curiosity, not at all disconcerted. She handed him the letter and the card and did not take her eyes off him while a very serious Fonchito, the tip of his tongue between his teeth, read the letter as if he were spelling it out word by word. His alert eyes moved back and forth, reading the lines again and again.

"There are two words I don't understand," he said at last, bathing her in his limpid glance. "Helen and batik. A girl at the academy is named Helen. But it's used with a different meaning here, isn't it? And I've never heard of batik. What do they mean, Stepmamá?"

"Don't play the fool," Doña Lucrecia said irritably. "Why did you write this to me? Did you think I wouldn't know it was you?"

She felt rather uncomfortable at the open perplexity now displayed by Fonchito, who, after shaking his head a few times in bewilderment, began to read the letter again, silently moving his lips. And she was caught completely off guard when the boy raised his head and she saw that he was grinning from ear to ear. In a transport of joy he held out his arms, threw himself on her, and embraced her with a little cry of triumph.

"We did it, Stepmamá! Don't you see?"

"What is it I'm supposed to see, smarty?" She pushed him away.

"But Stepmamá," he said, with a tender, pitying look. "Our plan. It's working. Didn't I say we had to make him jealous? Be happy, we're doing very well. Don't you want to make up with my papá?"

"I'm not so sure this anonymous letter is from Rigoberto," said a dubious Doña Lucrecia. "I tend to suspect you, you little hypocrite."

She fell silent, because the boy was laughing, looking at her with the affectionate benevolence due someone not very bright.

"Did you know that Klimt was Egon Schiele's teacher?" he exclaimed suddenly, as if responding to a question that had not yet crossed her lips. "He admired him. He sketched him on his deathbed. A very nice charcoal, *Agony*, 1912. And that same year he also painted *The Hermits*, where he and Klimt appear in monks' habits."

"I'm convinced you wrote it, Mr. Know-it-all." Doña Lucrecia felt angry again, torn by conflicting suppositions, irritated by Fonchito's untroubled face and the way he spoke, so pleased with himself.

"But Stepmamá, instead of thinking the worst, be happy. My papá has sent you this note to let you know he's forgiven you and wants to make up. As if you didn't know that already."

"Nonsense. It's nothing but an insolent anonymous letter, and a dirty one at that."

"Don't be so unfair," the boy protested vehemently. "It compares you to a painting by Klimt; it says that when he painted that girl he was foreseeing what you would look like. What's dirty about that? It's a very pretty compliment. A way for my papá to be in touch with you. Are you going to answer it?"

"I can't, I have no proof it's from him." But now Doña Lucrecia was more convinced. Did he really want them to reconcile?

"You see, making him jealous worked brilliantly," the boy repeated happily. "Ever since I told him I saw you arm in arm with a gentleman, he's been imagining all kinds of things. It scared him so much he wrote you this letter. Aren't I a good detective, Stepmamá?"

A thoughtful Doña Lucrecia folded her arms. She had never taken seriously the idea of a reconciliation with Rigoberto. She had played along with Fonchito simply to pass the time. Suddenly, for the first time, it seemed a possibility rather than a remote daydream. Is that what she wanted? To go back to the house in Barranco and take up the old life again?

"Who else but my papá could compare you to a painting by Klimt?" the boy insisted. "Don't you see? He's reminding you of those little picture games you two played at night."

Señora Lucrecia felt as if she were suffocating.

"What are you talking about?" she stammered, too faint to deny it.

"But Stepmamá," the boy replied, gesturing with his hands. "You know the games. When he would say today you're Cleopatra, or Venus, or Aphrodite. And you'd imitate the paintings to give him pleasure."

"But, but . . ." In her utter mortification, Doña Lucrecia could not even become angry; she felt as if anything she said would incriminate her further. "Where did you get that idea; your imagination is very twisted, very, very . . ."

"You told me so yourself," the boy said, confounding her. "What a scatterbrain, Stepmamá. Did you forget so soon?"

She fell silent. Had she told him? She raked her memory, but it was useless. She did not remember bringing up the subject with Fonchito, not even indirectly. Never, not ever, of course not. But then how did he know? Could Rigoberto have taken him into his confidence? Impossible; Rigoberto never spoke to anyone about his fantasies and desires. Not even to her, during the day. That had been a rule both had respected during their ten years of marriage; never, either in jest or seriously, to allude during the day to what they said and did at night in the privacy of their bedroom. So as not to trivialize their love, in order to preserve its magical, sacred aura, Rigoberto would say. Doña Lucrecia recalled their early days together, when she was first discovering the hidden side of her husband's life and they'd had a conversation about the book by Johan Huizinga, *Homo Ludens*, one of the first he had asked her to read, assuring her that in the notion of life as play, and the sacred space, she would find the key to their future happiness. The sacred space turned out to be our bed, she thought. They had been happy playing those nocturnal games, which at first merely intrigued her but gradually won her over, spicing her life—her nights—with endlessly renewed fictions. Until her moment of lunacy with this boy.

"He who laughs alone remembers evil things he's done." The impudent voice of Justiniana, who was carrying in the tea tray, brought her back from her ruminations. "Hello, Fonchito."

"My papá has written a letter to Stepmamá and they'll be making up any day now. Just like I told you, Justita. Did you fix sweet buns for me?"

"Nicely toasted, with butter and strawberry marmalade." Justiniana turned to Doña Lucrecia, her large eyes opening wide. "You're going to make up with the señor? So we'll be moving back to Barranco?"

"It's all foolishness," said Señora Lucrecia. "Don't you know him yet?"

"We'll see if it's foolishness," Fonchito protested, attacking the buns while Doña Lucrecia poured his tea. "How about a bet? What will you give me if you make up with my papá?"

"Burnt crumbs," said Señora Lucrecia, already beginning to yield. "And what will you give me if you lose?"

"A kiss." The boy laughed, winking at her.

Justiniana burst into laughter. "I'd better go and leave you two lovebirds alone."

"Be quiet, you fool," Doña Lucrecia chided her, but the girl was out of hearing.

They drank their tea in silence. Doña Lucrecia, still imbued with reminiscences of her life with Rigoberto, grieved over everything that had happened. The break could not be repaired. It had been too awful, there was no way back. Would it even be possible for the three of them to live together again under one roof? Then it occurred to her that Jesus, at the age of twelve, had confounded the doctors in the temple when he discussed theological matters with them as their equal. Yes, but Fonchito was not a child prodigy like Jesus. He was more like Lucifer, Prince of Darkness. Not she but he, he, the supposed child, was to blame for everything.

"Do you know another way I'm like Egon Schiele, Stepmamá?" The boy brought her out of her reverie. "He and I are both schizophrenics."

She could not suppress her laughter. But it broke off abruptly because, as on other occasions, Doña Lucrecia sensed that beneath apparently childish chatter something darker might be lurking.

"Do you even know what a schizophrenic is?"

"It's when you're only one person but think you're two different people, or even more." Fonchito was pompously reciting a lesson. "My papá explained it to me last night."

"Well then, you might be one," Doña Lucrecia said softly. "Because there's a grown man and a boy inside you. An angel and a devil. What does that have to do with Egon Schiele?"

Once again Fonchito's face broke into a satisfied smile. And after murmuring a rapid "Wait just a minute, Stepmamá," he pawed through his bag to find the inevitable book of reproductions. Books, rather, for Señora Lucrecia recalled having seen at least three. Did he always have one in his bag? He was carrying his mania too far, always identifying in everything with that painter. If she were in touch with Rigoberto, she would suggest he take him to a psychologist. But she immediately laughed at herself. What an insane idea, giving advice to her estranged husband about rearing the boy who had caused the rift between them. Lately she was becoming downright idiotic.

"Look, Stepmamá. What do you think of that?"

She took the book, open at the page Fonchito was pointing to, and for some time she turned the pages, trying to concentrate on those hot, unsettling images, those male figures in groups of two or three who looked at her impassively, fully dressed or draped in tunics, naked or half-naked, sometimes covering their sex or displaying it, erect and enormous, with a total lack of shame.

"Well, they're self-portraits," she commented at last, for the sake of saying something. "Some good, others not so good."

"He did more than a hundred," the boy informed her. "After Rembrandt, Schiele is the artist who painted the most self-portraits."

"That doesn't mean he was a schizophrenic. More like Narcissus. Aren't you a narcissist too, Fonchito?"

"You haven't looked carefully enough." The boy opened to another page, and then another, explaining as he pointed. "Don't you see? He doubles, even triples himself. This one, for example. *The Seers of Themselves*, 1911. Look. It's him, naked and dressed. *Triple Self-portrait*, 1913. Him, three times. And three more over here, very small, on the right. That's how he saw himself, as if he had several Egon Schieles inside him. Isn't that being schizophrenic?"

He spoke in a rush, his eyes flashing, and Doña Lucrecia attempted to mollify him.

"Well, he may have had a tendency to schizophrenia, like many artists," she conceded. "Painters, poets, musicians. They have many things inside, so many that sometimes they don't all fit in a single person. But you, you're the most normal boy in the world."

"Don't talk to me as if I were retarded, Stepmamá," Alfonso said angrily. "I'm like him and you know I am, because you just told me so. A grown man and a child. An angel and a devil. In other words, a schizophrenic."

She caressed his hair. The soft, tousled blond ringlets slipped between her fingers, and Doña Lucrecia resisted the temptation to take him in her arms, sit him on her lap, and croon a lullaby.

"Do you miss your mamá?" she blurted out. She tried to amend the question: "I mean, do you think about her often?"

"Hardly ever," said Fonchito very calmly. "I wouldn't remember her face except for photographs. The person I miss is you, Stepmamá. That's why I want you to hurry and make up with my papá."

"It's not that easy. Don't you see? Some wounds are difficult to heal. What happened with Rigoberto is one of those wounds. He was deeply offended, and with good reason. What I did made no sense, it was inexcusable. I don't know, I'll never know what came over me. The more I think about it, the more incredible it seems. As if it hadn't been me, as if another person had been inside me, taking my place."

"Then you're schizophrenic too, Stepmamá." The boy laughed, and again the expression on his face was the look of someone catching her in a mistake.

"A little, no, a lot," she agreed. "Let's not talk about sad things. Tell me about you. Or your papá."

"He misses you too." Fonchito became serious, almost solemn. "That's why he wrote you that anonymous letter. His wound has healed and he wants to make up."

She did not have the heart to argue with him. Now she felt overwhelmed by melancholy, and rather gloomy.

"How is Rigoberto? Living his usual life?"

"From the office to home, and from home to the office, every day," Fonchito agreed. "Sitting in his study, listening to music, looking at his pictures. But it's all an excuse. He doesn't go in there to read or look at paintings or listen to his records, but only to think about you."

"How do you know?"

"Because he talks to you," the boy declared, lowering his voice and looking toward the interior of the house to see if Justiniana was nearby. "I've heard him. I sneak up very slowly and put my ear to the door. It never fails. He's always talking when he's alone. And saying your name, I swear."

"I don't believe you, you're lying."

"You know I wouldn't make up a thing like this, Stepmamá. Do you see now? He wants you to come back."

He spoke with so much certainty that it was difficult not to feel pulled toward his world, so seductive and false, so full of innocence, of good and evil, purity and vileness, spontaneity and calculation. Since this happened, I've stopped grieving about not having my own child, Doña Lucrecia thought. She believed she understood why. The boy, sitting back on his heels, the book of reproductions open at his feet, was scrutinizing her.

"Do you know something, Fonchito?" she said, almost without thinking. "I love you very much."

"And I love you, Stepmamá."

"Don't interrupt. And because I love you, it hurts me that you're not like other boys. Acting so grown-up, you miss something you can only have at the age you are now. The most wonderful thing that can happen to anyone is being young. And you, you're wasting it."

"I don't understand you, Stepmamá," Fonchito said impatiently. "Just a minute ago you said I was the most normal boy in the world. Did I do something wrong?"

"No, no," she reassured him. "I mean that I'd like to see you playing soccer, going to the stadium, going out with kids from the neighborhood and from school. Having friends your own age. Having parties, dancing, falling in love with girls. Aren't you interested in any of those things?"

Fonchito shrugged disdainfully.

"They're so boring," he replied, not giving her words too much importance. "I play soccer at recess, and that's enough. Sometimes I go out with guys from the neighborhood. But I'm bored by the dumb things they like to do. And the girls are even dumber. Do you think I could talk to them about Egon Schiele? When I'm with my friends I feel as if I'm wasting my time. But with you, I'm making good use of it. I like being here and talking to you a thousand times more than smoking with the kids on the Barranco Seawalk. And what do I need girls for if I have you, Stepmamá?"

She did not know what to say. The smile she attempted could not have been more false. The boy, she was sure, was perfectly conscious of the embarrassment she felt. Looking at his upturned face, the features transformed by euphoria, the eyes devouring her with a manly light, she had the impression he was about to get up and kiss her on the mouth. She was relieved to see Justiniana come in just then. But her relief did not last very long, because when she saw the small white envelope in the girl's hand, she guessed what it was.

"Somebody slipped this envelope under the door, Señora."

"I bet it's another anonymous letter from my papá," Fonchito exclaimed, clapping his hands.

An Exaltation and Defense of Phobias

From this remote corner of the world, dear friend Peter Simplon—if that really is your last name and not a perverse alteration by some viper from the journalistic snakepit intending to ridicule you even further—I send you both my solidarity and my admiration. This morning, on my way to the office, I heard the newscast on Radio America reporting that a court in Syracuse, New York, had sentenced you to three months in prison for repeatedly climbing to the roof of your neighbor's house in order to spy on her as she bathed, and since then I have been counting the minutes until the day was over and I could return to my house and write these lines to you. I wish to tell you right now that these effusive feelings for you exploded in my chest (this is not a metaphor, I felt a grenade of friendship go off inside my ribs), not when I learned the sentence, but when I heard your reply to the judge (a reply that the wretched man considered an aggravating factor): "I did it because I found the hair under my neighbor's arms irresistibly attractive." (The rattlesnake of an announcer, when he read this part of the report, put on a mellifluous, joking voice, to let his listeners know he was even more of an imbecile than his profession would oblige one to suppose.)

My fetishist friend, I have never been in Syracuse, a city about which I know nothing except that it is devastated by snowstorms and arctic cold in the winter, but it must have something special at its very core to give birth to a man of your sensibility and fantasy, possessed of the courage you have displayed, risking disgrace and, I imagine, your livelihood, as well as the mockery of friends and family, to defend your small eccentricity (when I say small, I clearly mean inoffensive, benign, exceedingly healthful and beneficial, since you and I both know that no manias or phobias lack grandeur, for they constitute a human being's originality and the supreme expression of his sovereignty).

This being said, and in order to avoid any misunderstanding, I feel obliged to inform you that what you find a delicacy is inedible to me, for in the rich universe of desires and dreams, those clumps of fleece in feminine armpits, the sight (and, I suppose, the taste, touch, and smell) of which brings you the most sublime joy, demoralize and disgust me, and repel me sexually. (Looking at Ribera's *Bearded Woman* made me impotent for three weeks.) This is why my beloved Lucrecia always made certain that her soft underarms never revealed even the premonition of fleece, and the skin always seemed, to my eyes, tongue, and lips, like the smooth bottom of a cherub. In the matter of a woman's fleece, I find delight only in the pubic, as long as it is well groomed and does not grow excessively dense and long on the sides, or in unkempt tangles that make the act of love difficult and turn cunnilingus into an undertaking that threatens asphyxiation and choking.

Following your lead, having begun this intimate confession, I will add that not only underarms soiled by fleece ("hair" is a word that makes the reality even worse by adding sebaceous material and dandruff) provoke antisexual horror in me, comparable only to that produced by the disgraceful spectacle of a woman who chews gum, or has whiskers on her upper lip, or bipeds of either sex who root about their teeth with that ignoble object called a toothpick, searching for excrescences, or who gnaw at their nails, or who, in full view of the world and without scruple or shame, eat a mango, an orange, a pomegranate, a peach, grapes, custard apples, or any fruit having ghastly hard things—stems, fibers, pits, skins, rinds—the mere mention (not to mention the sight) of which makes my skin crawl and infects my soul with furious homicidal impulses. I in no way exaggerate, my dear companion-in-pride regarding our phantoms, if I say that each time I observe someone eating a fruit and removing the inedible parts from his mouth, or spitting them out, I feel nausea, and even find myself wishing for the death of the guilty party. By the same token, I have always considered any diner to be a cannibal if, when he brings the fork up to his mouth, he raises his elbow at the same time as his hand.

This is how we are, we are not ashamed, and I admire nothing so much as people willing to go to prison and expose themselves to ignominy for the sake of their manias. I am not one of them. I have organized my life secretly, within the bosom of the family, to reach the moral heights you have reached in public. In my case, everything is accomplished with discretion and prudence, with no missionary or exhibitionist spirit, in the most evasive manner, so as not to provoke sarcasm and hostility in those around me, people with whom I am forced to coexist because of professional or familial obligations, or for reasons of social servitude. If you are thinking there is a good deal of cowardice in me—above all when compared to your audacity in standing before the world as the man you are—then you are absolutely correct. I am much less a coward now than when I was young with regard to my phobias and manias—I don't like either term because of the pejorative implications and the association with psychologists or psychoanalytic couches, but what name can I use that would not injure them: eccentricities? private desires? For the moment, let us say that the second is less bad. In those days I was very Catholic, a member, then a leader, of Catholic Action, influenced by thinkers like Jacques Maritain; in other words, a worshipper of social utopias, certain that by means of an energetic apostolate inspired in the Gospels, we could wrest control of human history away from the spirit of evil—we called it sin—and build a homogeneous society based on spiritual values. I spent the best years of my youth working to realize the Christian Republic, that collectivist utopia of the spirit, enduring with all the zeal of a convert the brutal refutations endlessly inflicted on me and my companions by a human reality vexed at the lunacy of every effort to construct something coherent and egalitarian out of the vortex of incompatible particularities which constitute the human conglomerate. It was during those years, my dear Peter Simplon of Syracuse, that I discovered, at first with a certain affection and then with embarrassment and shame, the manias that distinguished me from others and made me a unique specimen. (Many years would have to go by, countless experiences would be necessary, before I finally understood that all human beings are a case apart, which is what makes us creative and gives meaning to our freedom.) How amazed I was when the mere sight of a man, who until then had been a close friend, peeling an orange with his hands, putting the sections into his mouth, not caring that repellent strings of pulp were hanging from his lips, and spitting inedible whitish seeds in all directions, was enough to turn fondness into unconquerable dislike, and a short while later I broke off my friendship with him on some pretext or other.

My confessor, Father Dorante, a good-natured Jesuit of the old school, listened without undue concern to my anxieties and scruples, considering those "little manias" as minor, venial sins, the unavoidable whims of any child of a well-off family who had been excessively catered to by his parents. "You want to be a freak, Rigoberto." He laughed. "Except for your monumental ears and anteater's nose, I've never seen anyone more normal than you. And so when you see someone eating fruit with pulp or pits, look the other way and don't lose any sleep over it." But I did lose sleep, I was frightened and troubled. Above all, after breaking with Otilia on some trivial pretext, Otilia of the braids, the skates, and the little turned-up nose, whom I loved so much and whom I pestered so much to make her notice me. Why did I quarrel with her? What crime was committed by the beautiful Otilia in her white uniform from the Villa María Academy? She ate grapes in front of me. She put them in her mouth one by one, showing her delight, rolling her eyes and sighing to mock my horrified grimaces, for I had already shared my phobia with her. She opened her mouth and made my disgust complete by using her hands to remove the repulsive seeds and obscene skins and tossing them into the garden of her house—we were sitting there, on the fence—with a defiant gesture. I detested her! I hated her! My longtime love melted away like a snowball in the sun, and for many days I hoped she would be hit by a car, knocked down by waves, infected by scarlet fever. "That's not a sin, my boy," Father Dorante thought he was reassuring me. "That's raving lunacy. You don't need a confessor, you need a keeper."

But, dear friend and *beau idéal* from Syracuse, this all made me feel abnormal. At the time the thought devastated me, because like so many hominids—the majority of them, I fear—I did not associate the notion of being different with a vindication of my independence but only with the social sanctions that inevitably fall on the black sheep of the flock. Being the pariah, the exception to the rule, seemed to me the worst of calamities. Until I discovered that not all manias were phobias; some were also a mysterious source of pleasure. The knees and elbows of girls, for example. My friends liked pretty eyes, a slim or a voluptuous body, a slender waist, and the boldest among them relished a prominent bottom or shapely legs. I alone gave a privileged place to those joints which, as I now confess with no shame in the tomblike intimacy of my notebooks, I valued more than all the rest of a girl's physical attributes. I say it and will not retract it. Well-cushioned, rounded, satiny knees with no bony protuberances; glossy elbows, unwrinkled, unroughened, smooth and soft to the touch, endowed with the spongy quality of cake; these arouse me to the point of delirium.

I am overjoyed to see and touch them; if I kiss them, I am transported to seventh heaven. You probably will not have the opportunity to do so, but if you needed confirmation from Lucrecia, my beloved, she would tell you how many hours I have spent—as many as at the foot of the cross when I was a boy—in ecstatic adoration, contemplating the perfection and unparalleled smoothness of her geometric knees and enchanting elbows, kissing them, biting them like a puppy playing with his bone, utterly intoxicated, until my tongue going to sleep or a labial cramp brings me back to pedestrian reality. Dear Lucrecia! Of all the graces that adorn her, I am most grateful for her understanding of my weaknesses, her wisdom in helping me to realize my fantasies.

On account of this mania, I found myself obliged to examine my conscience. A friend from Catholic Action who knew me very well and was aware of what attracted me most in girls—their knees and elbows—warned me that something was wrong. He was very fond of psychology, which made matters worse, for, in his orthodox way, he wanted to bring human behavior and motivation into harmony with the morality and teachings of the Church. He spoke of deviancy and pronounced the words "fetishism" and "fetishist." They now seem two of the most acceptable in the dictionary (that is what we are, you and I and all sensitive people), but in those days they sounded to me like depravity and abominable vice.

You and I know, my Syracusan friend, that fetishism is not the "cult of fetishes," as the Dictionary of the Academy so unfortunately defines it, but a privileged form of expression of human particularity that allows men and women to define their space, mark their difference from others, exercise their imagination, express their anti-herd spirit, and be free. I would like to recount to you, as we sit in a little cottage in the countryside surrounding your city, which I picture as full of lakes, pine groves, and hills white with snow, and drink a glass of whiskey together and listen to the logs crackling in the hearth, how discovering the central role of fetishism in the individual's life played a decisive role in my disenchantment with social utopias —the idea that it was possible to collectively create happiness and goodness or realize any ethical or aesthetic value—in my journey from faith to agnosticism and the belief that moves me now: since man and woman cannot live without utopias, the only realistic way to create them is by transferring them from the social to the individual sphere. A collective cannot organize to achieve any kind of perfection without destroying the freedom of many and obliterating beautiful individual differences in the name of horrifying common denominators. On the other hand, the solitary individual can—by acting on his appetites, manias, fetishes, phobias, or preferences—create his own world, one that approaches (or eventually incarnates, as it does in saints and Olympic champions) the supreme ideal in which experience and desire are one. Naturally, in certain privileged instances, a happy coincidence—for example, the sperm and ovum meeting to produce fertilization—allows two people to realize their dreams in complementary fashion. This was true in the case (I've just read it in the biography written by his understanding widow) of the journalist, playwright, critic, entertainer, and professionally frivolous man, Kenneth Tynan, a secret masochist to whom chance granted the opportunity of meeting a girl who happened to be a shameless sadist, a fact that allowed them both to be happy two or three times a week in a Kensington basement, he receiving the lash of the whip and she dispensing it, in a bruising game that transported them to heaven. I respect but do not practice games that have Mercurochrome and arnica as their corollaries.

Since we are relating anecdotes—in this sphere there are hundreds of them—I cannot resist describing for you the fantasy that afflicts the libido of Cachito Arnilla, a champion in the verbose profession of selling insurance, with the frenzy of Saint Vitus' dance; it consists—he confessed this to me at one of those abominable Patriotic Festival or Christmas cocktail parties that I cannot avoid attending—of seeing a woman, naked except for stiletto heels, smoking and playing billiards. This image, which he thinks he saw as a boy in some magazine, was associated with his first erections, and since then it has been the polestar of his sexual life. Dear Cachito! When he married a dark little hussy from Accounting, capable, I am sure, of complying with his wishes, I slyly presented him, in the name of La Perricholi Insurance Company—I am the director—with a full-size billiard table, delivered to his house in a van on the day of his wedding. Everyone thought it was an inane gift, but the look in Cachito's eye and the anticipatory salivation with which he expressed his thanks told me I had hit the bull's-eye.

My dear friend from Syracuse, lover of underarm bushes, the exaltation of manias and phobias must have limits. One needs to recognize certain restrictions, for without them crime would be unleashed and we would return to the bestiality of the jungle. But in the private domain, the domain of these phantoms, everything should be permitted between adults who consent to the game and its rules for their mutual pleasure. And though I find many of these games unbearably repugnant (for example, the little pills that produced the noisy farts so beloved of the gallant French century and, in particular, of the Marquis de Sade, who, not content with mistreating women, also demanded that they make him dizzy with artillery explosions of gases) it is equally true that in this sphere such differences deserve consideration and respect, for nothing else so well represents the unfathomable complexity of the human person.

Did you infringe upon the human rights and freedom of your hairy neighbor when you climbed to her roof in order to pay admiring homage to the tufts under her arms? No doubt. Did you deserve to be punished in the name of social harmony? Oh my, of course you did. But you knew that and took the risk, prepared to pay the price for peeping at the overgrown armpits of your neighbors. I've already told you I cannot emulate your courageous extremes. My sense of the ridiculous and my contempt for heroics, not to mention my physical clumsiness, are too great, and I would never dare to climb someone else's roof even for a glimpse, on a hairless body, of the roundest knees and most spherical elbows known to the female gender. My natural cowardice, which may be nothing more than an unhealthy legalistic instinct, leads me to find a propitious corner for my manias, phobias, and fetishes within the confines of what is commonly called the licit. Does this deprive me of a succulent treasure trove of lasciviousness? Of course. But what I do have is sufficient, as long as one derives the pleasure one should from it, which I attempt to do.

May your three months be easy, and may your dreams behind bars be filled with forests of fleece, avenues of silky hair—black, blond, red—along which you gallop, swim, run, frantic with joy.

Goodbye, my brother.

The Professor's Panties

Don Rigoberto opened his eyes: there, draped between the third and fourth stairs, blue and shiny and edged in lace, provocative and poetic, were her panties, the professor's panties. He trembled like one possessed. He had not slept despite spending a long time in the dark, lying in bed, listening to the murmur of the sea, lost in elusive fantasies. Until, suddenly, that phone had rung again, waking him with a violent start.

"Hello, hello?"

"Rigoberto, is that you?"

He recognized the voice of the aging professor, though he spoke very quietly, covering the mouthpiece with his hand and muffling his words. Where were they? In an old university town. In what country? The United States. In which state? Virginia. What university? The state university, the beautiful school built in neoclassic style with rows of white columns and designed by Thomas Jefferson.

"Is that you, Professor?"

"Yes, yes, Rigoberto. But speak slowly. Forgive me for waking you."

"Not at all, Professor. How was your dinner with Professor Lucrecia? Have you finished?"

The voice of the venerable jurist and philosopher, Nepomuceno Riga, broke into hieroglyphic stammering. Rigoberto realized that something serious had happened to his old teacher of Philosophy of Law at Catholic University in Lima, who had come to attend a symposium at the University of Virginia, where Rigoberto was doing graduate work (in legislation and insurance) and acting as his former teacher's chauffeur and guide: he had taken him to visit Monticello, Jefferson's home, now a museum, and to the historical sites of the Battle of Manassas.

"Rigoberto, I apologize for imposing on you, but you're the only person here I can trust. You were my student, I know your family, and you've been so kind these past few days . . ."

"Please, Don Nepomuceno, don't mention it," the young Rigoberto said encouragingly. "Is something wrong?"

Don Rigoberto sat up in bed, shaken by an anticipatory little laugh. It seemed to him that at any moment the bathroom door would open and the figure of Doña Lucrecia would be sketched there, surprising him with an exquisite pair of panties, in colors, or black or white, with embroidery, openings, silk trim, backstitched or smooth, the kind that covered just enough of her mound of Venus to emphasize it, and at the edges, peeking out to tempt him—wayward, coquettish—some stray pubic hairs. An undergarment like the one that lay so unexpectedly, as if it were a provocative object in a surrealist painting by the Catalonian Joan Ponc or the Romanian Victor Brauner, on the staircase which that good soul, that innocent spirit, Don Nepomuceno Riga, had to climb to reach his bedroom—Don Nepomuceno, who, in his memorable classes, the only ones worth remembering in seven dry-as-dust years studying law, would erase the blackboard with his tie.

"It's just that I don't know what to do, Rigoberto. I find myself in an awkward situation. In spite of my age, I have absolutely no experience in these matters."

"In which matters, Professor? Tell me, don't be embarrassed."

Why, instead of lodging him at the Holiday Inn or the Hilton along with the other scholars attending the symposium, why had they arranged for Don Nepomuceno to stay at the home of the woman who taught International Law II? Surely out of deference to his prestige. Or because the two enjoyed a friendship based on their encounters at law schools throughout the world, and their presence at the same conferences, lectures, and round tables, or perhaps because they had collaborated on an erudite paper abounding in Latin phrases that appeared, with a profusion of notes and an oppressive bibliography, in a professional journal published in Buenos Aires, Tübingen, or Helsinki? Whatever the reason, the esteemed Don Nepomuceno, instead of staying in an impersonal windowed cubicle at the Holiday Inn, spent his nights in Professor Lucrecia's comfortable, rustic-modern house, which Rigoberto knew quite well because this semester he was taking her seminar on International Law II and had gone several times to knock on her door and deliver his papers or return the dense treatises that she, very kindly, had lent him. Don Rigoberto closed his eyes and felt goose bumps as he once again saw the musical hips of the jurist's well-proportioned, erect figure walking away from him.

"Are you all right, Professor?"

"Yes, yes, Rigoberto. Really, it's very silly. You're going to laugh at me. But, as I say, I have no experience. I'm bewildered and confused, my boy."

He did not have to say so; his voice quavered as if he were about to lose it and his words had to be pulled out with forceps. He must have been drenched in icy perspiration. Would he find the courage to tell him what had happened?

"Well, just imagine. Tonight, when I returned from the cocktail party in our honor, Dr. Lucrecia prepared supper here in her house. Just for the two of us; yes, it was very considerate of her. An extremely pleasant meal, served with a bottle of wine. I'm not accustomed to alcohol, and so my befuddlement is probably due to the wine going to my head. A nice little California wine, apparently. Though rather strong, I must say."

"Stop beating about the bush, Professor, and tell me what happened."

"Wait, wait. Think of it, after supper and the bottle of wine, Professor Lucrecia insisted we drink cognac. I couldn't refuse, of course, it would have been impolite. But I saw stars, my boy. It was liquid fire. I began to cough and even thought I might go blind. But something ridiculous happened instead. I fell asleep. Yes, yes, son, right in the chair, right in the living room that is also a library. And when I awoke, I don't know how much later, perhaps ten or fifteen minutes, the professor was not there. She must have gone to bed, I thought. And I prepared to do the same. And then, then, just think, as I was climbing the stairs, whoosh, out of the blue, right in front of my eyes, you can't imagine what I saw. Panties! Yes, right in my path. Don't laugh, my boy, because even if it is laughable, I'm terribly upset. I tell you, I don't know what to do."

"Of course I'm not laughing, Don Nepomuceno. You don't think that intimate article of clothing was there by accident?"

"By accident? Not at all! Son, I may not be experienced, but I'm not in my dotage yet. She left it there ex professo, so that I would find it. Only she and I are under this roof. She put it there."

"But then, Professor, the best thing that can happen to a guest is happening to you. You've received an invitation from your hostess. It's as clear as day."

The professor's voice broke three times before he could articulate anything intelligible.

"You think so, Rigoberto? Well, that's what I thought too when I finally could think, after the shock. You'd call it an invitation, wouldn't you? It can't be accidental; this house is a paragon of order, like the professor herself. That garment was placed there intentionally. Even its arrangement on the staircase is no accident, because it is highlighted and carefully displayed, I swear."

"The intent was to trip you up, if you'll permit me the joke, Don Nepomuceno."

"Rigoberto, I'm laughing too, inside. Despite my confusion, I mean. That's why I need your advice. What should I do? I never dreamed I'd find myself in a situation like this."

"What you should do is very clear, Professor. Don't you like Dr. Lucrecia? She's a very attractive woman; I think she is, and so do my classmates. She's the best-looking woman on Virginia's faculty."

"No doubt she is, nobody can deny it. She's a very beautiful lady."

"Then don't lose any more time. Go and knock on her door. Don't you see? She's waiting for you. Go before she falls asleep."

"Can I take that liberty? Knock on her door, just like that?"

"Where are you now?"

"Where would I be? In the living room, at the foot of the stairs. Why do you think I'm talking so quietly? So I just go up and knock on her door? Just like that?"

"Don't waste a second. She's left you a sign, you can't pretend not to understand. Above all, if you like her. Because she appeals to you, doesn't she, Professor?"

"Of course. It's what I must do, yes, you're right. But I feel somewhat constrained. Thank you, my boy. I needn't remind you to keep this in strictest confidence? For my sake, and especially for the sake of the professor's reputation."

"I'll be as silent as a tomb, Don Nepomuceno. Don't hesitate any longer. Go up those stairs, pick up the panties, and take them to her. Knock on her door and begin by making a joke about the surprise you found on your way up. It will all turn out wonderfully, you'll see. You'll always remember this night, Professor."

Before the sound of the click that ended the conversation, Don Rigoberto heard a rumbling stomach and an anguished belch that the aged jurist could not suppress. How nervous and alarmed he must have been in the darkness of that living room filled with law books, in the potency of the Virginia spring night, torn between his hope for an adventure—the first in a lifetime of purely matrimonial and reproductive coitus?—and his cowardice disguised as rigorous ethical principles, religious convictions, and social prejudices. Which of the forces struggling in his spirit would emerge victorious? Would it be desire or fear?

Don Rigoberto, almost without realizing it, engrossed in what had become the totemic image of the panties left on Professor Lucrecia's staircase, got out of bed and went to his study without turning on the light. His body avoided obstacles—the bench, the Nubian sculpture, pillows, the television set—with an ease acquired through assiduous practice, for since his wife's departure not a night had gone by when sleeplessness did not drive him to leave his bed while it was still dark and seek, among his papers and scrawled notes, a balm for his nostalgia and solitude. His mind still fixed on the figure of the venerable jurist assailed by circumstance (embodied in the undergarment of a perfumed and voluptuous woman, which lay before him between two steps of a jurisprudential staircase) and forced into Hamletian uncertainty, but sitting now before the large wooden table in his study and leafing through his notebooks, Don Rigoberto gave a start when the golden cone of light from the lamp revealed the German proverb written at the top of the page: *Wer die Wahl hat, hat die Qual* ("Whoever must choose must suffer"). Extraordinary! Wasn't this adage, copied from who knows where, a perfect depiction of the state of mind of poor, fortunate Don Nepomuceno Riga, tempted by that well-fleshed academic, Dr. Lucrecia?

His hands, turning the pages of another notebook, challenging chance to see if for a second time he could happen upon, or establish, a relationship between what he found and what he dreamed that would serve as fuel to his fantasy, suddenly stopped ("like the hands of a croupier setting the ball in motion on a spinning roulette wheel"), and he avidly leaned forward. Written on the page was his response to *Edith's Diary*, by Patricia Highsmith.

He raised his head, disconcerted. He heard the furious waves at the foot of the cliff. Patricia Highsmith? The novelist who wrote about boring crimes committed by Mr. Ripley, an apathetic, unmotivated criminal, did not interest him in the least. He had always reacted with yawns (comparable to the ones produced in him by the popular *Tibetan Book of the Living and the Dead*) when this crime writer (helped along by Alfred Hitchcock movies) was all the rage a few years back among the hundred or so people who comprised the Limenian reading public. What was a hack writer for movie fans doing in his notebooks? He could not recall when or why he had written his comments on *Edith's Diary*, a book he did not even remember.

"An excellent novel for understanding that fiction is a flight into the imaginary which emends life. Edith's familial, political, and personal frustrations are not gratuitous; they are rooted in the reality that causes her the greatest suffering: her son Cliffie. Instead of showing him in her diary as he actually is—a weak failure of a boy who was not accepted at the university and does not know how to work—Cliffie breaks free of the original and, in the pages written by his mother, leads the life Edith wanted for him: he is a successful journalist married to a girl from a fine family, he has children and a good job, he is the kind of son who fills his mother with pride.

"But fiction is only a temporary remedy, for though it consoles Edith and takes her mind off her troubles, it removes her from life's struggle, isolating her in a purely mental world. Relationships with her friends are weakened or ended; she loses her job and becomes destitute. Her death seems melodramatic, but from a symbolic point of view it has coherence; Edith moves physically to the place she had already occupied in life: unreality.

"The novel is constructed with deceptive simplicity, beneath which a dramatic context is depicted: the merciless struggle between reality and desire, those sisters who are bitter enemies separated by impassable distances except in the miraculous recesses of the human spirit."

Don Rigoberto felt his teeth chatter, his palms perspire. Now he remembered the insignificant novel and the reason for his reflections. Would he, like Edith, eventually slide into ruin because he abused fantasy? But behind this melancholy hypothesis, the fragrant rose of the panties remained at the center of his consciousness. What had happened to Don Nepomuceno? What did he do and what dilemmas did he encounter after his telephone conversation with the young Rigoberto? Had he followed his student's advice?

He began to tiptoe up the stairs in a relative darkness that permitted him to see bookshelves and the edges of furniture. On the second step he paused, leaned forward, grasped the precious object with stiff fingers—was it silk? linen?—brought it up to his face and buried his nose in it, like a small animal deciding if the strange object was edible. He closed his eyes and kissed it, feeling the beginnings of a vertigo that made him reel as he held on to the banister. He was determined, he would do it. He continued up the stairs, still on tiptoe, the panties in his hand, fearful he would be found out, as if a noise—the steps groaned slightly—might break the spell. His heart was pounding so hard that it crossed his mind how incredibly inopportune and stupid it would be if he were to suffer a heart attack just then. No, it was not an attack; it was curiosity and the sensation (unknown in his life) of tasting forbidden fruit that made his blood race through his veins. He had reached the hall, he was at the jurist's door. He pressed his jaw with both hands, because his grotesquely chattering teeth would make a terrible impression on his hostess. Steeling himself ("summoning all his courage" whispered Don Rigoberto, trembling and dripping with perspiration) he knocked, very slowly. The door was ajar and it opened with a hospitable creak.

What the venerable professor of the Philosophy of Law saw from the carpeted threshold changed his ideas about the world, the human race—

most certainly the law—and forced a moan of desperate pleasure from Don Rigoberto. A gold and indigo light (Van Gogh? Botticelli? Some Expressionist like Emil Nolde?) radiating from a round yellow moon in the starry Virginia sky fell, as if arranged by a demanding set designer or a skillful lighting technician, directly on the bed, its sole purpose to highlight the naked body of Dr. Lucrecia. Who could have imagined that the severe clothing she wore at her professor's lectern, those tailored suits in which she expounded her arguments and made her motions at conferences, the waterproof capes she wrapped around herself in winter, concealed a body that would have been claimed by Praxiteles for its harmony, and Renoir for the sumptuous modeling of the flesh. She lay facedown, her head resting on her crossed arms, in a long, extended pose, but it was not her shoulders, morbid arms ("morbid in the Italian sense of the word," Don Rigoberto specified, since he had no liking for the macabre but did relish softness), or curved back that drew the eyes of a dumbfounded Don Nepomuceno like a magnet. Not even her ample milky thighs or small rosy-soled feet. It was those firm spheres which, with a happy lack of shame, rose prominently like twin mountaintops ("the mist-shrouded peaks of mountain ranges in Japanese prints of the Meiji period," Don Rigoberto made the association with satisfaction). But Rubens, Titian, Courbet, Ingres, Urculo, and a half-dozen other master painters of feminine posteriors also seemed to have banded together to give reality, consistency, abundance, and, at the same time, softness, delicacy, spirit, and a sensual vibration to that rump whose whiteness seemed opalescent in the semidarkness. Incapable of restraining himself, not knowing what he was doing, the bedazzled ("corrupted forever after?") Don Nepomuceno took two steps and, when he reached the bed, fell to his knees. The old floorboards groaned.

"Excuse me, Doctor, I found something of yours on the stairs," he stammered, feeling streams of saliva flowing out of the corners of his mouth.

He spoke so softly that not even he could hear what he was saying, or perhaps he moved his lips without making a sound. Neither his voice nor his presence had disturbed the jurist. She breathed quietly, rhythmically, in innocent sleep. But that pose, the fact that she was naked and had left her bedroom door open, had loosened her hair—black, straight, long—so that it swept across her shoulders and back, its blue-tinged darkness contrasting with the whiteness of her skin, could that be innocent? "No, no" was the judgment of Don Rigoberto. "No, no," echoed the stupefied professor, moving his eyes along the undulating surface that, at her flanks, sank and rose like a stormy sea of feminine flesh glorified by moonlight ("more like the oily light and shadow of Titian's bodies," Don Rigoberto amended) a few centimeters from his stunned face: Not innocent, not at all. I'm here because she planned it and brought me here.

And yet he could not derive from that theoretical conclusion sufficient strength to do what his reawakened instincts demanded: pass his fingertips along the satiny skin, rest his matrimonial lips on those hills and dales that he expected to be warm, fragrant, with a taste in which the sweet and salty coexisted but did not combine. Petrified with happiness, he could do nothing but look, look. After traveling back and forth many times between the head and feet of this miracle, passing over it again and again, his eyes stopped moving and rested, like the exquisite palate that does not need to taste any further after identifying the *ne plus ultra* of the wine cellar, on the independent spectacle of her spherical hindquarters. They stood out from the rest of her body like an emperor among his vassals, Zeus among the minor gods of Olympus. ("A happy union of nineteenth-century Courbet and the modern Urculo," Don Rigoberto ennobled the scene with references.) The eminent professor, overwhelmed by emotion, observed and adored the prodigy in silence. What was he saying to himself? He was repeating the line from Keats ("Beauty is truth, truth beauty"). What was he thinking? "And so these things do exist. Not only in evil thoughts, in art, in the fantasies of poets, but in real life. And so an ass like this is possible in flesh-and-blood reality, in women who inhabit the world of the living." Had he ejaculated yet? Was he about to befoul his shorts? Not yet, though the jurist was aware of new sensations in his groin, an awakening, a roused caterpillar stretching. Was he thinking anything else? This: "And where else would it be but between the legs and torso of my old and respected colleague, this good friend with whom I corresponded so often regarding abstruse philosophical-juridical, ethical-legal, historical-methodological issues?" How was it possible that never, until tonight, not in any of the forums, lectures, symposia, seminars they had both attended and where they had conversed, discussed, and argued, he had never even suspected that those boxy suits, shaggy coats, lined capes, ant-colored raincoats hid a splendor like this? Who could have imagined that this lucid mind, this Justinian intelligence, this legal encyclopedia also possessed a body so overwhelming in its form and abundance? For a moment he imagined—did she see him, perhaps?—that, indifferent to his presence, liberated in the abandon of Morpheus, those serene mountains of flesh released a joyful, muffled little wind that burst under his nose and filled his nostrils with a pungent aroma. It did not make him laugh, it did not make him uncomfortable (It did not excite him either, thought Don Rigoberto). He felt acknowledged, as if, in some way, for intricate reasons difficult to explain ("like the theories of Kelsen that he clarified so well for us" was his comparison), the little fart was a kind of acquiescence shared with him by the splendid body that displayed so intimate an intimacy, the useless gases expelled by an intestinal serpent whose hollows he imagined as pink, moist, free of dross, as delicate and well modeled as the untrammeled buttocks just millimeters from his nose.

And then, in terror, he realized that Doña Lucrecia was awake, for though she had not moved, he heard her say, "What are you doing here, Professor?"

She did not seem angry, much less frightened. The voice was hers, of course, but charged with additional warmth. Something languid, insinuating, a musical sensuality. In his embarrassment, the jurist managed to wonder how his old colleague could have undergone so many magical transformations in a single night.

"Forgive me, forgive me, Doctor. I implore you not to misinterpret my presence here. I can explain everything."

"Didn't the meal agree with you?" she asked reassuringly. She spoke with absolutely no irritation. "Would you like a glass of water and some bicarbonate?"

She turned her head slightly, and with her cheek still pillowed on her arm, her large eyes, shining through black strands of hair, observed him.

"I found something that belongs to you on the stairs, Doctor, and I came to give it to you," the professor mumbled. He was still kneeling, and now he became aware of a sharp pain in his knees. "I knocked, but you did not answer. And since the door was ajar, I ventured in. I did not mean to wake you. I beg you not to take it the wrong way."

She moved her head, nodding, forgiving him so gently, pitying his confusion. "Why are you crying, my dear friend? What's wrong?"

Don Nepomuceno, defenseless in the face of her fond deference, the caressing cadence of her words, the affection in those eyes gleaming in the shadows, broke down. What until then had been only great silent tears rolling down his cheeks turned into resounding sobs, wrenching sighs, a cataract of slobber and snot that he tried to contain with his hands—in his disordered mental state he could not find his handkerchief, or even the pocket where he kept his handkerchief—while, in a strangled voice, he opened his heart to her.

"Oh, Lucrecia, Lucrecia, forgive me, I cannot control myself. Don't look upon this as an insult. Quite the contrary. I had never imagined anything like this, anything so beautiful, I mean, anything as perfect as your body. You know how much I respect and admire you. Intellectually, academically, juridically. But this, tonight, seeing you like this, it is the best thing that has ever happened to me. I swear, Lucrecia. In exchange for this moment I would throw away all my degrees, the doctorates *honoris causa* that have been conferred upon me, my decorations and diplomas. ("If I weren't as old as I am, I would burn all my books and go to sit like a beggar at the door of your house"—Don Rigoberto read the poet Enrique Peña in his notebook—"Yes, my child, understand me: like a beggar at the door of your house.") I have never felt such great happiness, Lucrecia. Seeing you like this, without clothes, like Ulysses looking at Nausicaa, is the greatest prize, a glory I don't believe I deserve. I am so moved, so overwhelmed. I am crying because I am moved, because I am grateful. Don't find me contemptible, Lucrecia."

Instead of relieving him, his words moved him even more, and now his sobs were choking him. He rested his head on the edge of the bed and continued to cry, still on his knees, sighing, feeling sad and happy, afflicted and fortunate. "Forgive me, forgive me," he stammered. Until, seconds or hours later—his body arched as if he were a cat—he felt Lucrecia's hand on his head. Her fingers stroked his gray hair, consoling him, accompanying him. With a cool caress her voice also soothed the raw wound in his soul.

"Calm yourself, Rigoberto. Don't cry anymore, my love, my heart. It's over, it's finished now, nothing has changed. Haven't you done as you wished? You came in, you saw me, you came near, you wept, I forgave you. Can I ever be angry with you? Dry your tears, sneeze, go to sleep. Hush, baby, hush."

Down below, the sea crashed against the cliffs of Barranco and Mira-flores, and a thick cover of clouds hid the stars and moon in the sky over Lima. But the night was coming to an end. Day would break any moment now. One day less. One day more.

What Is Forbidden to Beauty

You will never see a painting by Andy Warhol or Frida Kahlo, or applaud a political speech, or permit the skin on your elbows or knees to roughen, or the soles of your feet to grow hard.

You will never listen to a composition by Luigi Nono or a protest song by Mercedes Sosa, or see a film by Oliver Stone, or chew directly on the leaves of an artichoke.

You will never scrape your knees or cut your hair or have blackheads, dental caries, conjunctivitis, (much less) hemorrhoids.

You will never walk barefoot on asphalt, stone, gravel, flagstone, hard rubber, corrugated iron, slate, or metal, and you will never kneel on a surface that is not as spongy as a sweet bun (before toasting).

You will never use the words telluric, half-breed, consciousness-raising, visualize, statist, pips, rinds, or societal.

You will never own a hamster or gargle or wear dentures or play bridge or wear a hat or a beret or coil your hair in a bun.

You will never bloat with gas, or curse, or dance to rock-and-roll.

You will never die.

VII

Egon Schiele's Thumb

"All of Egon Schiele's girls are skinny and bony and look very pretty to me," said Fonchito. "But you're plump, and I think you're very pretty too. Can you explain the contradiction, Stepmamá?"

"Are you calling me fat?" Doña Lucrecia became livid.

She had been distracted, hearing the boy's voice as if it were background noise, thinking about the anonymous letters—seven in just ten days—and the letter she had written to Rigoberto the night before, which was now in the pocket of her robe. She recalled only that Fonchito had begun to talk and talk, about Egon Schiele, as usual, until "plump" had caught her attention.

"Not fat, no. I said plump, Stepmamá," he apologized, gesturing.

"It's your papá's fault I'm like this," she complained, looking at herself. "I was very slender when we married. But Rigoberto had the notion that being fashionably slim destroys a woman's body, that the great tradition in beauty is abundance. That's what he called it: 'the abundant form.' To make him happy I put on weight. And I haven't been thin since."

"You look terrific just the way you are, I swear, Stepmamá," Fonchito continued to apologize. "I said what I did about Egon Schiele's skinny girls because don't you think it's odd for me to like them and like you too when you're at least twice their size?"

No, he couldn't be the author. The anonymous letters complimented her figure, and in one of them, entitled "In Praise of the Beloved's Body,"

159

each part mentioned—head, shoulders, waist, breasts, belly, thighs, legs, ankles, feet—was accompanied by a reference to a poem or emblematic painting. The invisible lover of her abundant forms could only be Rigoberto. ("That man is crazy about you," Justiniana declared after reading it. "How well he knows your body, Señora! It must be Don Rigoberto. Where would Fonchito find those words no matter how grown-up he is? Though he knows you pretty well too, doesn't he?")

"Why are you so quiet? Why aren't you talking to me? You look at me as if you didn't see me. You're acting very strange today, Stepmamá."

"It's those letters. I can't get them out of my head, Fonchito. You have your obsession with Egon Schiele, and now I have mine: those damned letters. I spend the whole day waiting for them, reading them, remembering them."

"But why damned, Stepmamá? Do they insult you or say ugly things?"

"Because they're not signed. And because sometimes I think a phantom is sending them, not your papá."

"You know very well they're from him. Everything's working out perfectly, Stepmamá. Don't worry. You'll make up with him soon, you'll see."

The reconciliation of Doña Lucrecia and Don Rigoberto had become the boy's second obsession. He spoke of it with so much certainty that his stepmother no longer had the heart to argue or to tell him it was nothing but another daydream of the inveterate daydreamer he had become. Had she been right to show him the anonymous letters? Some were so bold in their intimate references that after reading them she promised herself: "I certainly won't let him see this one." And each time she did, watching his reaction to find out if some gesture betrayed him. But no. Each time he reacted with the same surprise, the same excitement, and he always came to the same conclusion: the letter was from his papá, one more proof he wasn't angry with her anymore. She noticed that now Fonchito also seemed distracted, far removed from the dining alcove and the Olivar, caught up in some memory. He was looking at his hands, bringing them close to his eyes. He clasped them, extended them, spread his fingers, hid the thumb, crossed and uncrossed them in unusual positions, as if projecting figures on the wall with his hands. But on this spring afternoon Fonchito was not trying to create shadow figures; he was scrutinizing his fingers like an entomologist examining an unknown species through a magnifying glass.

"Can I ask what you're doing?"

The boy's expression did not change, and he continued his movements as he replied with another question: "Do you think my hands are deformed, Stepmamá?"

What was the little devil up to today?

"Let's see, let's have a look at them," she said, playing at being a specialist. "Put them here."

Fonchito wasn't playing. He was very serious as he stood, walked over to her, and placed both hands on her extended palms. At the touch of smooth, soft skin, the fragile bones in his fingers, Doña Lucrecia felt a shiver run down her spine. He had delicate hands, thin pointed fingers, pale pink fingernails, neatly trimmed. But there were ink or charcoal stains on the fingertips. She pretended to subject his hands to a clinical examination as she stroked them.

"They're not at all deformed," she declared at last. "Though a little soap and water wouldn't hurt."

"What a shame," the boy said without a trace of humor, pulling his hands away from Doña Lucrecia's. "It means I don't resemble him at all as far as that's concerned."

"There it is. It was bound to happen." The game they played every afternoon.

"Explain what you mean."

The boy quickly complied. Hadn't she noticed that hands were Egon Schiele's mania? His hands and the hands of girls and men he painted. If not, she ought to now. And in the blink of an eye Doña Lucrecia had a book of reproductions on her knees. Did she see how much Egon Schiele hated thumbs?

"Thumbs?" and Doña Lucrecia began to laugh.

"Look at his portraits. The one of Arthur Roessler, for example," the boy insisted passionately. "Or this one: the *Double Portrait of Inspector General Heinrich Benesch and His Son Otto*; the one of Enrich Lederer; his self-portraits. He shows only four fingers. The thumb is always out of sight."

Why would that be? Why did he hide it? Was it because the thumb is the ugliest finger on the hand? Did he prefer even numbers and think that odd numbers brought bad luck? Was his own thumb disfigured, did it embarrass him? Something was wrong with his hands; if not, why, when he had his picture taken, did he conceal his hands in his pockets or twist them into such ridiculous poses, curling the fingers like a witch's, placing them right in front of the camera, or raising them over his head as if he wanted to let them fly away? His hands, the men's hands, the girls' hands. Hadn't she noticed? Those naked girls with their well-formed little bodies, wasn't it inconceivable for them to have masculine hands with rough bony knuckles? For example, this engraving from 1910: *Standing Nude with Black Hair*, weren't those mannish hands with their square-cut fingernails out of place, weren't they identical to the ones Egon painted in his self-portraits? Hadn't he done the same thing with almost all the women he painted? For example, *Standing Nude*, 1913. Fonchito took a breath. "I mean, he was Narcissus, just like you said. He always painted his own hands, even if the person in the painting was someone else, another man or a woman."

"Did you find this out on your own? Or did you read it somewhere?" Doña Lucrecia was disconcerted. She leafed through the book, and what she saw confirmed what Fonchito said.

"Anybody who looks at his pictures a lot can see it," the boy said with a shrug, not giving the matter much importance. "Doesn't my papá say that if an artist doesn't develop motifs he never becomes inspired? That's why I always pay attention to the manias that painters reflect in their pictures. Egon Schiele had three: he put the same out-of-proportion hands, with the thumb missing, on all his figures. He had the girls and men show their things by lifting their skirts and spreading their legs. And third, in his self-portraits, he shows his own hands in forced positions that are very conspicuous."

"All right, all right, if you wanted to leave me dumbfounded, you've succeeded. Do you know something, Fonchito? You certainly have your motif. If your papá's theory is correct, you already have one of the requirements for being inspired."

"All I need to do is to paint the pictures," he said with a laugh. He lay down again and resumed looking at his hands. He moved them about, imitating the extravagant poses displayed in Schiele's pictures and photographs. Doña Lucrecia was amused as she observed his pantomime. And suddenly she came to a decision: "I'm going to read him my letter and see what he says." Besides, if she read it aloud she would know if what she had written was all right, could decide if she should send it to Rigoberto or tear it up. But when she was about to begin, she lost her courage. Instead, she said, "It worries me that all you think of night and day is Schiele." The boy stopped playing with his hands. "I'm saying this with all the affection

I have for you. At first I thought it was nice for you to like his pictures so much and identify with him. But because you try to resemble him in everything, you're not being yourself anymore."

"But I am him, Stepmamá. Even though you take it as a joke, it's true. I feel that I'm him."

He smiled to reassure her. "Wait a minute," he murmured, and as he stood, he picked up the book of reproductions, turned the pages as he looked for something, and placed the open book on her knees again. Doña Lucrecia saw a plate in color; against an ocher background a sinuous woman wore a carnival costume with zigzag stripes of green, red, yellow, and black. Her dark hair was under a kind of turban, she was barefoot, she looked out with a languid sadness in her large dark eyes, and her hands were raised over her head as if she were about to play castanets.

"Looking at that picture, I knew," she heard Fonchito say with utter seriousness. "I knew I was him."

She tried to laugh but failed. What was the kid up to? Trying to frighten her? He plays with me like a little kitten with a big mouse, she thought.

"Is that so? And what in this picture revealed to you that you're the reincarnation of Egon Schiele?"

"You still don't understand, Stepmamá," Fonchito said with a laugh. "Look again, at each part. And you'll see that even though he painted it in his studio in Vienna in 1914, Peru is here in this woman. Repeated five times."

Señora Lucrecia examined the image again. From top to bottom. From bottom to top. Finally she noticed that on the multicolored clown costume of the barefoot model, there were five minute figures, at the height of both arms, on her right side, on her leg, and on the hem of her skirt. She raised the book to her eyes and examined the figures calmly. Well, it was true. They did look like Indian women. They were dressed like campesinas from Cuzco.

"That's what they are, little Indian women from the Andes," said Fonchito, reading her thoughts. "Do you see? Peru is there in Egon Schiele's paintings. That's how I knew. For me, it was a message."

He continued speaking, showing off a prodigious knowledge of the painter's life and work that left Doña Lucrecia with the impression of omniscience, and the suspicion of a scheme, a feverish ambush. "There's an explanation, Stepmamá. The lady was named Frederike María Beer. She was the only person whose portrait was painted by the two greatest painters in Vienna at the time: Schiele and Klimt. The daughter of a very wealthy cabaret owner, she had been a great lady who helped artists and found buyers for their work. A little while before Schiele painted her, she traveled to Bolivia and Peru and brought home those little Indian rag dolls that she probably bought at some fair in Cuzco or La Paz. And Egon Schiele had the idea of painting them into her dress. I mean, it was no miracle that made five little Indian women appear in the painting. But, but . . ."

"But what?" Doña Lucrecia encouraged him, fascinated by Fonchito's story, hoping for a great revelation.

"But nothing," the boy added, with a weary gesture. "The Indians were placed there so that I would find them one day. Five little Peruvians in a painting by Schiele. Don't you see?"

"Did they start talking to you? Did they say that you painted them eighty years ago? That you've been reincarnated?"

"Well, if you're going to make fun of me, let's talk about something else, Stepmamá."

"I don't like to hear you talking nonsense," she said. "Or thinking nonsense, or believing nonsense. You are you, and Egon Schiele was Egon Schiele. You live here, in Lima, and he lived in Vienna at the beginning of the century. There's no such thing as reincarnation. So unless you want me to get angry, don't say stupid things anymore. Okay?"

The boy nodded reluctantly. His face looked very sad, but he did not dare to respond, because she had spoken with unusual severity. She tried to make peace.

"I want to read you something I've written," she said softly, taking the rough draft of the letter from her pocket.

"You've answered my papá?" The boy was overjoyed and sat on the floor, craning his head forward.

Yes, last night. She didn't know yet if she would send it. She couldn't bear any more. Seven, that's a lot of anonymous letters. And the writer was Rigoberto. Who else could it be? Who else could speak to her in that familiar, exalted way? Who else knew her so well? She had decided to end the farce. She wanted to know what he thought of her letter.

"Read it to me right now, Stepmamá," the boy said impatiently. His eyes were shining and his face revealed enormous curiosity, as well as a hint, a hint of—Doña Lucrecia searched for the words—mischievous, even wicked, delight. Clearing her throat before she began, and not looking up until she had finished, Doña Lucrecia read:

Darling:

I've resisted the temptation of writing to you ever since I learned you were the author of the ardent letters that for the past two weeks have filled my house with flaming joy, nostalgia, and hope, and my heart and soul with the sweet fire that consumes without burning, the fire of love and desire joined in happy wedlock.

Why would you sign letters that you alone could write? Who has studied me, shaped me, invented me as you have? Who but you could speak of the little red marks under my arms, the pink tracery of nerves in the hidden spaces between my toes, that "puckered little mouth, bluish-gray, surrounded by a circle in miniature of happily wrinkled flesh to which one ascends by scaling the smooth marble columns of your legs"? Only you, my love.

From the first lines of the first letter, I knew it was you. And for that reason, before I finished reading it, I obeyed your instructions. I took off my clothes and posed for you, in front of the mirror, imitating Klimt's Danaë. *And once again, as on so many nights so profoundly missed in my present solitude, I soared with you through the realms of fantasy we explored together during the years we shared, years that are now, for me, a spring of consolation and life from which I drink again in memory in order to endure the empty routine that has replaced the adventure and plenitude I enjoyed at your side.*

To the best of my ability I have followed every detail of the demands—no, the suggestions and requests—in your seven letters. I have dressed and undressed, put on costumes and masks, lain on my back, bent, straightened, squatted, and incarnated—body and soul—all the whims in your letters, for what greater pleasure do I have than to please you? For you, because of you, I have been Messalina and Leda, Mary Magdalene and Salome, Diana with her bow and arrows, the Naked Maja, chaste Susanna surprised by the lecherous elders, and, in the Turkish bath, the odalisque of Ingres. I have made love to Mars, Nebuchadnezzar, Sardanapalus, Napoleon, swans, satyrs, slaves both male and female; I have emerged from the sea like a siren and assuaged and inflamed the desires of Ulysses. I have been a marquise by Watteau, a nymph by Titian, a Virgin by Murillo, a Madonna by Piero della Francesca, a geisha by Fujita, a poor wretch by Toulouse-Lautrec. It was difficult for me to go up on my toes like a ballerina by Degas, and believe me, in order not to cheat you, I even attempted, at the cost of many muscle cramps, to turn myself into what you call the voluptuous Cubist cube by Juan Gris.

Playing with you again, even at a distance, has been good for me, and bad for me. Once more I felt that I was yours and you were mine. But when the game was over, my solitude intensified and I grew even sadder. Have we lost everything forever?

Since receiving the first letter, I have lived for the next one, consumed by doubts, attempting to guess your intentions. Did you want an answer? Or does sending letters without a signature mean that you do not wish to engage in dialogue but want me only to listen to your monologue? Last night, however, after obediently playing the industrious housewife by Vermeer, I decided to respond. Something in the dark depths of my being, something that you alone have touched, demanded that I set pen to paper. Have I done the right thing? Have I broken the unwritten law that prohibits the figure in a portrait from stepping out of the painting and speaking to the painter?

You, my darling, know the answer. Tell me what it is.

"Golly, what a letter," said Fonchito. His enthusiasm seemed quite sincere. "Stepmamá, you love my papá very much!"

He was flushed and radiant, and, Doña Lucrecia also noticed—for the first time—even confused.

"I've never stopped loving him. Not even when what happened happened."

Fonchito immediately assumed the blank amnesiac expression that emptied his eyes, as he did whenever Doña Lucrecia referred in some way to that adventure. But she watched the pink drain from the boy's cheeks, replaced by a pearly whiteness.

"Because even though you and I wish it hadn't, and even though we never talk about it, what happened did happen. It can't be erased," said Doña Lucrecia, trying to look into his eyes. "And even though you stare at me as if you didn't know what I was talking about, you remember everything as well as I do. And must regret it even more."

She could not go on. Fonchito had begun to look at his hands again, moving them, imitating the exaggerated positions of Egon Schiele's figures: holding them rigidly parallel at shoulder height, the thumbs hidden as if they had been amputated, or placing them over his head and well forward, as if he had just hurled a lance. Doña Lucrecia finally started to laugh.

"You're not a devil, you're a clown," she exclaimed. "You ought to go into the theater."

The boy laughed too, stretching, making faces, constantly playing with his hands. And without stopping any of his tricks, he surprised Doña Lucrecia with this remark: "Did you write the letter in a sappy style on pur-

166

pose? Do you think, like my papá, that sappiness is inseparable from love?"

"I wrote it imitating your papá's style," said Doña Lucrecia. "Exaggerating, trying to be solemn, high-toned, elevated. He likes that. Do you think it's very sappy?"

"He's going to love it," Fonchito assured her, nodding several times. "He'll read it and reread it, over and over again, locked away in his study. You're not planning to sign it, are you, Stepmamá?"

In fact, she hadn't thought about it.

"Should I send it to him anonymously?"

"Of course, Stepmamá," the boy declared emphatically. "You have to play his game."

Perhaps he was right. If he had sent letters without signing them, why shouldn't she?

"You know all the tricks, kid," she said, almost to herself. "Yes, that's a good idea. I won't sign it. But he'll know exactly who wrote it."

Fonchito pretended to applaud. He had stood and was getting ready to leave. Today there had been no toasted sweet buns because Justiniana had gone out. As always, he picked up the book of reproductions and put it in his bag, buttoned the gray shirt of his uniform and straightened his tie, observed by Lucrecia, who was amused to see him repeat the same actions every afternoon when he arrived and when he left. But now, unlike other times when he would say only, "*Ciao*, Stepmamá," he sat very close to her on the sofa.

"I'd like to ask you something before I go. But I feel embarrassed."

He was speaking in the thin, sweet, timid little voice he used when he wanted to awaken her benevolence or her compassion. And though Doña Lucrecia never lost the suspicion that it was pure farce, sooner or later it always did awaken her benevolence or her compassion.

"Nothing embarrasses you, so don't tell me any stories or play the innocent," she said, giving the lie to her harsh words with a caress and a tug on his ear. "Go on, ask."

The boy turned and threw his arms around her neck. He buried his face in her shoulder.

"If I look at you I won't be able to," he whispered, lowering his voice into a barely audible murmur. "That puckered little mouth surrounded by wrinkles, in your letter, it's not this one, is it, Stepmamá?"

Doña Lucrecia felt his cheek move away from hers, felt two thin lips travel down her face and rest against her own. Cold at first, they instantly came to life. She felt their pressure, felt them kissing her. She closed her eyes and opened her mouth: a wet little viper came to visit, strolled across her gums and palate, and ensnared her tongue. For a time she was out of time, blind, transformed into sensation, annihilated, transported, doing nothing, thinking nothing. But when she raised her arms to clasp Fonchito to her, the boy, in one of those sudden changes of mood that were his most distinctive trait, released her and moved away. Now he was leaving, waving goodbye. His expression was quite natural.

"If you like, write out a clean copy of your anonymous letter and put it in an envelope," he said from the door. "Give it to me tomorrow and I'll slip it into the mailbox at home without my papá seeing me. *Ciao,* Stepmamá."

No Cattail Boat or Pucará Bull

I understand that the sight of the flag waving in the wind makes your heart beat faster, that the music and words of the national anthem produce the prickling in the veins and bristling of hairs called emotion. You do not associate the word "patria," or "fatherland" (which you always capitalize), with the irreverent verses of the young Pablo Neruda:

> *Patria,*
> *a melancholy word,*
> *like thermometer or elevator*

or with Dr. Johnson's lethal sentence ("Patriotism is the last refuge of a scoundrel") but with heroic cavalry charges, swords embedded in the bosoms of enemy uniforms, bugle calls, the sound of guns and cannon fire not caused by bottles of champagne. You belong, apparently, to the mass of males and females who look with respect upon the statues of leaders that adorn public squares, deplore the fact that pigeons shit on them, and are capable of rising before dawn and waiting for hours on national holidays so you'll find a good spot on the Campo de Marte for the armed forces parade, a sight that inspires you to appreciative comments sizzling with the words "martial," "patriotic," and "virile." Sir, madam: crouching inside you is a rabid beast that constitutes a danger to humanity.

You are living ballast that has dragged down civilization since the time of the tattooed, pierced cannibal with his phallic sheath, the pre-rational magician who stamped on the ground to bring rain and devoured the heart of his adversary to steal his power. In fact, behind your speeches and banners exalting this piece of geography blemished with boundary stones and arbitrary borders in which you see the personification of a superior form of history and social metaphysics, there is only an astute *aggiornamento* of the ancient primitive fear of separating from the tribe, of no longer being part of the mass, of becoming an individual, and a nostalgic longing for that ancestor for whom the world began and ended within the boundaries of the familiar, the clearing in the forest, the dark cave, the high plateau, the tiny enclave where sharing language, magic, confusion, customs, and, above all, ignorance and fear with his group gave him courage and made him feel protected against thunder, lightning, beasts, and the other tribes of this planet. Though centuries have passed since those distant times, and because you wear a jacket and tie or put on a tight skirt and have your face-lifts in Miami, you believe yourself far superior to that ancestor wearing a tree-bark loincloth and adornments dangling from lips and nose, you are he and she is you. The umbilical cord that connects you across the centuries is called terror of the unknown, hatred for what is different, rejection of adventure, panic at the thought of freedom and the responsibility it brings to invent yourself each day, a vocation for servitude to the routine and the gregarious, a refusal to decollectivize so that you will not be obliged to face the daily challenge of individual sovereignty. In ancient times, the defenseless eater of human flesh, submerged in metaphysical and physical ignorance regarding everything that happened around him, had a certain justification for refusing to be independent, creative, and free; in our day, when everything and more that needs to be known is already known, there is no valid reason for insisting on being a slave and an irrational being. You may think this judgment severe, even extremist, when applied to something that for you is simply a virtuous, idealistic feeling of solidarity and love for one's native land and one's memories ("the land and its dead," according to the French anthropoid Maurice Barrès), the frame of environmental and cultural references without which a human being feels empty. I assure you this may be one side of the patriotic coin, but the other side of the exaltation of one's own is the denigration of what belongs to someone else, the desire to humiliate and defeat others, those who are different from you because they have another skin color, another language, another god, even another way of dressing, another diet.

Patriotism, which actually seems to be a benevolent form of national-ism—for "patria" seems more ancient, deep-rooted, and respectable than "nation," that ridiculous politico-administrative contrivance manufactured by statists greedy for power and intellectuals in search of a master, that is, a Maecenas, that is, a pair of prebendal tits to suck on—is a dangerous but effective excuse for the countless wars that have devastated the planet, for despotic impulses that have sanctified the domination of the weak by the strong, and for an egalitarian smoke screen whose noxious fumes, indifferent to human beings, clone them and impose on them, under the guise of something essential and irremediable, the most accidental of common de-nominators: one's place of birth. Behind patriotism and nationalism there always burns the malignant fiction of collectivist identity, that ontological barbed wire which attempts to congregate "Peruvians," "Spaniards," "French," "Chinese," et cetera, in inescapable and unmistakable fraternity. You and I know that these categories are simply abject lies that throw a mantle of oblivion over countless diversities and incompatibilities, and at-tempt to abolish centuries of history and return civilization to those barbaric times preceding the creation of individuality, not to mention rationality and freedom: three things that are inseparable, make no mistake.

And therefore, when anyone says in my hearing, "the Chinese," "the blacks," "the Peruvians," "the French," "women," or any similar expression proposing to define human beings by membership in a collective of any kind rather than viewing that as a passing circumstance, I want to pull out a pistol—bang bang—and fire. (This is a figure of speech, of course; I've never held a weapon in my hand and never will, and have shot off nothing but semen, ejaculations to which I make claim with patriotic pride.) My individualism does not lead me, obviously, to a praise of the sexual soliloquy as the most perfect form of pleasure; in this area I am inclined toward dialogues between two persons, three at most, and of course, I declare myself a bitter enemy of the promiscuous *partouse*, which, in the realm of the bed and fornication, is tantamount to political and social collectivism. Unless the sexual monologue is practiced when one is not alone—in which case it becomes a highly baroque dialogue—as illustrated in the small wa-tercolor and charcoal sketch by Picasso (1902–1903) that you may view at the Picasso Museum in Barcelona, in which Sr. D. Ángel Fernández de Soto, fully dressed and smoking a pipe, and his distinguished wife, naked except for stockings and shoes, drinking a glass of champagne and sitting on her spouse's knees, engage in reciprocal masturbation; a picture, incidentally, that with no desire to offend anyone (least of all Picasso), I consider superior to *Guernica* and *Les Demoiselles d'Avignon*.

(If you think this letter is beginning to show signs of incoherence, think of Valéry's Monsieur Teste: "The incoherence of a discourse depends on the listener. The spirit apparently is not conceived in a way that allows it to be incoherent with itself.")

Do you want to know the origin of the bilious antipatriotic outburst in this letter? A speech by the President of the Republic, reported this morning in the press, according to which he stated, as he was opening the Handicrafts Fair, that Peruvians have the patriotic obligation to admire the work of anonymous artisans who, centuries ago, modeled the clay vessels of Chavín, wove and dyed the fabrics of Paracas, or threaded together the feather capes of Nasca, the *queros* of Cuzco; as well as contemporary makers of Ayacuchan altarpieces, little bulls from Pucará, figures of the Infant Jesus, rugs from San Pedro de Cajas, cattail boats from Lake Titicaca, tiny mirrors from Cajamarca, because—I quote the Commander-in-Chief—"crafts are popular art *par excellence*, the supreme display of a people's creativity and artistic skill, one of the great symbols and manifestations of the Fatherland, and none of the objects bears the individual signature of the artisan who made it because all of them bear the signature of the collectivity, of nationality."

If you are a man or woman of taste—that is, a lover of precision—you probably smiled at this artisanal-patriotic diarrhea from our Head of State. As for me, I find it, as you do, not only witless and vulgar but instructive as well. Now I know why I despise all the crafts of the world in general, and those of "my country" (I use the formula so that we understand each other) in particular. Now I know why my house has not seen and never will see a Peruvian pot, or a Venetian mask, or a Russian *matriuska*, or a little Dutch doll with braids and wooden shoes, or a miniature wooden bull, or a Gypsy girl dancing flamenco, or an Indonesian puppet with articulated joints, or a toy samurai, or an Ayacuchan altarpiece, or a Bolivian devil, or any figure or object of clay, wood, porcelain, stone, cloth, or bread manufactured serially, generically, and anonymously, usurping, despite the hypocritical modesty of calling itself popular art, the very nature of an artistic object, something that is the absolute domain of the private sphere, an expression of total individuality, and, consequently, the refutation and rejection of the abstract, the generic, everything that aspires to justify itself, directly or indirectly, in the name of an allegedly "social" lineage. Patriot, there is no impersonal art (and please don't talk to me about Gothic cathedrals). Crafts are a primitive, amorphous, fetal expression of what one day—when particular individuals separated from the mass begin to put a personal stamp on these objects and pour into them an untransferable intimacy—may reach the category of art. That crafts flourish, prosper, and reign in a "nation" should not make anyone proud, least of all so-called patriots. For flourishing handicrafts—that manifestation of the generic—is a sign of backwardness or regression, an unconscious desire not to progress through a devastating whirlwind of frontiers, picturesque customs, local color, provincial differences, rustic spirit, toward civilization. I know that you, Señora Patriot, Señor Patriot, hate civilization, if not the word itself then its devastating content. That is your right. It is also my right to love and defend it against all odds, knowing that the battle is difficult and that I may find myself—the indications are countless—in the army of the defeated. It does not matter. This is the only form of heroism permitted to those of us who oppose obligatory heroism: to die signing our first and last names, to have a personal death.

Let me say it, once and for all, and horrify you: the only "patria" I revere is the bed occupied by my wife, Lucrecia ("Noble lady, let your light, / Conquer my sightless, gloomy night," Fray Luis de León *dixit*), her splendid body the only flag or banner capable of drawing me into fearful combat, and the only anthem that can move me to tears are the sounds emitted by that beloved flesh, her voice, her laugh, her weeping, her sighs, and, of course (cover your ears and nose), her hiccups, belches, farts, and sneezes. Can I or can I not be considered a true patriot, *in my fashion*?

Damned Onetti! Blessed Onetti

Don Rigoberto awoke weeping (recently this had been happening fairly often). He had moved from sleep to wakefulness; in the dark his mind recognized the objects in his bedroom; his ears, the monotonous sea; his nostrils and the pores of his skin, the corrosive damp. But the horrible image, risen from some remote hiding place, was still there, swimming on the surface of his imagination, tormenting him just as it had a few moments earlier in the somnolence of his nightmare. "Stop crying, stupid." But the tears ran down his cheeks and he sobbed, seized with fear. What if it were telepathy? What if he had received a message? If, in fact, yesterday, that very afternoon, like a worm at the heart of the apple, they had discovered the lump in her breast that foretold catastrophe and Lucrecia had immediately thought of him, trusted in him, turned to him to share her sorrow and anguish? It had been a call *in extremis*. The day of the surgery had been set. "We caught it in time," the doctor declared, "on the condition we remove the breast, perhaps both breasts, immediately. I can almost, almost put my hand to the fire and say with certainty: it has not yet metastasized. On the condition we operate within a few hours, you will survive." The miserable wretch had begun to sharpen his scalpel, a glint of sadistic pleasure in his eyes. And at that instant Lucrecia thought of him, fervently desired to speak to him, to tell him, to be listened to and consoled by him, to have him at her side. "My God, I will crawl like a worm to her feet and beg her forgiveness." Don Rigoberto shuddered.

The image of Lucrecia lying on an operating table, subjected to that monstrous mutilation, caused another sharp stab of anguish. Closing his eyes, holding his breath, he recalled her firm, robust, identical breasts, the dark corollas with their granulate skin, the nipples, wooed and moistened by his lips, gallantly, defiantly standing erect at the hour of love. How many minutes, hours, had he spent contemplating them, weighing them, kissing them, licking them, toying with them, caressing them, fantasizing that he had been transformed into a Lilliputian who scaled those rosy hills to reach the high tower at the summit, or into a newborn who, sucking the white sap of life, received from those breasts his first lessons in pleasure when barely out of the womb. He recalled how, on certain Sundays, he would sit on the wooden bench in the bathroom to watch Lucrecia in the tub, submerged in bubbles. She would wrap a towel around her head like a turban and proceed with her toilette, very conscientiously, granting him an occasional benevolent smile as she washed her body with the large yellow sponge that she soaked in the foamy water and passed over her shoulders, her back, her beautiful legs raised for a few seconds from the creamy depths. At those times it was her breasts that drew all his attention, attracted all the religious fervor of Don Rigoberto. They appeared on the surface of the water, the white dome and bluish nipples gleaming in the foaming bubbles, and from time to time, to please and reward him (the distracted caress of his mistress stroking the docile dog stretched at her feet, he thought, more calmly) Doña Lucrecia would hold them and, on the pretext of soaping and rinsing them a little more, caress them with the sponge. They were beautiful, they were perfect. Their roundness, firmness, and warmth would fulfill all the desires of a lustful god. "Now pass me the towel, be my valet," she would say as she stood and rinsed her body with the hand shower. "If you're very good, perhaps I'll allow you to dry my back." Her breasts were there, glowing in the darkness of his room as if illuminating his solitude. Could a villainous cancer savage those creatures that ennobled the condition of women, justified their deification by the troubadours, vindicated the Marian cult? Don Rigoberto felt his earlier despair turn to fury, a feeling of savage rebellion against the disease.

And then he remembered. "Damned Onetti!" He burst into laughter. "Damned novel! Damned Santa María! Damned Gertrudis!" (Was that the character's name? Gertrudis? Yes, that was it.) That's where his nightmare came from, it had nothing to do with telepathy. He continued to laugh; he was liberated, excited, ecstatic. He decided, for a few moments, to believe in God (in one of his notebooks he had transcribed Quevedo's sentence from *El Buscón*: "He was one of those men who believed in God out of courtesy") in order to give thanks to someone because Lucrecia's beloved breasts were still intact, safe from the ravages of cancer, and because the nightmare had been no more than a reminiscence of a novel whose terrible beginning had shaken him with horror during the first months of his marriage to Lucrecia, filling him with the fear that one day his bride's delicious sweet breasts might fall victim to a surgical onslaught (the phrase appeared in his memory with all its obscene euphony: "ablation of the mammary") similar to the one described, invented, rather, in the opening pages by Brausen, the narrator of the unsettling novel by that damned Onetti. "Thank you, God, for making it not true, for keeping her breasts safe and sound," he prayed. And without putting on his slippers or robe he stumbled through the dark to his study to look at his notebooks. He was sure he had left some testimony to having read the disturbing novel that—why?—had risen from the depths of his unconscious to trouble his sleep tonight.

Damned Onetti! Uruguayan? Argentine? From the Río de la Plata region in any case. How he had made him suffer. What curious paths memory took, what capricious curves, baroque zigzags, incomprehensible hiatuses. Why now, tonight, had the fiction come to mind after ten years when he had probably not thought of it even once? With the lamp in his study projecting its golden light onto the table, he hurriedly leafed through the pile of notebooks which, he calculated, corresponded to the period when he had read *La vida breve*. Onetti's *vita brevis*. At the same time he continued to see, with increasing clarity, Lucrecia's breasts, snowy, high, warm, in their nocturnal bed, in their morning bath, peeking through the folds of her nightgown or her silk wrap or the deep plunge of her neckline. And coming back, returning with the memory of the ghastly impact the original image had made on him, was the story of *La vida breve* as clear and sharp as if he had only just read it. Why *La vida breve*? Why tonight?

He found it at last. Underlined, at the top of the page: *La vida breve*. And beneath that: "Superb architecture, highly refined, astute construction, prose and technique far superior to his impoverished characters and insipid plots." Not a very enthusiastic sentence. Why, then, the agitation when he remembered it? Simply because his unconscious mind had associated the surgically removed breast of Gertrudis in the novel with the longed-for breasts of Lucrecia? With great clarity he could see the first scene, the image that had come back and shaken him so. In his sordid apartment an ordinary clerk in a public-relations agency in Buenos Aires, Juan María Brausen, the narrator, agonizes over the idea of the mutilating breast surgery undergone by his wife, Gertrudis, the night before or that very morning, as he hears, on the other side of the thin wall, the stupid chatter of his new neighbor, Queca, a former or still-active whore, and vaguely imagines the plot for a movie that had been requested by his friend and superior, Julio Stein. Here were the dreadful citations: "I thought of how difficult it would be to look without disgust at the new scar Gertrudis would have on her chest, round, complex, with red or pink venations that time would perhaps transform into a pale confusion the same color as the other scar, thin, flat, as brisk as a signature, that Gertrudis had on her belly and that I had traced so often with the tip of my tongue." And this one, even more punishing, in which Brausen takes the bull by the horns and anticipates the only way he can really persuade his wife that the amputated breast did not matter: "Because the only convincing proof, the only source of joy and confidence I can give her is to turn on the light and raise and lower my face, rejuvenated by lust, over the mutilated breast, and kiss the spot and become wildly excited."

The man who writes sentences like these, sentences that after ten years can still make my hair stand on end and give me goose bumps like stalagmites, is a true creator, thought Don Rigoberto. He pictured himself naked, in bed with his wife, contemplating the almost invisible scar in the place where that goblet of warm flesh and silken curves had once reigned supreme, kissing it with exaggerated desire, pretending to an excitement, a passion he did not feel and would never feel again, and on his hair he recognized the hand—grateful? pitying?—of his beloved letting him know it was enough. There was no need to pretend. They, who each night had lived the truth of their desires and dreams down to the very marrow, why would they lie now, telling one another it did not matter when both of them knew it mattered tremendously, that the missing breast would continue to hover over all their successive nights? Damned Onetti!

"You would have had the surprise of your life," Doña Lucrecia laughed with the trill of an opera singer ready to go onstage. "As I did, when she told me. And even more so when I saw them. The surprise of your life!"

"The enchanting breasts of the Algerian ambassador?" Don Rigoberto was astounded. "Reconstructed?"

"The Algerian ambassador's wife," Doña Lucrecia corrected him. "Don't play the fool, you know very well who I mean. You spent the whole night looking at them at the dinner in the French embassy."

"It's true, they were lovely," Don Rigoberto admitted with a blush. And as he caressed, kissed, and looked with devotion on the breasts of Doña Lucrecia, he tempered his enthusiasm with a compliment: "But not as lovely as yours."

"I don't care," she said, ruffling his hair. "What can I do, they're better than mine. Smaller, but perfect. And firmer."

"Firmer?" Don Rigoberto had begun to swallow nervously. "I didn't know you had seen her naked. Or touched her breasts."

An auspicious silence fell, though it did coexist with the thunder of waves breaking against the cliffs down below, beneath the study.

"I have seen her naked, and I have touched them." His wife spelled it out for him, very slowly. "You don't care, do you? But that's not the point. The point is, they've been reconstructed. Really."

And now Don Rigoberto remembered that the women in *La vida breve*—Queca, Gertrudis, Elena Sala—wore silken girdles over their panties to control their waistlines and display better figures. What was the date of that novel by Onetti? Women didn't wear girdles anymore. He had never seen Lucrecia in a silken girdle. Or dressed as a pirate, a nun, a jockey, a clown, a butterfly, or a flower. But he had seen her as a Gypsy, wearing a scarf on her head, large hoops in her ears, a peasant blouse, a full multi-colored skirt, and strings of beads around her neck and arms. He remembered that he was alone, in the damp Barranco dawn, separated from Lucrecia for nearly a year, and he became saturated with the hideous novelistic pessimism of Juan María Brausen. He felt, too, what he read in the notebook: "the unforgettable certainty that nowhere is there a woman, a friend, a house, a book, not even a vice, that can make me happy." It was this awful solitude, not the scene of Gertrudis's cancerous breast, that had disinterred the novel from his unconscious; now he had sunk into a solitude as bitter as Brausen's, a pessimism as black.

"What does that mean, reconstructed?" he dared to ask after a long, uneasy parenthesis.

"It means she had cancer and they were removed," Doña Lucrecia informed him with surgical brutality. "Then they were gradually reconstructed at the Mayo Clinic in Minnesota. Six operations. Can you imagine? One. Two. Three. Four. Five. Six. It took three years. But they made them more perfect than before. They even made nipples, with little wrinkles and everything. Identical. I can tell you that because I saw them. Because I touched them. You don't care, do you, my love?"

"Of course not," Don Rigoberto quickly replied. But his haste betrayed him, as did the changes in the timbre, resonance, and implications of his voice. "Could you tell me when? Where?"

"When I saw them?" Doña Lucrecia put him off with professional skill. "Where I touched them?"

"Yes, yes," he pleaded, no longer observing the forms. "Only if you want to. Only if you think you can tell me, of course."

"Of course!" Don Rigoberto gave a start. He understood. It wasn't the emblematic breast, or the narrator's essential pessimism in *La vida breve*; it was the astute means Juan María Brausen had found to save himself that had provoked the sudden resurrection, the return of Zorro, Tarzan, or d'Artagnan, after ten years. Of course! Blessed Onetti! He smiled, relieved, almost happy. The memory had come back not to drown him but to help him or, as Brausen said when describing his own feverish imagination, to save him. Isn't that what he said when he transported himself out of the real Buenos Aires and into the invented Santa María, and fantasized a corrupt physician, Díaz Grey, who accepted money for injecting the mysterious Elena Sala with morphine? Didn't he say that this transposition, this move, this carefully elaborated act, this recourse to fiction, *saved him*? Here it was, in his notebook: "A Chinese puzzle box. In Onetti's work of fiction his invented character, Brausen, invents a fiction in which there is a doctor, Díaz Grey, based on himself, and a woman, Elena Sala, based on Gertrudis (though her breasts are still whole), and the fiction is more than the plot for a movie requested by Julio Stein; confronting reality with dream is his defense against reality, his way of annihilating the horrible truth of his life with the beautiful lie of fiction." He was overjoyed, ecstatic at his discovery. He felt as if he were Brausen, he felt redeemed and safe, and then another citation from his notebook, below the ones from *La vida breve*, troubled him. It was from "If," the poem by Kipling: "If you can dream—and not make dreams your master."

An opportune warning. Was he still master of his dreams, or did they now rule him because he had abused them so much since his separation from Lucrecia?

"We became friends after the dinner at the French Embassy," his wife was saying. "She asked me to her house for a steambath. A popular custom in Arabic countries, it seems. Steambaths. They're not the same as saunas, which use dry heat. A *hammam* had been built at the end of the garden at their residence in Orrantia."

A bemused Don Rigoberto still turned the pages of his notebook, but he was no longer completely there; now he was also in the densely planted garden filled with gaudy nightshade, white-and-pink-blossomed laurels, and the intense perfume of honeysuckle twined around the columns supporting the roof over a terrace. He was fully aroused as he spied on the two women—Lucrecia, in a flowered summer dress and sandals that revealed her powdered feet, and the Algerian ambassador's wife in a delicately colored silk tunic made iridescent by the luminous morning—walking through masses of red geraniums, green and yellow croton, and carefully trimmed grass, toward the wooden structure half-hidden by the leafy branches of a fig tree. "The *hammam*, the steambath," he said to himself, his heart pounding. He saw the two women from the rear and admired the similarity of their figures, their ample, unconfined buttocks moving in rhythm, their elegant backs, the graceful undulation of their hips as they walked, rippling their clothes. They strolled arm in arm, loving friends, and held towels in their hands. I am there, saving myself, and I am in my study, he thought, like Juan María Brausen in his apartment in Buenos Aires, who divides himself into the pimp Arce exploiting his neighbor Queca, and then saves himself by dividing into Dr. Díaz Grey in the nonexistent Santa María. But he was distracted from the two women when he turned a page in his notebook and found another quotation from *La vida breve*: "You appointed your breasts plenipotentiaries."

"This is a night for breasts," he said tenderly. "Are Brausen and I nothing but a couple of schizophrenics?" He didn't care in the least. He had closed his eyes and could see the two friends undressing, without shame, with easy assurance, as if they had celebrated this ritual many times in the small, wood-paneled antechamber to the steamroom. They hung their clothes on hooks and wrapped themselves in large towels, talking animatedly about something that Don Rigoberto did not understand and did not wish to understand. Now, pushing open a wooden door with no latch, they passed into a small room filled with clouds of steam. On his face he felt a blast of humid heat that dampened his pajamas and made them cling to his back, his chest, his legs. The steam entered his body through his nostrils, his mouth, his eyes, and it seemed to be scented with pine, sandalwood, mint. He trembled, afraid the two friends would find him out. But they paid no attention to him, as if he were not there, as if he were invisible.

"Don't think they used anything artificial, silicone or any junk like that," Doña Lucrecia explained. "Not at all. They were reconstructed with skin and flesh from her own body. Taking a bit from her stomach, another from her buttock, another from her thigh. And leaving no scars. She looked terrific, terrific, I swear."

It was true, he could see for himself. They had removed the towels and were sitting very close because there was not much space on the slatted wooden bench attached to the wall. Don Rigoberto contemplated the two naked bodies through the undulating clouds of steam. It was better than *The Turkish Bath* by Ingres, for in that picture the crowd of nudes divided one's attention—"Damned collectivism," he cursed—while here his perception could focus, take in the two friends at a single glance, scrutinize them without missing their tiniest gesture, possess them in a complete vision. Besides, in *The Turkish Bath*, the bodies were dry, but here, within a few seconds, Doña Lucrecia and the ambassador's wife were covered with brilliant beads of perspiration. How beautiful they are, he thought, deeply moved. Even more so together, as if the beauty of one empowered the beauty of the other.

"Not even the shadow of a scar," Doña Lucrecia insisted. "Not on her belly, her buttock, or her thigh. And, of course, not on the breasts they made for her. It was incredible, darling."

Don Rigoberto believed everything she said. How could he not, when he was seeing those two perfect women at such close range that if he stretched out his hand he would touch them? ("Oh, oh," he groaned in self-pity.) His wife's body was whiter and the ambassador's wife was tanned, as if she had spent her life outdoors; Lucrecia's hair was straight and dark, while her friend's was curly and auburn, but despite these differences, they resembled one another in their rejection of the modern taste for lanceolate thinness, in their Renaissance sumptuousness, in their splendid abundance of breasts, thighs, buttocks, arms, in the magnificent rounded forms that were—he did not need to caress them to know—firm, hard, taut, compressed, as if molded by invisible bodices, girdles, corselets, brassieres. "The classical model, the great tradition," he rejoiced.

"She suffered a great deal with so many operations, so much convalescence," Doña Lucrecia said compassionately. "But her vanity, her will not to be conquered or defeated by nature, to go on being beautiful, helped her. And finally, she won the war. Don't you think she's beautiful?"

"I think you are too," Don Rigoberto responded.

The heat and their perspiration had excited them. Both were taking slow, deep breaths that raised and lowered their breasts like the ocean's tides. Don Rigoberto was entranced. What were they saying? Why had a devilish gleam appeared in their eyes? He pricked up his ears and listened.

"I can't believe it," Doña Lucrecia was saying, looking at the breasts of the ambassador's wife and exaggerating her amazement. "They would drive any man crazy. They couldn't look more natural."

"That's what my husband says." The ambassador's wife laughed, not innocently, raising her torso slightly to show off her breasts. She pouted as she spoke, and her accent was French, though the *j*'s and *rr*'s were Arabic. ("Her father was born in Oran and played soccer with Albert Camus," Don Rigoberto decided.) "He says they're better than before, he likes them better now. And don't think the surgery made them insensitive. Not at all."

She laughed, feigning embarrassment, and Lucrecia laughed too and gave her a gentle pat on the thigh, which startled Don Rigoberto.

"I hope you don't take it the wrong way or think badly of me," she said a moment later. "Could I touch them? Would you mind? I'm dying to know if they're as real to the touch as they are to the eye. You must think I'm crazy to ask. Would you mind?"

"Of course not, Lucrecia," the ambassador's wife answered warmly. Her pout had become accentuated, and then she smiled broadly, displaying, with legitimate pride, her brilliant white teeth. "You'll touch mine and I'll touch yours. We'll compare. There's nothing wrong with two friends caressing each other."

"You're right, you're right," Doña Lucrecia exclaimed with enthusiasm. And, out of the corner of her eye, she glanced at Don Rigoberto. ("She knew from the very beginning that I was here." He sighed.) "I don't know about your husband, but mine adores this kind of thing. Let's play, let's play."

They had begun to touch, at first very cautiously, very lightly; then more boldly; now they were openly fondling one another's nipples. They moved closer. They embraced, their hair became entwined. Don Rigoberto could barely see them. Drops of sweat—or, perhaps, tears—irritated his eyes so much he had to blink constantly and close them. I am happy, I am sad, he thought, aware of the incongruity. Was that possible? Why not. It was like being in Buenos Aires and in Santa María, or alone, at dawn, in the solitary study, surrounded by notebooks and pictures, and in that spring-like garden, in clouds of steam, dripping with perspiration.

"It began as a game," Doña Lucrecia explained. "To pass the time as we rid ourselves of toxins. I immediately thought of you. If you would approve. If it would excite you. If it would bother you. If you would make a scene when I told you."

He, faithful to his promise to spend the whole night paying homage to his wife's plenipotentiary breasts, had knelt on the floor between Lucrecia's parted legs as she sat on the edge of the bed. With amorous solicitude he held each breast in one of his hands, showing exaggerated care, as if they were made of fragile crystal and could break. He kissed them with the surface of his lips, millimeter by millimeter, a conscientious farmer who does not leave a speck of earth unturned.

"In other words, I was moved to touch them to find out if her breasts felt artificial. And she touched mine because she's responsive, because she didn't want to sit there like an idiot and do nothing. But we were playing with fire, of course."

"Of course," Don Rigoberto agreed, tireless in his search for symmetry, moving, in fairness, from one breast to the other. "Why did you both get excited? Why did you go from touching to kissing? From kissing to sucking?"

He repented immediately. He had violated the strict rules that established the incompatibility between pleasure and the use of vulgar words, especially verbs (suck, nurse) that did harm to any illusion.

"I didn't say sucking," he apologized, trying to bring back the past and correct it. "Let's stop at kissing. Who began? Did you, love of my life?"

He heard her faint voice but could no longer see her because she was fading quickly, like vapor on the mirror when it is rubbed or touched by a breath of cool air: "Yes, I did, isn't that what you told me to do, isn't that what you wanted?" No, thought Don Rigoberto. What I want is to have you here, flesh and blood, not a phantom. Because I love you. Sadness had fallen on him like a heavy rain, a downpour of impetuous water that washed away the garden, the residence, the scent of sandalwood, pine, mint, honeysuckle, the steambath, the two affectionate friends. As well as the heat and humidity of a moment ago, and his dream. The cold dawn chilled his bones. The sea crashed furiously against the cliffs with monotonous regularity.

And then he remembered that in the novel—damned Onetti! blessed Onetti!—Queca and Gorda had kissed and caressed behind the back of Brausen, the false Arce, and that the whore, or ex-whore, his neighbor Queca, the one they killed, thought her apartment was filled with monsters, gnomes, dragons, invisible metaphysical terrors who were pursuing her. Queca and Gorda, he thought, Lucrecia and the ambassador's wife. Schizophrenic, just like Brausen. Now not even his phantoms could save him, but buried him each day in deeper solitude, leaving his study, like Queca's apartment, sown with ravening beasts. Should he burn this house? With him and Fonchito in it?

In the notebook there gleamed an erotic dream of Juan María Brausen ("taken from paintings by Paul Delvaux that Onetti could not have known when he wrote *La vida breve* because the Belgian surrealist had not even painted them yet," said a brief note in parentheses: "I lean back in the chair, resting on the girl's shoulder, and imagine I am leaving a small city made up of houses of assignation; a secretive village where naked couples stroll through small gardens, along moss-covered paving stones, hiding their faces with their open hands when the lights go on, when they cross paths with pederastic servants . . ." Would he end up like Brausen? Was he Brausen already? A failed man, a mediocre man who could not succeed as a Catholic idealist or an evangelical social reformer, as an irredeemable libertine individualist and agnostic hedonist or a creator of private enclaves of the highest fantasy and artistic good taste, a man defeated by everything, the woman he loved, the son he fathered, the dreams he tried to embed in reality, decaying day after day, night after night, behind the repellent mask of an executive in a successful insurance company, transformed into the "purely desperate man" mentioned in Onetti's novel, into a copy of the pessimistic masochist in *La vida breve*. At least Brausen finally succeeded in escaping from Buenos Aires and, by train, car, ship, or bus, had managed to reach Santa María, the city of his invention in the region of the Río de la Plata. Don Rigoberto was still lucid enough to know he could not traffic in fictions, leap headlong into dreams. He was not Brausen yet. There was still time to react, to do something. But what, what?

Invisible Games

I enter your house by the chimney, though I am not Santa Claus. I float to your bedroom and, very close to your face, imitate the buzz of a mosquito. As you sleep you begin to swat in the darkness at a poor insect that does not exist.

When I tire of playing the mosquito, I uncover your legs and blow a breath of cold air that numbs your bones. You begin to shiver, you curl up, you tug at the blanket, your teeth begin to chatter, you cover your head with the pillow and even begin to sneeze sneezes not caused by your allergy.

Then I become a Piuran, Amazonian heat that soaks you in perspiration from head to toe. You look like a little wet chick, kicking the sheets to the floor, pulling off your pajama tops and bottoms. Until you are stark naked, sweating, sweating and panting like a bellows.

Then I become a feather and tickle you, on the soles of your feet, in your ear, under your arms. Hee hee, ha ha, ho ho, you laugh without waking up, making desperate faces and twisting to the right, the left, trying to ease the cramps caused by your laughter. Until, at last, you wake, frightened, not seeing me but sensing that someone is moving in the darkness.

When you get up to go to your study and spend time with your pictures, I lay traps for you. I move chairs and objects and tables from their place so that you will trip over them and shout "Owowowww!" rubbing your shins. Sometimes I hide your robe, your slippers. Sometimes I spill the glass of water you leave on the night table to drink when you wake up. How angry you are when you open your eyes and feel around for it and find it in the middle of a puddle on the floor!

This is how we do it, how we play with the men we love.

Yours, yours, yours,
A Phantom in Love

VIII

Beast in the Mirror

"I went off last night," Doña Lucrecia said without thinking. Before fully realizing what she had said, she heard Fonchito: "Where to, Stepmamá?" She blushed to the roots of her hair, consumed by shame.

"I meant to say I couldn't sleep a wink," she lied, because for some time she had not enjoyed so deep a sleep, though one, it must be said, shaken by storms of desire and the phantoms of love. "I'm so tired I don't know what I'm saying."

The boy was concentrating again on a page in the book about the painter he adored, which displayed a photograph of Egon Schiele looking at himself in the large mirror in his studio. He was shown full-length, his hands in his pockets, his short hair uncombed, his slender boyish body encased in a white, high-collared shirt and tie, but no jacket, and his hands hidden, of course, in the pockets of a pair of trousers with the bottoms rolled as if he were about to wade across a river. Since he had arrived, Fonchito had done nothing but talk about that mirror, attempting over and over again to initiate a conversation about the photograph; but Doña Lucrecia, lost in her own thoughts and still caught up in the confused exaltation, the doubts and hopes that had dominated her since yesterday's surprising development in her anonymous correspondence, had paid no attention. She looked at Fonchito's head of golden curls and saw his profile, his solemn scrutiny of the photograph as if he were trying to wrench some secret from it. "He doesn't realize, he didn't understand." Though one never knew with him.

He had probably understood perfectly and was pretending he hadn't so as not to increase her embarrassment.

Or, perhaps, "to go off" didn't have the same meaning for the boy? She recalled that some time ago she and Rigoberto had engaged in one of those salacious conversations that the secret laws governing their lives permitted only at night and in bed during the prologue, main text, or epilogue of love. Her husband had assured her that the younger generation no longer used "to go off" but "to come," a clear demonstration, even in the delicate realm of Venus, of the influence of English, for when gringos and gringas made love they "came" and didn't go off anywhere, as Latins do. In any event, Doña Lucrecia had gone off, come, or finished (this was the verb she and Don Rigoberto had used during their ten years of marriage after agreeing never to refer to that beautiful conclusion to the erotic encounter as an uncivil, clinical "orgasm," much less a dripping-wet, belligerent "ejaculation") the night before, enjoying it intensely, with an acute, almost painful pleasure—she had awakened bathed in sweat, her teeth chattering, her hands and feet convulsed—dreaming that she had gone to the mysterious appointment indicated in the anonymous letter, following all the extravagant instructions, and in the end, after the most intricate routes along dark streets in both the center and outlying districts of Lima, she had been— wearing a blindfold, naturally—admitted to a house whose odor she recognized, led up a flight of stairs to the second floor—from the first moment she was certain it was the house in Barranco—undressed, and made to lie down on a bed that she also identified as their old one, until she felt herself held tightly, embraced, penetrated, and filled to overflowing by a body which, of course, was Rigoberto's. They had finished—going off or coming—together, which did not happen to them very often. Both had thought it a positive sign, a happy omen for the new life opening before them following this abracadabraesque reconciliation. Then she woke, wet, languorous, confused, and had to struggle for some time before she could accept that her intense happiness had been only a dream.

"The mirror was a gift to Schiele from his mother." Fonchito's voice returned her to her house, to a drab San Isidro, to the shouts of children kicking a soccer ball in the Olivar; the boy's face was turned toward her. "He begged her and begged her to give it to him. Some people say he stole it from her. That he wanted it so much that one day he went to his mother's house and just walked out with it. And finally she agreed and left it in his studio. His first one. He always kept it. He moved that mirror to every studio he ever had, until he died."

"Why is the mirror so important?" Doña Lucrecia made an effort to show interest. "We know he was like Narcissus. The photograph proves it. Looking at himself, in love with himself, putting on a victim's face. So the world would love and admire him just as he loved and admired himself."

Fonchito burst into laughter.

"What an imagination, Stepmamá!" he exclaimed. "That's why I like talking to you; you can think of things, just like I do. You can find a story in everything. We're alike, aren't we? I never get bored with you."

"You don't bore me either." She blew him a kiss. "I told you what I think, now it's your turn. Why are you so interested in the mirror?"

"I dream about that mirror," Fonchito admitted. And, with a little Mephistophelian smile, he added, "It was very important to Egon. How do you think he painted a hundred self-portraits? With that mirror. And he used it to paint his models reflected in it. It wasn't a whim. It was, it was . . ."

He made a face, searching, but Doña Lucrecia guessed it wasn't words he lacked but a way to articulate a formless idea still gestating in that precocious little head. The boy's passion for the painter, she was certain now, was pathological. But perhaps, for that very reason, it might also shape an exceptional future for Fonchito as an eccentric creator, an unconventional artist. If she kept the appointment and reconciled with Rigoberto, she would tell him so. "Do you like the idea of having a neurotic genius for a son?" And she would ask him if it wasn't dangerous for the boy's psychic health to identify so strongly with a painter like Egon Schiele, whose inclinations were so perverse. But then Rigoberto would reply: "What? Have you been seeing Fonchito? While we were separated? While I was writing you love letters, forgetting what had happened, forgiving what had happened, you were seeing him behind my back? The boy you corrupted by taking him to your bed?" My God, my God, what an idiot I've turned into, thought Doña Lucrecia. If she went to the appointment, the one thing she couldn't do was mention Alfonso's name even once.

"Hi, Justita," he greeted the girl as she came into the dining alcove, looking neat as a pin in a starched apron and carrying the tea tray and the requisite toasted buns with butter and marmalade. "Don't go, I want to show you something. Here, what do you see?"

"What else but more of that dirty stuff you like so much." Justiniana's darting eyes lingered on the book for a long time. "A fresh guy having a great time looking at two naked girls who are wearing stockings and hats and showing off for him."

"That's what it looks like, doesn't it?" exclaimed Fonchito with a triumphant air. He handed the book to Doña Lucrecia so that she could examine the full-page reproduction. "They're not two models, it's just one. Why do we see two, one from the front, the other from the back? Because of the mirror! Do you get it now, Stepmamá? The title explains everything."

Schiele Painting a Nude Model Before the Mirror, 1910 (Graphische Sammlung Albertina, Vienna), read Doña Lucrecia. As she examined the picture, intrigued by something she could not name except that it was not in the picture itself—it was a presence, or rather an absence—she half-heard Fonchito, who by now was in the state of growing excitement that talking about Schiele always brought him to. He was explaining to Justiniana that the mirror "is where we are when we look at the picture." And that the model seen from the front wasn't flesh and blood but an image in the mirror, while the painter and the model seen from the back were real and not reflections. Which meant that Egon Schiele had begun to paint Moa from the rear, in front of the mirror, but then, drawn by the part he did not see directly but only in projection, he decided to paint that too. And so, thanks to the mirror, he painted two Moas, who were really only one: the complete Moa, the two halves of Moa, the Moa no one could see in reality because "we only see what we have in front of us, not the part behind that front." Did she understand why the mirror was so important to Egon Schiele?

"Don't you think he's missing something upstairs, Señora?" Justiniana said in an exaggerated way, touching her temple.

"I have for a long time," Doña Lucrecia agreed. And then, in the same breath, she turned to Fonchito: "Who was this Moa?"

A Tahitian. She had come to Vienna and lived with a painter who was also a mime and a madman: Erwin Dominik Ose. The boy quickly turned pages and showed Doña Lucrecia and Justiniana several reproductions of the Tahitian Moa, dancing, draped in multicolored tunics through whose folds one could see small breasts with erect nipples, and, like two spiders crouching under her arms, the small tufts of hair in her armpits. She danced in cabarets, she was the muse of poets and painters, and in addition to posing for Egon, she had also been his lover.

"I guessed that from the start," remarked Justiniana. "That bandit always went to bed with his models after he painted them, we all know that."

"Sometimes before, and sometimes while he was painting them," Fonchito assured her calmly, approvingly. "Though not all of them. In his journal for 1918, the last year of his life, he mentions 117 models who visited his studio. Could he have gone to bed with so many in so short a time?"

"Not even if he contracted tuberculosis." Justiniana laughed. "Did he die of consumption?"

"He died of Spanish influenza at the age of twenty-eight," Fonchito explained. "That's how I'm going to die too, in case you didn't know."

"Don't say that even as a joke, it's bad luck," the girl reprimanded him.

"But something here doesn't fit," Doña Lucrecia interrupted.

She had taken the book of reproductions from the boy and was looking again, very carefully, at the drawing, with its sepia background and precise, thin lines, of the painter and the model duplicated ("or divided?") by the mirror, in which the intense, almost hostile eyes of Schiele seem to find their response in the melancholy, silken, flashing eyes of Moa, the dancer with blue-black lashes. Señora Lucrecia had been disturbed by something she had just identified. Ah yes, the hat glimpsed from the rear. Except for this detail, in everything else there was perfect correspondence between the two parts of the delicate, thrusting, sensual figure of the Tahitian with hair like spiders at her pubis and under her arms; once you were aware of the presence of the mirror, you recognized the two halves of the same person in the two figures observed by the artist. But not the hat. The figure seen from the rear wore something on her head which, from that perspective, did not seem to be a hat at all but something uncertain, unsettling, a sort of cowl, even, even, the head of a wild animal. That was it, some kind of tiger. In any case, nothing even remotely like the coquettish, feminine, charming little hat so flattering to the Moa seen from the front.

"How odd," the stepmother repeated. "In the rear view, the hat turns into a mask. The head of a beast."

"Like the one my papá asks you to put on in front of the mirror, Stepmamá?"

Doña Lucrecia's smile froze. Suddenly she understood the reason for the vague uneasiness that had engulfed her ever since the boy showed her *Schiele Painting a Nude Model Before the Mirror*.

"What is it, Señora?" Justiniana was looking at her. "You're so pale."

"Then it's you," she stammered, staring in disbelief at Fonchito. "You're sending me anonymous letters, you little hypocrite."

He was the one, of course he was. It had been in the letter before last, or the one before that. She didn't have to look for it; the sentence, with all its commas and periods, was etched in her memory: "You will undress before the mirror, except for your stockings, and hide your lovely head behind the mask of a wild animal, preferably a tigress or a lioness. You will thrust out your right hip, flex your left leg, rest your hand on your other hip, in the most provocative pose. I will be watching you, sitting in my chair, with my usual reverence." Isn't that exactly what she was looking at? The damn kid was playing with her! She seized the book of reproductions and, blind with fury, hurled it at Fonchito. The boy could not get out of the way in time. The book hit him full in the face, he screamed, and a startled Justiniana screamed too. With the impact, he fell back onto the carpet, holding his face and looking up at her, wide-eyed, from the floor. Doña Lucrecia did not think she had done anything wrong in losing her temper. She was too angry to regret anything. While the girl helped him to his feet, she continued to shout, beside herself with rage.

"You liar, you hypocrite, you fake. Do you think you have the right to play with me like that, when I'm a grown woman and you're nothing but a snot-nosed kid still wet behind the ears?"

"What's the matter, what did I do to you?" Fonchito stuttered, trying to free himself from Justita's arms.

"Calm down, Señora, you've hurt him; look, his nose is bleeding," said Justiniana. "And you be still, Foncho, and let me have a look."

"What, what did you do to me, you phony!" shouted an even angrier Doña Lucrecia. "You think it doesn't matter? Writing me anonymous letters? Making me think they came from your papá?"

"But I never sent you any anonymous letters," the boy protested, while the girl, on her knees, wiped the blood from his nose with a paper napkin. "Don't move, don't move, you're bleeding all over everything."

"Your damned mirror gave you away, and your damned Egon Schiele!" Doña Lucrecia was still shouting. "You thought you were so clever, didn't you? Well, you're not, fool. How do you know he asked me to put on an animal mask?"

"You told me, Stepmamá," Fonchito stammered, but fell silent when he saw Doña Lucrecia get to her feet. He protected his face with both hands, as if she were going to hit him.

"I never told you about the mask, you liar," his enraged stepmother exploded. "I'm going to bring you that letter, I'm going to read it to you. You're going to eat it, you're going to apologize. And I'll never let you set foot in this house again. Do you hear? Never!"

Like a bolt of lightning she shot past Justiniana and Fonchito, wild with indignation. But before going to the dressing table where she kept the anonymous letters, she went to the bathroom to splash cold water on her face and rub her temples with cologne. She could not calm down. This kid, this damn brat. Playing with her, yes, the little kitten with the big mouse. Sending her daring, elaborate letters to make her think they were from Rigoberto, encouraging her to hope for a reconciliation. What was he after? What scheme was he devising? Why the farce? For the fun, the sheer fun of manipulating her emotions, her life? He was perverse, sadistic. He enjoyed leading her on and then watching her crumbling hopes, her disillusionment.

She returned to her bedroom, still not herself, and did not have to look very long in her dressing-table drawer to find the letter. The seventh one. There was the sentence that had alerted her, more or less as she had remembered it: ". . . you will hide your lovely head behind the mask of a wild animal, preferably the tigress in heat in Rubén Darío's *Azul* . . . or a Sudanese lioness. You will thrust out your hip . . ." et cetera, et cetera. The Tahitian Moa in the drawing by Schiele, no more, no less. That precocious little troublemaker, that schemer. He'd had the gall to play out a whole drama about Schiele's mirror, even showing her the picture that betrayed him. She wasn't sorry she had thrown the book, even though it did give him a bloody nose. Good! Hadn't the little devil ruined her life? Because she had not been the seducer, though the difference in their ages condemned her. He, he had been the seducer. With his youth and cherubic face, he was Mephistopheles, Lucifer in person. But that was all over. She'd make him eat this anonymous letter, yes, and throw him out of the house. And he'd never come back, never interfere in her life again.

But she found only a dejected Justiniana in the dining alcove. She showed her the bloodstained napkin.

"He left crying, Señora. Not because of his nose. But because when you threw it at him you tore the book about that painter he likes so much. He's really sad, I can tell you."

"Go on, now you're feeling sorry for him." Señora Lucrecia dropped to

191

the sofa, exhausted. "Don't you realize what he did to me? He, he's the one who sent me those anonymous letters."

"He swore he didn't, Señora. He swore by all that's holy that it was the señor who sent them."

"He's lying." Doña Lucrecia felt utterly exhausted. Was she going to faint? How she longed to go to bed, close her eyes, sleep for an entire week. "He gave himself away when he mentioned the mask and the mirror."

Justiniana came over to her and spoke almost in a whisper. "Are you sure you didn't read him that letter? That you didn't tell him about the mask? Fonchito is a clever little scamp, Señora. Do you think he'd let something so stupid trip him up?"

"I never read him that letter, I never told him about the mask," Doña Lucrecia declared. But at that same moment she began to have doubts.

Had she? Yesterday, or the day before? Her mind wandered so these days; ever since the flood of anonymous letters she had been lost in a forest of conjectures, speculations, suspicions, fantasies. Wasn't it possible? That she had told him, mentioned it, even read him that strange command to pose nude, wearing stockings and an animal mask, in front of a mirror? If she had, she had committed a grave injustice by insulting and hitting him.

"I can't take any more," she murmured, making an effort to hold back her tears. "I'm sick of it, Justita, sick of it. I probably told him and forgot. I don't know where my head is. Maybe I did. I want to leave this city, this country. Go where nobody knows me. Far away from Rigoberto and Fonchito. Because of those two I've fallen into a pit and I'll never climb out."

"Don't be sad, Señora." Justiniana put her hand on her shoulder, stroked her forehead. "Don't be bitter. And don't worry. There's a way, a very easy way, to find out if it's Fonchito or Don Rigoberto who's writing all that nonsense to you."

Doña Lucrecia looked up. The girl's eyes were flashing.

"Of course there is, Señora." She spoke with her hands, her eyes, her lips, her teeth. "Didn't the last letter arrange a date with you? That's the answer. Go where it says, do what it asks."

"Do you really think I'm going to do things that belong in a cheap Mexican movie?" Doña Lucrecia pretended to be shocked.

"And that's how you'll find out who's writing the letters," Justiniana concluded. "I'll go with you, if you like. So you won't feel so alone. And because I'm dying of curiosity too, Señora. Sonny or daddy? Which one can it be?"

She laughed with all her usual boldness and charm, and Doña Lucrecia finally began to smile as well. After all, perhaps this lunatic was right. If she kept the mysterious appointment, her doubts would be over at last.

"He won't show up, I'll be playing the fool again," she argued, not very convincingly, knowing deep down that she had made her decision. She would go, do every silly thing daddy or sonny asked. She'd go on playing the game that, willingly or not, she had been playing for so long.

"Shall I fix you a nice warm bath with salts, so you'll get over your temper?" Justiniana was extremely animated.

Doña Lucrecia nodded. Damn it, now she had the feeling she had been too hasty and very unfair to poor Fonchito.

Letter to the Reader of Playboy, or A Brief Treatise on Aesthetics

Since eroticism is the intelligent and sensitive humanization of physical love, and pornography its cheapening and degradation, I accuse you, reader of *Playboy* or *Penthouse*, frequenter of vile dens that show hard-core movies, and sex shops where you purchase electric vibrators, rubber dildos, and condoms adorned with rooster crests or archbishops' mitres, of contributing to the rapid regression to mere animal copulation of the one attribute granted to men and women that makes them most like gods (pagan ones, of course, who were neither chaste nor prudish regarding sexual matters, like the one we all know about).

You transgress openly each month when, aroused by the flames of your desires, you renounce the exercise of your own imagination and succumb to the municipal vice of permitting your most subtle drives, those of the carnal appetite, to be reined in by products that have been cloned, and by seeming to satisfy your sexual urges actually subjugate them, watering them down, serializing and constricting them in caricatures that vulgarize sex, strip it of originality, mystery, and beauty, and turn it into a farcical, ignoble affront to good taste. To let you know who your accuser is, perhaps I can clarify my thinking for you by stating (monogamist that I am, though looking kindly on adultery) that I consider the late and highly respected Israeli leader Doña Golda Meir, or the austere Señora Margaret Thatcher of the United Kingdom, not one of whose hairs moved for the entire time she was Prime Minister, as more delectable sources of erotic desire than any of those interchangeable pimp's dolls, breasts swollen by silicone, pubises trimmed and dyed, the same fraud mass-produced out of a single mold, who, blending stupidity with the ridiculous, appear in the centerfold of *Playboy*, that enemy of Eros, wearing plush ears and a tail and flourishing their scepter as "Bunny of the Month."

My hatred for *Playboy*, *Penthouse*, and others of their ilk is not gratuitous. This kind of magazine symbolizes the corruption of sex, the disappearance of the beautiful taboos that once surrounded it and against which the human spirit could rebel, exercising individual freedom, affirming the singular personality of each human being, gradually creating the sovereign individual in the secret and discreet elaboration of rituals, actions, images, cults, fantasies, ceremonies which, by ethically ennobling the act of love and conferring aesthetic distinction upon it, progressively humanized it until it was transformed into a creative act. An act thanks to which, in the private intimacy of bedrooms, a man and a woman (I cite the orthodox formula, but clearly this also applies to a gentleman and a web-footed creature, two women, two or three men, and all imaginable combinations as long as the company does not exceed three individuals or, at most, two couples) could spend a few hours emulating Homer, Phidias, Botticelli, or Beethoven. I know you don't understand me, but that is not important; if you understood me, you would not be imbecilic enough to synchronize your erections and orgasms with the watch (surely solid gold and waterproof?) of a man named Hugh Hefner.

The problem is more aesthetic than ethical, philosophical, sexual, psychological, or political, though it goes without saying that such divisions are unacceptable to me because *everything* that matters is, in the long run, aesthetic. Pornography strips eroticism of its artistic content, favors the organic over the spiritual and mental, as if the central protagonists of desire and pleasure were phalluses and vulvas and these organs not mere servants to the phantoms that govern our souls, and segregates physical love from the rest of human experience. Eroticism, on the other hand, integrates it with everything we are, everything we have. Pornographer, while for you the only thing that counts when you make love is the same thing that counts for a dog, a monkey, or a horse—that is, to ejaculate—Lucrecia and I, go on, envy us, *also* make love when we are having breakfast, dressing, listening to Mahler, talking with friends, and contemplating the clouds or the sea.

When I say aesthetic you may, perhaps, think—if pornography and thinking are compatible—that with this shortcut I fall into the trap of gregariousness, and, since values are generally shared, in this domain I am less myself and more the other, in short, a part of the tribe. I acknowledge that the danger exists, but I battle it unceasingly, day and night, defending my independence against all odds through the constant exercise of my freedom.

You can judge this for yourself by reading a small sample of my personal treatise on aesthetics (which I hope I do not share with many people, which is flexible, which is shaped and reshaped like clay in the hands of a skilled potter).

Everything brilliant is ugly. There are brilliant cities, like Vienna, Buenos Aires, and Paris; brilliant writers, like Umberto Eco, Carlos Fuentes, Milan Kundera, and John Updike; brilliant painters, like Andy Warhol, Matta, and Tàpies. Though all of them shine, for me they are dispensable. Without exception, all modern architects are brilliant, and for this reason architecture has been marginalized from art and transformed into a branch of advertising and public relations, and therefore it would be a good idea to reject architects en masse and have recourse only to masons, master builders, and the inspiration of laymen. There are no brilliant musicians, though composers like Maurice Ravel and Erik Satie struggled to achieve brilliance and almost succeeded. Cinema, a diversion like judo or wrestling, is post-artistic and does not deserve to be included in any considerations regarding aesthetics, despite a few Western anomalies (tonight I would save Visconti, Orson Welles, Buñuel, Berlanga, and John Ford) and one Japanese (Kurosawa).

Every person who writes "nuclearize," "I submit," "raise consciousness," "visualize," "societal," and, above all, "telluric," is a son/daughter of a bitch. As are those who use toothpicks in public, inflicting on their neighbors a repellent sight that defaces the landscape. As are those repulsive creatures who pull off pieces of bread and knead them into little balls that they leave on the table. Don't ask me why the perpetrators of these hideous acts are sons/daughters of bitches; such knowledge is intuited and assimilated through inspiration; infused, not studied. The same term applies, of course, to the mortal of any sex who, in an attempt to Castilianize drink, writes *guisqui* for whiskey, *yinyerel* for ginger ale, or *jaibol* for highball. These men/women should probably die, for I suspect their lives are superfluous.

The obligation of a film or a book is to entertain me. If I am distracted, if I begin to nod or fall asleep when I watch or read them, they have failed in their duty and are bad books, bad films. Conspicuous examples: *The*

Man without Qualities, by Musil, and all the movies made by those charlatans called Oliver Stone and Quentin Tarantino.

With regard to painting and sculpture, my criterion for making an artistic judgment is very simple: everything I could paint or sculpt myself is shit. The only artists of value are those whose works, far beyond the reach of my creative mediocrity, I could not reproduce. This criterion has allowed me to determine, on first viewing, that all work by "artists" like Andy Warhol or Frida Kahlo is trash, and, on the contrary, even the quickest sketch by George Grosz, Chillida, or Balthus is a work of genius. In addition to this general rule, the obligation of a picture is to excite me (an expression I am not fond of but use because I like even less, since it introduces a comic element into something very serious, our Latin American allegory: "almost get me off"). If I like it but it leaves me cold, if my imagination is not overwhelmed by theatrical-copulatory desires and that tickling buzz in the testicles that precedes a tender new erection, then even if it is the *Mona Lisa, The Man with His Hand on His Chest, Guernica,* or *The Night Watch,* the picture holds no interest for me. And so you may be surprised to learn that in Goya, another sacred monster, I like only the little shoes with golden buckles, pointed heels, and satin adornments worn with white mesh stockings by the marquises in his oil paintings, and that in Renoir's paintings I look with benevolence (sometimes with pleasure) only on the pink behinds of his peasant girls and avoid his other bodies, above all those kewpie-doll faces and firefly-eyes that anticipate—*vade retro!*—the *Playboy* bunnies. In Courbet, I am interested in the lesbians and that gigantic posterior that made the prudish Empress Eugénie blush.

In my opinion, the obligation of music is to plunge me into a vertigo of pure sensation that makes me forget the most boring part of myself, the civil, municipal part, clears away preoccupations, isolates me in an enclave untouched by the sordid reality surrounding it, and in this way allows me to think clearly about the fantasies (generally erotic and always with my wife in the starring role) that make my existence bearable. Ergo, if the music makes its presence felt too strongly and, because I begin to like it too much or because it is very loud, distracts me from my own thoughts and demands and captures my attention—I quickly cite Gardel, Pérez Prado, Mahler, every merengue, and four-fifths of all operas—it is bad music and is banished from my study. This principle, of course, makes me love Wagner despite the trumpets and annoying English horns, and respect Schoenberg.

I hope these brief examples, which, naturally, I don't expect you to share with me (and I desire it even less), illustrate what I mean when I state that eroticism is a private game (in the highest sense given to the word by the great Johan Huizinga) in which only I and phantoms and other players can participate, and whose success depends on its secrecy and imperviousness to public curiosity, for this can lead only to its regimentation and perverse manipulation by forces that would nullify erotic play. Underarm hair on a woman disgusts me, but I respect the amateurs who persuade their companion, male or female, to water and cultivate it so that they may play there with lips and teeth until achieving ecstasy, howling in C major. But I absolutely cannot respect, cannot feel anything but pity for the poor shithead who bastardizes this whim of his phantom by buying—for example in one of the pornographic department stores sown all over Germany by the former aviatrix Beate Uhse—an artificial hairy armpit or pubis (made with "natural hair," boast the most expensive) sold in various shapes, sizes, flavors, and colors.

The legitimization and public acceptance of eroticism municipalizes it, nullifies it, debases it, turning it into pornography, that sad business which I define as eroticism for the poor in purse and spirit. Pornography is passive and collectivist, eroticism is creative and individual even when practiced in twos or threes (I repeat, I oppose raising the number of participants, so that these functions do not lose their inclination to be individualistic celebrations and exercises of sovereignty, and are not soiled by appearing to be meetings, sporting events, or circuses). Consequently, I can only laugh like a hyena at the arguments of the Beat poet Allen Ginsberg (see his interview with Allen Young in *Consuls of Sodom*) defending collective couplings in dimly lit bathhouses with the tall tale that such promiscuity is democratic and fair because the egalitarian darkness permits the ugly and the attractive, the skinny and the fat, the young and the old to have the same opportunities for pleasure. The absurd reasoning of a constructivist commissar! Democracy has to do only with the civil dimension of a person, while love—desire and pleasure—belongs, like religion, to the private sphere, where differences, not similarities to others, matter more than anything else. Sex cannot be democratic; it is elitist and aristocratic, and a certain amount of despotism (mutually agreed upon) tends to be indispensable. The collective copulations in dark pools recommended as erotic models by the Beat poet too closely resemble the intercourse of stallions and mares in pastures or the indiscriminate skirmishes of roosters and hens in noisy henhouses to be confused with the beautiful creation of animated fictions and carnal fantasies in which there is equal participation of body and spirit, imagination and hormones, the sublime and the base in the human condition, which is what eroticism means to this modest epicurean and anarchist concealed in the civil body of a man who insures property.

Sex practiced *Playboy*-style (I return to this subject and will continue to do so until my death, or yours, stops me) eliminates two ingredients essential to Eros, as I understand it: risk and modesty. Let us be clear. The terrified little man on the bus who, conquering his shame and fear, opens his overcoat and for a few seconds offers the sight of his erect penis to the unwary matron whom fate has placed in front of him, is recklessly indecent. He does what he does knowing that the price of his fugitive whim can be a beating, a lynching, prison, and a scandal that would reveal to public opinion a secret he would prefer to take with him to the grave, condemning him to the status of reprobate, psychopath, and a menace to society. But he risks all this because the pleasure he receives from his minimal exhibitionism is inseparable from fear and his transgression against modesty. What an interstellar distance—precisely the distance that separates eroticism from pornography—separates him from the executive basted in French cologne, his wrist encircled by a Rolex (what other watch could it be?), who, in a trendy bar enlivened by the sound of the blues, opens the latest issue of *Playboy* and exhibits himself and the magazine, convinced he is displaying his penis to the world, showing himself as worldly, unprejudiced, modern, pleasure-seeking, *in*. The poor imbecile! He does not suspect that what he is exhibiting is the sign and seal of his servitude to the commonplace, to advertising and a deindividualizing fashion, his abdication of freedom, his renunciation of emancipation, by means of his personal phantoms, from the atavistic slavery of serialization.

For this reason I accuse you and the aforementioned magazine and others like it and all of you who read them—or even leaf through them—and with that miserable prefabricated pap nourish—I mean, kill—your libidos, of spearheading the great campaign, the manifestation of contemporary barbarism, to desacralize and banalize sex. Civilization hides and nuances sex in order to better enjoy it, surrounding it with rituals and rules that enrich it to an extent undreamed of by pre-erotic men and women, copulators, progenitors of offspring. After traveling a long, long road whose backbone, in a sense, was the progressive distillation of erotic play by an unexpected route—the permissive society, the tolerant culture—we have returned to our ancestral starting point: lovemaking has again become physical, semi-public, thoughtless gymnastics performed to the rhythm of stimuli created not by the unconscious mind and the soul but by market analysts, stimuli as stupid as the false cow's vagina passed under the noses of stabled bulls to make them ejaculate so that their semen can be collected and used for artificial insemination.

Go on, buy and read your latest *Playboy*, you living suicide, and bring your grain of sand to the creation of that world of ejaculating male and female eunuchs where imagination and secret phantoms will vanish as the pillars of love. For my part, I am going now to make love to the Queen of Sheba and Cleopatra, both at the same time, in a play whose script I do not intend to share with anyone, least of all you.

A Tiny Foot

It is four in the morning, my darling Lucrecia, thought Don Rigoberto. As he did almost every day, he had risen in the mournful damp of dawn to celebrate the ritual he had monotonously repeated ever since Doña Lucrecia had gone to live near the Olivar de San Isidro: dreaming while awake, creating and re-creating his wife under the magic spell of those notebooks where his phantoms hibernated. And where, from the first day I met you, you have been queen and mistress.

And yet, unlike other desolate or ardent early mornings, today it was not enough for him to imagine and desire her, chat with her absence, love her with his fantasy and the heart she had never left; today he needed more material, more certain, more tangible contact. Today I could kill myself, he thought without anguish. And if he wrote to her? Finally answered her suggestive anonymous letters? The pen slipped from his fingers, he barely managed to catch it. No, he couldn't do it, and in any case, he wouldn't be able to send her the letter if he did.

In the first notebook he opened, an exceedingly opportune phrase leaped off the page and bit him: "My savage awakenings at dawn are always spurred on by an image of you, real or invented, which inflames my desire, maddens my nostalgia, suspends me in midair, and drives me to this study to defend myself against annihilation, finding sanctuary in the antidote of my notebooks, pictures, and books. This alone cures me." True. But today the usual remedy would not have the beneficial effect it had at other dawns. He felt bewildered, tormented. He had been awakened by a mixture of sensations: a generous rebelliousness, similar to the feeling that at the age of eighteen had led him to Catholic Action and filled his spirit with the missionary urge to change the world, armed with the Gospels, was confused with a melting nostalgia for an Asian woman's tiny foot glimpsed in passing over the shoulder of a passerby who stood beside him for a few moments while waiting for the red light to change at a midtown intersection, and with the appearance in his memory of an eighteenth-century French scribbler named Nicolas-Edme Restif de la Bretonne; he had only one of his books in his library—he would look for it and find it before the morning began—a first edition bought many years before in an antiquarian bookshop in Paris, costing him an arm and a leg. "What a hodgepodge."

On the surface, none of this had anything directly to do with Lucrecia. Why, then, this urgent need to communicate with her, to recount to her in minute detail every thought boiling inside him? I am lying, my love, he thought. Of course it has to do with you. Everything he did, including the stupid managerial tasks that kept him shackled eight hours a day, Monday through Friday, in an insurance company in downtown Lima, had a profound connection to Lucrecia and to no one else. But above all, and even more slavishly, his nights and the exaltations, fictions, and passions that filled them were, with chivalrous fidelity, dedicated to her. There was the proof—intimate, incontrovertible, painful—on each page of the notebooks he now leafed through.

Why had he thought about rebellions? The thing that had awakened him a few moments earlier was surely an intensification of that morning's indignant anger, his consternation when he read the newspaper article that Lucrecia must have read as well; in a cramped hand, he began to transcribe it onto the first blank page he found:

Wellington (Reuters). A twenty-four-year-old teacher from New Zealand has been sentenced by a judge in this city to four years in prison for sexual assault after it was learned that she had been having carnal relations with a ten-year-old boy, a friend and classmate of her son's. The judge declared that he had given her the same sentence he would have imposed if a man had raped a girl of that age.

My love, my darling Lucrecia, please do not find in this even the shadow of a reproach for what happened between us, he thought. No distasteful allusion, nothing that might seem accusatory or vindictive. No. She ought to see exactly the opposite. Because when the few lines of this dispatch unfolded beneath his eyes this morning as he was taking the first sips of his bitter breakfast coffee (not because he drank it without sugar but because Lucrecia was not beside him and he could not talk over the news with her), Don Rigoberto felt no anguish or pain, much less gratitude or enthusiasm for the judge's statement. Rather, he felt the impetuous, startling solidarity of an adolescent attending a rally for that poor New Zealander so brutally punished because she had introduced the delights of Muslim heaven (the most carnal of those offered in the marketplace of religions, as far as he knew) to that fortunate boy.

Yes, yes, my beloved Lucrecia. He was not pretending or lying or exaggerating. All day he had been aflame with the same indignation he had felt that morning at the judge's foolishness and its unfortunate symmetry with certain feminist doctrines. Could an adult male violating a prepubescent girl of ten, a punishable crime, be the same as a woman of twenty-four disclosing bodily joy and the miracles of sex to a ten-year-old boy already capable of timid erections and simple seminal emissions? If in the first case the presumption of violence against the victim by the victimizer was obligatory (even if the girl had sufficient use of reason to give her consent, she would still be the victim of physical aggression against her hymen), in the second it was simply inconceivable, for if copulation did take place it could happen only with the boy's enthusiastic acquiescence, without which the carnal act would not have been consummated. Don Rigoberto picked up his pen and wrote in a fever of rage: "Although I despise utopias and know they are catastrophic for human life, I now embrace this one: let all boys in this city be deflowered when they reach the age of ten by married women in their thirties, preferably their aunts, teachers, or godmothers." He breathed deeply, feeling somewhat relieved.

For the entire day he was tormented by the fate of that teacher from Wellington, feeling immense sympathy for the public condemnation she must have been exposed to, the humiliation and mockery she must have suffered in addition to losing her job and having that cacographic, electronic, and now digital obscenity, the press, the so-called media, treat her as a corruptor of youth, a degenerate. He was not lying to himself, he was not perpetrating a masochistic farce. "No, dear Lucrecia, I swear I'm not." Throughout the day and into the night the teacher's face, incarnated as the face of his ex-wife, had appeared to him many times. And now, now he felt a driving need to let her know ("to let you know, my love") of his regret and shame. For having been as insensitive, obtuse, inhuman, and cruel as that magistrate in Wellington, a city he would never set foot in except to lay fragrant red roses at the feet of that admired, admirable teacher who would pay for her generosity, her great heart, locked away with fili- cides, thieves, swindlers, and pickpockets (Anglophiles and Maori).

What would the teacher's feet be like? If I could obtain her photograph I would not hesitate to light candles and burn incense to her, he thought. He hoped and prayed her feet were as beautiful and delicate as Doña Lucrecia's, or the foot he had seen on the glossy page of *Time* magazine over the shoulder of a passerby one afternoon when he was stopped by a traffic light at the corner of La Colmena on his way to the Miguel Gray room at the Club Nacional, where he had a meeting with one of those necktied imbeciles who hold their meetings at the Club Nacional and provide a living for imbeciles like him who earn their bread insuring personal property and real estate. The vision lasted only a few seconds but was as illuminating, as bright, as convulsive and overwhelming as it must have been for that girl from Galilee when she had her vision of the winged Gabriel announcing the news that would inflict so many outrages upon the human race.

It was a tiny foot, viewed in profile, with a semicircular heel and a high instep rising proudly from an elegantly shaped sole and ending in meticulously modeled small toes, a feminine foot unblemished by calluses, rough spots, corns, or hideous bunions, a foot where nothing seemed inharmonious and nothing limited the perfection of the whole and the part, a small foot raised and apparently surprised by the alert photographer an instant before it came to rest on a soft carpet. Why Asian? Perhaps because the page it adorned advertised an airline from that part of the world—Singapore Airlines—or possibly because, in his limited experience, Don Rigoberto believed he could affirm that the women of Asia had the loveliest feet on the planet. He was shaken as he recalled the times he had kissed the delectable extremities of his beloved, calling them "little Filipino feet," "Malaysian heels," "Japanese insteps."

All day, in fact, along with his rage over the misfortunes of his new friend, the teacher from Wellington, the tiny feminine foot in the advertisement in *Time* had troubled his mind, and later had disturbed his sleep, unearthing from the depths of memory the recollection of Cinderella, a story told to him when he was a child, and it was precisely the detail of the heroine's emblematic slipper that only her tiny foot could wear which had awakened his first erotic fantasies ("Some wetness and a partial erection, if I must be technical," he said aloud, in the first good-humored impulse of the night). Had he ever discussed with Lucrecia his theory that the amiable Cinderella had undoubtedly done more than all the corrupt mountains of antierotic pornography produced in the twentieth century to create legions of male fetishists? He could not remember. A lapse in his matrimonial relationship that he must correct one day. His state of mind had improved considerably since he had awakened, filled with vexation and longing, dying of rage, solitude, and sorrow. For the past few moments he had even authorized—it was his way of not succumbing to the despair of each day—certain fantasies that had to do not with the eyes, hair, breasts, thighs, or hips of Lucrecia but exclusively with her feet. He now had beside him—it had been difficult to find on the shelves where it had been mislaid—that first edition, in three small volumes, of the novel by Nicolas-Edmé Restif de la Bretonne (in his own hand he had noted on an index card: 1734–1806), the only one he owned of the dozens and dozens badly written by that incontinent polygraph: *Le Pied de Franchette ou l'orpheline française: Histoire intéressante et morale* (Paris, Humblot Quillau, 1769, 2 parties en 3 volumes, 160–148–192 pages). Now I leaf through it, he thought. And now you appear, Lucrecia, barefoot or shod, in every chapter, page, word.

Only one thing in this overwrought scribbler deserved his sympathy and made him associate, in the middle of this misty night, Restif de la Bretonne with Lucrecia, while a thousand other things (well, perhaps not quite so many) made him forgettable, transitory, even unpleasant. Had he ever talked about him to her? Had his name ever come up in their nightly conjugal celebrations? Don Rigoberto could not remember. "But even if it is too late, my dearest, I present him to you, offer him, lay him at your feet (an appropriate turn of phrase)." He had been born into a time of great upheavals, the French eighteenth century, but it was unlikely that the good Nicolas-Edme realized that the entire world around him was falling apart and being put back together again in the pendulum swings of the revolution, obsessed as he was with his own revolution, not the one in society, the economy, and the political regime—"the ones, in general, that get good press"—but the one that concerned him personally: the revolution in carnal desire. That is what he found sympathetic, what led him to buy the first edition of *Le Pied de Franchette*, a novel of cruel coincidences and comic iniquities, absurd entanglements and mindless exchanges, which any respectable literary critic or reader of good taste would find execrable but for Don Rigoberto had the high merit of exalting to deicidal extremes the right of the human being to rebel against the establishment for the sake of his desires, to change the world by making use of his fantasy even for the ephemeral duration of his reading or dreaming.

He read aloud what he had written in the notebook about Restif after reading *Le Pied de Franchette*: "I do not believe that this provincial, the son of peasants, an autodidact, despite his having attended a Jansenist seminary, who taught himself languages and doctrines, all of them badly, and earned his living as a typesetter and maker of books (in both senses of the word, for he wrote them and manufactured them, though he did the second more artfully than the first), ever suspected the transcendental importance his writings would have (symbolic and moral importance, not aesthetic) when, in his incessant explorations of poor working-class neighborhoods in Paris, which fascinated him, or the villages and countryside of France, which he documented like a sociologist, taking time away from his amorous entanglements—adulterous, incestuous, mercenary, but always orthodox, for homosexuality produced a Carmelite consternation in him—he wrote on the run, guided, horror of horrors, by inspiration, never correcting, in a prose that poured out of him overblown, vulgar, burdened with all the detritus of the French language, confused, repetitive, labyrinthine, conventional, cheap, bereft of ideas, insensitive, and—in a word that defines his style better than any other—underdeveloped."

Why, then, after so severe a judgment, was he wasting the dawn recalling this aesthetic imperfection, a crude scribbler who, to make matters worse, even plied the ugly trade of informer? The notebook overflowed with information about him. He had produced nearly two hundred books, all of them unreadable as literature. Why, then, did he persist in bringing him close to Doña Lucrecia, his polar opposite, perfection made woman? Because, he answered himself, no one but this uncouth intellectual could have understood his midday emotion on glimpsing so fleetingly, in a magazine advertisement, the Asian girl's tiny swift foot that tonight had brought him the memory of, the desire for, the queenly feet of Lucrecia. No, no one but Restif, amateur and supreme adept of the cult that an abominable race of psychologists and psychoanalysts preferred to call fetishism, could have understood him, accompanied him, counseled him in this homage and act of gratitude to those adored feet. "Thank you, my beloved Lucrecia"—he prayed fervently—"for the hours of pleasure they have given me since I first discovered them on the beach at Pucusana and kissed them beneath the water and the waves." Overcome with emotion, Don Rigoberto once again felt the salty, agile toes wriggling inside the grotto of his mouth, and his retching because of the seawater he had swallowed.

Yes, that was Don Nicolas-Edmé Restif de la Bretonne's predilection: the feminine foot. And, by extension and "affinity," as an alchemist would say, everything that clothes and covers it: stocking, shoe, sandal, boot. With the spontaneity and innocence of what he was, a rustic who migrated to the city, he practiced and proclaimed his predilection for that delicate extremity and its wrappings without a trace of shame; with the fanaticism of the convert, in his innumerable writings he replaced the real world with a fictitious one as monotonous, predictable, chaotic, and stupid as the first, except that in the one shaped by his bad prose and monothematic singularity, what shone brilliantly, what stood out and unleashed the passions of men, was not the charming faces of ladies, their cascading hair, graceful waists, ivory necks, or haughty bosoms but, inevitably and exclusively, the beauty of their feet. (If he were still alive, it occurred to him, Don Rigoberto would take his friend Restif, with Lucrecia's consent, of course, to the little house by the Olivar and, hiding the rest of her body, show him her feet enclosed in a pair of darling granny boots and even permit him to remove her shoes. How would this forebear have reacted? With a transport of ecstasy? With trembling and howling? Rushing forward, like a happy bloodhound, tongue hanging out, nostrils dilated, to smell and lick the delicacy?

Although he wrote so badly, wasn't he to be respected as a man who paid so much reverence to pleasure and defended his phantom with such conviction and coherence? Wasn't the good Restif, despite his indigestible prose, "one of us"? Of course he was. That is why he had appeared tonight in his dream, drawn by that furtive little Burmese or Singaporean foot, to accompany him through the dawn. A sudden feeling of demoralization gripped Don Rigoberto. The cold penetrated his bones. How he wished at this moment that Lucrecia could know all the repentance and pain tormenting him because of the stupidity, or obstinate incomprehension, that had driven him a year ago to behave just as the ignoble judge in Wellington across the sea had when he sentenced that teacher, that friend ("She is also one of us") to four years in prison for having allowed that fortunate child, that New Zealander Fonchito, to glimpse—no, to inhabit—heaven. "Instead of suffering, instead of reproaching you, I should have thanked you, adorable nursemaid." He did so now, in a dawn filled with resounding, turbulent waves and an invisible, corrosive drizzle, seconded by an obliging Restif, whose little novel deliciously entitled *Le Pied de Franchette*, and stupidly subtitled *ou l'orpheline française: Histoire intéressante et morale* (after all, there was good reason to call it moral), he held on his lap and caressed with both hands, like a pair of beautiful feet.

When Keats wrote, "Beauty is truth, truth beauty" (the citation reappeared constantly in every notebook he opened), was he thinking of Doña Lucrecia's feet? Yes, though the unhappy man did not know it. And, when Restif de la Bretonne wrote and printed (at the same speed, probably) *Le Pied de Franchette*, in 1769, at the age of thirty-five, he too had been inspired, from the future, by a woman who would come into the world nearly two centuries later, in a barbarous region of America called (seriously?) Latin. Thanks to his commentaries in the notebook, Don Rigoberto began to remember the plot of the little novel. As conventional and predictable as could be, written with his feet (no, this he should not think or say), the true protagonist was not the beautiful adolescent orphan Franchette Florangis but the maddening feet of Franchette Florangis, and this elevated and individualized the novel, giving it the wisdom and persuasiveness of a true work of art. The opalescent feet of the young Franchette caused unimaginable disturbances, ignited unimaginable passions. Her tutor, Monsieur Apatéon, a foolish old man who loved to buy exquisite shoes for them and took advantage of any excuse to caress them, was so inflamed by his pupil's feet that he even tried to rape her, the daughter of his dearest friend. They turned the painter Dolsans, a decent young man who was smitten from the first time he saw them encased in little green slippers adorned with a golden flower, into a desperate madman full of criminal designs who lost his life because of them. The fortunate young man, the wealthy Lusanville, before his arms and mouth ever held the beautiful girl of his dreams, took solace in one of her shoes which he, another amateur, had stolen. Every living male who saw them—financiers, merchants, landowners, noblemen, plebeians—succumbed to their charms, pierced by the arrows of carnal love and prepared to do anything to possess them. And therefore the narrator was correct when he stated the words that Don Rigoberto had transcribed: *"Le joli pied les rendait tous criminels."* Yes, yes, those tiny feet made them all criminals. The slippers, sandals, boots, shoes of the beautiful Franchette, those magical objects, moved through the story and illuminated it with a dazzling, seminal light.

Though stupid people might speak of perversion, he, and Lucrecia of course, could understand Restif, celebrate his having the audacity, the lack of shame, to display to others his right to be different, to remake the world in his own image. Hadn't they done the same, he and Lucrecia, every night for ten years? Hadn't they disarranged and rearranged life according to their desires? Would they ever do so again? Or would all of it remain confined to the past, along with the images that memory treasures in order not to succumb to the despair of the real, the actual?

On this night-dawn, Don Rigoberto felt like one of the men driven mad by Franchette's foot. His life was empty; each night, each dawn, he replaced Lucrecia's absence with phantoms, but they were not enough to console him. Was there any solution? Was it too late to turn back and correct the error? Couldn't a Supreme Court or Constitutional Tribunal in New Zealand revoke the sentence of the obtuse magistrate in Wellington and pardon the teacher? Couldn't an unprejudiced New Zealander governor declare an amnesty and even present her with a civilian heroine's medal to honor her demonstrated sacrifices for the sake of youth? Couldn't he go to the little house by the Olivar de San Isidro and tell Lucrecia that stupid human justice had been wrong, had condemned her with no right to do so, and give her back her honor and the freedom to . . . to? To what? He hesitated, but went forward the best he could.

Was this a utopia? A utopia like the ones also fantasized by the fetishist Restif de la Bretonne? No, no, for those of Don Rigoberto, when, borne away by the languid sweetness of a mind at play, he sometimes gave himself over to them, were private utopias incapable of infringing on the free will of others. Couldn't these be legitimate utopias, very different from the collective ones, the rabid enemies of freedom, the ones that always carried in them the seed of catastrophe?

This had been the weak and dangerous side of Nicolas-Edmé as well: a disease of the age, to which he had succumbed, as had so many of his contemporaries. Because the appetite for social utopias, the great legacy of the Enlightenment together with new horizons and bold vindications of the right to pleasure, had also brought historical apocalypses. Don Rigoberto remembered none of this; his notebooks did. They contained the accusatory data, the implacable fulminations.

In Restif, the refined devotee of tiny feet and women's shoes—"May God bless him for that, if He exists"—there was also a dangerous, messianic thinker (a cretin if one wished to judge him harshly, a misguided dreamer if one preferred to spare his life), a reformer of institutions, a savior from social ills who, among the mountains of paper he scribbled, dedicated a few hills and highlands to erecting those prisons, his public utopias, whose purpose was to regulate prostitution and impose happiness on whores (the hideous enterprise appeared in a book with the deceptively attractive title of *Le Pornographe*), improve the operation of theaters and the behavior of actors (*Le Mimographe*), organize the life of women by assigning them duties and setting limits on them so that there would be harmony between the sexes (this fearsome aberration also bore a title that seemed to promise pleasure—*Les Gynographes*—when it actually proposed stocks and chains for freedom). Much more ambitious and threatening, of course, had been his attempt to regulate—to suffocate, in fact—the behavior of the human race (*L'Andrographe*) and introduce an intrusive, sharp-edged legal system that would attack intimacy and put an end to free initiative and the free disposition of human desires: *Le Thermographe*. In the face of these interventionist excesses worthy of a secular Torquemada, Restif's regulatory madness seemed mere child's play, causing him to recommend a total reform of orthography (*Glossographe*). He had collected these utopias in a book he called *Idées singulières* (1769), which they undoubtedly were, but in the sinister, criminal interpretation of the notion of singularity.

The sentence inscribed in the notebook was unappealable, and Don Rigoberto agreed with it: "There is no doubt that if this diligent printer, writer of documents, and refined amateur of feminine pedal appendages had ever attained political power, he would have turned France, and perhaps all of Europe, into a well-disciplined concentration camp in which a fine mesh of prohibitions and obligations would have vaporized the last trace of freedom. Fortunately, he was too much of an egotist to lust after power, concentrating instead on reconstructing human reality in fiction, reshaping it to suit his desires, so that, as in *Le Pied de Franchette*, the supreme value, the greatest aspiration of the male biped was not to perform heroic feats of military conquest, or achieve sainthood, or discover the secrets of matter and life, but consisted instead of that delectable, delicious, divine as the ambrosia that nourished the gods on Olympus, tiny, feminine foot." Like the one Don Rigoberto had seen in the advertisement in *Time*, which reminded him of Lucrecia's feet and held him here, in the first light of morning, sending his beloved this bottle that he would throw into the sea, hoping it would find her, knowing very well it would not, for how could something that did not exist, something shaped by the evanescent brush of his dreams, ever reach her?

Don Rigoberto, his eyes closed, had just asked himself this desperate question when, as his lips murmured the amorously vocative "Ah, Lucrecia!" his left arm knocked one of the notebooks to the floor. He picked it up and glanced at the page it had opened to in the fall. He gave a start: chance provided marvelous details, as he and his wife had often had occasion to discover in their flirtatious pursuits. What had he found? Two notes, written many years ago. The first, a forgettable reference to a small, anonymous, turn-of-the-century engraving of Mercury ordering the nymph Calypso to free Odysseus—with whom she had fallen in love and whom she was holding prisoner on her island—and allow him to continue his voyage back to Penelope. And the second, how marvelous, an impassioned reflection on: "The delicate fetishism of Johannes Vermeer, who, in *Diana and Her Companions*, pays plastic tribute to that scorned member of the female body by showing a nymph given over to the amorous task of using a sponge to wash—or rather, caress—Diana's foot, while another nymph, in sweet abandon, caresses hers. Everything is subtle and carnal, imbued with a delicate sensuality masked by the perfection of the forms and the soft mist that bathes the scene, endowing the figures with the magical unreality that you possess, Lucrecia, every night in flesh and blood, as does your phantom when you visit my dreams." How true, how real, how relevant.

And if he were to answer her anonymous letters? And if he actually were to write to her? And if he were to knock on her door this very afternoon, as soon as he had completed the last turn on the treadmill of his insuring and managerial servitude? And if, as soon as he saw her, he were to fall to his knees and humble himself, kissing the ground she walked on, begging her forgiveness and calling her, until he made her laugh, "My beloved nursemaid," "My teacher from New Zealand," "My Franchette," "My Diana"? Would she laugh? Would she throw herself into his arms and, offering him her lips, make him feel her body, let him know that everything lay behind them, that they could begin again to build, all by themselves, their secret utopia?

Tiger Stew

With you I have a Hawaiian romance in which you dance the hula-hula for me on nights when the moon is full, wearing little bells on your hips and ankles, imitating Dorothy Lamour.

And an Aztec romance in which I sacrifice you to coppery, avid gods, serpentine and feathered, at the top of a pyramid made of rust-streaked stones, surrounded by the teeming, impenetrable jungle.

An Eskimo romance in freezing igloos illuminated by torches burning whale blubber, and a Norwegian one in which we love each other on skis, racing a hundred kilometers an hour down the slopes of a white mountain erupting in totems with runic inscriptions.

My conceit tonight, beloved, is modernist, bloodthirsty, and African.

You will undress before the mirror, keeping on your black stockings and red garters, and conceal your beautiful head beneath the mask of a wild animal, preferably the tigress in heat in Rubén Darío's *Azul . . .* , or a Sudanese lioness.

You will thrust out your right hip, flex your left leg, rest your hand on the opposite hip, in the most savage, provocative pose.

Sitting in my chair, and lashed to its back, I will be looking at you and adoring you with my customary servility.

I will not move even an eyelash, I will not scream as you sink your claws into my eyes and your white fangs tear out my throat and you devour my flesh and slake your thirst with my enamored blood.

Now I am inside you, now I am you, beloved who feeds on me, your stew.

IX

The Date at the Sheraton

"Just so I could, just to find the courage to do it, I had a couple of whiskeys neat," said Doña Lucrecia. "Before I started to put on my costume, I mean."

"You must have been good and tight, Señora," Justiniana remarked in amusement. "We know you have no head for liquor."

"You're shameless, you were right there," Doña Lucrecia scolded her. "All excited at what might happen. Pouring the drinks, helping me dress up, laughing out loud while I was turning myself into a tart."

"A hooker," the maid echoed, touching up her rouge.

This is the craziest thing I've ever done in my life, thought Doña Lucrecia. Worse than what I did with Fonchito, worse than marrying a madman like Rigoberto. If I do this I'll be sorry till the day I die. And yet she was doing it. The red wig suited her perfectly—she had tried it on in the shop where she had ordered it—and its high, ornate piles of curls and ringlets seemed to be aflame. She barely recognized herself as that incandescent woman in her curled false eyelashes and tropical hoop earrings, heavily made up with fiery red lips larger than her real ones, and the beauty marks and blue eye shadow of a femme fatale in the style of a Mexican movie from the 1950s.

"Well, I'll be darned, I can't believe it, nobody would know it's you." An astonished Justiniana, her hand covering her mouth, examined her. "I don't know who you look like, Señora."

"A hooker, I guess," declared Doña Lucrecia.

The whiskey had its effect. The doubts of a few moments before evaporated and now, intrigued and amused, she observed her own transformation in the mirror in her room. Justiniana was more and more amazed as she handed her the articles of clothing laid out on the bed: the miniskirt that clung so tightly she could hardly move; the black stockings topped by red garters with gold ornaments; the glittering blouse that exposed her breasts down to the nipples. She helped her, too, to put on the silver spike-heeled shoes. Stepping back to look her over from top to bottom, bottom to top, she exclaimed again in stupefaction, "It's not you, Señora, it's someone else, another woman. Are you really going out like that?"

"Of course," Doña Lucrecia declared. "If I'm not back by morning, notify the police."

And without another word she called for a taxi from the Virgen del Pilar station and said to the driver, in an authoritative voice, "Hotel Sheraton." Two days ago, yesterday, this morning, as she prepared her outfit, she'd had her doubts. She had told herself she wouldn't go, wouldn't lend herself to this kind of spectacle, to what was surely a cruel joke; but once in the taxi she felt absolutely sure of herself, and determined to live out the adventure to its conclusion. And whatever happened would happen. She looked at her watch. The instructions said to come between eleven-thirty and midnight, and it was only eleven; she'd arrive early. Serene and somewhat removed because of the alcohol, she asked herself, as the taxi sped down the semideserted Zanjón expressway toward the center of the city, what she would do if someone recognized her at the Sheraton despite her disguise. She would deny what they saw, making her voice higher, using the honeyed, vulgar tone those women used: "Lucrecia? My name's Aída. She looks like me? A distant relative, maybe." She would lie with utter brazenness. Her fear had vanished totally. You're under a spell and have to play a whore for one night, she thought, pleased with herself. She noticed that the cabdriver was constantly raising his eyes to the rearview mirror to look at her.

Before going into the Sheraton, she put on the dark glasses with pearly-white frames that ended in a kind of trident, which she had bought that afternoon in a little shop on La Paz. She had chosen them for their coarse bad taste and because they were big enough to seem like a mask. She hurried across the lobby toward the bar, afraid that one of the uniformed bellboys, eyeing her scornfully, would ask who she was and what she wanted, or throw her out no questions asked because of her tawdry appearance. But no one approached her. She walked up the steps to the bar at an unhurried pace. The dim light restored the confidence she had almost lost in the glare of the entrance, that vast hall under the oppressive rectangle of the hotel, a prisonlike skyscraper of floors, walls, corridors, balustrades, and bedrooms. In the half-light, through a haze of cigarette smoke, she saw that only a few tables were occupied. She heard an Italian tune sung by a prehistoric singer—Domenico Modugno—that reminded her of an old movie with Claudia Cardinale and Vittorio Gassman. Silhouettes stood at the bar against a bluish-yellow background of glasses and rows of bottles. At one table voices rose in the strident early stages of drunkenness.

Once again she felt self-assured and certain of her ability to confront any unforeseen turn of events, and she crossed the room and claimed a bar stool. The mirror in front of her showed a grotesque figure that deserved tenderness, not revulsion or laughter. She could not have been more amazed when she heard the mestizo bartender, his hair stiff with pomade, wearing a vest several sizes too large and a string tie that seemed to be strangling him, say with loutish familiarity, "Order or get out."

She was about to make a scene, but thought better of it, and said to herself with satisfaction that his insolence proved the success of her disguise. And, testing her new affected, sugary voice, she said, "A Black Label on the rocks, if you don't mind."

He stared at her, dubious, trying to decide if she was serious. Finally he murmured, "On the rocks, right," and moved away. She thought that her disguise would have been complete if she had added a long cigarette holder. Then she would have asked him for a pack of Kool 100's and blown smoke rings toward the ceiling of winking stars.

The bartender brought the bill with the whiskey, and she did not protest this show of distrust either but paid, leaving no tip. She had barely taken her first sip when someone sat down beside her. She shuddered slightly. The game was turning serious. But no, it wasn't a man but a woman, fairly young, wearing pants and a dark sleeveless polo with a high neck. Her straight hair hung loose, and she had an impudent, rather common face, the kind that Egon Schiele's girls had.

"Hello." The thin Mirafloran voice sounded familiar. "Haven't we met?"

"I don't think so," Doña Lucrecia replied.

"I thought we had, I'm sorry," said the girl. "I really have a terrible memory. Do you come here often?"

"Once in a while," Doña Lucrecia said hesitantly. Did she know her?

"The Sheraton isn't as safe as it used to be," the girl lamented. She lit a cigarette and exhaled a mouthful of smoke that took some time to dissipate. "I heard they raided it on Friday."

Doña Lucrecia imagined herself pushed into a police van, taken to the station, charged with prostitution.

"Order or get out," the bartender warned her neighbor, threatening her with a raised finger.

"You go to hell, you stinking half-breed," the girl said, not even turning to look at him.

"You're always ready with the backtalk, Adelita," the bartender said with a smile, showing teeth that Doña Lucrecia was sure were green with tartar. "All right, go on. Make yourself at home. You know I have a soft spot for you, and you take advantage."

That was when Doña Lucrecia recognized her. Adelita, of course! Esthercita's daughter! Well, well, so this was the daughter of Esther the prude.

"Señora Esthercita's daughter?" Justiniana doubled over with laughter. "Adelita? Little Adelita? The daughter of Fonchito's godmother? Picking up tricks at the Sheraton? I can't swallow that, Señora. I can't swallow that even with Coca-Cola or champagne."

"Adelita in person, and you can't imagine what she was like," declared Doña Lucrecia. "Tough as nails. Using filthy language, moving as easily as a fish in water there at the bar. Like the oldest tart in Lima."

"And she didn't recognize you?"

"No, fortunately. But you haven't heard anything yet. We were sitting and talking when this man appeared, out of the blue. Adelita knew him, apparently."

He was tall, strong, a little heavy, a little drunk, a little of everything a man needs in order to feel fearless and in command. Wearing a suit and a loud tie with a pattern of diamonds and zigzags. Breathing like a bellows. He must have been about fifty. Placing himself between the two women, he put his arms around them both, and as if they were lifelong friends, he said by way of greeting, "Are you two coming to my suite? I have good booze and a little something for the nose. And lots of dollars for girls who know how to be nice."

Doña Lucrecia felt dizzy. The man's breath hit her in the face. He was so close to her that with the slightest movement he could have kissed her.

"You all alone, honey?" the girl asked flirtatiously.

"What do you need anybody else for?" The man sucked in his lips, touching the pocket where he must have carried his wallet. "A hundred green ones apiece, okay? Paid in advance."

"If you don't have tens or fifties, I'll take *soles*," Adelita said immediately. "The hundred-dollar bills are always counterfeit."

"Okay, okay, I have fifties," the man promised. "Let's go, girls."

"I'm expecting someone," Doña Lucrecia apologized. "I'm sorry."

"Can't he wait?" the man said impatiently.

"I can't, really."

"If you want, just the two of us can go up," Adelita interrupted, taking him by the arm. "I'll be nice to you, honey."

But the man turned her down, disappointed.

"Not just you, no. Tonight I'm giving myself a present. My ponies won three races and the daily double. Want me to tell you what the present is? I'm going to do something that's been making me crazy for days. Know what it is?" He looked first at one and then the other, very seriously, loosening his collar, and then, without waiting for an answer, eagerly continued: "I'm going to fuck one while I eat the other. And watch them in the mirror, feeling each other up, kissing each other, while they sit on the throne. And I'll be the throne."

Egon Schiele's mirror, thought Señora Lucrecia. She felt less repelled by his vulgarity than by the pitiless glint in his eyes as he described his desire.

"Your eyes will pop out of your head if you look at so many things at once, honey." Adelita laughed, pretending to punch him.

"It's my fantasy. Thanks to the ponies, tonight it'll come true," he said proudly, by way of farewell. "Too bad you're busy, babe, I like your looks, even with all the war paint. *Ciao*, girls."

When he had disappeared among the tables—the bar was more crowded than before, the smoke denser, the sound of conversations louder, and now the music on the loudspeakers was a merengue by Juan Luis Guerra—Adelita leaned toward her with a dejected look on her face.

"Do you really have a date? With our friend there it would have been a bargain. What he said about the horses is a lie. He's a dealer, everybody knows him. And he comes right away, a hundred miles an hour. Premature ejaculation, they call it. So damn fast he hardly gets started sometimes. It was a present, honey."

Doña Lucrecia tried without success to put on a knowing smile. How could any daughter of Esther's be saying such things? A woman so fastidious, so rich, so vain, so elegant, so Catholic. Esthercita, Fonchito's godmother. The girl went on with the self-assured remarks that astounded Doña Lucrecia.

"What a pain in the ass missing a chance to earn a hundred dollars in half an hour, more like fifteen minutes," she complained. "Going up with you to do that guy sounded good to me, I swear. It would have been over one two three. I don't know about you, but what I can't stand is doing those damn couples. The husband bug-eyed while you make the little woman hot. Honey, I hate those bitches! Dumb cunts always dying of embarrassment. They giggle, they're ashamed, you have to give them booze and plenty of stroking. Shit, I tell you it makes me sick to my stomach. Especially when they start to cry and feel sorry for what they did. I swear I could kill them. You waste half an hour, an hour with those broads. First they want to, then they don't, and you lose a lot of money. I don't have any patience for it, honey. It's happened to you, hasn't it?"

"Sure it has," Doña Lucrecia felt obliged to say, having to force each word out of her mouth. "Sometimes."

"Now, what's even worse is two guys, bosom buddies, pals, know what I mean?" Adelita said with a sigh. Her voice had changed and Doña Lucrecia thought that something awful must have been done to her by sadists, madmen, monsters. "They feel so macho when there are two of them. And they begin to ask for all the crazy shit. Blow jobs, the sandwich, up-the-ass. Why don't you ask your old lady for that one, babe? I don't know about you, honey, but as far as I'm concerned, up-the-ass is something I won't touch with a ten-foot pole. I don't like it. It's disgusting. And it hurts too. So I won't do it even for two hundred dollars. What about you?"

"The same goes for me," Doña Lucrecia declared. "It makes me sick and it hurts, just like you said. Up-the-ass is a killer, not for two hundred, not for a thousand."

"Well, for a thousand, who knows?" The girl laughed. "See? We're alike. Well, there's your date, I think. Let's see if next time the two of us can do that moron with his ponies. *Ciao*, have fun."

She moved away, leaving her seat free for the slender figure who was approaching. In the dim light Doña Lucrecia saw that he was young, with dark blond hair and boyish features and a vague resemblance to . . . to whom? Fonchito! A Fonchito with ten years added, whose eyes had hardened and whose body had lengthened and toughened. He wore an elegant blue suit, and the pink handkerchief in his jacket pocket was the same color as his tie.

"The inventor of the word 'individualism' was Alexis de Tocqueville," he said by way of greeting, in a harsh voice. "True or false?"

"True." Doña Lucrecia broke into a cold sweat: what was going to happen now? Determined to see it through to the end, she added, "I am Aldonza, the Andalusian from Rome. Whore, sorceress, and mender of maidenheads, at your service."

"The only thing I understand is whore," observed Justiniana, her head spinning at the words she was hearing. "Were you serious? How could you keep from laughing? Excuse the interruption, Señora."

"Follow me," said the newcomer, without a hint of humor. He moved like a robot.

Doña Lucrecia slid off the bar stool and could imagine the bartender's evil-minded glance as he watched her leave. She followed the blond young man, who moved quickly among the crowded tables, cutting through the smoke-filled atmosphere on his way to the exit. Then he crossed the corridor to the elevators. Doña Lucrecia saw him press the button for the twenty-fourth floor, and her heart skipped a beat and the pit of her stomach felt hollow because of how quickly the elevator rose. A door was opened as soon as they walked out into the hallway. They were in the foyer of an enormous suite: through the large picture window, a sea of lights with dark patches and banks of fog spread out at her feet.

"You can take off the wig and get undressed in the bathroom." The boy pointed to a room off the sitting room. But Doña Lucrecia could not take a step, for she was intrigued by that youthful face, the steely eyes, the tousled ringlets—she had thought his hair was blond, but it was light to medium brown—that fell on his forehead and were modeled by the cone of light from a lamp. How was it possible? He looked exactly like him.

"Do you mean Egon Schiele?" Justiniana interrupted. "The painter that Fonchito's so crazy about? That good-for-nothing who painted his models doing dirty stuff?"

"Why do you think I was so shocked? I mean him and no one else."

"I know I resemble him," the boy explained in the same serious, businesslike, dehumanized tone he had used with her from the first. "Is that why you're so disconcerted? All right, I resemble him. What about it? Or do you think I'm Egon Schiele come back to life? You're not that foolish, are you?"

"It's just that I'm dumbfounded by the resemblance," Doña Lucrecia acknowledged as she stared at him. "It's not just the face. It's your body

217

too, thin, tall, rachitic. And your hands, they're so big. And the way you play with your fingers, hiding the thumbs. Exactly the same, identical to all the photographs of Egon Schiele. How is it possible?"

"Let's not waste any more time," the boy said coldly, with a look of irritation. "Take off that disgusting wig and those horrible earrings and beads. I'll wait for you in the bedroom. Come in naked."

There was something defiant and vulnerable in his face. He looked, thought Doña Lucrecia, like a spoiled, brilliant little boy who, in spite of his pranks and impudence, his audacity and insolence, needed his mamá very much. Was she thinking of Egon Schiele or Fonchito? Doña Lucrecia was absolutely certain that the boy prefigured what Rigoberto's son would be in a few years.

"Now the hard part begins," she said to herself. She was sure that the boy who resembled Fonchito and Egon Schiele had double-locked the door, and that even if she wanted to, there was no escape from the suite. She would have to remain there the rest of the night. Along with the fear that had overwhelmed her, she was consumed with curiosity, and even a hint of arousal. Giving herself to this slender youngster with the cold, rather cruel expression would be like making love to a Fonchito-youth-almost-man, or to a rejuvenated and beautified Rigoberto, a Rigoberto-youth-almost-boy. The idea made her smile. The mirror in the bathroom reflected her relaxed, almost happy expression. She had trouble taking off her clothes. Her hands felt stiff, as if they had been in snow. Without the absurd wig, free of the miniskirt that had confined her, she could breathe freely. She kept on her panties and minimal black lace bra, and before walking out she fluffed and arranged her hair—she had been wearing a hairnet— pausing for a moment in the doorway. Again she felt panic. "I may not get out of here alive." But not even that fear made her regret coming here or acting out this cruel farce in order to please Rigoberto (or Fonchito?). When she walked into the sitting room, she saw that the boy had turned off all the lights in the room except for a small lamp in a far corner. Through the enormous window, thousands of fireflies were winking down below, in an inverted sky. Lima wore the disguise of a great city; the darkness wiped away its rags, its filth, even its bad smell. The soft music of harps, flutes, and violins washed over the shadows. As she walked, still apprehensive, toward the door the boy had indicated, she felt a new wave of excitement that stiffened her nipples ("Rigoberto likes that so much"). She moved

218

silently across the thick-piled carpet and knocked on the closed door. It opened without a sound.

"And they were there, the ones from before?" exclaimed Justiniana, even more incredulous. "I can't believe it. Both of them? Adelita, Señora Esther's daughter?"

"And the man with the horses, the dealer, or whatever he was," Doña Lucrecia confirmed. "Yes, they were there. Both of them. In bed."

"And stark naked, of course." Justiniana giggled, raising a hand to her mouth and brazenly rolling her eyes. "Waiting for you, Señora."

The room seemed larger than usual for a hotel, even one in a luxury suite, but Doña Lucrecia could not make an exact estimate of its dimensions because only the lamp on one of the night tables was lit, and the circular light, reddened by the large, scorpion-colored shade, clearly illuminated only the couple lying in an embrace on the coal-black spread with the dark brownish markings that covered the king-size bed. The rest of the room lay in shadow.

"Come in, baby," the man welcomed her, waving a hand as he continued to kiss Adelita, whom he had partially mounted. "Have a drink. There's champagne on the table. And some coke in that silver snuffbox."

Her surprise at finding Adelita and the horse lover did not make her forget the slender young man with the cruel mouth. Where had he gone? Was he spying on them from the shadows?

"Hi, honey." Adelita's mischievous face appeared over the man's shoulder. "I'm glad you got rid of your date. Come on, hurry up. Aren't you cold? It's nice and warm in here."

She lost all her fear. She went to the table and poured a glass of champagne from a bottle resting in an ice bucket. And if she did a line of cocaine as well? As she sipped her drink in the semidarkness, she thought, It's magic or witchcraft. It can't be a miracle. The man was fatter than he had seemed in clothes; his pale body, spotted with moles, had rolls of fat around the middle, smooth buttocks, and very short legs covered with tufts of dark hair. Adelita, on the other hand, was even thinner than Lucrecia had thought; her body was long, lean, and dark, with an extremely narrow waist and protruding hipbones. She allowed herself to be kissed and embraced, and also embraced the horse-loving dealer, but though her gestures simulated enthusiasm, Doña Lucrecia noticed that she did not kiss him, and even avoided his mouth.

"Come on, come on, I can't hold out much longer," the man pleaded suddenly, vehemently. "My fantasy, my fantasy. It's now or never, girls!"

Though her earlier excitement had ebbed and she felt a certain revulsion, after she drained her glass, Doña Lucrecia obeyed. Going toward the bed, she again saw the archipelago of lights through the window, below and above her, in the hills where the distant Cordillera began. She sat on a corner of the bed, not fearful but bewildered and increasingly repelled. A hand grasped her arm, pulled her, forced her to lie beneath a small, soft body. She gave in, she did not resist, she was disheartened, demoralized, disillusioned. She told herself, over and over again, like an automaton: "You're not going to cry, Lucrecia, you're not going to cry." The man embraced her with his left arm and Adelita with his right, and his head pivoted from one to the other, kissing them on the neck, on the ears, searching for their mouths. Adelita's face was very close to hers; she was disheveled and flushed, and in her eyes she detected a mocking, cynical sign of complicity, urging her on. His lips and teeth pressed against hers, forcing her mouth open. His tongue slithered in like an asp.

"You're the one I want to fuck," she heard him beg as he nibbled and caressed her breasts. "Get on, get on. Hurry, I'm going to come."

She hesitated, but Adelita helped her mount him, and then she squatted too, passing one of her legs over him and adjusting her position so that his mouth was at her depilitated sex, where Doña Lucrecia saw no more than a sparse line of hair. At that moment, she felt herself impaled. Had that tiny, barely erect thing that seconds before had been rubbing against her legs grown so much when it entered her? Now it was a rod, a battering ram that raised her up, pierced her, wounded her with cataclysmic force.

"Kiss each other, kiss each other," the pony man was moaning. "I can hardly see you, damn it. We don't have a mirror!"

Drenched with perspiration from head to foot, stupefied, in pain, not opening her eyes, she stretched out her arms and searched for Adelita's face, but when she found her thin lips the girl, though she pressed them hard against Lucrecia's, kept them closed. They did not open even when she applied pressure with her tongue. And then, through the lashes of her half-closed eyes and the beads of sweat falling from her brow, she saw the young man with the steely eyes, above them, near the ceiling, balancing at the top of a ladder. Half-hidden by what seemed to be a lacquered screen that had Chinese characters on it, his ears attentive, his eyes ablaze, the small cruel mouth puckered, he was furiously drawing her, drawing them, with a long stick of charcoal on snow-white paper. He looked, in fact, like a bird of prey crouched at the top of the ladder, observing them, measuring them, putting on the finishing touches with long, energetic strokes, those fierce, sharp eyes darting back and forth from the pad to the bed, the bed to the pad, not paying attention to anything else, indifferent to the lights of Lima spread out beneath the window, and to his own virile member that had forced its way out of his trousers, popping the buttons, and stretched and grew like a balloon filling with air. A flying serpent, it hovered over her, contemplating her with its great Cyclopean eye. It did not surprise her or matter to her. She was riding, overflowing, intoxicated, grateful, full to the brim, thinking now of Fonchito, now of Rigoberto.

"Why are you still bouncing around, can't you see I've come?" whimpered the lover of horses. In the semidarkness his face looked ashen. He was pouting like a spoiled child. "Damned luck, the same thing always happens. Just when things get going, I come. I can't hold it back. No way, no way. I went to a specialist and he prescribed mud baths. Pure crap. They gave me a stomachache and made me puke. Massages. More crap. I went to a witch doctor in La Victoria and he put me in a tub with herbs that smelled like shit. What good did it do me? None at all. Now I come faster than I did before. Why do I have such rotten luck, damn it?"

He moaned and began to sob.

"Don't cry, *compadre*, didn't you have your fantasy?" Adelita consoled him, passing her leg again over the sniveler's head and lying beside him.

Apparently neither of them could see Egon Schiele, or his double, balancing a meter above them at the top of the ladder, who kept from falling and maintained his center of gravity thanks to that immense penis waving gently over the bed, displaying in the dim light its delicate rose-colored creases and the merry veins on its back. And they undoubtedly did not hear him either. She did, very clearly. Between clenched teeth he was repeating, like a harsh, belligerent mantra, "I am the most timid of men. I am divine."

"Take a rest, honey, what are you doing, the show's over," Adelita said to her affectionately.

"Don't let them leave, hit them if you have to. Don't let them go. Hit them, hit them hard, both of them!"

It was Fonchito, naturally. No, not the painter absorbed in the task of sketching them. It was the boy, her stepchild, Rigoberto's son. Was Rigoberto there too? Yes. Where? Somewhere, hidden in the shadows in that room of miracles. Lying still, feeling awkward, no longer excited, terrified, covering her breasts with her hands, Doña Lucrecia looked to the right, peered to the left. And at last she found them, reflected in a great oval mirror where she saw herself as well, repeated like one of Egon Schiele's models. The half-light did not dissolve them; instead, it revealed father and son, sitting next to each other—the former observing them with benevolent affection, the latter overexcited, his angelic face red with so much shouting—"Hit them, hit them"—on a settee that seemed like a box in a theater perching over the stage of the bed.

"You mean the señor and Fonchito were there too?" said Justiniana in a rather sharp tone of utter disbelief. "Now that's something nobody could believe."

"Sitting right there watching us." Doña Lucrecia nodded. "Rigoberto, very well-bred, understanding, tolerant. And the boy out of control, up to his usual mischief."

"I don't know about you, Señora," said Justiniana abruptly, cutting the narration short and getting to her feet, "but right now I need a cold shower. So I won't spend another sleepless night tossing and turning. I love having these conversations with you. But they leave me hot and bothered and charged with electricity. If you don't believe me, just put your hand here and see what a shock you'll get."

The Slimy Worm

Although I know all too well that you are a necessary evil without which communal life would not be livable, I must tell you that you represent everything I despise, in society and in myself. Because for more than a quarter of a century, Monday through Friday, from eight in the morning until six in the evening, with some ancillary activities (cocktail parties, seminars, inaugurations, conferences) which are impossible for me to avoid without risk to my livelihood, I too am a kind of bureaucrat though I work in the private, not the public sector. But, like you, and because of you, in the course of these twenty-five years my energy, time, and talent (I had some, once) have been swallowed up in large part by transactions, negotiations, applications, petitions, the procedures invented by you to justify the salary you earn and the desk where your rear end grows fat, leaving me barely a few crumbs of freedom to take certain initiatives and engage in work that may deserve to be called creative. I know that insurance (my professional field) and creativity are as far apart as the planets Saturn and Pluto in the vast reaches of space, but this distance would not be so vertiginous if you, regulationist hydra, red tapist caterpillar, king of seal-bearing documents, had not made it into an abyss. For even in the arid desert of insurers and underwriters the human imagination could play an enthusiastic part and derive intellectual stimulation and even pleasure if you, imprisoned in that dense chain mail of suffocating regulations—meant to lend an air of necessity to the bloated bureaucracy that gorges itself at the public trough and creates myriad alibis and justifications for its blackmail, bribery, trafficking, and theft—had not transformed the work of an insurance company into a mind-numbing routine similar to that followed by Jean Tinguely's complicated, hardworking machines, which move chains, pulleys, rods, blades, scoops, and pistons, and eventually give birth to a Ping-Pong ball (you don't know who Tinguely is, nor should you, though I am sure that if you ever happened to run across his creations, you would have taken every precaution to not understand, to trivialize the savage sarcasm aimed at you by the works of this sculptor, one of the few contemporary artists who understand me).

If I tell you that I started at the firm soon after receiving my law degree, in an insignificant position in the legal department, and that in the past quarter century I have moved up through the hierarchy to become a manager, a member of the Board of Directors, and the owner of a good share of stock in the company, you will say that under these circumstances I have nothing to complain about, that I suffer from ingratitude. Don't I live well? Don't I form part of the microscopic portion of Peruvian society that owns a home and a car, has the opportunity to vacation once or twice a year in Europe or the United States, and enjoys the kind of comfortable, secure life that is unthinkable, undreamable, for four-fifths of our compatriots? All this is true. It is also true that because of my successful career (isn't that what you people call it?) I have been able to fill my study with books, etchings, and paintings that protect me from rampant stupidity and vulgarity (that is, from everything you represent) and create an enclave of freedom and fantasy where every day or, rather, every night, I have been able to detoxify, shedding the thick crust of dulling conventionality, vile routine, castrating gregarious activities that you manufacture and that nourish you, and live, truly live and be myself, opening wide to the angels and demons that live inside me the iron-barred doors behind which—and you, you are to blame—they are obliged to hide for the rest of the day.

You will also say, "If you hate office routine so much, and letters and policies, legal reports and protocols, claims, permits, and allegations, then why did you not have the courage to shake it off and live your true life, the life of your fantasy and desires, not only at night but in the morning, afternoon, and evening too? Why did you give more than half your life to the bureaucratic animal that enslaves you and your angels and demons?" The question is pertinent—I have asked it many times—but so is my reply: "Because the world of fantasy, pleasure, and liberated desire, my only homeland, would not have survived unscathed subjected to the rigors of need, deprivation, economic worries, the stifling weight of debts and poverty. Dreams and desires are inedible. My existence would have been impoverished, would have become a caricature of itself." I am no hero, I am not a great artist, I lack genius, and consequently I would not have been able to console myself with the hope of a "work" that would outlive me. My aspirations and aptitudes do not go beyond knowing how to distinguish—in this I am superior to you, whose adventitious condition has reduced to less than nothing your sense of ethical and aesthetic discrimination—within the thicket of possibilities that surround me, between what I love and what I despise, what makes my life beautiful and what makes it ugly and besmirches it with stupidity, what exalts me and what depresses me, what gives me joy and what makes me suffer. Simply to be in a position to constantly differentiate among these contradictory options, I require the economic peace of mind provided by this profession so blemished by the culture of red tape, that noxious miasma produced by you as the worm produces slime, which has become the air the entire world now breathes. Fantasies and desires—mine, at least—demand a minimum of serenity and security to manifest themselves. Otherwise they would wither and die. If you wish to deduce from this that my angels and demons are defiantly bourgeois, that is absolutely true.

Earlier I mentioned the word "parasite," and you probably asked yourself if I, a lawyer who for the past twenty-five years has applied the science of jurisprudence—the most nourishing food for bureaucracy and the primary begetter of bureaucrats—to the specialty of insurance, have the right to use it disparagingly about anyone else. Yes, I do, but only because I also apply it to myself, my bureaucratic half. In fact, to make matters even worse, legal parasitism was my first area of specialization, the key that opened the doors of the La Perricholi Company—yes, that is its ridiculous South Americanized name—and got me my first few promotions. How could I avoid being the most ingenious tangler or disentangler of juridical arguments when I discovered in my first law class that so-called legality is, in great measure, an intricate jungle in which technicians of obfuscations, intrigues, formalisms, and casuistries would always come out ahead? And that the profession has nothing to do with truth and justice but deals exclusively with the fabrication of incontrovertible appearances, with sophistries and deceptions impossible to clarify. It is true, I have engaged in this essentially parasitic activity with the competence needed to reach the top, but I have never deceived myself. I have always been aware that I was a boil feeding on the defenselessness, vulnerability, and impotence of others. Unlike you, I make no claims to being a "pillar of society" (it is useless to refer you to the painting of that name by George Grosz: you don't know the painter, or, worse yet, you know him only for the splendid Expressionist asses he painted and not his lethal caricatures of your colleagues in the Weimar Republic): I know what I am and what I do, and I have as much or more contempt for that part of myself as I have for you. My success as an attorney is derived from this understanding—that the law is an amoral technique that serves the cynic who best controls it—and from my discovery, a precocious one as well, that in our country (in all countries?) the legal system is a web of contradictions in which each law, or ruling with the force of law, can be opposed by another, or many others, that amend or nullify it. Therefore all of us are always violating some law and transgressing in some way against the legal order (chaos, actually). Thanks to this labyrinth, you bureaucrats subdivide, multiply, reproduce, and regenerate at a dizzying pace. And we lawyers live and some of us—*mea culpa*—prosper.

Well, even if my life has been the torment of Tantalus, a daily moral struggle between the bureaucratic rubble of my existence and the secret angels and demons of my being, you have not conquered me. Faced with what I do from Monday through Friday, from eight to six, I have always maintained sufficient irony to despise the job and despise myself for doing it, so that in the remaining hours I could make amends, redeem and indemnify myself, humanize myself (which, in my case, always means separating from the herd, the crowd). I can imagine the tingle running through you, the irritable curiosity with which you ask yourself, "And what does he do at night that immunizes him against me, that saves him from being what I am?" Do you want to know? Now that I am alone—separated from my wife, I mean—I read, look at my pictures, review and add to my notebooks with letters like this one, but, above all, I fantasize. I dream. I construct a better reality purged of all the scum and excrescences—you and your slime—which make the actual one so sinister and sordid that we wish for another. (I've spoken in the plural and I'm sorry; it won't happen again.) In this other reality, you do not exist. All that exists is the woman I love and will love forever—the absent Lucrecia—my son, Alfonso, and a few variable, transitory secondary players who come and go like will-o'-the-wisps, spending only the time needed to be useful to me. Only when I am in that world, in that company, do I exist, for then I am joyful and content.

Now, these strands of happiness would not be possible without the immense frustration, arid tedium, and crushing routine of my real life. In other words, without a life dehumanized by you, without everything you weave and unweave with all the machinery of power you possess. Do you understand now why I began by calling you a *necessary evil*? You thought, master of the stereotype and the commonplace, that I described you in this way because I believed that a society must function, must have at its disposal order, legality, services, authority, in order not to run aground on confusion. And you thought this regulatory Gordian knot, this saving, organizing mechanism of the anthill, was you, the *necessary* man. No, my awful friend. Without you, society would function much better than it does now. But without you here to prostitute, poison, and hack away at human freedom, I would not appreciate it nearly as much, my imagination would not soar as high, my desires would not be as powerful, for they are born in rebellion against you, as the reaction of a free, sensitive being against an entity who is the negation of sensitivity and free will. Which means that however one looks at this rocky terrain, without you I would be less free and less sensitive, my desires more pedestrian, my life emptier.

I know you will not understand this either, but it does not matter at all if your puffy batrachian eyes never see this letter.

Bureaucrat, I curse you and thank you.

Bathed in perspiration, not yet completely emerged from that narrow frontier where sleep and wakefulness were indistinguishable, Don Rigoberto could still see Rosaura, dressed in a jacket and tie, as she carried out his instructions: she approached the bar and leaned over the bare back of the flashy mulatta who had been flirting with her since she had seen them walk into that cheap hookers' club.

They were in Mexico City, weren't they? Yes, after a week in Acapulco, making a stop on their way home to Lima following a brief vacation. It had been Don Rigoberto's whim to dress Doña Lucrecia in men's clothes and then go with her to a whores' cabaret. Rosaura-Lucrecia was whispering something to the woman and smiling—Don Rigoberto saw with what authority she squeezed the bare arm of the mulatta, who looked at her with alert, malicious eyes—and finally led her out to dance. They were playing a mambo by Pérez Prado, of course—"*El ruletero*"—and on the narrow, smoky, crowded dance floor, where shadows were fitfully distorted by a reflector with colored lights, Rosaura-Lucrecia played her part very well: Don Rigoberto nodded approvingly. She did not seem a stranger in her men's clothing, or different in her *garçon* haircut, or uncomfortable leading her partner when they tired of doing their own steps and danced with their arms around each other. In an increasingly feverish state, Don Rigoberto, filled with grateful admiration for his wife, risked a stiff neck in order not to lose sight of them among the heads and shoulders of so many other people. When the out-of-tune but intrepid band moved from the mambo to a bolero—"*Dos almas*," which reminded him of Leo Marini—he felt that the gods were with him. Interpreting his secret desire, he saw Rosaura immediately press the mulatta to her, passing her arms around her waist and obliging the girl to place hers on her shoulders. Even if he could not make out the details in the half-light, he was sure that his beloved wife, the counterfeit male, had begun to kiss and gently bite the mulatta's neck, rubbing up against her belly and breasts like a true man spurred on by desire.

He was awake now, no doubt about it, but though all his senses were alert, the mulatta and Lucrecia-Rosaura were still there, in a close embrace, in a nighttime brothel crowd, in that harsh, cruel place where the gaudily made-up women displayed tropical rumps and the male patrons had drooping mustaches, fat cheeks, and the eyes of marijuana smokers. Ready to pull out their pistols and start shooting at the first false move? Because of this excursion to the lower depths of the Mexican night, Rosaura and I may lose our lives, he thought with a happy shudder. And he anticipated the headlines in the gutter press: DOUBLE HOMICIDE: BUSINESSMAN AND TRANSVESTITE WIFE MURDERED IN MEXICAN BROTHEL; MULATTA WAS BAIT, VICE THEIR DOWNFALL; UPPERCRUST LIMENIAN COUPLE KILLED IN MEXICO'S UNDERWORLD; WHITE-HOT SCANDAL: GO TOO FAR, PAY IN BLOOD. He brought up a chuckle as if it were a belch: "If they kill us, the worms can worry about the scandal."

He returned to the aforementioned club, where the mulatta and Rosaura, the counterfeit man, were still dancing. Now, to his joy, they were shamelessly caressing and kissing each other on the mouth. But wait: weren't the professionals reluctant to offer their lips to clients? Yes, but did any obstacle exist that Rosaura-Lucrecia could not overcome? How had she gotten the fleshy mulatta to open that huge mouth with its thick scarlet lips to receive the subtle visit of her serpentine tongue? Had she offered her money? Had she aroused her? It didn't matter how, what mattered was that her sweet, soft, almost liquid tongue was there in the mulatta's mouth, wetting it with her saliva and absorbing the saliva—which he imagined as thick and fragrant—of that lush woman.

And then he was distracted by a question: Why Rosaura? Rosaura was also a woman's name. If it was a question of disguising her completely, as he had disguised her body by dressing it in men's clothes, then Carlos, Juan, Pedro, or Nicanor would have been preferable. Why Rosaura? Almost without realizing it, he got out of bed, put on his robe and slippers, and went to his study. He did not need to see the clock to know that the light of dawn would soon appear, seeming to rise out of the sea. Did he know any flesh-and-blood Rosaura? He ransacked his memory, and the answer was a categorical no. She was, then, an imaginary Rosaura who had come tonight to appear in his dream about Lucrecia, to merge with her, leaving the forgotten pages of some novel, or some drawing, oil painting, or engraving he could not recall. In any case, the pseudonym was there, clinging to Lucrecia like the man's suit they had bought, laughing and whispering, that afternoon in a shop in the red-light district after he had asked Lucrecia if she would agree to concretize his fantasy and she—"as always, as always"—had said she would. Now Rosaura was a name as real as the couple who, arm in arm—the mulatta and Lucrecia were almost the same height—had stopped dancing and were approaching the table. He stood to greet them and ceremoniously offered his hand to the mulatta.

"Hello, hello, delighted to meet you, please have a seat."

"I'm dying of thirst," said the mulatta, fanning herself with both hands. "Shall we order something?"

"Whatever you want, baby," Rosaura-Lucrecia said, caressing her chin and calling a waiter. "You order, go ahead."

"A bottle of champagne," the mulatta said with a triumphant smile. "Is your name really Rigoberto? Or is that your alias?"

"That's my name. Pretty unusual, isn't it?"

"Very unusual." The mulatta nodded, looking at him as if instead of eyes she had two coals burning in her round face. "Well, original at least. You're pretty original too, and that's the truth. Want to know something? I've never seen ears and a nose like yours. My God, they're enormous! Can I touch them? Will you let me?"

The mulatta's request—she was tall and curvaceous, with incandescent eyes, a long neck, strong shoulders, and a burnished skin set off by her canary-yellow dress with its deeply plunging neckline—left Don Rigoberto speechless, incapable of even responding with a joke to what appeared to be a serious request. Lucrecia-Rosaura came to his rescue.

"Not yet, baby," she said to the mulatta, pinching her ear. "When we're alone, in the room, you can touch anything of his you want."

"The three of us are going to be alone in a room?" the mulatta asked with a laugh, rolling her eyes beneath their silken false lashes. "Thanks for letting me know. And what will I do with the two of you, my angels? I don't like odd numbers. I'm sorry. I'll call a friend and then we can be two couples. But me alone with two men? Not on your life."

However, when the waiter brought the bottle of what he called champagne but was in reality a sweetish spumante with hints of turpentine and camphor, the mulatta (she said her name was Estrella) seemed to become more enthusiastic about the idea of spending the rest of the night with the disparate pair, and she made jokes, laughing boisterously and distributing playful slaps between Don Rigoberto and Rosaura-Lucrecia. From time to time, like a refrain, she would laugh about "the gentleman's ears and nose" and stare at them, her fascination charged with a mysterious covetousness.

"With ears like that you must hear more than normal people," she said. "And smell more with that nose than ordinary men do."

Probably, thought Don Rigoberto. What if it were true? What if he, thanks to the munificence of those organs, heard more and had a more acute sense of smell than other people? He did not like the comic turn the story was taking—his desire, inflamed only a moment ago, was fading, and he could not revive it, for Estrella's jokes obliged him to move his attention away from Lucrecia-Rosaura and the mulatta to concentrate on his outsized auditory and nasal instruments. He tried to abbreviate certain stages, skipping over the bargaining with Estrella that lasted as long as the bottle of supposed champagne, the arrangements to have the mulatta leave the club—a token had to be purchased with a fifty-dollar bill—the rattling taxi afflicted with the tremors of tertian fever, their registering at the filthy hotel—CIELITO LINDO said the red-and-blue neon sign on its façade—and the negotiation with the squint-eyed clerk, who was picking his nose, to let them occupy only one room. It cost Don Rigoberto another fifty dollars to calm his fears that there might be a police raid and the establishment would be fined for renting one bedroom to three people.

As they crossed the threshold of the room, and in the dim light of a single lightbulb saw the king-size bed covered with a bluish spread, and next to it a washstand, a basin with water, a towel, a roll of toilet paper, and a chipped chamber pot—the squint-eyed clerk had just left, handing over the key and closing the door behind him—Don Rigoberto remembered: Of course! Rosaura! Estrella! He slapped his forehead, relieved. Naturally! Those names came from the performance in Madrid of *La vida es sueño*, Calderón de la Barca's *Life Is a Dream*. And once again he felt, bubbling up from the bottom of his heart like a spring of clear water, a tender feeling of gratitude toward the depths of memory from which there endlessly poured forth surprises, images, phantoms, and suggestions to give body, backdrop, and storyline to the dreams with which he defended himself against his solitude, the absence of Lucrecia.

"Let's get undressed, Estrella," Rosaura was saying, standing up and then sitting down. "You'll have the surprise of your life, so get ready."

"I won't take off my dress if I can't touch your friend's nose and ears first," replied Estrella, utterly serious now. "I don't know why, but I want to touch them so much it's killing me."

This time, instead of anger, Don Rigoberto felt flattered.

Doña Lucrecia and he had seen the play in Madrid on their first trip to Europe a few months after they were married, a performance of *La vida es sueño* so old-fashioned that open laughter could be heard in the darkened theater. The tall skinny actor who played Prince Segismundo was so bad, so clearly overwhelmed by the role, and his voice so affected, that the spectator—"well, *this* spectator," Don Rigoberto was more precise—felt inclined to look favorably upon his cruel, superstitious father, King Basilio, for keeping him, throughout his childhood and youth, chained like a wild beast in a solitary tower, fearful that if his son came to the throne the cataclysms predicted by the stars and his learned mathematicians would come true. The entire performance had been ghastly, dreadful, clumsy. And yet Don Rigoberto recalled with absolute clarity that the appearance in the first scene of the young Rosaura dressed as a man, and later, with a sword at her waist, ready to go into battle, had touched his soul. And now he was sure he had been tempted several times since then by the desire to see Lucrecia attired in boots, plumed hat, a soldier's tunic, at the hour of love. *La vida es sueño!* Though the performance was awful, the director unspeakable, the actors even worse, it was not only that one actress who had lived on in memory and often inflamed his senses. Something in the work intrigued him as well, because—his recollection was unequivocal—it had led him to read the play. He must still have his notes from that reading. Down on all fours on the rug in the study, Don Rigoberto looked through and discarded one notebook after another. Not this one, or this one. It had to be this one. That was the year.

"I'm naked, honey," said Estrella the mulatta. "Now let me touch your ears and nose. Don't make me beg. Don't make me suffer, don't be mean. Can't you see I'm dying to do it? Just this one favor, baby, and I'll make you happy."

She had a full, abundant body, shapely though somewhat flabby in the belly, with splendid breasts that barely sagged and Renaissance rolls of flesh at her hips. She did not even seem to notice that Rosaura-Lucrecia, who had also undressed and lay on the bed, was not a man but a beautiful woman with well-delineated curves. The mulatta had eyes only for him, or rather, for his ears and nose, which she now—Don Rigoberto had sat on the edge of the bed to facilitate the operation—caressed avidly, furiously. Her ardent fingers desperately kneaded, pressed, and pinched, first his ears, then his nose. He closed his eyes in anguish because he sensed that very soon the fingers on his nose would provoke one of those allergic attacks that would not stop until he had sneezed—lascivious number—sixty-nine times. His Mexican adventure, inspired by Calderón de la Barca, would end in a grotesque outburst of nasal excess.

231

Yes, this was it—Don Rigoberto brought the notebook into the light of the lamp: a page of quotations and comments he had made as he read the play, its title at the top of the page: *La vida es sueño* (1638).

The first two citations, taken from speeches by Segismundo, affected him like the lashes of a whip: "Nothing to me seems right/if it counters my delight." And the other: "And I know that I am/compounded of beast and man." Was there a cause-and-effect relationship between the two quotations he had transcribed? Was he compounded of man and beast because nothing that opposed his pleasure seemed right? Perhaps. But when he read the play after their trip, he was not the old, tired, solitary, dejected man he had become, desperately seeking refuge in his fantasies so as not to go mad or commit suicide; he was a happy fifty-year-old brimming with life who, in the arms of his bride, his second wife, was discovering that joy existed, that it was possible to construct, at the side of his beloved, a singular citadel fortified against the stupidity, the ugliness, the mediocrity, and the routine where he spent the rest of his day. Why had he felt the need to make these notes as he read a work that, at the time, had no bearing on his personal situation? Or did it?

"If I had a man with ears and a nose like these, I'd really go wild. I'd be his slave," exclaimed the mulatta, resting for a moment. "I'd make him happy no matter what he wanted. I'd lick the floor clean for him."

She was squatting on her heels, and her face was flushed and sweaty, as if she had been bending over a boiling pot of soup. Her whole body seemed to vibrate. As she spoke she greedily passed her tongue over the wet lips with which she had been interminably kissing, nibbling, and licking Don Rigoberto's auditory and olfactory organs. He used the time to take in air and dry his ears with his handkerchief. Then he blew his nose with a good deal of noise.

"This man is mine; I'm just lending him to you for the night," said Rosaura-Lucrecia firmly.

"But don't these marvels belong to you?" asked Estrella, not paying the slightest attention to the dialogue. Her hands had taken hold of Don Rigoberto's alarmed face, and her thick, determined lips were advancing again toward their prey.

"Haven't you even noticed? I'm not a man, I'm a woman," an exasperated Rosaura-Lucrecia protested. "Look at me, at least."

But with a slight movement of her shoulders the mulatta ignored her and passionately continued her work. She had Don Rigoberto's left ear in her large, hot mouth, and he, unable to control himself, laughed hysterically. In fact he was very nervous. He had a presentiment that at any moment Estrella would move from love to hate and tear off his ear in one bite. "If I'm earless, Lucrecia won't love me anymore." He grew sad. He heaved a deep, cavernous, gloomy sigh similar to those of the bearded Prince Segismundo, chained in his secret tower, as he demanded of heaven, with great strident shouts, what sin he had committed by being born.

"That's a stupid question," Don Rigoberto said to himself. He had always despised the South American sport of self-pity, and from that point of view, the sniveling prince of Calderón de la Barca (a Jesuit, in all other respects), who presented himself to the audience moaning, "Ah, woe is me, most wretched of men," had nothing that would appeal to the spectators or make them identify with him. Why, then, in his dream, had his phantoms structured the story by borrowing from *La vida es sueño* the names of Rosaura and Estrella and Rosaura's masculine disguise? Perhaps because his life had become nothing but a dream since Lucrecia's departure. Was he even *alive* during the gloomy, opaque hours he spent in the office discussing balances, policies, renewals, judgments, investments? His one corner of real life was provided by the night, when he fell asleep and the door of dreams was opened, which is what must have happened to Segismundo in his desolate stone tower in that dense forest. He too had discovered that true life, the rich, splendid life that yielded and bent to his will, was the life of lies, the life his mind and desires created—awake or asleep—to free him from his cell, allow him to escape the asphyxiating monotony of his confinement. The unexpected dream was not gratuitous after all: there was a kinship, an affinity, between the two miserable dreamers.

Don Rigoberto remembered a joke in diminutives whose sheer stupidity had made him and Lucrecia giggle like two children: "A teeny-tiny elephant came to the edge of a teeny-tiny lake to drink, and a teeny-tiny crocodile bit off his teeny-tiny trunk. With teeny-tiny tears, the teeny-tiny pug-nosed elephant sobbed, 'Is that your teeny-tiny idea of a goddamn joke?' "

"Let go of my nose and I'll give you anything you want," he pleaded in terror, in a nasal Cantinflas voice, because Estrella's teeny-tiny teeth were interfering with his breathing. "All the money you want. Let me go, please!"

"Quiet, I'm coming," stammered the mulatta, letting go for a second and then seizing Don Rigoberto's nose again with her two rows of carnivorous teeth.

A violent hippogriff, she came indeed, flying before the wind, shuddering from head to toe, while Don Rigoberto, drowning in panic, saw out of the corner of his eye that Rosaura-Lucrecia, distressed and disconcerted, sitting up in bed, had caught the mulatta around the waist and was trying to move her away, gently, without forcing, surely afraid that if she pulled too hard Estrella would bite off her husband's nose in reprisal. They remained this way for a while, docile, joined together, while the mulatta reared and moaned and licked without restraint the nasal appendage of Don Rigoberto, who, in dark clouds of anxiety, recalled Bacon's monstrous *Man's Head*, a shocking canvas that had long obsessed him, and now he knew why: it was how Estrella's jaws would leave him after she bit him. It was not the mutilation of his face that horrified him but a single question: Would Lucrecia still love an earless and noseless husband? Would she leave him?

Don Rigoberto read this excerpt in his notebook:

> *What could have befallen*
> *my fantasy in sleep*
> *that I find myself now*
> *in this castle keep?*

Segismundo declaimed this when he awoke from the artificial sleep into which (with a mixture of opium, poppy, and henbane) King Basilio and old Clotaldo had plunged him when they mounted the ignoble farce, moving him from his prison tower to court to have him rule for a brief time and leading him to believe that the transition was also a dream. What happened to your fantasy as you slept, poor prince, he thought, is that they put you to sleep with drugs and killed you. For a moment they returned you to your true state, making you believe that you dreamed. And then you took the liberties one takes when he enjoys the impunity of dreams. You gave free rein to your desires, you threw a man off a balcony, you almost killed old Clotaldo and even King Basilio himself. And so they had the pretext they needed—you were violent, foul-tempered, base—to return you to the chains and solitude of your prison. Despite this, he envied Segismundo. He too, like the unfortunate prince condemned by mathematics and the stars to live in dreams so as not to die of imprisonment and solitude, was, he had written in the notebook, "a living skeleton," an "animate corpse." But unlike the prince, he had no King Basilio, no noble Clotaldo, to remove him from his abandonment and solitude, to put him to sleep with opium, poppy, and henbane and allow him to wake in the arms of Lucrecia. "Lucrecia, my Lucrecia," he sighed, realizing that he was weeping. What a sniveler he had become this past year!

Estrella was crying too, but hers were tears of joy. After her final gasp, during which Don Rigoberto felt a simultaneous jolt to every nerve ending in his body, she opened her mouth, released his nose, and fell back onto the blue-covered bed with a disarmingly pious exclamation: "Mother of God, I came so good!" And crossed herself in gratitude without the slightest sacrilegious intention.

"Sure, good for you, but you almost took off my nose and ears, you outlaw," Don Rigoberto complained.

He was positive that Estrella's caresses had turned his face into the face of Arcimboldo's plant man, who had a tuberous carrot for a nose. With a growing sense of humiliation he saw, through the fingers of the hand he was using to rub his bruised and battered nose, that Rosaura-Lucrecia, without a shred of compassion or concern for him, was looking at the mulatta (serenely stretching on the bed) with curiosity, a pleased little smile floating across her face.

"So that's what you like in men, Estrella?" she asked.

The mulatta nodded.

"It's the only thing I do like," she stated more precisely, panting and exhaling a dense, vegetal breath. "The rest they can stick where the sun never shines. Usually I hold back, I hide it because of what people might say. But tonight I let myself go. I've never seen ears and a nose like the ones on your man. You two made me feel right at home, sweetie."

She looked Lucrecia up and down with the eyes of a connoisseur and seemed to approve. She extended one of her hands and placed her index finger on the left nipple—Don Rigoberto thought he could see the small wrinkled button harden—of Rosaura-Lucrecia and said, with a little laugh, "I knew you were a woman when we were dancing in the club. I could feel your tits, and I saw you didn't know how to lead. I led you, not the other way around."

"You hid it very well. I thought we had you fooled," Doña Lucrecia congratulated her.

Still rubbing his well-caressed nose and offended ears, Don Rigoberto felt a new wave of admiration for his wife. How versatile and adaptable she could be! It was the first time in her life that Lucrecia was doing things like this—dressing like a man, visiting a tarts' dive in a foreign country, going to a cheap hotel with a whore—and yet she did not show the slightest discomfort, unease, or annoyance. There she was, chatting so familiarly with the otolaryngological mulatta, as if they were equals who shared the same background and profession. They looked like two good friends gossiping during a break in their busy day. And how beautiful, how desirable she seemed! In order to savor the sight of his naked wife in the oily half-light, next to Estrella on the wretched bed with the blue spread, Don Rigoberto closed his eyes. She was lying on her side, her face resting on her left hand, in a state of abandon that highlighted the delicate spontaneity of her posture. Her skin looked much whiter in the dim light, her short hair blacker, the bush of pubic hair tinted with blue. And as he amorously followed the gentle meanders of her thighs and back, scaled her buttocks, breasts, and shoulders, Don Rigoberto began to forget his afflicted ears, his abused nose, as well as Estrella, the cheap little hotel where they had taken refuge, and Mexico City: Lucrecia's body was colonizing his mind, displacing, eliminating every other image, consideration, or preoccupation.

Rosaura-Lucrecia and Estrella did not seem to notice—or, perhaps, they attributed no importance to it—when he mechanically began to remove his tie, jacket, shirt, shoes, socks, trousers, and shorts, tossing them onto the cracked green linoleum. Or even when he knelt at the foot of the bed and started to run his hands along his wife's legs and kiss them deferentially. They were involved in their confidences and gossip, indifferent to him, as if they did not see him, as if he were a phantom.

I am, he thought, opening his eyes. His excitement remained, beating him about the legs without much conviction, without a shred of joy or decisiveness, like a rusted clapper striking an old bell made dissonant by time and routine in the little church with no parishioners.

And then memory brought back the profound displeasure—the bad taste in his mouth, really—caused in him by the sycophantic ending, so abjectly subservient to principles of authority and the immorality of reasons of state, in that work by Calderón de la Barca: the soldier who initiated the uprising against King Basilio, thanks to which Prince Segismundo comes to occupy the Polish throne, is condemned by the new, ignoble, ungrateful king to rot away for the rest of his life in the same tower where Segismundo had suffered, with the argument that—his notebook reproduced the ghastly lines—"the traitor is not needed once the treason is complete."

A horrendous philosophy, a repugnant morality, he reflected, temporarily forgetting his beautiful naked wife, though he continued to caress her mechanically. The prince pardons Basilio and Clotaldo, his oppressors and torturers, and punishes the valiant anonymous soldier who incited the troops against the unjust ruler, freed Segismundo from his cave, and made him monarch because, more than anything else, it was necessary to defend obedience to established authority, to condemn the principle, the very notion, of rebellion against the sovereign. It was disgusting!

Did a work poisoned by an inhuman doctrine so opposed to freedom deserve to occupy and nourish his dreams, to populate his desires? And yet there had to be some reason why, on this particular night, these phantoms had taken full, exclusive possession of his dreaming. Again he looked through his notebooks, searching for an explanation.

Old Clotaldo called the pistol a "viper of metal," and the disguised Rosaura asked herself "if sight does not suffer deceptions that fantasy creates/ in the fainthearted light still left to day." Don Rigoberto looked toward the sea. There, in the distance, on the line of the horizon, a fainthearted light announced the new day, the light that each morning violently destroyed the small world of illusion and shadows where he was happy (happy? No, where he was merely a little less unfortunate) and returned him to the prison routine he followed five days a week (shower, breakfast, office, lunch, office, dinner) with barely an opening for his inventions to seep through. A note in the margin—it said, "Lucrecia"—had an arrow pointing at some brief verses written on the page: ". . . joining/the costly finery of Diana, the armor/of Pallas." The huntress and the warrior, combined in his beloved Lucrecia. Why not? But this evidently was not what had embedded the story of Prince Segismundo in the depths of his unconscious and materialized it in tonight's fantasies. What, then?

"It cannot be that so many things/are contained within a single dream," the Prince had said in amazement. "You are an idiot," replied Don Rigoberto. "A single dream can contain all of life." It moved him that Segismundo, transported under the effects of the drug from his prison to the palace, and asked what, in his return to the world, had made the greatest impression on him, should reply: "Nothing has surprised me,/for all was foreseen; but if one thing/in the world were to amaze, it would be/the beauty of women." And he hadn't even seen Lucrecia, he thought. He could see her now, splendid, supernatural, flowing across that blue spread, delicately purring as the tickling lips of her amorous husband kissed her underarms. The amiable Estrella had moved away, ceding to Don Rigoberto her place next to Rosaura-Lucrecia, sitting at the corner of the bed previously occupied by Don Rigoberto when she had labored so enthusiastically over his ears and nose. Discreet, motionless, not wanting to distract or interrupt them, she observed with sympathetic curiosity as they embraced, entwined, and began to make love.

> *What is life? Confusion.*
> *What is life? Illusion,*
> *a shadow, a fiction;*
> *its greatest goods are small,*
> *life is a dream, and all*
> *our dreams another dream.*

"It's a lie," he said aloud, slamming the desk in his study. Life was not a dream, dreams were a feeble lie, a fleeting deception that provided only temporary escape from frustration and solitude in order that we might better appreciate, with more painful bitterness, the beauty and substantiality of real life, the life we ate, touched, drank, the rich life so superior to the simulacrum indulged in by conjured desire and fantasy. Devastated by anguish—day had come, the light of dawn revealed gray cliffs, a leaden sea, fat-bellied clouds, crumbling brickwork, a leprous pavement—he clung desperately to Lucrecia-Rosaura's body, using these last few seconds to achieve an impossible pleasure, with the grotesque foreboding that at any moment, perhaps at the moment of ecstasy, he would feel the impetuous hands of the mulatta landing on his ears.

The Viper and the Lamprey

Thinking of you, I have read *The Perfect Wife* by Fray Luis de León, and understand, given the idea of matrimony he preached, why this fine poet preferred abstinence and an Augustinian habit to the nuptial bed. And yet, in those pages of good prose abounding in unintentional humor, I found this quotation from the blessed Saint Basil that fits like a glove on the ivory hand of can you guess which exceptional woman, model wife, and sorely missed lover?

The viper, an exceptionally fierce animal among serpents, diligently goes to wed the marine lamprey; having arrived, he whistles, as if signaling that he is there, thus calling her from the sea in order to engage her in conjugal embrace. The lamprey obeys, and with no fear couples with the venomous beast. What do I mean by this? What? That no matter how violent the husband, how savage his habits, the woman must endure, must not consent for any reason to be divided from him. Oh! He is a tyrant? But he is your husband! A drunkard? But the bonds of matrimony made you one with him. A harsh man, an unpleasant man! But your member, your principal member. And, so that the husband may also hear what he must: the viper, respectful of their coupling, sets aside his venom, and will you not abandon the inhuman cruelty of your nature in order to honor your marriage? This is from Basil.

—Fray Luis de León, *The Perfect Wife*, Chapter III

Conjugally embrace this viper, dearly beloved lamprey.

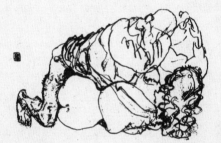

EPILOGUE

A Happy Family

"The picnic wasn't so disastrous after all," said Don Rigoberto with a broad smile. "And it taught us a lesson: there's no place like home. Especially if no place is the countryside."

Doña Lucrecia and Fonchito applauded his witticism, and even Justiniana, who at that moment was bringing in the sandwiches—chicken, and avocado-with-egg-and-tomato—to which their lunch had been reduced because of the frustrated picnic, also burst into laughter.

"Now, my dear, I know what it means to think positively," Doña Lucrecia congratulated him. "And to have constructive attitudes in the face of adversity."

"And to make the best of a bad situation," Fonchito said conclusively. "Bravo, Papá!"

"The fact is that nothing and nobody can cloud my happiness today." Don Rigoberto nodded, contemplating the sandwiches. "Certainly not a miserable picnic. Not even an atomic bomb could make a dent. Well, cheers."

With visible pleasure he drank some cold beer and took a bite of his chicken sandwich. The Chaclacayo sun had burned his forehead, face, and arms, which were reddened by its rays. He did seem very content, enjoying the improvised lunch. It had been his idea, the night before, for the entire family to have a Sunday picnic at Chaclacayo, to escape the fog and damp of Lima and enjoy good weather, in touch with nature, on the banks of the river. The idea surprised Doña Lucrecia, for she recalled the holy horror everything rural had always inspired in him, but she willingly agreed. Weren't they beginning a second honeymoon? They would begin new habits too. That morning they left at nine—as planned—furnished with a good supply of drinks and a complete lunch, prepared by the cook, that included blancmange with crêpes, Don Rigoberto's favorite dessert.

The first thing to go wrong was the highway in the center of town; it was so crowded that they made very slow progress, when they could move at all, surrounded by trucks, buses, and all kinds of shabby vehicles that not only clogged the highway and brought traffic to a standstill for long periods of time but also belched out of their exhausts a thick black smoke and a stink of burning gasoline that made them dizzy. They were exhausted and flushed when they finally reached Chaclacayo after twelve o'clock.

Finding a clear space near the river turned out to be more difficult than they had imagined. Before taking the secondary road that would bring them close to the banks of the Rímac—as opposed to its appearance in Lima, out here it seemed a real river, broad and full, the water foaming and forming playful little waves when it ran into stones and rocky places—they had to make turn after turn that always brought them back to the damned highway. When, with the help of a kindly Chaclacayan, they found a turn-off that led down to the river, things got worse, not better. In that spot the Rímac was used as a garbage dump (as well as a urinal and outhouse) by local residents, who had tossed every imaginable kind of trash there—from papers and empty cans and bottles to rotting food, excrement, and dead animals—so that in addition to the depressing view, the place was tainted by an unbearable stench. Swarms of aggressive flies obliged them to cover their mouths with their hands. None of this appeared to conform to the pastoral expedition anticipated by Don Rigoberto. He, however, armed with unassailable patience and a crusader's optimism that astounded his wife and son, persuaded his family not to let themselves be disheartened by difficult circumstances. They continued their search.

After some time, when it seemed they had found a more hospitable spot—that is, one free of foul smells and garbage—it was already taken by countless family groups who sat under beach umbrellas, ate pasta smeared with red sauces, and played tropical music at full volume on portable radios and cassette players. Don Rigoberto held sole responsibility for their next mistake, though his motive was sound: to find a little privacy and move away from the crowd of pasta eaters, who apparently could not conceive of leaving the city for a few hours without bringing along noise, that urban product *par excellence*. Don Rigoberto thought he had found the solution. As if he were a Boy Scout, he proposed that they take off their shoes, roll up their trousers, and wade a small stretch of river out to what looked like a tiny island of sand, rock, and sparse undergrowth which, by some miracle, was not overrun by the large Sunday collectivity. And that is what they did. Rather, that is what they began to do, carrying the bags of food and drink prepared by the cook for their rustic outing. Just a few meters from the idyllic little island, Don Rigoberto—the water came only to his knees, and until this point they had followed their route without incident—slipped on something cartilaginous. He lost his balance and sat down in the cool waters of the Rímac River, which, in and of itself, would have been of no importance considering the hot weather and how much he was perspiring if, at the same time, the picnic basket had not also gone down and, adding a comic touch to the accident, had not scattered everything it contained before coming to rest on the riverbed, strewing spicy ceviche, rice and duck, and crêpes with blancmange, along with the exquisite red-and-white-checkered cloth and napkins selected by Doña Lucrecia for the picnic, all across the turbulent waters that were already carrying them away toward Lima and the Pacific.

"Just go ahead and laugh, don't hold back, I won't be angry," said Don Rigoberto to his wife and son, who, as they helped him to his feet, were making grotesque faces in an effort to suppress their howls of laughter. The people on shore, seeing him soaked from head to toe, were laughing too.

Inclined toward heroism (for the first time in his life?), Don Rigoberto suggested they persevere and stay on, claiming that the Chaclacayo sun would dry him before they knew it. Doña Lucrecia was categorical. That she would not do, he could catch pneumonia, they were going back to Lima. And they did, defeated, but not despairing. And laughing affectionately at poor Don Rigoberto, who had taken off his trousers and drove in his shorts. It was almost five when they reached the house in Barranco. While Don Rigoberto showered and changed, Doña Lucrecia, with the help of Justiniana, who had just returned from her day off—the butler and cook would not be back until later that night—prepared chicken and avocado-with-tomato-and-egg sandwiches for their belated and eventful lunch.

"Since you made up with my stepmamá you've become so good, Papá."

Don Rigoberto moved the half-eaten sandwich away from his mouth. He grew thoughtful. "Are you serious?"

"Very serious," the boy replied, turning toward Doña Lucrecia. "Isn't it true, Stepmamá? For two days he hasn't grumbled or complained about anything, he's always in a good mood and saying nice things. Isn't that being good?"

"It's only been two days," Doña Lucrecia said with a laugh. But then, becoming serious and looking tenderly at her husband, she added, "In fact, he always was very good. It's just taken you a while to realize it, Fonchito."

"I don't know if I like being called good," Don Rigoberto reacted at last, his expression apprehensive. "All the good people I've known were pretty imbecilic. As if they were good because they lacked imagination and desire. I hope I'm not becoming more of an imbecile than I already am simply because I feel happy."

"No danger of that." Señora Lucrecia put her face close to her husband's and kissed him on the forehead. "You may be everything else in the world, but not that."

She looked very beautiful, her cheeks colored by the Chaclacayo sun, her shoulders and arms bare in a light dress of flowered percale that gave her a fresh, healthy air. How lovely, how youthful, thought Don Rigoberto, delighting in his wife's slender throat and the charming curve of one of her ears where a stray lock of hair curled, having escaped the ribbon—the same yellow as the espadrilles she had worn on the outing—that held her hair at the nape of her neck. Eleven years had gone by, and she looked younger and more attractive than on the day he met her. And this health and physical beauty that defied time, where were they best reflected? "In her eyes," he answered his own question. Eyes that changed color from pale gray to dark green to soft black. Now they looked very light under her long, dark lashes, and animated by a merry, almost flashing sparkle. Unaware that she was the object of contemplation, his wife ate her second avocado-with-egg-and-tomato sandwich with good appetite, and from time to time took sips of cold beer that left her lips wet. Was it happiness, this feeling that overwhelmed him? This grateful admiration and desire he felt for Lucrecia? Yes. Don Rigoberto wished with all his heart that the hours till nightfall would fly by. Once again they would be alone and he would hold in his arms his adored wife, here, in flesh and blood, at last.

"The only thing that sometimes makes me think I'm not so similar to Egon Schiele is that he liked the country a lot, and I don't at all," said

Fonchito, speaking a thought he'd begun to turn over in his mind some time before. "I'm a lot like you that way, Papá. I don't like seeing trees and cows either."

"That's why our picnic turned out topsy-turvy," Don Rigoberto philosophized. "Nature's revenge against two of her enemies. What did you say about Egon Schiele?"

"I said that the only way I don't resemble him is that he liked the country and I don't," Fonchito explained. "He paid a price for loving nature. They arrested him and put him in prison for a month, and he nearly lost his mind. If he had stayed in Vienna, it never would have happened."

"You're very well informed about the life of Egon Schiele, Fonchito," Don Rigoberto said in surprise.

"You can't imagine," Doña Lucrecia interjected. "He knows by heart everything he did, said, wrote, everything that happened to him in his twenty-eight years. He knows all the paintings, drawings, engravings, their titles and dates too. He even thinks he's the reincarnation of Egon Schiele. I swear, it frightens me."

Don Rigoberto did not laugh. He nodded, as if pondering this information with the greatest care, but, in fact, he was concealing the sudden appearance in his mind of a tiny worm, the stupid curiosity that was the mother of all vices. How did Lucrecia know that Fonchito knew so much about Egon Schiele? Schiele! he thought. A perverse variant of Expressionism whom Oskar Kokoschka rightly called a pornographer. He found himself possessed by a visceral, biting, bilious hatred for Egon Schiele. Blessed be the Spanish influenza that carried him off. How did Lucrecia know that Fonchito thought he was this misbegotten hack spawned in the death throes of the Austro-Hungarian Empire that, just as fortunately, had been carried off by deceit? Worst of all, unaware she was sinking into the fetid waters of self-incrimination, Doña Lucrecia continued to torture him.

"I'm glad the subject has come up, Rigoberto. I've wanted to talk to you about this for a long time; I even thought of writing to you. The boy's mania for that painter has me very worried. Yes, Fonchito. Why don't the three of us talk it over? Who can give you better advice than your father? I've already said it several times. I don't think there's anything wrong with your passion for Egon Schiele. But it's becoming an obsession. You don't mind if the three of us discuss it, do you?"

"I don't think my papá's feeling very well, Stepmamá" was all that

Fonchito would say, with an innocence that Don Rigoberto took as a further affront.

"My God, how pale you are. You see? I told you so. That little dip in the river has made you sick."

"It's nothing, nothing," Don Rigoberto vaguely reassured his wife in a strangled voice. "Too big a mouthful and I choked. A bone, I think. It's gone down, I'm all right now. I'm fine, don't worry."

"But you're trembling," Doña Lucrecia said in alarm, touching his forehead. "You've caught a cold, I knew it. A nice hot cup of tea and a couple of aspirin, right now. I'll get it for you. No, don't say anything. And straight to bed, no arguments."

Not even the word "bed" could raise Don Rigoberto's spirits, for in just a few minutes his mood had changed from vital joy and enthusiasm to bewildered demoralization. He saw Doña Lucrecia hurrying to the kitchen. Fonchito's transparent glance made him uneasy, and to break the silence he said, "Schiele was arrested because he went to the country?"

"Not because he went to the country, what an idea," his son said, bursting into laughter. "Because he was accused of immorality and seduction. In a little village called Neulengbach. It never would have happened if he had stayed in Vienna."

"Really? Tell me about it," Don Rigoberto urged, aware that he was trying to gain time, though he didn't know for what. Instead of the glorious, sunny splendor of the past two days, his state of mind was now a disastrous storm with heavy rain, thunder, lightning. Calling on a remedy that had worked on other occasions, he tried to calm himself by mentally listing mythological figures. Cyclops, sirens, Lestrigons, lotus-eaters, Circes, Calypsos. He got no further.

It happened in the spring of 1912, in the month of April, to be exact, the boy rambled on. Egon and his lover Wally (a nickname: her real name was Valeria Neuzil) were out in the country, in a rented cottage on the outskirts of the village whose name was so difficult to pronounce. Neulengbach. Egon would frequently paint outdoors, taking advantage of the good weather. And one afternoon a young girl appeared and struck up a conversation with him. They talked, that was all. The girl returned several times. Until one stormy night, when she showed up soaking wet and announced to Wally and Egon that she had run away from home. They tried to change her mind, you've done a bad thing, go home, but she said no, no, let me at least spend the night with you. They agreed. The girl slept with Wally; Egon Schiele was in another room. The next day . . . But the return of Doña Lucrecia, carrying a steaming infusion of lemon verbena and two aspirin, interrupted Fonchito's story, which, as a matter of fact, Don Rigoberto had barely heard.

"Drink it all up while it's nice and hot," Doña Lucrecia pampered him. "And take the two aspirin. Then beddy-byes. I don't want you to catch a cold, baby."

Don Rigoberto felt—his great nostrils inhaled the garden fragrance of the lemon verbena—his wife's lips resting for a few moments on the sparse hairs at the top of his skull.

"I'm telling him about Egon going to prison, Stepmamá," Fonchito explained. "I've told you so many times you'd be bored hearing it again."

"No, no, of course, go on," she urged him. "Though you're right, I do know it by heart."

"When did you tell your stepmother this story?" The question escaped between Don Rigoberto's teeth as he blew on the lemon verbena tea. "She's been home barely two days and I've monopolized her day and night."

"When I visited her in her little house at the Olivar," the boy replied with his customary crystalline frankness. "Didn't she tell you?"

Don Rigoberto felt the air in the dining room turn electric. So he wouldn't have to talk to his wife or look at her, he took a heroic swallow of the burning lemon verbena, scalding his throat and esophagus. The inferno settled in his innards.

"I haven't had time," he heard Doña Lucrecia whisper. He looked at her and—oh! oh!—she was livid. But of course she intended to tell him. There was nothing wrong about those visits, was there?

"Of course there was nothing wrong," Don Rigoberto declared, swallowing another mouthful of the hellish perfumed liquid. "I think it's fine that you went to your stepmamá's house to give her my news. And the story about Schiele and his lover? You stopped in the middle, and I want to know how it ends."

"Can I go on?" Fonchito asked happily.

Don Rigoberto felt his throat as a burning wound; his wife stood mute and frozen at his side, and he guessed that her heart was racing. Just like his.

Well, so . . . The next day Egon and Wally took the girl by train to

Vienna, where her grandmother lived. She had promised she would stay with that lady. But in the city she changed her mind and spent the night with Wally, in a hotel. The next morning Egon and his lover took the girl back to Neulengbach, and she stayed with them another two days. On the third day her father showed up. He confronted Egon outdoors, where he was painting. He was very angry and said he had denounced him to the police, accusing him of seduction, because his daughter was a minor. While Schiele tried to calm him, explaining that nothing had happened, the girl spied her father from inside the house, picked up a pair of scissors, and tried to slash her wrists. But Wally, Egon, and her father all stopped her, they helped her, and she and her father talked and made up. They left together, and Wally and Egon thought everything had been settled. But of course it wasn't. The police came to arrest him a few days later."

Were they listening to his story? Apparently they were, for both Don Rigoberto and Doña Lucrecia found themselves petrified, and seemed to have lost the ability not only to move but even to breathe. Their eyes were fixed on the boy, and throughout his tale, recited without hesitation, with the pauses and emphasis of a good storyteller, neither one blinked an eye. But what about their pallor? Those intense, absorbed stares? Were they so moved by an old story about a painter long ago? These were the questions that Don Rigoberto thought he could read in the great, sparkling eyes of Fonchito, who was now calmly looking from one to the other, as if waiting for some comment. Was he laughing at them? At him? Don Rigoberto looked into his son's clear, limpid eyes, searching for the malevolent glint, the wink, the flicker of light that would betray his Machiavellian duplicity. He saw nothing: only the healthy, innocent, beautiful gaze of a clear conscience.

"Shall I go on or are you bored, Papá?"

He shook his head and, making a great effort—his throat was as dry and rough as sandpaper—he murmured, "What happened to him in prison?"

"They kept him behind bars for twenty-four days, charged with immorality and seduction. Seduction because of the episode with the girl and immorality because of some paintings and drawings of nudes that the police found in the house. It was proven that he hadn't touched the girl, and he was cleared of the first charge. But not the second. The judge ruled that since girls and boys who were minors visited the house and could have seen the nudes, Schiele deserved to be punished. How? By having his most immoral drawings burned.

"In prison his suffering was unspeakable. The self-portraits he painted in his cell show him as terribly thin, with a beard, sunken eyes, a cadaverous expression. He kept a diary, and in it he wrote (wait, wait, I know the sentence by heart): 'I, who am by nature one of the freest of creatures, am bound by a law that is not the law of the masses.' He painted thirteen watercolors, and that saved him from going mad or killing himself: he painted the cot, the door, the window, and a luminous apple, one of those that Wally brought him every day. Every morning she would stand outside the prison, strategically placed so that Egon could see her through the bars of his cell window. Wally loved him dearly and behaved wonderfully during that terrible month, giving him all her support. But he must have loved her less. He painted her, yes; he used her as a model, yes; but not only her, many others too, especially those little girls he picked up in the streets and kept there, half naked, while he painted them in every imaginable pose from the top of his ladder. Little girls and boys were his obsession. He was crazy about them, and, well, not only about painting them, it seems he really liked them, in the good and bad senses of the word. That's what his biographers say. He may have been an artist, but he was also something of a pervert, because he had a predilection for boys and girls . . ."

"Well, well, I think I have caught a bit of a chill after all," Don Rigoberto interrupted, standing so abruptly that the napkin on his lap fell to the floor. "I'd better follow your advice and lie down, Lucrecia. I don't want to get one of those awful colds of mine."

He spoke, not looking at his wife but only at his son, who, when he saw him on his feet, stopped speaking, an alarmed expression on his face, as if he were anxious to help. Don Rigoberto did not look at Lucrecia as he passed her on his way to the stairs, though he was consumed by curiosity to know if she was still livid, or bright red perhaps, with indignation, surprise, uncertainty, unease, asking herself, as he was, whether what the boy had said and done was part of some plan or the work of chance, scheming and labyrinthine, frustrating and mean-spirited, the enemy of happiness. He realized he was dragging his feet like a broken old man and stood erect. He climbed the stairs at a brisk pace, as if to prove (to whom?) that he was still a vigorous man in his prime.

Removing only his shoes, he lay on the bed, face up, and closed his eyes. His body was on fire with fever. He saw a symphony of blue spots in the darkness behind his eyelids and thought he could hear the belligerent buzzing of the wasps he had heard during their failed picnic that morning. A short while later, as if he had taken a powerful barbiturate, he fell asleep. Or did he pass out? He dreamed he had mumps and that Fonchito, a boy with a grown man's voice and specialist's air, warned him, "Watch out, Papá! This is a filtering virus, and if it travels down to your balls they'll get as big as two tennis balls and will have to be pulled out. Like wisdom-come-too-late teeth!" He awoke gasping for breath, bathed in sweat—Doña Lucrecia had put a blanket over him—and realized that night had fallen. It was pitch-black, there were no stars in the sky, the fog hid the lights along the Seawalk in Miraflores. The door to the bathroom opened, and in the flood of light that poured into the darkened room, Doña Lucrecia appeared in her robe, ready for bed.

"Is he a monster?" Don Rigoberto asked in anguish. "Does he realize what he's doing, what he's saying? Does he do what he does knowingly, weighing the consequences? Is that possible? Or is he simply a mischievous boy whose mischief turns out to be monstrous without his intending it to?"

His wife dropped onto the foot of the bed.

"I ask myself that question every day, many times a day," she said, sighing dejectedly. "I don't think he knows the answer either. Do you feel better? You've slept a couple of hours. I fixed you a hot lemonade, there in the thermos. Shall I pour you a glass? Listen, speaking of that, I never meant to keep anything from you, or not tell you that Fonchito visited me at the Olivar. It just kept slipping my mind, these two days have been so busy."

"Of course," Don Rigoberto said quickly, with a wave of his hand. "Let's not talk about it, please."

He stood, and murmuring, "This is the first time I've fallen asleep when it wasn't my bedtime," he walked to his dressing room. He took off his clothes; in a robe and slippers he went into the bathroom to perform his usual meticulous ablutions before retiring. He felt depressed, bewildered, with a buzzing in his head that seemed to portend a bad flu. He began to run warm water in the tub and poured in half a bottle of salts. As the tub was filling he flossed his teeth, brushed them, and with a tweezers plucked the new-grown hairs in his ears. How long was it since he had abandoned the habit of devoting one day a week to the specialized hygiene of each organ, in addition to his daily bath? Since his separation from Lucrecia. A year, more or less. He would resume that salutary weekly routine: Monday, ears; Tuesday, nose; Wednesday, feet; Thursday, hands; Friday, mouth and teeth. Et cetera. Lying in the bath, he felt less demoralized. He tried to guess if Lucrecia was already under the sheets, what nightgown she had put on, could she be naked? and for moments at a time he managed to eclipse the ominous presence from his mind: the little house by the Olivar de San Isidro, a childish figure standing at the door, a slim finger ringing the bell. A decision had to be made about the boy, once and for all. But what decision? All of them seemed unsuitable or impossible. After getting out of the tub and drying himself, he rubbed his body with cologne from the Floris shop in London; a colleague and friend at Lloyd's periodically sent him their soaps, shaving creams, deodorants, talcs, and perfumes from there. He put on clean silk pajamas and left his robe hanging in the dressing room.

Doña Lucrecia was already in bed. She had turned off the lights in the room except for the lamp on her night table. Outside, the sea crashed against the cliffs of Barranco, and the wind howled in lugubrious lament. He felt his heart pounding as he slipped under the sheets, next to his wife. A gentle aroma of fresh herbs, of flowers wet with dew, of spring, entered his nostrils and reached his brain. Almost levitating with the tension he felt, he could detect his wife's thigh just millimeters from his left leg. In the scant, indirect light he saw that she was wearing a pink silk nightgown with spaghetti straps and a lace edging, through which he could see her breasts. He sighed, and was transformed. Impetuous, liberating desire filled his body and seeped out of his pores. He felt dizzy, intoxicated by his wife's perfume.

And then, intuiting this, Doña Lucrecia stretched out her hand, turned off the small lamp, and in the same movement turned toward him and embraced him. A sigh escaped his lips as he felt Doña Lucrecia's body, which he eagerly embraced, press against him, arms and legs enfolding him. He, in turn, kissed her neck, her hair, murmuring words of love. But when he began to strip and to remove his wife's nightgown, Doña Lucrecia whispered words into his ear that had the effect of a cold shower.

"He first came to see me six months ago. He showed up one afternoon, with no warning, at the house near the Olivar. And from then on he visited me constantly, after school, slipping away from the painting academy. Three, even four times a week. He had tea with me, stayed for an hour or two. I don't know why I didn't tell you yesterday, the day before yesterday. I was going to. I swear I was going to."

"I beg you, Lucrecia," Don Rigoberto implored. "You don't have to tell me anything. By what you hold most dear. I love you."

"I want to tell you. Now, right now."

She was still holding him, and when her husband searched for her mouth, she opened it and kissed him avidly. She helped him to take off his pajamas and remove her nightgown. But then, as he was caressing her and moving his lips along her hair, her ears, her cheeks, her neck, she spoke again: "I didn't go to bed with him."

"I don't want to know anything, my love. Do we have to talk about this now?"

"Yes, now. I didn't go to bed with him, but wait. Not because of any virtue in me, but because of him. If he had asked, if he had made the slightest suggestion, I would have done it. With the greatest of pleasure, Rigoberto. Many afternoons I felt sick because I hadn't. You won't hate me? I have to tell you the truth."

"I'll never hate you. I love you. My darling, my dear wife."

But she interrupted with another confession: "And the truth is that if he doesn't leave this house, if he goes on living with us, it will happen again. I'm sorry, Rigoberto. It's better that you know. I have no defenses against that boy. I don't want it to happen, I don't want to make you suffer the way you suffered before. I know you suffered, my love. But there's no reason for me to lie. He has a power, something, I don't know what it is. If he gets the idea into his head again, I'll do it. I won't be able to stop. Even if it destroys our marriage, this time forever. I'm sorry, I'm sorry, but it's the truth, Rigoberto. The raw truth."

His wife had begun to cry. The last shreds of his excitement disappeared. He embraced her, deeply troubled.

"Everything you're telling me I know all too well," he said softly, fondling her. "What can I do? Isn't he my son? Where will I send him? To whom? He's still very young. Don't you think I've thought about it? When he's older, of course. But let him finish school, at least. Doesn't he say he wants to be a painter? Fine. He'll study art. In the United States. In Europe. Let him go to Vienna. Doesn't he love Expressionism? He'll go to the academy where Schiele studied, the city where Schiele lived and died. But how can I send him away now, at his age?"

Doña Lucrecia pressed against him, entwined her legs with his, attempted to rest her feet on her husband's.

"I don't want you to send him away," she whispered. "I realize he's only a boy. I never could tell if he knows how dangerous he is, the catastrophes he can provoke with his beauty, that sly, terrible intelligence of his. I'm telling you only because, because it's true. With him, we'll always be in danger, Rigoberto. If you don't want it to happen again, then watch me, guard me, hover over me. I never want to go to bed with anybody but you, my dear husband. I love you so much, Rigoberto. You don't know how I've needed you, how I've missed you."

"I know, my love, I know."

Don Rigoberto turned her onto her back and positioned himself over her. Doña Lucrecia too seemed to have regained her desire—there were no more tears on her cheeks, her body was hot, her breathing heavy—and as soon as she felt him on top of her she parted her legs and let him enter. Don Rigoberto closed his eyes and gave her a long, deep kiss, immersed in total surrender, happy once more. Fitting perfectly, touching and rubbing from head to foot, their perspiration mixing, they rocked slowly, rhythmically, prolonging their pleasure.

"In fact, you've gone to bed with many people all year," he said.

"Oh, really?" she purred, as if speaking with her belly from some secret gland. "How many? Who? Where?"

"A zoological lover who put you into bed with cats"—"How awful, that's disgusting," his wife protested weakly. "A love of your youth, a scientist who took you to Paris and Venice and who sang when he came . . ."

"I want details," Doña Lucrecia gasped, speaking with difficulty. "All of them, even the tiniest. What I did, what I ate, what was done to me."

"That asshole Fito Cebolla almost raped you, and Justiniana too. You saved her from his raging lust. And ended up making love to her in this very bed."

"Justiniana? In this bed?" Doña Lucrecia laughed. "Life is so strange. Well, because of Fonchito, one afternoon I almost made love to Justiniana in San Isidro. The only time my body betrayed you, Rigoberto. But my imagination has done it a thousand times. As has yours."

"My imagination has never betrayed you. But tell me, tell me," and her husband accelerated the rocking, the swaying.

"I'll tell you later, you go first. Who? How? Where?"

"With a twin brother of mine whom I invented, a Corsican brother, in an orgy. With a castrated motorcyclist. You were a law professor in Virginia, and you corrupted a saintly jurist. You made love to the wife of the Algerian ambassador in a steambath. Your feet maddened a French fetishist of the eighteenth century. The night before our reconciliation, we were in a Mexican brothel with a mulatta who pulled off one of my ears in a single bite."

"Don't make me laugh, you fool, not now," Doña Lucrecia protested. "I'll kill you, I'll kill you if you stop me."

"I'm coming too. Let's come together. I love you."

Moments later, when they were calm, he on his back, she curled at his side with her head on his shoulder, they resumed their conversation. Outside, along with the crash of the sea, the night was disturbed by the shrieks and howls of cats fighting or in heat, and, at intervals, the blare of car horns and the roar of motors.

"I'm the happiest man in the world," said Don Rigoberto.

She nestled against him demurely. "Will it last? Will we make our happiness last?"

"It can't last," he said gently. "All happiness is fleeting. An exception, a contrast. But we have to rekindle it from time to time, not allow it to go out. Blowing, blowing on the little flame."

"I'll start exercising my lungs right now," Doña Lucrecia exclaimed. "I'll make them like bellows. And when it begins to go out, I'll puff out a blast of wind that will make it grow bigger and bigger. Phhhhewwww! Phhhhewwww!"

They lay silent, in each other's arms. His wife was so still that Don Rigoberto thought she had fallen asleep. But her eyes were open.

"I always knew we would reconcile," he said into her ear. "I wanted to, tried to, for months. But I didn't know where to begin. And then your letters began to arrive. You read my thoughts, my love. You're better than I am."

His wife's body stiffened. But it immediately relaxed again.

"An ingenious idea, those letters," he went on. "The anonymous letters, I mean. A baroque scheme, a brilliant strategy. To pretend I was sending you anonymous letters so you would have an excuse to write to me. You're always surprising me, Lucrecia. I thought I knew you, but no. I never would have imagined your sweet head involved in machinations and tangled schemes. They turned out well, didn't they? Lucky for me."

There was another long silence in which Don Rigoberto counted the beats of his wife's heart, which sounded in counterpoint and at times were confused with his own.

"I'd like us to take a trip," he digressed a little while later, feeling that he was succumbing to sleep. "Somewhere far away, totally exotic. Where we don't know anybody and nobody knows us. Iceland, for example. Maybe at the end of the year. I can take a week, ten days. Would you like that?"

"I'd rather go to Vienna," she said, stumbling over the words—because she was tired? feeling the languor that love always caused in her? "And see Egon Schiele's work, visit the places where he worked. For all these months I haven't done anything but hear about his life, his paintings, his drawings. And now my curiosity is piqued. Doesn't Fonchito's fascination with this painter surprise you? You've never liked Schiele very much, as far as I know. So why does he?"

He shrugged. He didn't have the slightest idea where that passion might have sprung from.

"Well then, in December we'll go to Vienna," he said. "To listen to Mozart and see the Schieles. I never liked him, it's true, but perhaps now I'll start to. If you like him, I'll like him. I don't know where Fonchito's enthusiasm comes from. Are you falling asleep? I'm keeping you up with my talking. Good night, love."

She murmured "Good night," turned on her side, and pressed her back against her husband's chest; he turned on his side as well, flexing his legs so that she seemed to be sitting on his knees. This is how they had slept for the ten years before their separation. And how they had slept since the day before yesterday. Don Rigoberto passed an arm over Lucrecia's shoulder and rested one hand on her breast, clasping her waist with the other.

The cats in the vicinity had stopped their fighting, or their lovemaking. The last horn and raucous motor had long since fallen silent. Warm, and warmed by the nearness of the beloved body so close to his, Don Rigoberto had the sensation that he was floating, gliding, moved by a pleasant inertia through tranquil, delicate waters, or, perhaps, through deep, empty space on his way to the icy stars. How many more days or hours would it last without shattering, this sensation of plenitude, of harmonious calm, of equilibrium with life? As if responding to his silent question, he heard Doña Lucrecia: "How many anonymous letters did you receive, Rigoberto?"

"Ten," he replied with a start. "I thought you were asleep. Why do you ask?"

"I received ten from you, too," she said, not moving. "That's called love by symmetry, I guess."

255

Now it was he who tensed. "Ten letters from me? I never wrote to you, not once. Not anonymous letters, or signed ones, either."

"I know," she said, sighing deeply. "You're the one who doesn't know. You're the one whose head is in the clouds. Now do you understand? I didn't send you any anonymous letters either. Only one letter. But I'll bet that one, the only genuine one, never reached you."

Two, three, five seconds passed without his speaking or moving. The only sound came from the sea, but it seemed to Don Rigoberto that the night had filled with furious tomcats and she-cats in heat.

"You're not joking, are you?" he said at last, knowing very well that Doña Lucrecia had spoken with absolute seriousness.

She did not answer. She remained as still and silent as he, for another long while. What a short time it had lasted, how brief that overwhelming happiness. There it was again, harsh and cruel, Rigoberto, real life.

"If you can't sleep, and I can't sleep," he finally proposed, "maybe we could try to straighten this out, the way other people count sheep. We'd better do it now, once and for all. If you agree, if you want to. Because if you'd rather forget it, we'll forget it. We won't talk about those letters again."

"You know very well we'll never be able to forget them, Rigoberto," his wife declared, with a trace of weariness. "Let's do now what you and I both know we'll eventually do anyway."

"All right, then," he said, sitting up. "We'll read them."

The temperature had dropped, and before they went to the study they put on their robes. Doña Lucrecia brought the thermos of hot lemonade for her husband's supposed cold. Before showing one another their respective letters, they drank some warm lemonade from the same glass. Don Rigoberto had kept his anonymous letters in the last of his notebooks, which still had blank pages free of commentaries and annotations; Doña Lucrecia had hers in a portfolio, tied with a thin purple ribbon. They found that the envelopes were identical as well as the paper, the kind of envelopes and paper that sold for four *reales* in little Chinese grocery stores. But the writing was different. And, of course, the letter from Doña Lucrecia, the only authentic one, was not among them.

"It's my writing," Don Rigoberto murmured, going beyond what he believed was the limit of his capacity for astonishment, and then feeling even more astounded. He had read the first letter with great care, almost ignoring what it said, concentrating only on the calligraphy. "Well, the fact is that my handwriting is the most conventional in the world. Anybody can imitate it."

"Especially a young boy with a passion for painting, a child-artist," concluded Doña Lucrecia, flourishing the anonymous letters supposedly written by her, which she had just leafed through. "On the other hand, this is not my writing. That's why he didn't give you the only letter I really wrote. So you wouldn't compare it to these and discover the deception."

"They're vaguely similar," Don Rigoberto corrected her; he had picked up a magnifying glass and was examining the letter, like a collector with a rare stamp. "It is, in any case, a round hand, very clear. The writing of a woman who studied with nuns, probably at the Sophianum."

"And you didn't know my handwriting?"

"No, no, I didn't," he admitted. It was the third surprise on this night of great surprises. "I realize now that I didn't. As far as I recall, you never wrote me a letter before."

"I didn't write these to you, either."

Then, for at least half an hour, they sat in silence, reading their respective letters, or more precisely, each one read the other, unknown half of this correspondence. They were sitting next to one another on the large leather sofa with pillows, beneath the tall floor lamp whose shade had drawings of an Australian tribe. The wide circle of light reached both of them. From time to time they drank warm lemonade. From time to time one of them chuckled, but the other asked no questions. From time to time the expression on one of their faces would change, showing amazement, anger, or a sentimental weakness, tenderness, indulgence, a vague melancholy. They finished reading at the same time. They looked at one another obliquely; they were exhausted, perplexed, indecisive. Where should they begin?

"He's been in here," Don Rigoberto said at last, pointing at his desk, his shelves. "He's looked through my things and read them. The most sacred, secret things I have, these notebooks. Not even you have seen them. My supposed letters to you are, in reality, mine. Though I didn't write them. Because I'm certain he transcribed all those phrases from my notebooks. Making a mixed salad. Combining thoughts, quotations, jokes, games, my own reflections and other people's."

"And that's why those games, those orders, seemed to come from you," said Doña Lucrecia. "But these letters, I don't know how you could have thought they were mine."

"I was going crazy, wanting to know about you, to receive some sign from you," Don Rigoberto apologized. "Drowning men grab on to whatever's in front of them, they don't turn up their noses at anything."

"But all that vulgarity, that sentimentality? Don't they sound more like Corín Tellado?"

"They are Corín Tellado, some of them," said Don Rigoberto, remembering, associating. "A few weeks ago her novels began to show up around the house. I thought they belonged to the maids or the cooks. Now I know whose they were and what they were used for."

"I'm going to murder that boy," exclaimed Dona Lucrecia. "Corín Tellado! I swear I'll murder him."

"You're laughing?" he said in astonishment. "You think it's funny? Should we congratulate him, reward him?"

She really laughed now, for a longer time, more openly than before.

"The truth is, I don't know what I think, Rigoberto. It certainly is nothing to laugh at. Should we cry? Get angry? All right, let's get angry, if that's what must be done. Is that what you'll do tomorrow? Scold him? Punish him?"

Don Rigoberto shrugged. He wanted to laugh as well. And he felt stupid.

"I've never punished him, much less hit him, I wouldn't know how to do it," he confessed with some embarrassment. "That's probably why he's turned out the way he has. To tell you the truth, I don't know what to do with him. I suspect that whatever I do, he'll always win."

"Well, in this case we've won something too." Doña Lucrecia leaned against her husband, who put his arm around her shoulders. "We're together again, aren't we? You never would have dared to call me or ask me to tea at the Tiendecita Blanca without those letters. Isn't that so? And I wouldn't have gone if it weren't for the letters. I'm sure not. They prepared the way. We can't complain, he helped us, he brought us together. I mean, you're not sorry we made up, are you, Rigoberto?"

In the end, he laughed too. He rubbed his nose against his wife's head, feeling her hair tickling his eyes.

"No, I'll never be sorry about that," he said. "Well, after so many emotions, we've earned the right to sleep. All of this is very nice, but tomorrow I have to go to the office, my dear wife."

They returned to the bedroom in the dark, holding hands. And she still had the heart to make a joke: "Are we taking Fonchito to Vienna in December?"

Was it really a joke? Don Rigoberto immediately pushed away the evil thought as he proclaimed: "In spite of everything we're a happy family, aren't we, Lucrecia?"

MAKING WAVES
Essays
Edited and Translated by John King

Spanning thirty years of writing, the essays here trace the development of Vargas Llosa's thinking on politics and culture and show the breadth of his interests and passions. A *Publishers Weekly* Best Book of 1997, a *New York Times* Notable Book, and a National Book Critics Circle Award nominee.   ISBN 0-14-027556-8

AUNT JULIA AND THE SCRIPTWRITER
Translated by Helen R. Lane

Sexy Aunt Julia finds forbidden love with her lusty nephew Varguitas, who works for a ramshackle radio station with a new hotshot scriptwriter of racy soap operas. Vargas Llosa merges reality with fantasy in this "wonderfully comic novel almost unbelievably rich in character, place, and event." (*Los Angeles Times Book Review*)   ISBN 0-14-024892-7

DEATH IN THE ANDES
Translated by Edith Grossman

In a remote Andean village, two soldiers investigating the disappearances of three local men encounter the resentment and superstitions of the townspeople. Vargas Llosa evocatively melds past and present, the sensual and the spiritual, a political allegory and a suspense story in a surreal portrait of contemporary Peru.   ISBN 0-14-026215-6

A FISH IN THE WATER
A Memoir
Translated by Helen R. Lane

Vargas Llosa entwines the story of his run for the presidency of his native Peru with an intimate look at his intriguing life. With the same artistry he brings to his fiction, he recounts vividly the events that formed the basis of his novels.   ISBN 0-14-024890-0

IN PRAISE OF THE STEPMOTHER
Translated by Helen R. Lane

Vargas Llosa lures readers into a passionate world of family life and erotic love with the tale of Don Rigoberto, his second wife Lucrecia, and his young son Alfonso. Meticulously, seductively, he turns the proverbial romantic triangle on its ear in a novel that is both "a genuinely erotic story and a wicked parody of one." (*Los Angeles Times*)   ISBN 0-14-015708-5

THE STORYTELLER
Translated by Helen R. Lane

Mesmerized by a photograph in a Florence gallery of a tribal storyteller, a Peruvian writer is overcome by the impression that the grainy figure is not an Indian at all, but a friend from his past. "Vargas Llosa's most engaging and accessible book." (*The New York Times Book Review*)
                ISBN 0-14-014349-1

THE WAR OF THE END OF THE WORLD
Translated by Helen R. Lane

In the backlands of nineteenth-century Brazil lies Canudos, home to social outcasts, a libertarian paradise that the nation-state cannot tolerate. This retelling of a crucial historical event, is "the most powerful and ambitious Latin American epic novel since Gabriel García Márquez's *One Hundred Years of Solitude*." (*The Boston Globe*)   ISBN 0-14-026260-1

FOR THE BEST IN PAPERBACKS, LOOK FOR THE 🐧

In every corner of the world, on every subject under the sun, Penguin represents quality and variety—the very best in publishing today.

For complete information about books available from Penguin—including Puffins, Penguin Classics, and Arkana—and how to order them, write to us at the appropriate address below. Please note that for copyright reasons the selection of books varies from country to country.

In the United Kingdom: Please write to *Dept. EP, Penguin Books Ltd, Bath Road, Harmondsworth, West Drayton, Middlesex UB7 0DA.*

In the United States: Please write to *Penguin Putnam Inc., P.O. Box 12289 Dept. B, Newark, New Jersey 07101-5289* or call 1-800-788-6262.

In Canada: Please write to *Penguin Books Canada Ltd, 10 Alcorn Avenue, Suite 300, Toronto, Ontario M4V 3B2.*

In Australia: Please write to *Penguin Books Australia Ltd, P.O. Box 257, Ringwood, Victoria 3134.*

In New Zealand: Please write to *Penguin Books (NZ) Ltd, Private Bag 102902, North Shore Mail Centre, Auckland 10.*

In India: Please write to *Penguin Books India Pvt Ltd, 11 Panchsheel Shopping Centre, Panchsheel Park, New Delhi 110 017.*

In the Netherlands: Please write to *Penguin Books Netherlands bv, Postbus 3507, NL-1001 AH Amsterdam.*

In Germany: Please write to *Penguin Books Deutschland GmbH, Metzlerstrasse 26, 60594 Frankfurt am Main.*

In Spain: Please write to *Penguin Books S. A., Bravo Murillo 19, 1° B, 28015 Madrid.*

In Italy: Please write to *Penguin Italia s.r.l., Via Benedetto Croce 2, 20094 Corsico, Milano.*

In France: Please write to *Penguin France, Le Carré Wilson, 62 rue Benjamin Baillaud, 31500 Toulouse.*

In Japan: Please write to *Penguin Books Japan Ltd, Kaneko Building, 2-3-25 Koraku, Bunkyo-Ku, Tokyo 112.*

In South Africa: Please write to *Penguin Books South Africa (Pty) Ltd, Private Bag X14, Parkview, 2122 Johannesburg.*